For Fiona

THE SALT FARMER

All The Best

Francis J Glynn

Frank x

ISBN-10: 1984912062
ISBN-13: 978-1984912060

By the Same Author

Veneer of Manners (2016)

<u>A note on usage</u>

I have attempted to mimic Sixteenth Century language use while maintaining a style that is accessible to the modern reader. One aspect of this is the use of the word *self.* In the Sixteenth Century, *self* meant *itself,* or *the same*. It did not have the modern association with inner identity. This explains usage such as “one's self”, or “my self” within dialogue. (See Anne Ferry, 'The Art of Naming', Univ. of Chicago Press, 1988)

The Quikbeme Tree

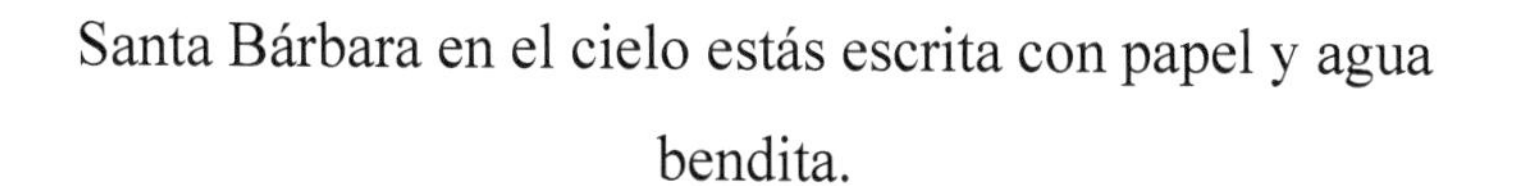

Santa Bárbara en el cielo estás escrita con papel y agua bendita.

Saint Barbara, you are written in the sky with paper and holy water.
(To be recited during a thunderstorm)

In memory of my parents, Mary and Shay Glynn

A Sea Battle

The Myth of the Cordelière

On St Lawrence Day, ill met at Brest,
Great ships for trial and test:
Mary Rose, Regent, Sovereign,
Grand Louise, Cordelière, and more;
Boats, full seven and two score,
Captained by Knyvet, Howard, Portzmoguer.
But on the Cordelière, were land-people of quality,
Women, men, and children, in finest for society,
Knowing not their day's end.

So, the ships engaged and new cannon roared,
And spat flame and iron
from new-fangled mouths.
Regent and Cordelière met, grappled, inseparable.
Women and boys fought,
Swinging staff and blade and cutlass,
on gore, split mast and ruined sail.

The Salt Farmer

When near lost, Portzmoguer ordered to fire the magazine
For the glory of St Lawrence, who, too, died in flame,
Which eruption engulfed the Cordelière, dragged poor Regent down
Harnessed together, conjoined in cord and chain,
With fifteen hundred souls, below.

Timbers tore and shivered,
Sheet and masts, and men.
And women and children rent asunder,
Their bodies cracked, in flame and tears and torment,
As the two ships met their doom,
Under the dread sea.

Or was all this so true? Who lit that fuse,
That gave death to those gallant innocents, entwined?
Was it Portzmoguer indeed?
Who heard his oath to St Lawrence's end?
Why such sacrifice?
Perchance it was another: a shot wildly fired, or misadventury,
Who lit that fuse?
Shall that Captain be remembered for this?
Or is there another narration?
What history shall fate tell?
What history shall fate tell?

Extract from 'Le Mythe du Cordelière' (Lyons, 1642), an epic poem by Rolande de Ville d'Fin (1590-1666) of The Battle of St Matthieu at Brest, on the feast of St Lawrence, 10th August, 1512. Translated from Latin by Archibald Clett of Canmore (1721-1799), from the collection of letters and documents in Kirkwall Library, Orkney.

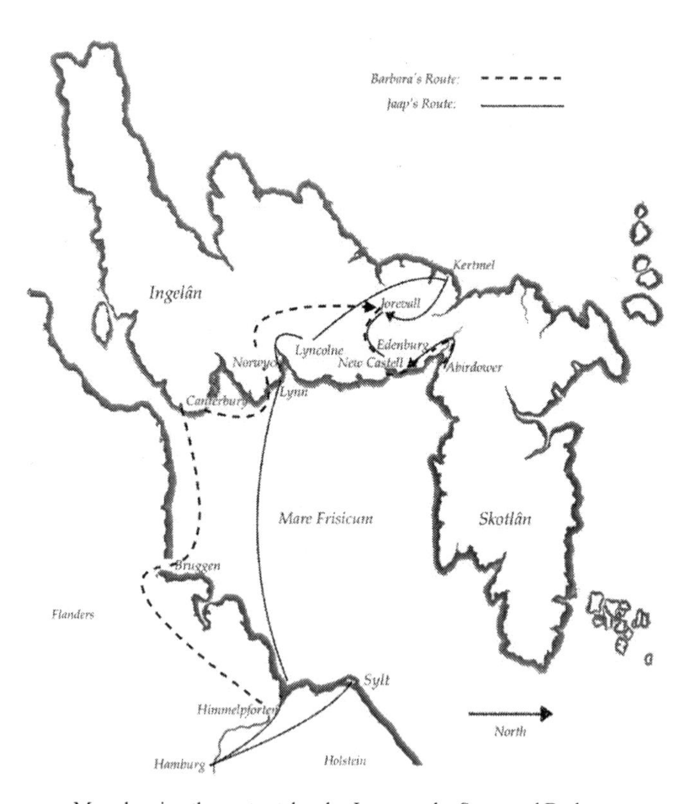

Map showing the routes taken by Jaap van der Staen and Barbara

I

Sylt

The Feast day of St Appolonius the Apologist,

18th April, 1536

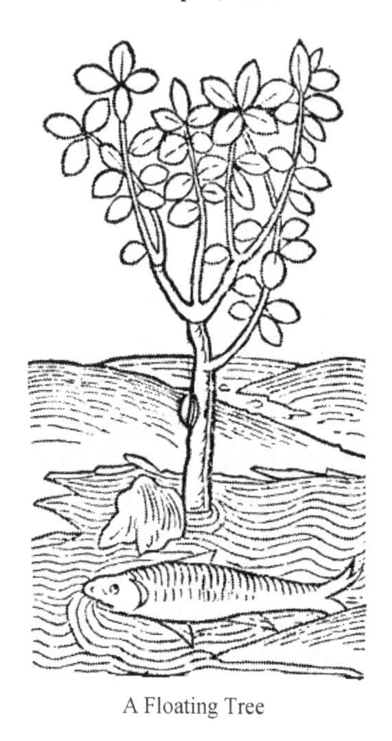

A Floating Tree

The pain in his hip was keeping Jaap van der Staen awake. Silently, he reached over and touched his wife's hair, then her cheek; it was cold. Now, here, the act was complete: Gertje was dead. Jaap hobbled to the basin, splashed water on his face and drank; he looked back at Gertje in the thin dawn light, at the lumps that had grown under her skin, the lumps he had touched and known. Gertje was now free with the gift of death.

Jaap lit a fire, but it offered no comfort. He lifted his wife from their bed, placed her on the table and washed her body. He spoke softly, apologising as he raised her delicate limbs; she didn't shiver when he dabbed with the cold water. He put down the cloth and looked to the lightening sky. Touching her shoulder, he covered her with their blanket. He opened the door and the bitter haar rolled into their home; he sucked in the salt-sharp air.

"I have to catch the tide my love."

Jaap walked south, into the enveloping mist, the little hamlet of Keitum soon behind him, past the church of St Severin. He stopped to watch four horses, the large black Frisians that roamed free in these parts. Silhouetted in the fog, they galloped in the haar, the sound of their hooves increasing, fading, rising again as they raced this way and that, unable to see more than a few feet in front of them. Jaap felt the thumping on the ground as they appeared and disappeared in the mist. A large stallion approached, its head high. It bent down, whispering hot breath in his ear. As Jaap looked into its eyes for meaning, rubbing under its jaw, it whinnied, moving its huge head from side to side. The animal turned away, returning to its companions, and became a ghost in the mist. Jaap moved on, quickening his pace, pushing past the pain in his hips and knees. He passed small homes sheltered from the sea by the dunes. That morning, there had been no sunrise, only a slow development of grey light as the morning sun attempted to pierce the thick haze that would be constant until dusk. Jaap came to the crossroads, where the old quikbeme tree was covered with spring blossom. Gertje once told him that people had been coming to this tree since the beginning of time. It had three trunks, each separate, pleated, twined together. Somebody had placed rocks in the gaps, and it was dressed in offerings of rags, flowers and trinkets. The quikbeme had grown around the older offerings: a spoon, a withered piece of clothing, a clay bowl; all these things had grown into the tree; embedded in the bark. Jaap van der Staen placed the palm of his hand on the quikbeme; this tree that contained human residue. He made the Sign of the Cross before going on, past St Martin's at Morsum. As he approached the salt marshes on this first morning of the season, he breathed in the familiar stench.

Jaap arrived expecting the usual chatter, but the salt farmers were silent, peering out into the quiet murk. A tree, a young oak, was floating out on the retreating tide. It stood upright, attached by its roots to a piece of earth, moving with a slow rocking motion on the water. Some crows flew to the tree; others left it to return to the safety of home. The light changed, and the dull haar was briefly broken by a beam of sunlight that illuminated the tree. The people gasped. For that moment, the tree was ablaze in gold and green, immense in the morning; then its colour drained once more, returning to its dull green and brown-grey in the Frisian fog. Jaap felt the chill air on his neck, stretching his shoulders to ease his aching bones.

The other salt farmers watched as the tree faded in the fog, disappearing in the near distance. Some made the Sign of the Cross, some shook their heads.

"It be the will of God."

Above, the crows called to the salt farmers who were aware of Jaap behind them.

"God's day, Jaap van der Staen. Have you said your prayers this morning?"

They laughed, and then it was quiet again. Jaap took his lousse, the long-handled rake for gathering the brittle salt from the thick brine.

"Are you for a pilgrim today then Jaap?"

More laughter.

"Why don't you stay here on Sylt to work to pay your debts?"

"Yes, your debts", said one man loudly; again, the quiet: just the cold morning air brushing their faces. Another man approached Jaap; smiling only with his lips, he whispered:

"I know you. I know what you have done. You and I are the same."

The man walked off into the gloom. The others remained in the silence. Old Tom spoke:

"Enough, fools. Jaap, my friend, come farm salt with me."

Jaap looked at the patch of marsh in front of him, out into the mist. The oak tree was gone.

"How could that happen?" thought Jaap. "What was it? A ship? No, it had been too close in the shallow water." There was no explaining it. The distant tide was on the turn.

"Please my friend, come. Let us make salt together."

Jaap shook his head and twisted his waist against the pain in his joints. Old Tom placed his hand on his arm.

"Tell me what troubles you?"

Jaap looked out into the impenetrable morning.

"Gertje. God has taken my Gertje."

The older man made the sign of the cross, touching his forehead, navel, and left and right shoulders, mumbling the short blessing. The wet air blew between them.

"I am sorry, my friend."

"This morning. She was in bed beside me."

"And so soon after your little boy was taken?"

Out in the thick white air, a crow called. Jaap felt the marsh mud chill rise from his feet through his body, seeping into his bones. He closed his eyes.

"Just a year ago. Little Anders."

Jaap wiped his dripping nose and peered through the fog to the ponds. Each pond held brine in increasing concentration. Out at the edge of the sea there was the new water, and closer in you could see the green and orange algae; and further in, away from the sea were the smaller inner ponds, with thick white encrusted brine.

"Why don't you go home? These people are not helping you."

"I want to work."

Jaap walked towards the pond containing the most orange-tinged algae, the solution that would supply the sweetest, strongest salt. This salt would be harvested later when the summer sun evaporated the water to make the brine strong. In the distance the sea turned, and the salt farmers worked in the cold breeze that blew through the still mist. They sent the boy to close the watergate at the outer pond. With their lousses, they started at the half-tide mark and worked their way inland, scraping the surface of the scummy water, one rakeful at a time, towards the brittle sludge lying by the edge of the inner ponds. Later they would separate the good salt from the poisonous black mineral mud below, and mix it with salted peat, increasing the concentration, and it would be boiled and burned to make the salt they would sell for a florin a peck: the beautiful bounty formed as a result of the rhythm of the sea and the sun and the moon, combined with the toil of the salt farmers.

Jaap worked in the penetrating damp, the pain in his joints subsiding. Now he stood upright, he was almost lithe in the cold, salt-laden air. The marshes stretched out before him, the mist blurring the close horizon. After a while, he stopped, bent down and scooped up a handful of the wet salt from his pan and shook it dry. He filled three muslin bags and walked away from the others.

"Off for some more prayers then, Jaap?"

Again they laughed.

"But we've not seen you at Mass."

Jaap turned northwards, towards Gertje and home, away from the sulphurous air of the marshes. At the crossroads, he stopped again at the quikbeme. Taking one of the muslin bags, he sprinkled salt around the trunk and muttered a short Ave Maria. He returned home to Keitum and opened his door.

"Hello, my little fish."

Gertje lay on the table, covered with their blanket. Jaap tidied her hair and put on her best cap. He opened her mouth and filled it with the contents of the second bag of salt from the marsh.

"There you are, my love. You will have an easier road now."

He kissed her cold forehead.

"Why did you have to suffer – you and our little Anders? Why does God punish the innocent so? It is my sin that has brought you to this."

Even the previous night, her last night, when she was in pain and couldn't breathe, Gertje had told Jaap that this was not true, that her illness was the will of God, and his reasons beyond our ken. But Jaap knew his own sin. He had lived with it since he was ten years old. It was the reason for the pain in his joints that woke him every morning; but why she and Anders had to suffer, he could not fathom. He alone was responsible. Why should anyone else suffer? What kind of God allowed such cruelty?

He carried Gertje out to the patch of soil where they grew their vegetables; under the old yew, away from the sea, where the earth was not yet sandy. Jaap dug the familiar ground, where he had placed his son, not a year ago.

"Hello, my Anders, my little puppy. Here is your Mummy to lie beside you."

Jaap lowered Gertje's body down beside the bag containing his son's remains. He put earth on their bodies and said a prayer, and fashioned a cross and placed it at the head of the grave, facing out to the mudflats and the Wadden Zee in the east.

"There you are, my loves. Here you will see the dawn through the haar each morning, and when there is no haar, you will be warmed by the bounty of the sun."

~ ~ ~ ~ ~

Jaap opened the huge oak door of St Severin's and went straight to the triptych with its little saints sitting on either side of the little Christ; he knelt and said a Pater Noster. When he had finished, he stood up and found the priest beside him.

"Majstro Siemen."

"My son, it is good to see you. Have you come for confession?" Jaap was irritated by the interruption.

"No, Majstro."

"But you must have confession, Jaap. How will you die without the succour of Christ? I fret for your soul. You have not had confession since your boy died."

"It is my sin. I will be answerable – I alone."

"That is bad talk, Jaap. You will burn in the eternal fires of Hell."

Jaap looked up at the triptych. Beneath Christ's right foot was a serpent.

"Gertje is dead."

Tiny rays of light shone from the timber roof, illuminating motes in the air. Majstro Siemen made the Sign of the Cross.

"May almighty God forgive her and her sins. I am sorry to hear of your loss. I will say a Mass for her. We will bring her here to be buried."

"No, Majstro. I have seen to it."

"How so?"

"I put her in the ground."

"Where?"

"Somewhere she wanted to be."

"Sweet Blood of Christ, their immortal souls!"

The priest made the sign of the cross, reciting the Latin incantation.

"My son, I can say no Mass for her if she is not buried in consecrated ground. We shall move her."

"No, you shall not."

"Then I cannot say a Mass for her."

"I will give you money."

"No. God's succour cannot be bought."

Jaap walked away.

"Jaap, you cannot turn your back on God. You must repent your sins."

Jaap continued walking.

~ ~ ~ ~ ~

Jaap went home and ate a little cheese and bread and beer and stirred the ashes of the morning's fire, trying to glean some heat. Looking out to the low evening tide that exposed the mud flats as far as the eye could see, he considered the first part of his journey, across the flats of the Wadden Zee; away from Sylt, the island that had been his home with Gertje and Anders. He took the remaining salt, placed it with some food into a small bag and put on his coat. It was getting dark and a complete moon was rising.

But first, he blew on some embers from the hearth and made a torch of twigs, blowing on the flame. He walked around the house and, using the light from the torch, examined the walls and roof. The outer thatch was damp, but Jaap held the flame to the dry material underneath and waited. The thatch took, and he blinked against the hot sparks from the salty straw. He moved around the house, lighting the roof. Within a few minutes, the flames reached into the night, crackling and spurting and splashing into the sky. In the distance he heard voices.

Jaap walked away from his burning home, past the dunes, out on to the mudflats towards the retreating tide. He put his shoes around his neck and stepped onto the wet sand. Looking back to Sylt, to the tower of fire that was his home, he heard the distant babble of the townsfolk. But now the huge expanse of absent sea was before him. He stepped into a small puddle of chilly water left by the outgoing tide and shivered. The water guttered in the dark, filling the space left by each step, gurgling in the mute night. In the light of the moon, he saw birds congregating near a dead salmon on a sandbank. Its silver scales shone in the moonlight; it jerked as crows and peewits and seagulls poked their beaks into the eyes and the open gap in its belly. As Jaap approached, they turned as one.

"This is our prize," they called, proudly. "Leave us. All of this is not yours, it is ours."

Jaap found himself in a squealing frenzy of hungry confused birds, fighting for the dead fish, cawing and mobbing him in the night. In the middle of it all, he felt a thump as the belly of a huge seagull collided with his head. There was a sharp peck and blood dribbled down his face. He ran, stumbling away from the scene, splashing and tripping in the pools of water, the whole spectacle lit by the incoherent moon.

Jaap carried on towards the distant tide, across the causeway that would take him away from Gertje and Anders. On and on, his feet hurt on the hard, rippled sand. But still the sea receded. Then, with the turning tide, he knew he was half way across the Wadden Zee. Looking back on Sylt, through the haar, he saw the distant glow of his burning home. The light from the dark red of the fading fire and the white of the shadowing moon illuminated the darker patches of quicksand. Here were colder pools of water; here the sand was softer – so soft that he had to stop his thoughts – he could so easily allow himself to sink into the ground that might embrace him in darkness.

He tripped in the pools of water, gasping with the cold; with each step, an explosion of small shining fish; each tiny creature speeding away in a chaos of movement, leaving behind little scars in the sand. New birds fed in the bright night, stuffing themselves with the worms and little creatures now unprotected by the deep. Jaap continued east, across the wide sands soon to disappear under a new sea.

~ ~ ~ ~ ~

Back in Keitum, Majstro Siemen joined the salt farmers in angry discussion.

"Jaap had driven his wife to.... Well, it was obvious."

"Had he poisoned her?"

"Those lumps on her face? He must have beaten her."

"And that boy of his, how did he die?"

"The fire. What kind of man would burn his own home?"

The townsfolk appeared in front of the priest at St Severin's. Majstro Siemen raised his hand.

"My children, none of us has slept. We are tired."

"Where is he, Majstro?"

"His wife is dead."

"Our poor Gertje. She was our girl before he came to this island. He murdered her, it's as obvious as the nose on your face. He killed her son too."

"You don't know that."

"Yes I do. He set fire to his home. This proves it. The man is evil. He killed our Gertje."

"When was the last time anyone saw her?"

A woman's voice came from the back of the crowd.

"I saw her last week. She was sick. You could see it."

"See, he killed her."

The man looked at the priest.

"You must do something, Majstro."

Old Tom spoke.

"You can't say that. The poor man was beside his self".

"Yes, I can say that. He killed his son, he killed his wife, and he burned his house. I see it all now; and to think that I loaned him money."

"He never spoke to anyone. He was always a strange one."

"He brought nothing but evil fortune to Sylt. Him with his foreign ways and strange ways of talking. What about that name of his? 'Van der Staen'; who calls themselves with such a name? How can I tell who his father was? How Gertje put up with him I don't know. And little Anders. How did that happen? Eh? I say again, how did that happen? Tell me that?"

"Where is he anyway? He wasn't on the marshes until this last tide."

"I just saw the new grave at his burned house; must have dug it just before he burned it down."

The townsfolk were quiet, and the priest spoke.

"It would seem that he has buried his wife and son in unconsecrated ground."

There was a short silence as they took in the enormity of what Majstro Siemen had just said. They blessed themselves, and there were gasps and cries of 'No', 'Shame', and 'Murderer'.

"But their poor immortal souls."

"He is a witch!"

"When were they ever at Mass?"

"There was evil in that family!"

The priest held up his hand.

"Does anyone know where Jaap is?"

"He has gone on a pilgrimage."

"Blasphemer!"

"What? Yes, of course. He said he wanted to be a pilgrim."

"Where has he gone? To Santiago? To Jerusalem?"

"His son's name was Anders. He will go to Skotlân, I am sure of it. Go home, all of you. I will write to my friend, the Abbess at Porto Coeli."

II

Himmelpforten

St Abdiesus' Day

22nd April 1536

A Benedictine Abbess and nun

Abbess Lücke von Sandbeck blew her nose. She found a dry part of a handkerchief and dabbed at her sore nostrils. Her secretary waited a few steps away, holding a letter. The Abbess's cold was clearing, and she was grateful that it had not been more serious. She had just sung for Terce, but her voice had not been at its best. The other Sisters of Porto Coeli, however, made a grand sound and God had been well praised. She blessed her self and returned her handkerchief to a pocket in her habit. She took the letter to the open window, sucking in the spring air, admiring the view over Himmelpforten and the Oste Marsh. The hamlet was an assortment of red roofs, each chimney sending a silent plume of smoke into the windless sky. The seal on the letter made Lücke von Sandbeck smile. She sniffed at it gingerly. Its scent brought back memories of her childhood on Sylt, of the sea, of the bitter winters and searing summers. She detected the smell of salt on the paper and felt the sand embedded in the wax seal. She dismissed her secretary. The letter was from her old friend Siemen in Keitum, but when she read it, her mood changed. It told a terrible story of witchcraft, blasphemy and murder. She read that a Dutchman, Jaap van der Staen, had murdered his wife and his young son, that he had buried their bodies in unconsecrated ground, and that he had fled the island after burning his home. That Sylt, the place of her childhood had been insulted so; that her remembered haven of tranquillity and beauty could contain such events was shocking. Outside, a breeze rose, rattling tiles on the roof; wisps of smoke from the hearths now rippled in the air.

She placed the letter on the desk and turned her mind to the current difficulties with her young novitiate, Barbara, soon to be obedientiary. The Abbess reflected on the irony in that title. Obedience was not a quality that one associated with Barbara. Keen to please, and biddable to a degree, yes; but if she didn't want to carry out a task, no authority on this earth could force her to do what she did not want to do. Abbess Lücke von Sandbeck sneezed. Wincing, she blew her nose once more. She wiped the water from her eyes and blessed her self. With reform in the air, this girl's continued presence at Porto Coeli would impede progress. She had many good points: she was popular; she had the common touch; and she was strangely charismatic for one so young. More to the point was the perception among the townsfolk that she was blessed. They called her their Jeanne d'Arc, their 'Maid of Himmelpforten'; and then there was the problem of Barbara's visions: not a desirable situation when the monastery was assimilating the new ideas of reform, unshackling old magic and superstition. But as she leaned back in her chair and stretched her legs, Lücke von Sandbeck made a connection between the problem posed by Barbara and the new information from Sylt. Once again, she held Siemen's letter to her nose and breathed in the salt. She returned to the window. Out in the courtyard she saw the Provost of Porto Coeli, Martin Reiff, crossing the cloister, talking to a man she had not seen before. The man was tall and strong, with a beard knotted beneath his chin. He handed some papers to the Provost. The Abbess watched as the man leaned over into the rose border and spat. She went out into the yard, stepping briskly to catch up with Reiff as he passed the Chapter House; he was alone again.

"My dear Provost."

"Abbess. How are you this morning?"

"I am better, for which God be praised."

"For he is bountiful."

They blessed themselves. The Abbess held up the letter from Sylt.

"I may have a solution to our problem."

"The girl? Tell me, for we must take the Ox Road to Bremervörde to meet the Prince Archbishop."

"First I must speak with the girl."

~ ~ ~ ~ ~

"Ah, Barbara. Enter."

The novitiate stepped into the Abbess's office, avoiding the lines in the floorboards. She stared at the light from the coloured windows, the little pools of red and blue and green that flooded the room. In the corner was a tiny chapel; like a little cathedral.

Abbess Lücke von Sandbeck examined her: habit dishevelled, a coif propped on top of her unkempt red hair; her fingernails dirty and hands ingrained with soil; she had a face full of freckles, and her green eyes danced as she glanced around the room, moving from foot to foot, wringing her hands. It seemed inconceivable that this clumsy twitching child could have been the cause of such trouble. The Abbess placed her hand on a small Book of Hours that lay on her desk. She touched the inlaid leather binding under her fingers, so comfortable in her hand, like an old friend. She flicked through the pages and the colours flashed from the little book. The greens and yellows glinted in the light, and the familiar words came to her as she glimpsed the fragments of text, page after page; this memory that would always be a part of her, that represented the past and old comfort. She put it aside and returned to the letter from Sylt and to Barbara.

"I have information about a man, a man who has lost his way. He has sinned grievously. He has sinned mortally and he must atone. Tell me, girl, how will he atone?"

Barbara stood up straight, crossed her self and took a breath.

"If he has sinned, he must receive confession. If he does not do so, he will burn in the fires of Hell for all eternity. If he receives confession, he must atone by carrying out his penance on this earth and by suffering in the fires of Purgatory, until our Almighty God sees fit to release him to the eternal bounty of the Kingdom of Heaven."

"Thank you, child. And how will we servants of Christ ensure that God's will is carried out?"

"By ensuring that he receives confession, and that his penance is enacted upon this earth."

"And, tell me, how will we do that my child?"

"Why Abbess, it is not for me, that is, absolution is not my..."

"I wish to know what you would do about this sinner, child."

Lücke von Sandbeck stopped and raised her right hand. In the silence, outside her window, a skein of honking geese flew north, and the breeze rattled the roof tiles once more. She took her friend's letter, breathing in the vapours of her childhood, the vapours of freedom – the freedom she once had from such determinations. She and the Provost, Martin Reiff, had already made the decision to send the girl in pursuit of the sinner: Barbara would follow Jaap van der Staen. It might be that the benefit to her would be great, and she might escape from the uncertain future that would be her destiny if she stayed at Porto Coeli. She simply did not belong at the monastery in these changing times. Barbara could use this opportunity to her advantage, for she was capable and resourceful. Lücke von Sandbeck had no doubts as to the girl's ability, only concern for the dangers she would face. This man, van der Staen, was going to Skotlân. To get there, he would follow the pilgrims' road through Ingelân, a dangerous place with menace in the air. The Abbess straightened the letter on her desk and looked up at her novice, nervously fingering the cord on her habit, biting her lip.

"This man's name is Jaap van der Staen. He murdered his wife and son, he buried them in unconsecrated ground, he burnt down his house and now he has fled."

Barbara put her hand to her mouth, her eyes wide. Lücke von Sandbeck continued:

"He is from Keitum, on the Island of Sylt: my home, and not three days walk from here."

She felt again the sand on the paper between her fingers.

"This letter tells me he has gone with the pilgrims."

"To Jerusalem?"

"No, child; to Sintanders."

"I have heard of this place. It is in the North."

"Yes my child. It is in Skotlân. It will be many months travelling."

"But how can I do God's work? If he is a pilgrim, he is performing his own penance."

"Of this, we cannot be sure. I want you to take the pilgrim roads and find him. I know you speak the tongue of the Ingelânders, and your Latin is good, is it not?"

"Yes, but Abbess, I am to take my vows. I have waited for this. I wish to become a novitiate, a bride of Christ. I want to work in the infirmary."

"I know, my child. I have observed you since you were eight years old when you became tithed to the monastery by your mother. I have seen many such girls go on to take their vows; but you are different. I can see so much potential in you, perhaps more so outside this monastery."

"But Abbess, the monastery is all I have known."

"Not so. You worked in the town, ministering to the poor and the sick of Himmelpforten, and more. Is this not so?"

Barbara nodded, her arms fixed at her side, her thumb rubbing hard at the knuckle of her index finger, her stomach tight. She felt a twitch on her cheek.

"So Abbess, do you not wish me to become a sister at Porto Coeli?"

The Abbess sniffed, took her damp handkerchief and dabbed at her nose.

"I suggest you carry out this task and consider how you wish to serve God once it has been completed."

"So, I can still take my vows?"

Lücke von Sandbeck coughed and looked away from Barbara, down to the letter from Siemen, and again touched the surface of her Book of Hours.

"Perhaps."

Barbara's hopes could not be as they were, her plans for a secure future at Porto Coeli dashed. But this was the wish of her Abbess, so she now had to concentrate on the prospect of what was ahead of her. She blinked away a tear.

"So, you wish me to find this man; but what if he is not on the pilgrims' road?"

"My child, I know he is on the pilgrims' road. He will go to Sintanders, but we wish for you to intercept him and bring him to the nearest monastery where he will be examined, where his penance will be decided by the correct authorities."

"But Abbess, I am but a girl and you tell me this man is a man of evil."

"God will lead you to this sinner. You have his Grace, and you have a gift. You own talents beyond your years. I have seen how you have dealt with folk in the village, and with men whose behaviour posed a danger. People listen to you. You have their ear; you speak directly to them. You have helped many of them, the poor tortured men and their families to whom only you could speak. You remember Johann?"

"Yes, Abbess."

Barbara gazed down at her feet.

"Johann who beat his wife and children; it was you alone who pacified him. You spoke to that part of him that was his conscience, you persuaded him not to drink and to turn to love. He has stayed on that path because of you. He was a violent man, and you, my child, brought him and his family peace. You may be able to do the same for this man."

Barbara blushed.

"Yes."

"That is why you can carry out this assignment. Find Jaap van der Staen and have him confess his sins. I shall supply you with letters of credentials after you have had confession."

Lücke von Sandbeck smiled at the girl before her, the cause of so much trouble, but also so guileless, so well-meaning. She did seem almost blessed, but also in need of protection. However, the Abbess was not in a position to provide that protection. This solution would allow her to grow, to survive, and to offer the world something she could never do in the confines of Porto Coeli.

"You know, my child, there is great transformation afoot. The world will not be as you see it today. I have concerns for the future of our beautiful monastery that has stood for five hundred years. Our Brother, Martin Luther has put into motion changes which we ignore at our peril;

and there is the question of money. The spending of our Prince Archbishop in Bremen is of great concern to me. He is squandering our legacy. This leaves us vulnerable to dangers that go with the new ideas taking hold. We have a holy duty to the women in our charge; we must prepare for the enormity of the reform that is ahead of us. If we cling to the old ways, we will surely die. The way to ensure our future is to adapt. I can protect this monastery and the Sisters, but I wonder if you would ever find happiness here."

Barbara wiped a tear away with the cotton tie that hung from her coif, and she tucked a straggling lock of her red hair under the cap.

"You must learn to seek succour in the carrying out of this task. You will turn to dust if you do not embrace the change that is to engulf us all. I will pray for you and your success."

Lücke von Sandbeck lifted her Book of Hours again. It fitted in her palm. The little thing, bound in a coloured inlaid calfskin, forty pages of vellum, each containing words she knew by heart. She would never unlearn them, and this was the time.

"I was given this Book of Hours by my old Abbess when I was a novice. I think that you should have it."

"But Abbess, it is yours. How can I ...?"

"You can take it because I am giving it to you. So it now belongs to you."

Barbara took the book and examined the tiny images alongside the Latin text. It had a saint's day calendar showing the progression of the year, with a little painting of each saint. The book was heavy, dense, and despite its age, the coloured images remained vivid and alive.

"Go, my girl."

"Yes, Abbess."

Barbara left the Abbess's office holding the Book of Hours. What were these changes her Abbess had spoken of? What had they to do with her?

What was she to do? She was to follow a man she had never met, a powerful man, and, if the reports were correct, an evil man. She was to apprehend him, to bring him to a monastery to face up to his sins. How would she respond when she met face to face with such evil? How would she find him among thousands of other souls in a foreign country? She ran a finger over the warm calfskin binding of her Abbess's Book of Hours.

~ ~ ~ ~ ~

The Abbess and Martin Reiff exchanged few words as the carriage rumbled along the Ox Road. Lücke von Sandbeck observed the Provost of Porto Coeli, asleep, his head nodding with each bump in the road. She couldn't say she trusted him, and she wanted to know more about this man with the knotted beard who spat into her roses. What was their conversation about? What did it have to do with Barbara and the letter from Sylt?

At Schloss Bremervörde, they were met by an elegant young man, wearing a black velvet cap and a sleek doublet with rabbit collar. Clutching a bundle of papers and a quill, he walked in small steps, and took them to an antechamber. The Provost fidgeted as the young man left them alone.

"He's new: the Prince Archbishop's latest secretary."

"Ah."

The Abbess dabbed her nose and feigned interest in a tapestry showing peasants at harvest.

"Who were you talking to in the cloister? He spat in my roses."

Martin Reiff coughed.

"Just a man who helps me with the odd problem."

"I do not know him. He is not from Himmelpforten; an unusual bearing has he not; rough; no? That of a soldier perhaps?"

"I couldn't say, Abbess."

"What is his name?"

Reiff cleared his throat.

"His name?"

"Starter, Jan Starter."

"Not from Holstein, then. And what was the matter of your talk? He gave you documents."

Reiff took the papers from his pocket and handed them to the Abbess.

"Rhymes."

"Rhymes?"

"Yes, Rhymes. He writes poesy. Wedding songs, drinking songs and such."

The Abbess glanced at the rhymes and songs on the papers and handed them back.

"I thought him to have the bearing of a man who has been in battle."

"Indeed Madam."

"And this is all he spoke of?"

Reiff started to mumble a response as two guards swung open the doors. The Prince Archbishop Christoph von Braunschweig-Wolfenbüttel sailed through the ornate portal, with three hounds at his heels, waving his hand.

"Come, come, come, come!"

They entered a fabulous room, covered with paintings, tapestries, and elaborate carvings. At the entrance of the Prince Archbishop, a parley of viols struck up a galliard. In the centre of the room was a large throne, at its base a bronze carved lion; the Castle Lion of Brunswick. As he moved to the throne, the dogs lay at his feet. The Prince Archbishop's gowns draped over the bronze lion. Each layer of the gown was made of a more expensive fabric, the sleeves were slit to show the layers of ruff and velvet; he wore a bonnet studded with precious stones, sewn in thread of gold. As he sat into the throne, he allowed the Provost and the Abbess to kiss his ring. He snapped his fingers and a posse of servants came in carrying wine and figs and nuts, placing them on a small, onyx table. Lücke von Sandbeck considered the Provost, bowing low before the Prince Archbishop. He had not given her a satisfactory answer to her question about Starter, the man with the knotted beard. They took glasses of deep red wine from the servants; the Prince Archbishop lifted his glass.

"Tsjoch!"

"Tsjoch!", said the Provost.

Lücke von Sandbeck hesitated, sniffed, then lifted her glass and joined in the toast.

"Tsjoch!"

The viols played a gigue, and one of the dogs let out a soft whine.

Prince Archbishop Christoph von Braunschweig-Wolfenbuttel smiled. He tugged at the ornate ruff at his wrist.

"And may God be with you, my dear Abbess."

The dogs closed their eyes and dreamed dog dreams. The Prince Archbishop, the Provost and the Abbess drank the wine together, enjoying its warmth and potency, and their good fortune.

"Tell me, Abbess, do you like this wine? I had this cask from Bordeaux. Much more satisfying, more full-bodied than our Frankish libations, would you not say?"

"Indeed, Prince Archbishop."

"What about you, Provost? I will send you some — a gift."

"Well, I, eh, well, thank you, Prince Archbishop."

Martin Reiff glanced at the Abbess who did not smile. The Prince Archbishop stroked the ermine edging of his gown.

"You are preoccupied my dear Abbess. You are concerned about the girl?"

One of the hounds twitched in its sleep. Lücke von Sandbeck put down her wine and noticed the way the light sparkled in the grey glass.

"Yes; the girl. I am indeed concerned."

"But we all agree to this course of action, do we not Provost? She speaks the tongue of the Ingelânder. This is good, surely?"

"Yes Prince Archbishop, we taught her, that is, I, eh..."

The Abbess turned away and blew her nose.

"This suggestion was my own, but I have concerns; the Provost also has reservations, do you not?"

Reiff shuffled his feet.

"Yes, I em..."

"Out with it, man. In Heaven's name, speak your thoughts."

"It is, that she is simply not old enough to be exposed to such danger. If this man is such a sinner, she will never be able to apprehend him. Send for the Bailiffs instead, or I know a qualified man who will be able to deal with him. The Dutchman, van der Staen, is dangerous."

"Abbess, what do you say? Are we placing her in danger?"

"Your Holiness, I think that we are placing her in a position where she will need all her resourcefulness, all her gifts. I have seen these gifts. I have seen her pacify violent men, and she has used her gentle ways to dissolve peril. But Ingelân is a long way, and full of ignorance."

The Abbess paused while the musicians re-tuned their instruments.

"So you see, my Prince Archbishop, I have doubts; but with this opportunity, the girl has potential that she will never fulfil at Porto Coeli."

The Prince Archbishop fiddled with the gemstones sewn into the arm of his gown.

"So! As I see it, we have a dilemma. On one horn the girl's future, and upon the other, the risk she presents to the viability of our monastery in these changing times."

The servants filled their glasses while the parley played an allemande. The Prince Archbishop tapped his slippered foot on the head of the bronze Castle Lion of Brunswick.

"Let us turn to the nature of our position, and to the future of Porto Coeli. There is money to be made. Think of the prosperity. We all know that the new ideas will affect us all. They are not going to go away. The last thing we need is this mad girl."

The Abbess shook her head.

"She is not mad. She is gifted."

"It matters not. She has no place in our plans for the future of our monastery."

"She has done good. The townspeople love her. They have adopted her. They pray to her."

The three dogs woke suddenly and howled together, drowning out the music. The Prince Archbishop called, "Enough!", and the dogs lay down. The Provost held up his empty glass.

"They pray to her, well, there you have it. Blasphemy if ever I heard it."

Lücke von Sandbeck tore a piece of rye bread, and hesitated as she raised it to her mouth.

"They say she is blessed."

"She is mad."

"She has visions."

"Stop!"

The Prince Archbishop raised his hand and there was only the soft sound of a courante from the viols. As he brought his hand down again, he noticed how the light caught the emerald in his new ring. He moved it into the sunbeam from the coloured window, and back again. Rotating his wrist, he observed the green shimmering shaft play, as it swung through the room. Prince Archbishop Christoph von Braunschweig-Wolfenbüttel sighed.

"The novitiate *is* mad. She takes control away from us. If we have rid of her, we will have the space to change without interference.

How can we do what we need to do if she and her ideas hold back the people of Himmelpforten? Look what happened last year. She brought the whole town to a stop with her wailing and weeping, right there, in the marketplace, in the middle of a storm, thunder and lightning and rain all around. Nothing was sold, the merchants made no money; she sent everyone mad with their shouting and howling, raising their hands to the heavens; all because of their 'Maid of Himmelpforten' – indeed! Such stupidity."

"I know Prince Archbishop. I spoke to her about this, but the people still love her."

Provost Martin Reiff cleared his throat.

"Prince Archbishop, my opinion is that this child is not capable of this task."

"Thank you Provost. My decision is made. This sinner, van der Staen – the girl is to find him."

"With the greatest of respect, my very Gracious Prince Archbishop, I see no chance of success. She will be in a foreign country among thousands of strangers. This task is not possible."

The Prince Archbishop touched the side of his nose and smiled at Reiff, who looked away and coughed.

"Yes. She is unlikely to find him; and it is a good thing too. It will keep our little Barbara out of our way. My hope is that she does not return; and we can look to a future in the new ways without her magic, and the superstition she engenders in her followers."

The Prince Archbishop raised his index finger.

"And they will forget her."

Abbess Lücke von Sandbeck sat upright and coughed aloud.

"My most revered Prince Archbishop, I think not."

"Yes, they will, Abbess."

He raised his finger, and the musicians became silent.

"Once we show the people of Himmelpforten the way to a prosperous future, they will forget her."

Once more, Lücke von Sandbeck took her ornate handkerchief and dabbed at her nose.

"Your Grace, I do your bidding, but I fear this is a sin. Are we just to abandon this child of God, who has so much to offer, and so much of his work to do?"

"My dear Abbess, this is a sin, but it is a necessary sin."

One of the hounds shivered in its sleep, and growled softly.

III

Hamburg

The Feast of St Mellitus,

24th April 1536

The Drinkers

It took Jaap nearly four days to get to Hamburg. While he walked, he thought he saw Gertje and Anders beside him. Gertje would speak to him with Anders at her side. At night, he dreamed about the dog heads that lived in other countries, where strangers lived: did they live in Skotlân? Did he really want to visit the country of his nightmares? He dreamed about the fire and was woken each morning with the pain in his joints.

He arrived at Hamburg, where the huge expanse of the estuary of the Elbe allowed for an immense range of industry protected by the city walls. On the water were dozens of ships of all sizes loading and unloading on the massive stone piers. The reek of fish and pitch and sawdust filled the air. All of this; the shouting and hammering and clattering, the smoke and smells, brought Jaap back to his life as a sailor, his life before Gertje. But now that seemed a long way away – now he would atone for sins new and old. He would go to Sintanders, to the shrine of little Anders' Saint-name. Perhaps there he could pray for the souls of Anders and Gertje. He would go to Skotlân. First Ingelân, and then Skotlân.

Jaap stopped at one of the big caravelles at the quayside. The letters that made up the name on the prow appeared as a jumble of incoherent shapes, but here was a word he recognised – Purmurend.

"Purmurend", he said out loud.

"Aye. That's the Sanctus Andreas, out of Purmurend. Beautiful ship, don't you think?"

The voice came from the next ship. It was Frisian; Gertje's language.

"By the Virgin! You are from Sylt?", said Jaap in his best Frisian.

The man smiled at the sound of his own tongue.

"My friend, I hail from the South, near Hörnum; but you are not from Sylt. Your Frisian is good, but not true."

"I am from Purmurend."

"So, a Dutchman; like the Sanctus Andreas here."

"Yes. This ship is from my home – near Aemstelredamme. I lived in Keitum for a time. I am Jaap."

"And I am Bent."

They shook hands, and Bent threw a coil of rope on to his boat. The boat was a lugger, out of place among the dozens of weary old Hansa trading kogges, caravelles, and holks. The lugger was different. Even with the lugsail furled, it was ungainly. Its flat bottom and the rudder on the larboard made this boat ideal for rivers and shallow water; this did not look like a sea-going craft. Bent observed Jaap's disapproving look.

"Do you not like our ship? This is the Drie Magiërs. She is a fine beauty and a good friend. I would have her a thousand times over the Sanctus Andreas, even if it is from Purmurend."

"So you say."

Bent tied off some items on the deck and jumped down to the quay. He rubbed his hands together, looked to the sky and back to Jaap.

"So. Keitum, you say. What news? Is Majstro Siemen still king up there?"

Jaap smiled.

"He is."

Jaap examined the Drie Magiërs, walking around her as he spoke.

"Where are you sailing for?"

"To Ingelân; to Bishop's Lynn, in the morning. We have hemp and flax."

Once more, Jaap considered the lugger. A rough sea would make the crossing an uncomfortable prospect.

"On this boat? To Ingelân?"

"By the Virgin, yes. We sail there all the time. I tell you the Drie Magiërs can swim the Mare Frisicum on the lightest of breezes."

Jaap eyed the ship once more, hesitating.

"Do you need another hand?"

"You have sailed?"

"Yes, to the North; Jutland, for five years." Jaap coughed. "I started before the mast on the Cordelière."

The Frisian whistled.

"By God's Arms, the Marie la Cordelière! You saw the action at Brest?"

"At Saint-Matthieu. I was but a ship's boy."

Bent's smile disappeared. He clapped Jaap's back.

"Now I know it, you must sail with us."

"Good. How long will it take to sail to Ingelân?"

Bent looked towards the clear blue sky in the East and to the clouds in the West.

"It will take us four days, with the blessing of the Virgin!"

Bent made the sign of the cross.

"Will you return with us?"

"No. I am going to Sintanders."

"You are a pilgrim. You will have a long walk for your sins. You must meet the other mate, Geoff. He is from Ingelân. He is ... how can I say, well, he jests."

"Ah."

Jaap's stomach grumbled. He couldn't remember when he had eaten. Bent smiled.

"Come to the tavern my friend. You need food. We will meet with Geoff."

The two men walked through the empty market. The stink of rotting fish filled the air. Cats and dogs fought to claim fish heads, and birds swooped down to feast on scraps. A man with a knotted beard walked towards them carrying papers. He stared at Jaap.

"You know that man? He seems to know you."

"Never seen him before."

An old woman washed away fish guts, and cleaned the last few stalls with salt. Jaap picked a pinch of the salt, put it to his tongue and spat it out.

"Poor salt. Too bitter."

"You know salt?"

"I am a salt farmer now. The season has started."

Two cats quarrelled over a pile of fish heads. Jaap and Bent walked around them.

"You will find such work hard in Ingelân. It rains all the time there."

"Ah."

"Yes, but those sinning dogs deserve it. Their king is a madman you know."

"Dogs, you say. You have seen the English dog heads?"

"By the Rood, yes. They call Ingelân the Isle of Dogs."

Bent took Jaap by the elbow into a huge tavern, a large barn with tables full of people sitting together, eating, drinking, and laughing.

"Jaap, my friend, this is our mate for Ingelân in the morning. This is Geoff. He is one of those sinning English dogs I told you about."

Geoff laughed.

"Und ya learnig alt my sins from zu, Bent, you Dutch fool!"

"I am not Dutch, I am Frisian."

"You Dutch fool", Geoff repeated and laughed, clapping Bent on the back.

Geoff had long hair that hung down like ears, and his large teeth stuck out in front of his face. His laugh was a bark, his accent incomprehensible. He added bits of Dutch, Danish and French altogether in the same sentence. Whenever he didn't know a word, he would speak in what Jaap could only guess was English.

"You Jaap. You Frisian, ya?"

"No, I am from Aemstelredamme."

"Ah ya. Ein ander Dutch bastard. You volken ist ein distemper."

He laughed and clapped the others on the back and they all laughed. Jaap raised his eyebrows. Bent doubled up.

"Jaap, did I not say he was a jester!"

Jaap joined in the laughter and Geoff stood to let him in at the table.

"Sit en ze Jaap. If you are for England, I must teach you my tongue. You must listen to me. You will need to spraken English. For not everyone in England spraks your language; my countrymen do not have my talent for tongues."

Jaap looked at the Frisian and raised his eyebrows. Geoff continued:

"You will need meinen helfen. Ya?"

Jaap grinned at the man with long earlobes and a white skin jacket.

"Ya. Thank you Geoff."

Geoff nodded, helpfully.

"Now, sit en ze hier. Eat en ze."

A girl appeared carrying pitchers of beer. She poured the golden liquid into everyone's cups. Geoff smacked her behind.

"Hamburg serving mädchen. The besten in ze welt."

The girl winked at Jaap. The blood rose to his cheeks; he smiled and looked away.

"The sprats are sehr gut, und the salt cod and cabbage. They have radi."

Jaap ordered the salt cod and a radi, a large white root vegetable. It came sliced and dosed with salt. Jaap tasted it and nodded.

"Good."

The night grew full of laughter with these new friends. Jaap remembered what camaraderie was like, and forgot, for a while, his grief. This company of men, laughing and talking of nothing, of politics, of the price of things, of corruption in the church; but not saying anything to each other that told of who they were. No talk of children or wives or home. This comforting, happy exchange, a diversion from the individual unhappinesses that existed elsewhere in their lives. In this way Jaap forgot his grief and lived this time of beer and men.

"So Jaap, you were at Brest?"

"Yes, on the Cordelière."

They stopped laughing.

"God's Nails! See en zie the explosion?"

"I was a boy. It exploded."

"God in de Hemel!"

"So many died; families, children."

"Show en zie the action, here on ze taffel."

Geoff cleared a space on the table and gestured.

"Here ist Brest."

He placed a cup down.

"Let this be Cordelière. Wo ist 'Mary Rose'?"

Jaap shook his head.

"I am sorry. I am not a general."

Bent put down his beer.

"But this was a great sea battle. God's Arms! All those ships – the 'Mary Rose', the 'Petite Louise', the 'Saint-André', the 'Regent'. Fifty ships."

"Und our new English cannon."

"Yes Geoff, your cannon. But Jaap, it is natural we would want you to tell us what happened. You say you were on the Cordelière when it exploded. Tell us your mind. That captain – Portzmoguer – did he set the explosion deliberately? That's what we are told, it was an act of tribute to St Laurence; was he a martyr, or was he a coward?"

"Ya Jaap, They say he said – 'We shall celebrate St Lawrence by dying in the fire'."

Jaap looked up to the high rafters of the tavern.

"Come on, Jaap. Tell us."

"I was just a boy."

Jaap looked at his hands and placed them palm down on the table.

"I saw people burn on that ship; women and children. Fifteen hundred souls were on that boat."

The three were silent. Geoff waved to the serving girl for more beer. Jaap murmured:

"I still dream of it."

Bent clapped Jaap's back.

"Ah, the fighting sailor's life!"

The talk continued into the night and the passage of time was a blur. The girl brought more beer. As the night went on, they sang in uncertain harmony the one song they all knew, first in their French:

L'homme armé doibt on doubter.

On a fait partout crier

Que chascun se viengne armer

D'un haubregon de fer.

L'homme armé doibt on doubter.

Then Geoff sang in English in a loud baritone:

The armed man should be feared.

Everywhere it has been proclaimed

That each man shall himself be armed

With a coat of iron mail.

The armed man should be feared.

"Guter song, that 'L'homme armé'; think you nicht?"

Geoff clapped Jaap's back, he stumbled.

"Yes. Great song!"

At last, the three men, wise with drink, staggered back across the market that was now coming alive again before the dawn. The three helped each other up the narrow plank, back onto the lugger. Jaap found a quiet part of the open deck and slept between the ropes.

~ ~ ~ ~ ~

The pain in Jaap's back stabbed him into wakefulness. The Drie Magiërs lay still and flat on the harbour mud.

"Bent, Bent."

He shook the man lying dead to the world beside him.

"Bent, we slept through the tide."

Bent moaned:

"What?"

The water tumbled out of the harbour until it was a stream.

"Eh? Another tide will come."

It was clear from the mud below that the Drie Magiërs was going nowhere. The next high tide was many hours away, so Jaap walked into the town, along streets familiar to him from his sailing years. He passed the old Hansa Kontor building with its ornate brickwork and roof tiles, and headed towards the spires of St Mary's, and St Nicholas.

At St Mary's, he found its doors shut fast. He stopped a woman in the street

"What has happened? The doors are locked."

"They closed it."

"What? They closed a cathedral? How? When?"

"Where have you been? The reformers closed it six, no, seven years ago."

Jaap's head pounded as a result of the night's ale. He stared at the edifice before him. The once glorious cathedral had broken windows, and cranes nested in the dirty spire. He walked on to St Nicholas and found it open. He would pray to St Nicholas, the friend of sailors. He entered and found a service under way, but it was like no service Jaap had seen. There was no incense, no choir, no Latin. Instead, a man stood in the pulpit speaking to the congregation. He spoke in Plattdüütsch, the Low German of the people. Jaap stood at the back and listened, tuning his ear to the unfamiliar tongue. The man next to him whispered,

"My friend, have you heard Doctor Bugenhagen preach before?"

"No, I am not from here."

"He is a fine man. Where other reformers have created discord, he has governed the changes well. He is friend to Doctor Luther."

Jaap listened to this preacher talk of love and responsibility for our sins at the day of Judgement. There was no mention of confession or

Purgatory or praying for the dead. This talk of individual responsibility intrigued and disturbed him. In the world of the old ideas, Jaap could not accept that the suffering of one person in purgatory could be alleviated by the atonement of another in this world. How was this right? Majstro Siemen spoke of Gertje's suffering being the consequence of Jaap's sins, but that made no sense. Jaap could not believe this, but he had no way of knowing. Were Gertje and Anders suffering in Purgatory for his sins right now? Could they reach the Gates of Heaven without his prayers? But these new ideas that this preacher spoke of, of one's responsibility for one's own sins, for Jaap this remained unsatisfactory. Was sin to be defined by the sinner?

These questions troubled him, and he found satisfaction neither in the new, nor the old. His head continued to pound. He came out of the church and looked back down towards the river. The tide would be up soon.

Jaap returned to the harbour; Bent and Geoff were setting the Drie Magiërs, now floating on the rising water.

"Ah Jaap, we thought you had changed your mind."

"No."

"So, to Ingelân, to Ingelân!"

IV

Bruggen

The Feast Day of St Catherine of Sienna,

29th April 1536

Medieval Hospital, circa 1500

Barbara stumbled into Bruggen through the morning haze. At Mariapoort a leper sat in the rain: she gave him her last piece of bread; he mumbled a blessing. Barbara had been walking for three days, with little to eat, sleeping at the side of the roads in that wet spring northern weather that makes comfort impossible. She staggered, shivering, towards the harbour, a forest of ships' masts. There had to be a ship that was to sail for Ingelân. But the kogges and holks and caravelles merged into a single mass of shouting and gabble and thunk of sheets on rigging. A familiar white light appeared to illuminate her vision. Barbara was delirious and shaking. A sailor approached. She squinted and peered at him, murmuring:

"Will you take me to Ingelân?"

"Ingelân? Why do you want to go there? They are brutes."

Barbara shuffled and shook in the rain; her eyes darted to and fro. She didn't flinch as he placed the back of his hand on her forehead.

"Girl, you are sick. You must rest."

"I must to Ingelân, I must go to Ingelân."

"When did you eat?"

Barbara's head jerked as she tried to stay awake.

"I must go to Ingelân."

"Come this way."

The sailor guided Barbara through the lanes and bridges. She allowed her self to be led around the strangely named streets: Katerinastraat, Twijnstraat, Hoogstraat, Meestraat. The sound of the town, the chat, the rumble of carts on the cobbles, dogs barking; it was all as one noise in her head, getting fainter and fainter. And then came her little silence. Barbara became unaware of the world around her. If she were able to describe it, she would say that it was a peace, a small glimpse of heaven, a small familiar comfort. During this moment, she felt no pain, no hunger, no cold. She heard, she saw nothing. She did not know how long she had been walking. Who was this man guiding her? They came to a large building on the Mariastraat. The sailor beat on the two huge doors. Over the lintel was carved the inscription:

SINTJANSHOSPITAAL DOMUS BEATI JOHANNES

Barbara repeated the words on the lintel, turning them around in a nonsensical mumbling.

"Johann, Benedictus, SintJaap .... ubi peccátor? ... Hospitaal, Domus, Pater Noster Deus misereri peccatori... qui es in caelis ... Coeli, Porto ... peccator quaerere ... peccator quaerere ... turribus ignis ... saltatus ..."

They waited at the entrance to the Hospital, and Barbara uttered incomprehensible stuttering words in Latin and Plattdüütsch, and other tongues not known to the sailor. Her eyes rolled to the back of her head. The sailor blessed himself.

The door was opened by a nun. Barbara stooped, eyes dull and half-shut, swaying as men and women gathered around to hear her gabblings. She continued to mumble incomprehensible articulations, but the little crowd were listening. The nun shoo'ed them away.

"Begone, can't you see the girl is sick."

She placed a hand on Barbara's shoulder.

"Hush, my dear. You are ill."

"...turrib ... saltatus ..."

She whispered in her ear:

"Are you with child?"

"Gravidam ... infans ..."

The Nun examined the skinny half-starved girl, her hair a tumbled red tangle on her head. Barbara trembled, uncomprehending, her gaze fixed on a distant point.

"... because you have to go over the road to Sint Andreis if you are with child. They can care for you there."

The sailor coughed:

"I don't think she is with child. I remember with my wife, it was different. She is too skinny. Do you think she is with child?"

"No sir. I don't think so."

Louder, she spoke:

"Enter. Welcome to Sint-Janshospitaal."

The Sister embraced Barbara and gestured to the sailor.

"Thank you my son. Your deed will not go unnoticed on the day of judgement. God bless you."

The sailor crossed himself and said goodbye to Barbara, her gaze unfocussed and blank.

"You need to have your confession heard, my dear. Sin causes all sickness."

The nun brought Barbara into the warm hall; she continued to mumble, limply holding her Abbess's letters of credentials. The sister removed them from her hand, and studied Lücke von Sandbeck's brusque

Latin, mouthing as she read. She picked up her quill and scratched Barbara's name and condition in a ledger. Out of the rain and cold, Barbara became conscious of her surroundings. Her silence, her little absence, was now fading, and she found her self again in a sensible world. Around her there appeared to be more than a hundred large cots, each with two occupants. Masses were in progress around the hall. Triptychs and paintings glowed at each altar, and the silverware glinted in the light from the large coloured windows. At each cot, nuns helped the sick to take part in the worship, or in other ways tended to their needs. The singing of chants resonated, filling the space to the high airy roof. Barbara allowed her self to be bathed and dried, and she was dressed in a red gown.

"This means you are a fever patient. Stay with the others who are wearing red. Do you understand?"

Barbara nodded. She took some broth and rested. As she lay down, the other occupant of the large cot, an old woman turned from her. Barbara touched her shoulder. As she faded into sleep, she listened to her soft, persistent weeping.

The next few days at the Sint Jans-Hopitaal blurred into each other. Barbara was too weak to get out of her cot. When she slept, she was aware of the constant sound of the mass being sung that washed over her. The repetition of the Latin, the elevation of the host, the sound of the bells and the smell of the incense increased her sense of peace. If she was to die, this would help. Her soul was being tended in this place. However, Barbara soon knew that she would not die here. She found the Book of Hours given to her by her Abbess, and every day she would take its weight, open the embossed covers and contemplate its pages. As she grew stronger, she remembered her mission and the long way she had to go.

The old woman in the cot beside her was dying. When she was awake, she was in pain and the nuns would come to her, speaking softly, feeding her, praying with her. In time, the woman settled and Barbara drifted off into sleep once more. When she woke again, the space next to her in the cot was empty.

Barbara gained strength and didn't have to wear the gown that identified her as a patient. She could walk in the gardens where the smells from the bakery and the brewery mixed with the heady fragrance of the herbs and plants. She would sit, listening to the occasional plash of the fish in the pond. The spring sun through the trees gave her a sense of well-being. After a while, she was able to help the nuns in the pharmacy and with visitations to the other patients. She learned the ways of determining ailments and their cures.

"Have you met Karl?"

One of the nuns took Barbara to an old man in a cot on the men's side of the hall.

"Karl is a soul of doubtful health. He likes the music. It moderates his pulse and gives him peace."

"Sir, what is it that ails you?"

The old man looked at Barbara. The look of pain in his eyes subsided. She touched his forearm. He placed his hand over hers. His voice was weak and guttural.

"Who are you?"

He saw Barbara with her tangled red hair tied back, lit by the light from the illuminated coloured windows.

"Are you an Angel?"

Karl blessed himself. Barbara smiled.

"No sir, I am Barbara. You are Karl?"

"I am a sinner."

"We are all sinners."

"This is my punishment, to suffer."

"That is why you are here. We can relieve you of your spiritual torment. Your soul can be cleansed here."

"Thanks be to God."

"What happened to you?"

Karl responded in short breaths.

"I fell in the canal, and I was sick. I am a stonemason."

He was now gasping for air. His eyelids almost completely closed with swelling, his breaths small and laboured; there was a rattle in his chest.

"Sir, do you wish to live?"

"Why yes, it is all I wish for."

"Rest, Sir. I will be here."

Karl squeezed his eyes shut, coughing, as he shuffled to find a comfortable position.

The nun came and moved him onto his side and firmly tapped his ribs with her fingertips. There was a gurgling sound, and he coughed up green bilious matter into a bowl.

"Thank you Sister" he croaked.

The Nun spoke to Barbara.

"This treatment gives him peace. Can you do this?"

"Yes Sister."

~ ~ ~ ~ ~

Barbara visited Karl often. She helped him eat and made him comfortable so he could see the Masses. His rattled breathing seemed to ease as she sat him up.

"My friend, how has your afternoon been?"

"Please don't waste your time with me. I ..."

Karl spluttered and coughed, gasping. He clawed at the air, a look of terror in his face. Although he was a big man, Barbara placed her small arms around his large frame; gradually, he relaxed, and she wiped his tears. She turned him over and tapped at his back, the way she had been shown. Karl breathed easier.

"I thought I was to die here."

"I know."

"But I don't think I will die."

"No Karl."

Karl rubbed at his itchy, painful eyelids with his knuckles, digging hard in to the sockets. When he finished, he peered through the swollen slits.

"My friend, your eyes are a cause of pain to you."

"My girl, it is nothing. I have other problems. Others are in greater need of your succour."

"Come, Karl, we know each other better than that. Let me look at them."

Barbara examined Karl's eyelids, swollen and bleeding where he had rubbed too hard. She opened them further with her fingers and saw the whites streaked with blood.

"Karl, I would like to wash your eyes."

"What? No. I don't want you to touch."

"I can bathe them using a mussel shell with a mixture of water and salt. Please trust me."

"No girl. I am in no need of your help. Leave me alone."

~ ~ ~ ~ ~

Meanwhile, over the next few weeks, Barbara became part of the community. She got to know Karl more, and his condition improved. It was Barbara who now tapped his ribs to release his phlegm before each call of the canonical hours. Barbara was washing his eyes daily, and the swelling subsided.

"I am sorry I doubted you, my little one."

"It is of no consequence."

Karl talked easier with Barbara. She learned of his children and grandchildren in Ghent.

"And why are you here?" he said to Barbara.

"My Abbess gave me a task. I have to find a sinner. I have to resume this task."

"You mean leave the Hopitaal?"

"Yes. I leave in the morning."

"But who will administer to me?"

"My friend, you are better, and you will soon be home with your grandchildren."

"I thought I was for the afterworld. I have sinned so."

"Oh Karl, we have talked about that. This world you inhabit is, right now, the world you must embrace. When the time comes for you to embrace the next world, you must do so only at that time. I shall pray for you."

"Thank you, my blessed little one."

Barbara walked around the hall, praying with this patient, sitting with another, some knowing they were for death, and others, like her, who knew death was a long way away. The care, the touch she gave to each, was the same, and they gravitated to Barbara as a focus that helped them live their life for that day.

Here, in Sint-JansHopitaal, the proximity of life and death was manifest. All there would share the same fate; only the timing of one's death was not to be known. The profound sympathy for the dying was borne out of the potent realisation that death could be as close as the person in the next cot, or could be visited upon one with no warning; but there was only so much attention that Barbara could give. Sometimes she had to be alone. She would sit in the garden, and read books of physic – Hildegard, Vesalius, Paracelsus, Galen, Hilda of Presscott, and more. Today, she went to one of the triptychs, the paintings in front of the high altar. The triptych showed the two Sint-Jans, the Evangelist and the Baptist. She had seen these paintings many times and knew the stories, but now, tonight, in the dimming light, she saw something she had not seen before. In the painting, just to the left of St Catherine, she saw a girl; but it was as if she saw her self in a looking glass; her own self, that same Barbara, translated into the painting. The image, of course, was much more beautiful than Barbara. This painted angel was no clumsy foolish girl, she was perfect, with red hair brushed like silk, dressed in such garments that Barbara would never wear, robed in a joyful dress of green and cloth of gold. In the end, though, it was the face of the angel; it was Barbara's face; the soft warm features, her own smile. In the choir, Barbara couldn't hold a note, but the angel in the picture carried a little organ. She imagined singing like her, happy and consonant. She found an inscription on the frame.

OPUS JOHANNIS MEMLING ANNO M CCCCLXXIX

Barbara gazed again on the happy angel, as if alive, singing and playing her little organ. But this triptych had been created many years ago by someone long dead. How could this person have painted her? She went to the pharmacy and found the looking glass used for observing wounds. She observed her self in the wrinkled glass and saw the self, the same face as the angel; but where the angel had brushed locks, Barbara had a mess of red hair, tangled and bedraggled. How could she think that she resembled the beautiful being in the old painting? She had committed the sin of pride. Barbara opened her Abbess's book of hours to pray, running her fingers over the embossed images of the little saints. She remembered when she was never proud; when she was happy in Himmelpforten; and as she prayed, realised that she had to return to her task. She had to find van der Staen; but the image of the angel in the painting was to stay with her.

The next morning, Barbara confessed her new sin, collected together her things and went to the door and said her farewells to the nuns. Waiting outside was the sailor who had brought her to the Hopitaal.

“My little Angel, how good to see you well.”

Barbara flushed.

“Thank you, sir.”

“I have been hearing about your progress. You are well?”

“I am well now, with God's blessing. But how can I repay you? It is through your good works that I am here today.”

“You can repay me by allowing me to do something for you.”

“You are a sailor?”

“Yes.”

“I want to go to Ingelân.”

“I know someone that leaves tonight with a cargo of pilgrims for Dover.”

“To Dover then.”

V

Len Episcopi

The Feast Day of St Guido of Acqui,

4th May 1536

Unloading a Lugger

The lugger had rolled and pitched all the way from Hamburg to Len Episcopi – 'Bishop's Lynn' as Geoff called it. On the open deck of the Drie Magiërs, the persistent rain soaked into their bones. With clothes heavy and sodden, the simplest movement was a struggle. They were exhausted; their feet held no grip on the timbers, and the ropes were so swollen with water that the knots could not be undone. In the pernicious drizzle, with bloated fingers, every surface they touched was cold, coated in a salty watery film; their happy night of beer and laughter of a week past, a dim memory.

Jaap van der Staen stepped from the slippy plank to the moss covered quay, onto the muddy dock. After so many nights of sleeplessness, the pain in his soaking joints pierced his fatigue. As his feet sank in the mud, his balance lost, he swayed, staggering on the seeming unfirm ground.

He helped Bent, Geoff and the laders unload the saturated cargo of flax and hemp, and hauled it to the marketplace just by the quays, the Tuesday Market where the traders and merchants and hawkers set their stalls. With the rain dripping from their chins, they worked sullenly, without speaking, struggling with the bulky loads, struggling to keep their footing on the wet cobbles. For Jaap, the earth itself seemed to roll beneath him as he fought the land sickness.

When they finished, they separated with an unsmiling nod. As he walked away, the ground moved like a ship, each step inflicting spasms of pain. He used his staff, holding on to posts and walls to secure his balance. A small boy was playing fivestones at the side of the quay. When he saw the tall Dutchman, he put the stones away and followed him across the market place. Jaap tried out his new language with a passer-by.

"Here Len Episcopi?"

The man examined Jaap, staggering and bedraggled and soaked. He rolled his eyes, sneered and said something incomprehensible. Pointing at him, the little boy laughed. How was Jaap to get by in this soup of talk? There appeared to be no Dutch, no German here; the few bits of English taught to him by Geoff on the lugger, useless. There were no separate words in this foreign place, just the Ingelânders' babble, the meaning lost in the jabber and drizzle.

Jaap was relieved to be on his own; he couldn't get off the Drie Magiërs quickly enough, but, as he stepped out on this new, unstable land, fighting for balance in the rain, in the pain and exhaustion, once again he found himself dreaming in the daylight. There was Gertje, in front of him, walking away, holding hands with Anders, trotting beside her, smiling. At the side of the road, he was sure he saw prattling dog heads. He shook his head to clear it of these spirits; although he would have liked Gertje to stay.

Jaap held on to his staff and his scrip, the bag that contained money, food, and the pilgrim accoutrements: the shell, the votive offering and the miniature altar. He staggered on in the noise of the harbour, reeling on the muddy earth, followed by the scruffy boy singing a song.

He went into the town, stepping carefully, swaying on the slippy cobbles. Horses and carts appeared out of the gloom, splashing in the filthy puddles. The little lanes were drained of light by the overhanging houses; above, the sky, a thin sliver of dull grey; the rain pouring into the centre of the narrow streets, creating small torrents in the gutter. A man walking in the opposite direction stopped in front of Jaap, blocking his way. He had a knotted beard, his eyes hidden in shadow. He spat to the side, raising his eyebrows as if in recognition, and pushed past.

Jaap looked at the boy, who smiled. He pointed across the square to an inn called 'The Gryffen'. As he entered, he was relieved to hear familiar words.

"You speak Dutch?" said Jaap.

The innkeeper examined the bedraggled figure in front of him, dripping on the fresh rushes that covered the floor.

"Of course. I speak Dutch; Plaat, Hoch, Flemish, Slav and all tongues in between. This is a Hanse town."

It had not occurred to Jaap that the trading of Lubeck, Danzig, Bergen, Bremen and Hamburg stretched to this odd, ancient place. Now he recognised the shape of the houses and the rich dress of the merchants, and all that old familiar wealth. He paid the innkeeper of the Gryffen a groat for a cot, lay down and closed his eyes, but at once felt the world sway. He put aside the nausea and persevered; all he had to do was to sleep.

~ ~ ~ ~ ~

With the jumble of the descending peals of church bells and the pain in his shoulders, Jaap wakened. He couldn't tell the time. He went out of the inn into the street; the town cloaked in a damp fog. He walked down the Briggate, passing the old Hanse Steelyard trading buildings, the Ouse river on his right with its smelly salt workings all along the shore. In front of the striking chequerboard facade of the Trinity Guildhall, familiar looking merchants gathered, their assistants clutching rolls of bills and their boxes of quills. Across the busy sand-market was the Cathedral of St Mary of Antioch with its high twin spires lost in the mist. The crowds pushed past, gabbling in the drizzle. Where were the Dutch speakers the innkeeper spoke of? Everywhere was the speech of the Ingelânders; the sing-song of these people a sound not known to him. How was he to get by in this mad tongue?

In a space in the crowd, he became aware of the boy again, his back to him. The hair colour? No. Impossible. He turned and looked at Jaap.

"Anders!"

It couldn't be him, could it? Jaap walked towards him, but the gap in the mass of bodies closed over. He pushed through, but the boy had gone. Jaap tried to explain to himself what he had seen. Had he served his penance on that terrible sea crossing? Now Gertje had been taken away, was it possible that this God in all His seeming bountiful goodness was restoring Anders to him? But no, Jaap shook these thoughts from his head. He had been dreaming. Only in his dreams would he ever meet Gertje and Anders again.

He crossed the sand-market and down Friar's Street, all the while hoping to see the boy. He went into the Crown Inn, took some coin and pointed to his money and at the bread and beer and meat. He ate and felt full again. The rain had stopped and he saw now that the streets were lined with inns to accommodate traders, and stallholders shouting their wares.

As well as the great cathedral of St Mary, there was the usual collection of monasteries and churches, and the old Hanse presence could be seen in the grand designs of the merchants houses, in the kogges and holkes in the long harbour that lined the silty estuary. To the East, Dutch windmills reclaimed the land.

Jaap returned across the town to the Tuesday Market to find Bent and Geoff, all the while hoping to see the boy. He crossed the market with its callers and hawkers. Below the market cross were two miserable men shivering in the stocks, stinking of piss, surrounded by tiny puddles of spittle. He found the stall where they left their hemp and flax, but it was empty, and the Drie Magiërs was not at the quay. Jaap was not disappointed that the lugger had gone.

He re-crossed the square and went into the church of St. Nicholas. He had it in mind to pray to thank him for saving him from the sea journey, but as he entered, the noise of the town disappeared, he found himself in a heaven on earth. The smell of the incense, the blaze of colour, the bright light that emanated from beyond the rood screen contrasted with the damp dull day outside. His senses were overwhelmed. This place was so warm, so beautiful, so uplifting, so affirming, that he forgot his anger, his despair, his fatigue and his loss. He saw that his suffering, his pain and the awful events of the death of Anders and Gertje, had to have made some kind of sense. Monks sang a Benediction. Men and women stopped and prayed where they stood. Pilgrims prostrated themselves on the tiled floor, reciting their prayers again and again. A priest and deacons and acolytes walked among them, blessing the crowd with holy water. The sound resonated right to the roof, the painted canopy that seemed as heaven itself. This rich conjunction of beauty surely proof of the demonstrable bounty of God. In the centre of the aisle, he was absorbed in the wash of the music, the smells and the light. Whatever his difficulties, this was the reality. He recited a Pater Noster and walked out of the cathedral, once more into the manifest world. The smell of the crowd, the damp grey sky and the tumult contrasted with the joyous thrill he had just experienced, but now the ground was stable and Jaap stood taller. He heard a voice behind him speaking in Flemish. He turned and saw a man with green eyes and a knotted beard, carrying a stick with a heavy joint at its end. As if from outside himself, he observed the weapon coming slowly down upon his head. As he lost consciousness, he saw the boy, smiling at him; and then there was nothing; no Gertje, no Anders, and no dog heads.

~ ~ ~ ~ ~

Jaap woke to the sulphurous stench of a salt marsh. He was surely back on Sylt with Gertje and Anders. He kept his eyes closed against the ache in his hips and knees and dreamed of laughing and playing; but there was the throbbing in his head. He turned over, wakened by the usual pains. He held his hand against a bright light at the door and listened to the sound of the slow wooden clunk of windmill gears and the whoosh of sails. He heard soft voices; not Frisian, not Ingelânder. He recognised a familiar accent from Delft. Jaap relaxed and spoke in Dutch:

"Where am I?"

"You are in Lynn, my friend."

"Lynn? Len Episcopi?"

"Well, that's what the Pope calls it. I am van der Oosten."

Jaap peered at the silhouetted figure with the voice of a Delftman.

"I am van der Staen."

He continued:

"The Pope, you say?"

"Yes, Pope Clement."

Jaap's head throbbed. He looked out beyond the curtain of his pallet, out to the open door to the street, to the clatter of people passing by. The Delftman was sitting at a table writing with a quill. On one wall were two Dutch paintings; one of a polder and a modest house, a dog running past a sluice gate; the other of a child wearing a cap. On the other wall hung pots and jugs and plates. On the table were maps and drawings; truly, a Dutch home, here in Ingelân. Jaap coughed to attract the Delftman's attention.

"You said the Pope calls this place Len Episcopi. You do not agree. Are you a follower of the new ideas?"

His chair creaked as van der Oosten leaned across the table and placed his quill in an inkwell.

"Whether I am a supporter of reform or not is irrelevant. I am an engineer. I deal in what is real. If change comes, it comes. I can do nothing about it. But you are an outsider here. You have to know that the King has denied the Pope's authority here in Ingelân."

"Denied the.... but how? How can it be so? No one will stand for such a thing,"

"Nevertheless, the Pope has no rule here. Anyway, never mind these things. How is your head?"

"It pains me but it matters not. How did I come to be here?"

"You were beaten outside the cathedral and the thug ran away."

"I remember the man who hit me. He had a beard. Flemish, I think."

"He ran off with your purse, and your pilgrim's things are gone."

"Alas, I have nothing now, and I cannot pay you for your kindness."

"Kindness is never bought my friend. But you may wish to regain your independence."

"Indeed I do."

"Do not fret. We will come to an arrangement."

"You are a good man."

"So some say."

Both men smiled. The Delftman called at the door:

"Gertje. "

Jaap was taken aback.

"Gertje?"

"Yes, for Gertje is my wife."

"This was my wife's name also."

"Ah. I see."

Van der Oosten and his wife exchanged a nod.

"Gertje, broth for our visitor please?"

The Delftman's wife brought in a steaming dish of barley, peas and mutton, and a cup of beer. They both watched as Jaap finished the food without speaking. He put down the bowl; he had been staring at Gertje. The Delftman's chair creaked as he leaned back, folding his arms.

"I think your wife is no longer with us?"

"She died not two weeks ago."

"Two weeks! By the Rood! I am sorry to hear of that my friend. This is a bad time for you."

The three crossed themselves. There was a silence, but for the whoosh of the windmill sails outside.

Jaap sipped the beer and carefully returned the cup on top of the ring-mark on the table.

"You are from Delft, yes?"

"Indeed I am. I think you are from Aemstelredamme."

"Very good. I am from Purmurend, close by. I am pleased you can tell. I have not lived there since I was a child."

"I have an ear for tongues."

Jaap raised his cup.

"So, how did a Delftman find his way to Len Episcopi?"

"There you go. You should to be more careful. Calling this place by its Roman name will define you as one of the old faith."

"But I have no love of the Priests."

"Nevertheless my friend, it may even be the reason you were attacked. "

"But I spoke to no one. "

"You must take care. This is Lynn. They say they will change its name to King's Lynn. It is to be called the King's town. You know what that means?"

"That the old faith will not be practised here?"

"Indeed. Along with all the cathedrals, that church of St Nicholas will have all its fine gold, all its statues removed, sold for the King to pay for his wars and his palaces."

"That is not possible. The Pope would never allow it."

"I told you, the Pope has no authority here any more. Reform is slow, but it is inevitable."

Jaap stopped and shook his head, bewildered, and took another drink of his beer.

"So, how did you get here?"

The Delftman swept his hand across the chart on the table.

"See here; we are draining the water from the land. The whole area around here, south of The Waashe, could be more productive and we do what we have done in Holland. We stop the sea, we solidify the ground we have claimed, we plant salt-resistant crops, and build dunes and ditches and dykes. We steal land from the sea. In five years they will be able to plant any grain they wish. You know the saying – 'God made the world...'"

"'... but Dutchmen made Holland.'"

They both smiled. and the Delftman refilled Jaap's beer.

"Thank you. You have children?"

"Alas, God did not give us the gift of children."

"I see."

"And you? What about you and your poor Gertje?"

"Indeed we did. We had a boy. His name was Anders. God took him also."

Jaap made the sign of the cross and wiped his eyes.

"You have had it hard, my friend."

"I thought I saw my dead son, here, in this place."

The candle spurted and splashed.

"Grief is a force that we have no control upon."

"I should like to see that boy once more."

"Be careful, my friend. These children in the streets, they are skilled thieves."

They sat for a few minutes, sipping their beer, with only the sound of the wind in the rotating sails. Jaap cleared his throat and spoke.

"How do you understand the language of these Ingelânders? It sounds as if they sing everything, just like the Milanese, but they don't move their arms about; their faces are like masks."

The Delftman laughed.

"Yes, I thought so too, but it will come in time. There are many who speak Flemish and Dutch too. This is a Hanse town."

Jaap walked to the door, forcing a rhythm into his movements that would get him past the sharp stabbing of his joints. Gertje supported his arm over to the cool air outside.

"Thank you."

He sniffed at the evening breeze.

"Where are the salt farms?"

The Delftman stood at Jaap's side.

"They are everywhere. They call the workings salterns here. It is the start of the season. You know salt?"

"I am a salt farmer. I think the rain spoils the salt here."

"They use different ways. Where there are salt marshes, where there is wood to burn, they boil the sea. In the north, there is a place called

Moricambe, where I am told they sleech the seawater using salty sand before boiling it."

"Sleech? I understand. This would make strong brine. In Sylt, we burned peat which flavoured the salt, but burning wood would boil the brine faster."

Jaap sniffed the air again.

"In the far north, in Skotlân, they use iron pans and they burn the brine with black stones from the ground. The great heat makes salt more rapidly. I should like to see this."

"My friend, Skotlân is such a long way; it is dangerous. I have heard there are savages there."

"And dog heads?"

"Yes. Even dog heads."

Jaap sucked in the familiar stench of the salt workings.

"Did I say that I thought I saw my dead son here."

The Delftman placed his hand on Jaap's shoulder.

"Do you want to work the salterns here in Lynn?"

"Yes."

"I will introduce you to the guild."

VI
Kent
Feast Day of Saint Eadburha of Bicester, 20th June 1536

A Book of Hours

Barbara landed at Dover off an easy crossing from Bruggen, with a fine breeze. The morning sun reflected on the blinding white cliffs like a mirror. She disembarked and joined the throng of pilgrims on the harbour, singing psalms, praying, buying trinkets from vendors calling to the crowd. Many were to head inland to Walsingham and Winchester, some would venture beyond, to the shrines and sites scattered through the country. Those travelling in the other direction sought out crossings that would lead them to Santiago de Compostela, or to Rome, or to Jerusalem. The optimism in the faces of those embarking on their pilgrimage contrasted with the different reactions of those coming back. Some heading home beamed with joy and happiness, some would continue on to another journey, but others showed anxiety. They were returning to untended crops, or unsympathetic families; returning to the problems they hoped would disappear while on their wanderings.

The morning sunlight was amplified by the blinding reflection from the cliffs that lit this community of travellers, talking together in all languages.

"So, this is Ingelân. They say they have a mad king here."

"Quiet, someone will hear."

"He is building a mighty army; and look at those new towers."

Beyond the harbour, there was the sound of builders hammering and sawing and chiselling as they worked on the port defences, but down among the pilgrims, hawkers shouted out their wares, the indulgences, their holy trinkets. They sold from stalls, or walked in the crowd carrying their trays of votive altars, badges, shells and staffs at their waists, supported by twine around their necks.

"Welcome pilgrims. We call this place 'Little Paradise'. Buy new-blessed rosary beads here. They are no weight. You can carry them on your holy path."

Barbara picked up a miniature altar at a seller's stall. She tried her new tongue.

"It is beautiful indeed."

A woman who was standing near took the little altar and put it back.

"Do not waste your money on these silly gee-gaws my dear. These people are thieves."

The vendor swung his staff at her.

"To the Devil with you. Can't a poor man make a living? Don't listen to this old crone." He smiled a toothless smile at Barbara.

"Buy my holy things."

The woman took Barbara's arm and guided her away.

"You are a stranger to this land, my dear?"

"I am, madam."

"You have to learn to protect your self. Do you have far to go?"

"I am for Skotlân. I have to find a Dutchman."

"Well girl, you must look around you everywhere at all times, and keep your possessions hidden."

"Thank you madam. I will take care."

"God be with you, girl."

"God be with you, madam."

~ ~ ~ ~ ~

The Monastery of St Sepulchre's in Canterbury, on the Dover Road, was just short of the Riding Gate on the city wall, overlooked by the high spire of the Christ Church Priory. Barbara entered the tiny cloister of the modest little nunnery with timbered, flinted walls. A woman in a rough habit was throwing ashes on to the midden, scattering a pair of quarrelling dogs. Barbara waited eagerly, but the woman merely glanced at her, returning to her work.

"Madam, I am from Porto Coeli."

She pointed towards a door across the courtyard with a dismissive gesture.

"Go find the Prioress Philippa Jonys; over there, in the refectory."

Barbara introduced her self to the Prioress in her hesitant English and offered her letters of credentials. Philippa Jonys shut the ledger she had been examining, scanned the letters, and placed them on top of the closed book.

"This is an open order; our Benedictine ways are contrary to the practices of your wealthy Cistercians. Do you understand this, girl?"

Barbara strained to comprehend the Prioress's rapid sing-song English, so unlike the English she had learned at Porto Coeli.

"Yes, Lady."

"Why do you wish to stay with us?"

"I heard about the open orders at the Sint Jaan's Hopitaal in Bruggen."

"I know this place. They do good work. How long were you there?"

Barbara struggled with the unfamiliar tongue.

"In Bruggen I was sick; they took me in; I worked there. I left three weeks ago and crossed the Mare Frisicum."

"But why here, why St Sepulchre's?"

"To serve God, Lady."

"You will call me Sister."

"Yes, Sister. My Abbess at Porto Coeli has instructed me to find a man, an evil man."
Prioress Philippa Jonys glanced down at Barbara's letters.

"Ah yes, your Abbess, Lücke von Sandbeck. Her Latin is direct. This is good."

The Prioress put down Barbara's letter and placed her hands on the desk.

"I have to tell you, child, that we are not short of evil men in this land."
She smiled and Barbara relaxed.

"He is a pilgrim. He is for Saint Andrews."

"So your Abbess writes. You do realise that you will never find this man."

"With the Grace of God, Sister, I will."

"Girl, how do you intend to do this? There are thousands upon thousands of men in England, and this – what is his name, Jaap van der Staen, this pilgrim could be anywhere."

"It is my work, Sister. I must find him."

"You have been sent upon a fool's errand. Why do they wish you gone from Porto Coeli?"

"They do not wish me gone. I was happy there and my Abbess loved me. Look, she gave me this Book of Hours."

Barbara held out the calfskin bound volume. The Prioress examined it as the colours reflected the glinting of the light.

"She loved you? Perhaps she did, perhaps she did."

The Prioress was warming to this girl. She was reminded of her own enthusiasms when she first took orders.

"I cannot recognise you as a Novitiate until we know you better. You will assist in the work and prayer until I decide your position here. As we are an open order, I will expect you to go out into the town."

"I would like that, Sister."

The bells rang for Nones.

"May I sing in the Office?"

"You may."

"Sister, I am sometimes out of tune."

Philippa Jonys smiled.

~ ~ ~ ~ ~

St Sepulchre's in Canterbury was very different to Barbara's nunnery in Himmelpforten. Porto Coeli was a large, wealthy institution, catering for twenty Sisters, each with a maid, each housed in their own little cottage. It was run along Cistercian rules with its own kitchens, wine cellars and a scriptorium, supported by a hierarchy of workers. In contrast, the little Benedictine open monastery at Canterbury, at the edge of town, was but a few buildings, comprising a small chapel, a tiny infirmary that doubled as a school, a cloister, all surrounded by the garden that spread to the other side of the Dover Road. The six nuns lived together; there were no cells. Inside its black and white flint walls it was a bustling place with people coming and going, the poor and the needy attended to by the Sisters in black habits. There was a constant noise from the kitchens, the crackle of the fire in the oven, the chat and the chopping of wood, as well as the bleating of a goat. Outside the walls, pilgrims chatted and prayed as they passed St Sepulchre's, along with the traders and stockmen taking their sheep and cattle, bleating and lowing, to market. From Matins to Vigils, the bells rang for the Divine Office from all the town's monasteries and churches; the Benedictines, the Augustinians, and the Franciscans all announcing their simultaneous calls to prayer.

Barbara fitted in with the rhythm of the community, adapting to the work, rolling back the sleeves of her habit, digging in the garden, cooking, tending to the needy. She taught in the school and was soon well liked in the monastery and in the town, and became a familiar figure, a mascot, even. People warmed to her attentiveness and her generosity, asking for her blessing. She would sit with them, listen to their troubles, touch an arm or knee, and they grew to trust and respect her. She also mixed with the pilgrims and visited the statios and the other Hostels, asking about the Dutch pilgrim.

"Jaap? What kind of name is that?"

"It is Dutch for Jacob. He is for Saint Andrews."

"Never heard of him."

Wherever Barbara turned, there was no sign of Jaap van der Staen. Perhaps Prioress Philippa had been correct. Maybe this was a fool's errand.

Barbara often opened the little Book of Hours given to her by her Abbess. She would gaze at an image, mouthing the words on the page. She imagined the sound of the words coming from her old Abbess, and then she would close the book once more; by this little contemplation, she found peace.

~ ~ ~ ~ ~

Then there was the night of the storm. The threat in the dense day weighed down on everyone; unable to sleep in the heat, they complained of pains in the head and sore joints. Barbara went into the town to the beggars and pilgrims and townsfolk complaining in the close air, and she spoke to them, calming them. Back in the hospital, she held those in pain near to her.

The oppressive day turned to humid evening; Barbara continued to tend to the townsfolk, unaware that she was exhausted. The storm came, as it could not but fail to come. The rain turned into a dense downfall and

Barbara found her self at the Buttermarket, in front of the Cathedral Gate. Townsfolk huddled together, the rain on their faces glowing in the torchlight. For them, there was fear in the black clouds of the late evening. She saw one of the torches become a white light that filled the centre of her vision. Feeling that warmth, that familiar tingling on her skin; time slowed down. The torrent permeated her clothes, and she shivered, but not with the cold. Above the sound of the rainstorm, there was the constant babble from the crowd, first incoherent, then she heard her name;

"Speak, little one."

"Comfort us, oh Barbara."

"Give us succour."

Barbara stood in the storm and the rain poured from the sky. They screamed as the lightning flashed in silence; and then, when the thunder cracked, they whimpered and held each other. Once again, Barbara felt that familiar lightness of her being, the confusion in her head, the taste of iron on her tongue. There was nowhere for her to go, no getting away from her predicament. Her red hair stuck to her face. She perceived a decelerating world, watching the rain fall, drop by drop; observing her arms as she held them out in the slow deluge. The townsfolk called to her.

"Our little saint!", they cried.

"Give us a miracle!"

Unaware of her surroundings, Barbara was deaf to the cheers, her trance combining with the warmth she felt, even in the rain. The crowd fell silent. Barbara closed her eyes and raised her left hand. Above their heads, clouds opened up, and the night was clear. All at once, the rain stopped, the wind dropped; the moon was sharp and bright above them. They gasped and fell to their knees.

"Sweet Blood of Christ!"

"Barbara. Our little angel."

Barbara now raised her right hand and pointed upwards. Three silver shooting stars crossed the sky. Men and women and children fell to the ground. The crowd wailed and swooned as one.

Then there came a perfect silence. Barbara, in her warmth, spoke. There was no meaning or grammar, but yet there was expression and cadence. Her eyes rolled back in her head as her words rose and fell. The melody swelled and diminished, and there was a crescendo towards a climax; such a climax. She dropped to her knees, turned her head to the canopy above and called out. The rain fell again and the clouds obscured the sky once more and lightning cracked the air. The terrified crowd ran away in mortal fear.

~ ~ ~ ~ ~

All those present that night would say that they had understood what Barbara had said in the rain. Later, there was argument as to the actual words, but they would soon relate her utterances with certainty. Barbara had delivered a prophesy. Within days, men and women and little children on the streets were reciting the words attributed to her:

The Power of the King is a Flower that withers in the night.
Towers of Fire, the Flower of God,
The Power of God is a Flower that rages in the night.
The Towers of Fire will rage like Flowers in the night
And the people will dance in the flames.

~ ~ ~ ~ ~

In the days that followed, when Barbara was recovering from the fever and the delirium, she was told what everyone in the crowd heard that night in the storm. Criers read her words aloud on the streets from pamphlets.

"I did not say these things."

But whenever she went into the town, bringing food to the poor, they murmured,

"Our Holy Saint, Barbara."

They touched her habit, blessing themselves as she passed. Barbara was embarrassed and confused by the attention. Why was she being treated in this way? At the monastery, she spoke with Prioress Philippa Jonys.

"Holy Prioress, Sister, I have been guilty of the sin of pride."

"Why do you say this my child?"

"The townsfolk say things to me. They bless themselves and touch my clothes."

"I have heard this said."

"But what am I to do?"

Philippa Jonys placed her hand on Barbara's.

"We shall find a solution."

"But my sin, Prioress?"

"This is not a sin of your making. You have a gift and you use it unwittingly. When they see you in the town, they see their mortal state as through a lens. You have a duty to them. You must but act this part and respond in the way that comes to you. Pray with them, share things with them, attend to their needs. It is what you have done since you arrived at St Sepulchre's."

Outside, the little goat bleated, and a cat screeched. The Prioress took up her quill, paused, and spoke again.

"I heard that Erasmus of Rotterdam has died."

Barbara was surprised at the change of subject.

" Erasmus; yes Sister? I have heard of this man."

"God bless his eternal soul, for we will not see his like again. He was here you know."

"Here in St Sepulchre's?"

"Yes. He wrote about this city and of our Cathedral. I remember his words – 'What pompous sick vestments is here', he said, 'what possible excuse can there be for decorating and enriching churches, while our brothers and sisters waste away from hunger and thirst'."

Sister Philippa looked out of the window. The bell for Vespers was rung. Barbara waited to be dismissed to sing the Hours, but the Prioress continued.

"These are hard days, Barbara."

This was the first time that Sister Philippa had addressed Barbara by name. She was taken aback.

"Yes, Sister."

"I do not know what is to become of us. You have heard of the Valor Ecclestiasticus?"

"'The Value of the Church'? No. What does it mean?"

"Indeed. What does it mean? I forget you have not been long in England. The King sent counsellors to examine us. They want our gold and our land, although they found precious little of the former in our priory. Twenty nine pounds, twelve shillings and six pence. That is the value of this monastery. I fear they will close us."

"But what will happen to the sisters?"

The prioress shook her head and blessed her self.

"I cannot say. There is talk of a pension for those who have taken orders, and accommodation in houses in the town, but how can we Sisters live apart, away from our practices, away from this home of succour? What about our lay helpers? They will not obtain a pension. I don't know Barbara; perhaps nothing will come of it. What would they want from us? We are a poor order; all we do is provide help to those who need it. What King would wish to take that away from his subjects?"

Barbara left the Prioress and went out into the kitchen garden, still weak from her experience in the storm. She sat in an arbour, enjoying the feel of the sun on her face. Outside the monastery gates, she heard the trundling of carts along Dover Road. What would be the outcome of the Valor Ecclestiasticus? Would the monastery be safe? It was not Barbara's place to worry about such things, but Sister Philippa's concern was evident.

Barbara reflected on the night of the storm. What had happened? It was like at Himmelpforten, that time in the marketplace. She had no awareness of what she was doing; it was as if she was a puppet, her limbs operated by someone else. Was this God himself directing her actions? And those words. Where did they come from? She knew she spoke, for the utterances that came from her mouth were real, but she did not understand them; they were not words of intent, but somehow they appeared to be so. She had no wish to communicate anything to anybody, but many knew that she was transmitting a message.

And what of the prophesy, the 'Towers of Fire'? Did she really say these things? These were frightening words, disturbing words. What did they mean?

VII

Lynn

The Feast Day of St Zacharias of Jerusalem

23rd August 1536

The Making of Salt

In the morning sun that lit the low-lying fog on the fens, Jaap felt the warmth on his bones, easing his joints. He loved these mornings on the salt marshes; the flat open space, here at the wide plain between the land and the sea. With the breeze on his face, he moved between the ponds, estimating potential yield, lifting the gates to allow draining from one to another. At each pond, the hue on the brine changed with the increasing concentration of salt. The more orange there was further out, the sweeter the salt, and where the algae was dark green, was the bitter, cheap salt, for animal licks or fields. Close by were the snow-white ponds, where the salt coalesced. At the head of the salterns plumes of steam rose from large lead pans, heated with wood fires.

This morning, like every day now, the boy waited for Jaap, playing fivestones at the edge of the ponds. He had followed him around since Jaap's first day in Lynn. Jaap knew his name was Harry, but nothing more, he didn't seem to have a past, but he saw that even at his young age, the boy was able to protect himself by keeping such information to himself. This morning, in the light of the low mist he was so like his own Anders. Jaap waved as he approached across the ponds

"Hello, Jaap. Can we farm salt today? I brought an egg like you said."

"Good. We go."

The boy started to jumped up and down enthusiastically but realised the fragility of the egg he was holding in his little bag. He stopped and stepped carefully across the levees as Jaap led him out to where the water was fresh from the tide.

"Have you egg?"

The boy took an egg from its bag and held it in his hands.

"Put egg in water."

The egg sank.

"Look. It sinks."

"Yes. Now come."

They returned to where the clouds of white crystals floated in the water, lumps of salt piled up at the side.

"Put egg here."

Harry placed the egg in the brine.

"It floats, Jaap, it floats!"

The boy waved his arms up and down in excitement.

"It floats, it floats!."

"Why it float?"

Harry bit his lower lip.

"What colour is water?" prompted Jaap.

"White."

"Why water white?"

"Because it has more salt in it. There is no space in the water for the egg."

"Yes. When egg float, salt good for harvest."

They went to the whitest corner, where the crystals of salt clouded and crusted on the surface, glinting in the sun. Jaap dipped his lousse on the surface and drew the salt towards him. Harry attempted to copy, but struggled with the long handle. The large wooden rake splashed on the water, disturbing the gathered salt. Harry looked up at Jaap who stood close, saying nothing. He placed the boy's lousse once again on the surface, pulling the salty crust towards them. They repeated the action, each iteration increasing the boy's confidence. The growing pile of damp salt lay at the side of the pond. When he had finished, Harry smiled, and Jaap curtly nodded. Jaap placed his lousse, with the handle resting on the levee, out of the water. Harry mimicked Jaap's movements.

"Tell me about salt, Jaap."

"Salt. You want story about salt."

Jaap observed the ponds with their different concentrations of brine.

"You know why sea salty?"

"No Jaap."

Jaap stretched his creaking back. As he twisted his shoulders, turning his head fully to the left and right, he heard the clicks and cracks in his neck. He pointed.

"In far North, there is place in sea called Svelgr where the water turn round and round. Sea very angry. It very dangerous for ships."

He dipped his finger into the water and stirred it.

"A whirl-pool?"

"Yes, very good Harry. A whirl-pool, yes. This whirl-pool, there live witches."

"Witches?"

"Yes. They crush salt and turn it in the sea."

"They stir the sea?"

"Yes, they stir sea to make sea salty. They grind on Grotti. Grotti is, how do you say, Grotti is a big rock, a big quern under water."

"How many witches, Jaap? What are they called? Where do they come from?" Jaap smiled.

"They from the devil, Harry, they from the devil, and they are called Fenja and Menja. They make much trouble for ships. Many sailor killed."

"Were you a sailor, Jaap?"

"Yes I was sailor."

"Did you see the witches stirring the sea to make salt?"

"Yes. I saw witches, many times."

"You saw Fenja and Menja?"

Harry's eyes opened wide.

"Were you frightened Jaap?"

"Yes Harry, I much frightened."

Harry pointed to the pile of salt at the pond he had been working.

"Jaap, Is my salt good salt?"

They went to Harry's pile.

"You eat."

Harry took a pinch, put it on his tongue and smiled.

"It's nice Jaap, it's nice."

"Yes Harry, it nice."

"Tell me another story about salt Jaap."

"Not today. Another day."

Jaap bent and shook hands with the small boy in a mock formal fashion. Harry giggled.

The tide was on the turn and there was work to be done. The men stoking the fires were stripped to the waist, ladling thick white water from the inner ponds into the steaming pans edged with crusty salt crystals gleaming in the morning sun. The lumpman broke off the cakes of salt using a wooden shovel while the men ladled and poked at the fire. Harry followed Jaap at a distance and watched from the side.

"Jaap. Come and join us. Have you heard the news?"

The men shouted over the roar of the crackling fire.

"What news?"

"Parliament has supported the King. The Act has been passed. The monasteries will be dissolved."

The men cheered and raised their ladles and pokers.

"To the dissolution!"

"God Bless King Harry!"

Jaap looked at the men, puzzled.

"Dissolve? What this word?"

"God's Arms! Come on Jaap, you Dutch fool. Dissolve; get rid of them, destroy them. You know."

"But, the monasteries? What this mean? The Friaries? The Priories and Nunneries? God in de Hemel! What of great Abbeys? But there are so many. They are everywhere."

"By the Rood, my Dutch friend, these priests have had it coming. They have lost sight of all that is holy. You know Walsingham?"

" The shrine?" said Jaap

"You mean Falsingham, don't you", said another. The men laughed.

"You know that they can sell you the Virgin Mary's milk in Falsingham!" The men laughed again. Jaap raised his eyebrows as he translated these words in his head. He answered slowly, unsure of their meaning.

"But how can that be so? Why do you laugh? People think it a miracle?"

"Miracle my arse. They are thieves and are only interested in money. Trust us Jaap. The dissolution is wondrous news. We will have done with the monks and their sins and fornication and thievery."

"But this cannot be so. The monasteries ... where will sick go? Where will children be schooled? Where will succour be sought?"

" Our King has spoken. We no longer go with the old notions; forget the Pope and his foreign ways, this is England. We don't want to be ruled by these monks. They have no fealty to England. All they want to do is to take our money. Have you not seen the riches in the great Abbeys, all that gold and silver? How can they justify that? They are thieves and fornicators, thieves and fornicators, I tell you. Our Anointed Sovereign has spoken and we have a Holy duty. Are you with us, Jaap?"

"I, eh, I must think."

"We need men like you Jaap, men of honour and virtue."

'Honour and virtue', thought Jaap. 'How little you know of me'. He faced away, his cheeks flushing.

"The tide, it is turning. I must to the salterns."

~ ~ ~ ~ ~

Jaap sat down at the table with van der Oosten and Gertje.

"A good day?"

Jaap was relieved to hear his own tongue again. The Delftman's Dutch was rough and honest; you could tell what he felt when he spoke. These days, it was hard speaking the tongue of the Ingelânder. Jaap understood more, but he still couldn't tell what they thought. Hearing the Delftman speak was like breathing fresh air.

"Yes. A good day. I taught Anders how to farm salt."

"Anders? You mean Harry, don't you? Your new friend, that street boy."

"Ah yes, Harry. He is a clever boy."

"Where is he from? Where are his mother and father?"

"I do not know. He will tell me when he is ready."

"If he doesn't run off with your money first. I tell you, do not trust him."

"You do not know him. He is a good boy."

"Hmmm. Tell me, is there much salt?"

"Yes, my friend, the yield will be good, but as the weather gets colder, good days like today will be fewer. There will be more rain."

"But there is next year's harvest."

"With God's blessing."

The two men made the sign of the cross.

"Say grace with us?"

Jaap said the grace and they blessed themselves; they had rabbit stew and drowned it with beer. They said nothing, and they ate and drank; they smiled when their eyes met. Jaap put down his spoon.

"My friend, I heard today that the King is to – what was the word; yes – to dissolve, to dissolve the monasteries."

Van der Oosten put his finger to his mouth.

"You must be careful with such talk. We are outsiders here. Yes, they will destroy the monasteries. We live in changing times where the very earth beneath us moves."

"But the monasteries? It cannot be so? They cannot be destroyed."

"It is the wish of their King."

Van der Oosten poured beer into their cups.

"They say he is only dissolving minor monasteries – for now."

The Delftman went to the door, closed it and took the lamp to the table.

"You must whisper of such things; you must protect your self."

"Yes. yes, yes, but why? So much destruction because he hates the priests?"

Gertje glared at him. He put down his spoon.

"I will tell you because you are new in this country, and we must not speak of it again."

Gertje tutted and clattered the bowls and plates as she gathered them, deliberately leaning between the two men. Her husband patted her arm, addressing Jaap cautiously, whispering.

"Last Tuesday past, the King Henry beheaded his Queen, Anne, because she was guilty of adultery. He tired of her and wants a new Queen, but the Pope will not sanction a divorce. The Pope has no authority in England, so the King must have his own new religion with him as head of the church, so he can re-marry."

Van der Oosten moved the little dish of salt on the table to the side. He placed his forefinger on the space where the salt had been.

"Also, he needs money to finance his wars. He wants more ships and they are building new defences at all of the ports. He will get the money to pay for this by emptying the monasteries of their gold."

The Delftman took a drink of his beer.

"Folk are sick of the tyranny of Rome and the corruption in the church; they are sick of the monks that sell their prayers for indulgences. So you see, the King can use their hatred, the hatred they have for the monks who every day take the money from ordinary folk."

Jaap shook his head.

"No, no, no. The monks pray, as we pray, so to reduce the suffering of our loved ones tormented in Purgatory. Our forebears whom we love, their souls that are vital, they are as alive to us."

Jaap was raising his voice, gesturing wildly, illustrating each point by grasping the air between them with both hands.

"Ours is a community that is united with our dead. To take away the only means we have to help them is cruel. The dead rely on our prayers to alleviate their suffering. Do you tell me there is no Purgatory because of a few sinning monks?"

Van der Oosten held his finger to his mouth.

" Hush. Yes, but they do say it is many monks."

"But people are not stupid. They find honest confessors and avoid the bad ones. We all know who they are. If the king takes this away from us, how will we give succour to our loved ones who have passed on? Who cares if some churchmen become rich? It doesn't matter if the armies of monks praying for our poor dead are sinning. Even a prayer from a sinner is a worthy prayer. Is there to be no blessing of a man's memory?"

"The reformers tell us that each of us should keep his own balance sheet of sin and be responsible directly to God."

Jaap was breathing heavily, and his voice was raised.

"But what of our common love that is manifested in that prayer? What kind of world will it be where that bond is broken? How can we rely on each other for succour? We are all sinners, we need to support each other in the face of the punishment that awaits us."

Jaap wiped his eyes with his sleeve. The Delftman touched his hand.

"I know you grieve for your family, my friend. When it visits, grief governs all; we cannot but obey its commands."

Jaap took some beer and wiped his eyes. Van der Oosten lowered his voice.

"As to the reforms. many share your worries, but we have to be strong. We don't know how these changes will come about. Perhaps they will fail, but make no mistake: you must be circumspect. You have a good position here. You are respected; you are making improvements at the salterns, you can be wealthy. The price of the salt will go down for the townsfolk and what we sell in the markets will bring you money. Don't sacrifice this good business for your private worries. When it comes down to it, these changes we see around us are not driven by religion or by spiritual interests. They are borne out of mere political power; this is ever present in the world."

~ ~ ~ ~ ~

"Look, Jaap, Look."

They approached the Tuesday Market through Jews Lane, but the way was blocked by a large crowd at Stewards Hall. There was an air of anticipation in the light drizzle. Men came out of The Gryffen, drinking and shouting and crashing their cups, slopping their beer on the ground and on people's coats. They pushed to the front, cursing their way forward. The lowing of cattle mingled with shouts of men selling corn; the stink of wet beasts and dung hung pungent in the damp air, but there was something else. Harry looked at Jaap, blinking in the rain.

"Let's go and see. Please Jaap."

A man with a knotted beard pushed past carrying a cup of beer, he stared at Jaap, and down at Harry.

"They're burning an old witch. Remember this day, boy. You will see this sight again."

Their eyes locked together, and Harry felt his gaze pierce right through him. The man repeated, pointing at Harry's chest:

"Remember this day, I say. You will see another day like this. Remember this day."

Harry turned away, tugging at Jaap's sleeve.

"Jaap, please can we go and see."

"No Harry, this is not a good place."

The man with the knotted beard spat on the ground and, moving away, nodded knowingly to Jaap.

"The boy will see this sight again. Mark my words, Dutchman."

In his bewilderment, Jaap realised that he was no longer holding Harry's hand.

"Harry. Wait!"

The man with the knotted beard was gone; Harry ran towards the square and disappeared in the crowd. Jaap followed, but in an instant, the boy was lost.

All Harry could see were the bodies around him. He looked up at the falling rain and reached out for Jaap's hand. Harry felt the grip of cold fingers and stared into the wooden toothed grin of a woman wearing an old withered gown, face smeared with white, with pockmarked cheeks. Her breasts were wrinkled, and she smelled of beer and old sweat.

"Shall I lift you up to see, my lovely?"

Harry pulled away from her hand and wriggled further into the crowd. He shouted, but his voice was drowned in the noise of the mob. He was squeezed against the coarse linen of a man's coat, forced to smell his goaty odour. A woman next to him wore an embroidered dress and the beads and hard stitching pressed against his face. He was trapped in the terrifying clamour and confusion of crushing bodies.

"Jaap, Jaap, where are you?"

He looked up at a man with mad wide eyes, who shouted:

"Burn her!"

Others called out:

"Have Mercy!"

The noise of the crowd died down, and from the middle of the square, a man's voice could be heard. Harry couldn't make out what he was saying, but around him, people nodded and shook their heads, blessing themselves.

There was a crackling and Harry tried to push his way through the cheering mass of bodies, but it was impossible. A woman screamed and Harry smelled the reek of smoke. He saw nothing but the sky above and the bodies around him. There was no air; he started crying.

"Jaap, Jaap."

In the sound of the flames, there was a hissing of rain on the fire. A woman's voice croaked:

"For pity's sake help me. More fire."

A man's voice was heard:

"The rain's putting out the fire. It's taking too long. More fire, more fire."

There was a swelling in the crowd. Harry heard her scream again.

"Help me. For the Blood of Sweet Jesus, help me."

Now the fire had a new ferocity; Harry put his hands over his ears. The smell of the smoke joined with a strange stench of cooking meat. Not meat that Harry knew, but something sweeter and sicklier. Along with the rain falling, came ashes. Harry pressed his hands tighter against his ears, but the noise and smells were more intense. There was no air, and he gasped for breath. He tried to push the dark bodies away, but they closed in tighter. His senses dulled, he became drowsy. He licked his lips and felt the sharp gritty particles of ash. The air was full of smoke and bits of burnt sticks and burning cloth. He closed his eyes. His feet no longer touched the ground, and he was supported only by the mass of bodies pressed around him; he felt himself slip between them to the ground. Through the confusion, the haze and the ash, he heard the voice he wanted to hear more than anything else:

"Harry!"

Jaap pushed through the throng and lifted the boy free of the braying crowd. In the confusion, Jaap saw the man staring at him again, the man with green eyes and knotted beard; the man who had attacked him outside the cathedral. Staring at Jaap, he turned his head and spat. Jaap ignored him and carried the boy away, leaving the plume of black smoke behind them. The smell of the burning flesh was pungent and stuck in Harry's throat. The ashes and bits of cinders and twigs and cloth floated down onto his upturned face.

"Close your eyes", said Jaap.

Harry closed his eyes and Jaap covered his nose and he breathed easier. Jaap was carrying him and he knew he was safe. The rain turned into light drizzle, and they stopped at a well, away from the noisy crowd. Jaap gave Harry a drink of water.

"I'm sorry I ran away, Jaap."

"You must not do it again."

"No Jaap."

Jaap spat on his sleeve and wiped away the soot from the boy's face.

"What happened, Jaap?"

"They burned an old woman."

"I heard her shouting. Why did that man say I should remember it?"

"I don't want you to think about it. It is not what a boy should see."

"But why did she want more fire? The rain would have put out the fire."

"No, the rain would not have put the fire out. She wanted to die quicker, so they needed more fire."

Harry thought for a moment and said: "Oh".

Jaap thought about the despair in the woman's voice. This brutal public act he had witnessed. All this disturbing change. It was too much. Harry should not see such things.

"We need to go away from here. Would you like to go away from here?"

“I would like to go with you, Jaap. Can I come with you?”

“Yes. We should leave this place.”

Harry held Jaap's hand tight and looked up to him.

“I'm safe now.”

“Yes Harry, you safe.”

VIII

Lyncoln

The Feast Day of St Bavo of Ghent, 1st October 1536

The city of Taghaza

"Help me, Help me!"

It was Gertje, crying out, then Anders:

"Papa!"

Jaap awoke, but the screaming didn't stop. Across the room, Harry was sitting upright, his eyes wide open, staring ahead, wailing.

"There. Do not be frightened. You safe. I look after you."

The bed was wet. Jaap lifted the boy and held him until his sobbing subsided. He gently guided him to the side, where he swayed in his little waking dream, whimpering. Jaap changed his night clothes and put new linen and straw in the cot.

"You are safe here."

Jaap tucked Harry's blanket tight around the boy; he thought leaving Lynn would be good for them, but the nightmares and bedwetting were now every night. He told Jaap again and again of the smells and the shouts, of being lost in the crowd; the terror of the burning and being unable to breathe. Jaap could do nothing but comfort him.

"Where are your mother and father?"

"I don't know", croaked Harry.

"But everyone has a father and mother."

"I have no mother or father. I was stolen by my faerie uncle."
Harry yawned.

"He kept me with other boys and he made us do things. He had warm hands and a nice voice. He beat my friend. My friend died. My faerie uncle says that I am a hundred years old."

Jaap said nothing. Harry's eyes were half closed, and his head drooped.
Harry mumbled:

"Tell me a story about salt."
Jaap moved a piece of straw from his hair. He spoke in a quiet sing-song fluency.

"There was once city called Taghaza."

"Tagaz..." Drowsily, Harry repeated the word. "Taghaza. Where is Taghaza, Jaap?"

"In Barbary lands; Taghaza was wondrous city made of salt."
Harry lifted his head.

"A whole city, of salt?"

"Yes. But it was not always so. It was founded by a beautiful princess called Kinga. Before Kinga, there was no salt, only wooden huts and scrub. Kinga's father was a goodly ruler, and he loved his daughter; he wanted to give her a fabulous dowry, so he offered her a palace, but she refused. He offered her gold, and she refused. He offered her frankincense and myrrh and spices, and she refused.

'What can I give you, my daughter? You do not want my expensive gifts?'

'My Father, I cannot take these things for they will lead to injustice. I cannot have such things while my people are hungry.'

'These are fine words, but I must give you something for your dowry.'

'Give me salt', she said.

'Salt?' said her father.

'Yes, salt'.

'But salt is worthless'.

'No father, salt is not worthless. It is not as gold, but it can bring prosperity to our city'.

'Ah, I see', said her father.

So Kinga's father pointed to the West, to where the mountain stood.

'I will give you the mountain'."

Harry was awake.

"Why did the king give his daughter the mountain, Jaap?"

"He gave her the mountain because, in the mountain, there was a salt mine."

"Where you dig for salt?"

"Yes."

"Like we get salt from the water."

"Yes Harry."

Jaap continued.

"Kinga bowed, and as she did, her father kissed her and gave her a ring to wear when she married.

'My father, I thank you'.

And so Kinga left the city of Taghaza, but on her way, she went to the mountain and threw her wedding ring into the salt mine, and she walked away into the West. Eleven years, eleven months, and eleven days later, the Princess Kinga returned to the city with wise eyes. She was carried upon a palanquin, followed by a retinue of supporters, led by a man called Rodger. Rodger instructed the retinue to stop at the entrance to the mine – in those days, the mine was still and unworked. Men and women and children came from the city, for they remembered Kinga for her virtue and her innocence. She stood at the mine entrance and she spoke.

'My friends', she said, 'when I left this town, I threw my wedding ring into this mine. If you see fit, I would wish it returned to me'.
They all looked for Kinga's ring and at the same time, they learned to mine the salt. They found salt to be a fine building material, for they used water as mortar and the walls were polished like glass. And so, they built many new palaces and fine homes; and in their trading of salt with the outsiders, prosperity came to Taghaza. A wall of salt was built around the city, for they still had to protect themselves. When it was complete, the Princess led a procession to the gleaming palace of salt. It shone in the sun, sometimes white, sometimes blue, sometimes green, and in the evening it was red. As she walked among them, Princess Kinga thanked the people, enquiring after their children, or their parents and loved ones. When she was finished, she went up the steps to the open door of the palace. There, her companion, Rodger, raised his hand, and there was silence. He turned and presented the Princess with a box made of salt. It glinted with the colours of the palace walls. Kinga opened it; inside was her golden wedding ring they found in the salt mine. The Princess kissed Rodger and wept, for she was overcome with joy. She requested that the musicians play and that the children, and the men and women danced together. The music and dancing went on until the red light on the salt palace turned to the white blue of the moonlight. The city remained prosperous for many years, and they lived happy and healthy for a long, long time."

Harry's eyes drooped and his head jerked. Jaap moved the blanket to keep the sleeping boy warm.

"Where are your mother and father?" whispered Jaap once more.

"I don't know. The faeries took me."

~ ~ ~ ~ ~

The next day, under a grey sky, Jaap and Harry entered the city of Lincoln amongst the milling of pilgrims travelling up and down Ermine Street. They went through the Stonebow, climbing Steep Hill, past the quiet poultry market, towards the towering Cathedral of the Virgin Mary. There was no activity here, little sign of prosperity; the stalls were empty, broken boards hung loose from the traders' and guildsmen's shops; beggars and lepers filled the streets, and buildings were in need of repair. They joined a small group near a stall where they paid for poor bread and thin beer; listening to the murmurs of the run-down town. A man stood in front of Jaap, staring at him. Jaap recognised the knotted beard. Harry walked ahead into the market square; the man blocked Jaap's way.

"Who are you?" said Jaap. The man turned to the side and spat.

"The question is, my friend, who are you? A pilgrim? A Dutchman? Ha!"

He smiled with one half of his mouth, speaking English, but with the sound of one from Flanders. Jaap answered.

"I am from Aemstelredamme."

"I know who you are. I am Jan Starter. Do you not know my name? You see, you are so like me."

"What? How so?"

A woman pushed past. The man bent close to Jaap's ear and spoke in Flemish.

"My friend, we know things, we ken things; we have done things that others will never experience."

"What do you say?" said Jaap.

Starter continued.

"We – you and I, have committed that most mortal of sins."

Jaap was aghast.

"What?"

He examined the man – strong, tall, with the carriage of a soldier.

"I am just like you, my friend."

"But no ... you are not..."

"Don't say so. I ken, and you ken, and we see it in each other."

Starter took a piece of paper with writing and handed it to Jaap.

"It is a little rhyme. Think on it. Think on us."

Jaap took the paper and looked at it, uncomprehending. He crushed the paper and tossed it aside.

"You do not know me."

Starter bent to pick up his paper.

"Ah, But I do."

The man placed his hand on Jaap's shoulder, but Jaap threw it off. Starter smiled.

"You must know that I will always be there to remind you of who you are and what you have done. If not me, it will be another. You have sensed that thrill we have shared, that joy that makes us different."

"No", said Jaap. "Not me."

In an instant, the man disappeared in the small crowd. He had met this man before; Jaap was confounded. Was there something dark in his nature he himself could not see? Was it because of what he did as a boy, on the Cordelière, all those years ago? All that death? How could he have come through life for so many years and still not reconcile himself? It would seem that strangers in the street recognised him and saw these things in him. How could this be?

~ ~ ~ ~ ~

"Jaap, Jaap."

Harry was pulling at his arm.

"Jaap, I met a brave man. I am going to war to fight, just like him."

"Are you now?"

Rubbing Harry's head, Jaap laughed. He examined the boy's hair.

"Who have you met? Who is this brave man?"

"I have met Thomas Cade. He is a soldier. He fights for truth and against tyr, tyrr.."

"Against tyranny?"

"Yes, Jaap. Against tyranny."

Jaap smiled.

"Jaap, what's tyranny?"

"Where one person tells others what to do."

Harry allowed Jaap to pick a nit from his head.

"Where did you meet this man?"

Jaap cracked the nit between his thumbnails.

"At the marketplace at the cathedral steps."

"I see. Shall we visit this brave soldier?"

They walked with the pilgrims to the Chequer Gate at the top of Steep Hill, through the shabby little market in front of the Cathedral of the Virgin Mary, and heard a man's voice, clear and confident, speaking from the steps. Harry pointed.

"There he is. That is Thomas. Listen, listen."

Thomas Cade was addressing a growing crowd.

"It is for us, my brothers and sisters, to act. This moral corruption must not continue. The monks act irresponsibly, so we, yes, you and I, must hold the abbots to account. Let me tell you, I know of a man, Sedbar is his name, the Abbot at Jorevall. He is a tyrant, and like all tyrants, he will not answer to the people or our King, he will answer only to himself; those who line their own pockets at the expense of ordinary folk. He wants us to think that our sins must be paid for with money, and that you can buy your way into the kingdom of heaven. This is a travesty; these ideas must be shown to be the lies they are."

Across from the cathedral steps, Thomas Cade caught Jaap's eye.

"You sir, you have the bearing of a soldier. I think you have seen battle."

Harry grinned at Jaap, who stayed still, unsure of what was expected of him..

"Yes you sir, are you not ready to act on behalf of God's cause?"
Around him, men and women waited for Jaap's answer.

"Eh, I know nothing of your politics. I am Dutchman."
Thomas raised both arms to the air.

"My friend, these are difficult times, but we must take a stand. We cannot fail to take a part in these events. If good men, such as your self, sir, do nothing, the evil that grows amongst us will prevail."
Jaap responded, uncertain of his accented words.

"Yes, you are correct."

"My friend, of course I am correct. You and I and these good people around us are of a like mind."
Thomas pointed to a small group on the other side of the little marketplace.

"But see those fools yonder."
Across the empty stalls, a man addressed a group standing beneath a banner portraying the Five Wounds of Christ. They knelt, blessing themselves, exclaiming to God and the Virgin.

"These are the superstitious rebels who think they can turn the tide of progress; but they are weak. They are stuck in the past with their ignorance and corruption. They do nothing but pray. It is only by taking action that we can change the course of our world."
Jaap coughed.

"And, how so? What shall we do?"

"We are all soldiers my friend. We must act as soldiers act. We will assist the King's Commissioners in their lawful duty. Your son there, he is a fine lad. Come here my boy."
Harry ran to Cade's side, beaming back at Jaap.

"This young man is why we fight. We act not for ourselves, but for him. Stand by me."
Thomas Cade kneeled down and looked Harry in the eye.

"What is your name, son?"

"Sire, I am called Harry."

The crowd cheered.

"Ha! By God's Blood, he has our king's name! A name that befits a young man of the future. Young Harry here will fight with us, won't you, boy?"

Jaap was moving from foot to foot, clenching and unclenching his fist. The boy looked wide-eyed at Thomas.

"Yes, oh, yes sir, I want to fight with you."

Laughing, they lifted Harry into the air.

"We fight for Harry!"

Jaap followed the group as they left by the Chequer Gate, carrying Harry high, singing and calling:

"God Bless our Harry."

When they got to the turn at Bailgate, they put Harry down; Jaap took him by the arm and pulled him away.

"Jaap, you're hurting me."

"Come with me. These men very dangerous" Jaap said quietly through his teeth.

The boy stamped his foot on the ground.

"No Jaap, Thomas is a soldier fighting against evil, I want to join his band of brothers. I want to, I want to."

Thomas Cade and his men roared with laughter as Jaap dragged Harry wailing and shouting through the streets, back towards their lodging, hauling the boy by the arm.

"You must not listen to that man. He will cause trouble."

"But Thomas is a good man. I want to be like him. I hate you Jaap, I hate you."

As Jaap knelt down, Harry spat in his face. Instinctively, Jaap slapped him. The two were frozen for a moment; tears welled up in Harry's eyes and he wailed like a siren. Jaap stopped, dumbfounded.

"Harry, I..."

"I hate you. I hate you."

Jaap pulled the sobbing boy all the way down the hill, back to their room on the Briggate, near the Stonebow. Harry's exhausted little voice fading as he sniffed and whimpered.

"I hate you, I hate you."

~ ~ ~ ~ ~

'I hate you.' These words echoed through Jaap's sleeplessness. He turned over, seeking relief for his pained bones as his mind raced in the black night. He tried to control his breathing, but he couldn't settle, so he rose and felt his way out of their room into the night. Between the clouds, the intermittent stars punctuated the black sky; but there remained the words: 'I hate you', and Jaap's horror at his response; he had struck a defenceless child. Harry's words were hurtful, but they were guileless. What had he done? After all their shared experiences, their joy and growing together; these words had cut into Jaap worse than the pain in his bones. But worse, much worse, was his utter shame at striking the boy. Jaap hung his head. This boy's innate thirst for life was contagious, his ability to take from the moment the essence of everything. Jaap had not known such happiness since he had been with Gertje and Anders. He and Harry were happy; they seemed to meet each other's needs. But Harry's words seemed as a blade in Jaap's heart. He knew Harry didn't mean it; he knew he was responding in his childish way, but Jaap was still hurt. And that hurt was made solid by his disgust at what he had done. He gazed at his hands, at their dim outline in the dark. Whose hands were they, these that had perpetrated violence upon a small child? It was as if his skin was not his own skin. He put his fingers on the stone wall, but the very touch of things seemed remote; his actions distant, separate from him. But there it was. He had lost control and he had caused suffering and hurt to Harry.

Jaap closed his eyes and murmured, "No, no, no", holding on to the wall, rocking on his feet.

The clouds shifted to show more of the night sky, Jaap breathed deep in the cool air. How to protect Harry? This had been his singular purpose since the death of Gertje and Anders. Would Harry still trust him? Of course he knew that some kind of discipline was required and that he had to be firm, but this violence caused him more pain than he had ever known.

Jaap felt an urge to pray, but he made no prayer, or benediction. What was the point? There was nothing that could be done about his demons: all the people on the Cordelière; Gertje and Anders who were gone; and now he had struck little Harry. It was clear, as clear as each pinprick in the sky above him, as clear as the pain in each movement of his shoulder, or his hip, that his prayer was pointless. There was no one to hear, no one guiding his fate. Jaap governed his own actions. He alone made his choices upon a stage set by circumstance. Here he was, upon this little world, encircled by the horizon, with the sky shifting from the light of the day to the dark of the night, in his near constant pain. No creature, no being would offer him comfort in this world. Jaap knew that he was his own captain, without regard to the priests or reformers. Jaap was responsible for his own decisions; he chose his own path.

Jaap shook himself and straightened his creaking shoulders. The questions remained. Would Harry ever trust him again? And the upsets – Harry running off into the crowd at Lynn; witnessing the burning of that poor woman – this was what Jaap had to protect Harry from; from the dangerous influence of Thomas Cade. Here in this strange country, in these confusing politics of reform, where events and allegiances appeared spurious, who could tell who was for it and who opposed it. This man Cade had a logic of everything that seemed unassailable. Jaap could see how Harry was drawn to Cade's charisma. Jaap had met many such men;

their authority a given. In their company, Jaap could never gainsay them. There was nothing he could say that could change their ways, despite their manifest error. They were dangerous, and wrong in their dogmatic view of the world. In the past, he had walked away from men such as Majstro Siemen, or the other salt farmers in Sylt. But with Thomas Cade, he was forced into an unwelcome engagement. Somehow, Jaap would have to come to an understanding with Cade that would allow Harry some kind of accommodation with this disagreeable man. The alternative was that Harry would simply run off with him. This could not be allowed to happen.

Jaap shivered. The cold stars filled the sky in a gorgeous glow. The familiar patterns, creeping across the canopy, moving silently overhead; the Milky Way, the smear of stars that spread across the night sky from East to West, perpendicular to their northwards travel – here, they called it Watling Street – showed pilgrims their way.

"North", Jaap mouthed in the silent night.

Back in the darkness of their room, he heard the sound of Harry whimpering in his dreams.

~ ~ ~ ~ ~

The next morning Jaap's bones creaked, forcing him into unwelcome wakefulness. As he stretched, he saw that Harry's cot was empty. He dressed and ran into the street to the sound of the monastery bells ringing for Prime. The remains of the sliver of moon hung in the morning sky. Jaap ran up Steep Hill and around the square at the Chequer Gate. Had anyone seen a small boy? A woman took Jaap aside.

"I saw you and your boy in front of the Cathedral yesterday listening to that Thomas Cade. Stay away from that man. He is trouble."

"Have you seen my Harry?"

"The boy? He is with Cade."

"Mijn Gott! With Cade? I must find him. Where…?"

"They left the city", the woman pointed East. "...over the Wolds, to Louth. Look for the big spire. There are men in harness; a dozen or more. There is talk of trouble."

IX

Lowthe

The Feast Day of St Patusius of Meaux, 3rd October 1536

Marcuccio

Jaap ran, and walked, and ran again, the pain in his joints overwhelmed by the thought of Harry with Thomas Cade, caught up in a bewildering rebellion in which they had no part. And there were his worries; how could he regain Harry's trust? Was he lost to him? Was God punishing him yet again for his sins? What was Harry's dream of faeries?

The sun lit the fields on either side of the road to Louth. Men and women harvested the last meagre crops, their work for the season almost done; in the distance, he saw the high St James's spire. There was the near-constant peal of church bells, but this ringing sounded odd. Jaap had become familiar with the bells in England, their strange patterns, but this ascending sound was disturbing.

When he arrived in Louth, it was afternoon, the atmosphere heavy with threat. Jaap couldn't tell if those milling around were for the King or the rebels. He stood at the rear of a group of men who shouted "Glory to God", blessing themselves. A man standing next to Jaap spoke:

"Did you hear the Vicar Kendall preach on Sunday? Was it not such a joy? Did he not tell us what was in our hearts? He told us what we believed; that Purgatory was real, that we should continue to worship the Virgin, that we should protect and hide the beautiful things in the church before the Lord Thomas Cromwell's Commissioners come."

"Cromwell! Damn the Crumme in Hell!"

The danger was palpable. A man recognised Jaap as a newcomer, his features foreign.

"But you are not from here, are you? I think you did not hear our Vicar Kendall, eh?"

Jaap nodded. He wasn't listening to the man, he was listening to the rising sound of the upset bells.

"Why church bells ringing all the time; why they sound strange?"

"God's Arms, man. What is the matter with your ears? Can you not hear? They're ringing the changes awkward."

"But..." Jaap was puzzled.

"As a sign of danger man! God's Blood! Do you not know what is happening here? The bells are being rung backwards."

Another prodded Jaap in the chest.

"In the name of the Virgin, who are you? Why are you here?"

"Are you with the Commissioners?" said another.

Jaap was in the middle of an agitated mob with a worrying interest in him. What would he say? Out of the confusion, in the persistent sound of the disturbed bells, he recognised that here in Louthe, there appeared to be anti-reform rebels, and they thought that Jaap was the enemy, a king's man – like Thomas Cade.

"You know what we did to your friends at the Nunnery at St Mary's. We sent them packing."

"And yesterday, that Bishop's man, from Lincoln, Doctor Frankishe, God's Nails! Did we not show him a good time over at the High Cross?"

"To think he would strip our churches of the holy things."

"What a bonfire we made of his hateful accounts!"

"We made him burn his own books, Ha!"

"He won't come to tax Louthe again."

Jaap raised his voice:

"I not with Commissioners. I be not with King's men."

The men were silent.

"So, what do you want here?"

"I look for ..."

Jaap gazed down to the ground.

"I look for my son. He ran away with group of men. Their leader is called Thomas Cade."

"Thomas who? Who is this Thomas Cade?"

"He is with the Commissioners; he took my son."

"By God's Nails! Will these reformers stop at nothing? They steal honest men's children! Fetch the Captain."

A woman touched Jaap's arm.

"You poor man. You must be worried sick. When was your boy taken?"

"He wasn't in his bed this morning; a woman in Lincoln said they took him here to Louth."

"There be many strangers in town. The rebellion is gathering strength from all around, and we would know if there were any of the Commissioners' supporters here. They are all up at the Saracen's Head. Someone there will know if they have a child."

"Here's Captain Cobbler returned from Caister."

To cheers, a man approached wearing a coat of motley. With him was a taller man carrying a bundle of papers, wearing a kettle hat and a heavy leather jerkin. The Captain spoke to his companion behind his hand.

"What days of violence we have witnessed. First, Horncastle, today Caister. Such things will get us hanged, for I fear the King will hear of it."

The Captain's adjutant eyed Jaap as they sat at a table at the side of the road. He took a quill and scratched on a piece of paper. The Captain composed himself, gesturing towards the man with the kettle hat and jerkin.

"You all know Great James, my adjutant."

The Captain pulled the lapels of his coloured coat around him and stood straight.

"Friends, I have to tell you that we skirmished with the King's men in Caister today. One poor man is dead, and two are in the stocks for his murder. I fear there will be a reckoning, but that is tomorrow's work. Who will tell me what has been afoot in Louth?"

"They say we are to have forty thousand men at Hambleton Hill, and they are rising at Horncastle and in the north. There are Commissioners' Men at Market Rasen. We have the King's ear now."

Wearily, Captain Cobbler looked around at the men of Louth.

"Who is this man?"

Jaap came forward, and they told how Thomas Cade took Harry in Lincoln.

"What is your name Sir?"

"Jaap van der Staen. I am Dutchman."

"Indeed. I was in Ghent where I was gifted this here goodly coat of motley."

He exhibited the coloured garment; Jaap nodded approval.

"I saw a coat like this once, in Aemstelredamme. It is a fine coat."

"It becomes me, no?"

"It becomes you, sir."

"Thank you for your words. I like Dutchmen. You are direct; but enough of my coat; to business. What is your son's name?"

"Harry,"

Cobbler put his finger on his assistant's paper.

"Write it down, write it down".

Great James scratched the words on the paper with a quill, Captain Cobbler reading over his shoulder.

"We shall help you find your son, Dutchman, but first, you will take our oath."

Each man was listening to the Captain, waiting for Jaap's next move. There was to be no discussion on the matter. Cobbler took a Bible and placed Jaap's hand over it.

"Repeat after me: I Swear to be true to Almighty God, to Christ's Catholic Church, to our Sovereign Lord the King and unto the Commons of this Realm."

Jaap repeated, Cobbler continued:

"And so help me God and Holydam and by this book."

Jaap completed the oath. Captain Cobbler and the rest of the men made the sign of the cross and Great James recorded the proceedings. Cobbler addressed Jaap and the assemblage with a theatrical flourish.

"God bless you, Dutchman. We will go to the Saracen's Head and find your son."

The mob muttered approval and moved on, led by the Captain, his coat of motley swaying in his wake, Great James at his side. They passed along Mercer's Row, brandishing billhooks and pitchforks. At the door of St James's, another flock of people joined the group, adding to the collective outrage. When they arrived at the Saracen's Head, they pushed Jaap to the front beside Captain Cobbler.

"Cromwell's Commissioners have abducted this man's son. We demand he be freed before the night is out."

The innkeeper surveyed the angry mob.

"There are no Commissioners' Men here. You have frightened them away. They have gone to Market Rasen. They are staying at the Greyhound Inn."

"Market Rasen, you say. But this man says they stole his boy this morning."

"Well he isn't here. I have had no new Commissioners' men here today, and I have seen no boy."

Great James faced the innkeeper.

"By Christ's Blood. You had better not be lying my friend, for you know the consequences."

Their faces were an inch apart.

"Remember your oath, man."

"By God's Nails, I am telling the truth."

"You had better be, or we will return."

Cobbler clapped Jaap on the back.

"I believe this man. No Commissioners' men would come to Louthe today. They would be dead men. This man Cade and your son have turned back to safety, towards Lincoln by way of Market Rasen. You shall go to there, to the Greyhound Inn. If you ride, you will arrive this afternoon. The Commissioners' men are there. You shall have a horse. James, what spare horse do we have?"

The adjutant referred to his ledger.

"He may have Marcuccio."

"Ah yes, Marcuccio. I know him well. A horse with character, and not yet reformed; ha, ha! A fine beast."

Captain Cobbler and Great James laughed together and pointed to a large muzzled horse as black as night. The horse was tied up, but moved sideways, stepping its hooves one over the other.

"A Frisian!"

The horse pawed the ground.

"Indeed. A Frisian he is; Marcuccio will see you well."

Captain Cobbler became serious.

"I must think on the muster at Hambleton Hill where our army awaits. We are to ride on Lincoln tomorrow with our friends from the South. Good luck with your search for your son. Send me word of how you fare. You are to consider your self blessed you are in England at such a time. With the Grace of God, our rebellion will be a success. The King has no choice but to recant and halt these devilish reforms."

Jaap was trying to make sense of these confusing parties, and his apparent allegiance to both sides. He rode with two of Cobbler's men to Market Rasen. Marcuccio answered sweetly.

"What did Captain Cobbler mean about Marcuccio?"

"Ah now. You are a lucky man. Marcuccio is a horse with a history, a performing horse."

Jaap considered the large animal beneath him, black and lean, but massive, like a horse one would take into battle.

"A performing horse, you say? But this horse is too large."

"He used to dance and fly, some said he could sing and talk. A wondrous beast."

Indeed, the animal's gait was elegant, and he appeared to float. Not like a beast of burden at all.

"How did you come by him?"

"I heard he was with us rebels, then he was with the reformers, and now he is back with us. He is a horse that cannot make up his mind if he is a reformer or rebel, Ha, ha, ha!"

"But you say he is a performing horse! Good Marcuccio!"
A slight nudge from Jaap and the horse purred and moved forward.

"He likes you."

~ ~ ~ ~ ~

At the Greyhound Inn, they found no sign of Harry or of Cade. Market Rasen was full of rebels, loitering with their pitchforks and scythes, and again, the Commissioners' men had fled.

Jaap returned to Lincoln, with its tattered signs and beggars. He rubbed Marcuccio's nose as he left him with an ostler, and the horse gave a whinny. Jaap was sorry to leave the animal, but he had to find Harry. He asked at the taverns and alehouses as to the whereabouts of the King's men, and he found Thomas Cade and his followers drinking in the Ram's Inn, near the Cathedral. Harry sat at Cade's feet, playing fivestones. The man was laughing, with his hand on his shoulder. Jaap's relief was short lived as he took in the distasteful scene. Harry saw Jaap approaching.

"Jaap, Jaap, We are going into battle with Thomas."
The men laughed, Cade smiled at Jaap.

"My friend, you have come to join us after all."
There was a sense of menace in Thomas Cade's invitation, and Jaap knew that if he tried to remove Harry, he would lose him. Here he was, sitting with the King's Commissioners' Men, having just taken Captain Cobbler's oath for the rebels. Jaap was getting deeper into danger. He would have to bide his time. He addressed Cade:

"I wish to join you."

"Good man! Come and have some of this pottage."
Cade put his hands on Jaap's arm.

"So, Jaap. I can call you Jaap, can't I? Young Harry tells me you were a sailor; that you were in a sea battle. Is this true?"
Jaap hesitated.

"I was at the Battle of St Matthieu, at Brest."

"Ah, where our Mary Rose trounced you Frogges and Frenchies! But this is all good, for that was yesterday's war. You have seen fighting and you are welcome in our band."

Jaap nodded, and Cade put his arm around Harry.

"Your son is a fine boy. You should be very proud of him."

Harry beamed. Jaap strained with the pretence of friendship.

"Tell me Thomas, what do you think is to happen?"

"Why, we will follow the king's Commissioners and assist them with their work."

"Of destroying monasteries?"

"Dissolving them. God's Death! We are liberating these pathetic souls from their backward ideas. You can't eat a nut without breaking the shell. Have you any idea what has been happening here, my friend? The goodly Lord Burgh's servant was beaten and murdered by those animals at Caister, and another, a poor man, Bellow, his name was; they blinded him and sewed him into a raw cowhide and baited him to death with dogs; of what indiscretion were these honest men guilty? Why, they were doing their King's bidding, collecting the tax that is rightfully his. These are the curs we are dealing with. They are burning books, forcing good people to make oaths against the King's law. They have no respect."

Jaap flushed and said nothing. Another man in the troop spoke up.

"Their leader in these parts is not even a nobleman. He is a shoemaker. They call him Captain Cobbler. Ha!"

Jaap remained stonefaced. Cade continued:

"There are forty thousand of them, camped, waiting to attack. We are to wait for the King's men and engage them when they arrive. There will be a hundred thousand strong from the King. It is to be announced at the Chapter House at the Cathedral of the Virgin Mary tomorrow. Come with us to Lincoln and see history written."

Jaap nodded.

"When are they to arrive?"

"Soon, my friend, soon."

Jaap ate his pottage and Harry approached.

"Are you angry with me?", he whispered.

"No, Harry."

"But I ran away."

"That's all right. We are here now."

"I'm sorry. But we are all together, happy with Thomas, aren't we?"

"Yes."

Later, in the moonless night, Jaap turned over to ease the pain in his hips. He wanted to know more of Harry's dream of the Faeries. These worries kept him awake. Harry was so taken with Cade, and would follow him anywhere. Jaap had to stay close to protect him. He had to pretend to be with Cade's men. But what if he was to meet up again with Captain Cobbler and his rebels? He had taken their oath. He wanted nothing to do with all this confusion and danger but, to keep Harry safe, he had to appear to be loyal to both sides of this rebellion; this dangerous anarchy in a foreign country.

~ ~ ~ ~ ~

At the shabby market in front of the Cathedral, rebels and reformers mixed together to hear the King's proclamation. Incense filled the anxious air, mixing with the smell of animals and men and anticipation. A Mass had just finished, and the priest came down the steps of the cathedral, blessing the crowd with holy water. Some knelt and one of the King's men called:

"Ho, Priest. Go hence and look to your gold, for we will soon take it away to feed the people!"

Others shouted "Husht!", and "Shame on you." The priest returned to the safety of the cathedral. Jaap and Harry stayed out of sight at the back, observing the jostling of men with swords and armour, the nervous throng pushed aside by nobles on horseback and the going and coming from the Chapter House to hear the King's proclamation. Jaap recognised the colourful coat of motley of Captain Cobbler who approached with Great James.

"Well Dutchman, I see you found your son."

"Eh, Yes. Thanks to your fine horse."

"Indeed, I wonder what is to come of good Marcuccio. I do wonder, will he ever fly and sing again?"

The Captain placed his hand on Jaap's shoulder.

"These are troubling times, Dutchman."

"I must say to you, I am confounded. I know not which side is which. What is to happen? Among these men here, who is rebel and who is King's man? What will they say in the Chapter House?"

"We wait to hear the King's mind. Then we decide if we should march on London."

"On London. Mein Gott! This is a big thing?"

"Ha. Yes. It is indeed a big thing; forty thousand men to rise against the King! Who would have ever thought such a thing to happen? But first, the lawyer, Thomas Moigne, is to read the King's response to our letter so I must attend at the Chapter House. God's Bye, Dutchman. Remember your oath!"

"Aye! God's Bye, Captain Cobbler."

As Jaap raised his hand to say farewell, he saw Thomas Cade who had just seen him speak with Cobbler; Jaap moved deeper into the crowd where they talked of going to battle. Men were in harness, with various pieces of chain mail, breastplates, and gauntlets. Some were on horses, drinking ale and singing. In the throng, some prayed in the open. A nobleman wore an ancient full suit of rusty armour; children laughed and pointed, and their mothers took them by their ears and pulled them home, squealing. Along with Captain Cobbler in his coat of motley, the nobles and the leaders left the body of the cathedral, and processed into the huge Chapter house. The crowd jostled at the door, trying to hear. Jaap and Harry were carried along in the throng, unable to move. Thomas Cade was watching as Harry tugged Jaap's sleeve.

"What is happening Jaap? Are we going into battle?"

Distractedly, he rubbed the boy's head.

"I don't know."

While negotiations took place inside the Chapter House; rumours circulated about the King giving way, restoring the monasteries but, at the same time, there was talk of the King's army having already left London to engage the rebels. These conflicting reports spread with different little groups in the gathering hearing new and contradictory accounts. The murmuring crowd silenced as a noble wearing the King's colours left the Chapter House and walked down the nave and out to face the crowd at the Cathedral steps.

"That's Thomas Moigne, the lawyer. He's to read the King's proclamation."

He was sweating, and he mumbled his words.

"Speak up, King's man!"

Moigne raised his hand, but the first part of the reading was lost. He stopped, cleared his throat, started again, louder, and the King's words carried over the anxious throng:

"For doubt ye not that we and our nobles can nor will suffer this injury at your hand unrevenged. And thus we pray unto Almighty God to use yourselves towards us like true and faithful subjects, so as we may have cause to order you thereafter; and to consent amongst you to deliver unto the hands of our lieutenant one hundred persons, to be ordered according to their demerits at our will and pleasure."

Men and women gasped in shock. Jaap mouthed the words to himself:

"The King wants one hundred persons to be ransomed? Executed? Sweet Jesus, what King treats his people so?"

In the hush, Harry whispered:

"What does he mean Jaap, what does he mean?"

"It means we have to leave this place Harry."

X

Canterbury

The Feast Day of St Palmatius of Trier

5th October 1536

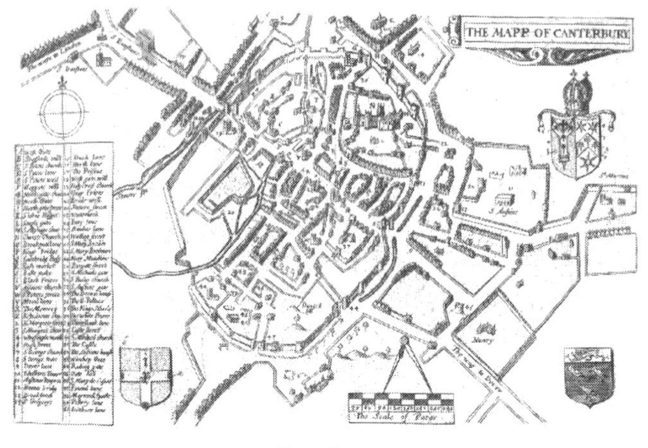

Canterbury

Philippa Jonys had a herring for her breakfast. She removed the flesh from the bones while surveying the scene from her window on this uncharacteristically cool October morning; a harbinger of the cold winter to come? Last winter, the town had done well. They had stored salt fish and smoked meat, and the beasts in the fields had survived. Then, in spring, the long dark nights ended and softer weather returned. The Prioress took a piece of the herring and put it in her mouth, removing a thin hair of bone and laying it aside. She looked to her ledgers for last year and thought of the plans for the winter to come. She placed the plate aside, took a fresh piece of paper and loaded her quill with ink.

As she worked, her thoughts returned to Barbara. She had kept her safe since the night of the storm, and she seemed less anxious. The regularity of life in St Sepulchre's, the observance of the Hours, the work, the prayer suited Barbara. However, outside the walls, the Prioress was concerned about the atmosphere in Canterbury. Barbara's fit – for Philippa Jonys knew it for what it was – had signalled the start of mutterings of unrest in the town; about Towers of Fire, and uncertainty. Nervous rumours abounded concerning the King's intentions. How could they enact such change? Indeed, now the Pope had no authority in England, surely reform was complete. What would be the point of further upset? Philippa Jonys shivered in this first hint of the chill to come.

There was a rattle at her door, and Barbara entered, flushed and shivering.

"Who was Elizabeth Barton?"

Barbara held a creased pamphlet that shook in her hand.

Philippa Jonys stopped her quill, placing it by her paper; she rubbed her inky fingers.

"Who told you about Elizabeth Barton?"

"They say that I am like her, that my prophesy is like hers."

She sniffed, wiping her eyes with the sleeve of her habit.

"Sweet Jesus, they say I am to suffer her fate."

The Prioress took Barbara's hand and looked into her eyes.

"You are not like her. She was a gullible serving girl that we took in to this monastery at the behest of our Grace, the Archbishop of Canterbury. I never thought for a moment that she had visions. She spoke carelessly. She was an unfortunate fool who believed her own imaginings, and she was taken in by those weak-wits, Edward Bocking and the others. What is more, she told the King not to marry again and to return to the Pope. Can you believe it? She spoke to our King and told him to his face that he was for Hell. Can you imagine such folly? In these times to be so foolhardy is perilous."

The Prioress eyed Barbara clutching the piece of paper.

"But how they loved her. They called her the 'Maid of Kent'."

"You say she spoke to the King?"

"Indeed. Here at St Sepulchre's."

"Where is she now?"

The Prioress blessed her self.

"May God Bless her immortal soul, Elizabeth Barton was executed at Tyburn, with six others, Easter Monday before last."

Barbara stopped, her mouth agape.

"Holy Mother of God!"

She held her hand to her mouth.

"But Prioress, what was her crime?"

"She was charged with treason, but they did not try her, may God in Heaven have mercy upon her; but you know, in the end, it was her own witlessness and her loose tongue that sealed her fate."

Trembling, Barbara placed the crumpled pamphlet on the Prioress's desk, smoothing it with the heel of her hand. Her tears dripped on the wrinkled paper, smudging the ink.

The Prophesy of Holy Barbara

The pow'r of the King, 'tis but a flower that withers in the night.
Towers of Fire, the Flower of God,
The Pow'r of God 'tis a Flower that rages in the night.
The Towers of Fire will rage like flowers in the night
And the people, they will dance in the flames.

The Prioress blessed herself.

"Where did you get this? Have you been in the town?"

"No Sister, the vittles boy gave it me."

Barbara was wringing her hands, shifting from one foot to the other.

"I did not say these words. God in Heaven; am I to share the fate of Elizabeth Barton? They speak of my 'Towers of Fire' prophesy, but I don't remember saying these things they say I said. I am in danger because of these words. They say I spoke these words. Oh Sweet Jesus, I am to be done at Tyburn."

Barbara was trembling; tears dripped from her nose and down her cheeks. Philippa Jonys held the shaking girl to her.

"My dear Barbara, I vow that we shall look after you. If you take care, and stay here at St Sepulchre's, we will protect you. Stay here; pray and read. Keep away from those outside our walls. You are not Elizabeth Barton. You will not share her fate. Be prudent, and do not speak of this to anyone."

Barbara carried out her duties mechanically for the rest of the day, but any time she stopped, her thoughts turned to the fate of the Maid of Kent. She slept badly, and dreamed fitfully; she saw her self offering the King flowers, telling him he would burn in a tower of fire. In her dream, the King read from the Abbess's book of hours in Flemish. He had a knotted beard.

~ ~ ~ ~ ~

The next morning still held the cold. As Philippa Jonys took another herring, she contemplated the new boatload of pilgrims to come from Dover. She thought on their needs, their sores and their lonelinesses: the men and women away from their loved ones, looking for new meaning; couples who had lost their children, wanting someone to tell them that they were not at fault, with no knowledge that the course of grief was something they had no control over, struggling to find meaning in their troubles; and there were the wasters who merely ran from life. On the other hand, there were the many genuine pilgrims, ordinary and devout, walking from one day to the next, on their mission for which they would sacrifice everything for redemption. These were the ones in undeniable need of succour, who prostrated themselves on chapel floors, the true pilgrims who had been lost to themselves. Here were the ones with torment in their eyes, the souls whose tears washed the steps of the shrines, so different from the fools who play-acted and went straight to the tavern.

There was a knock on the door of the Prioress's office. She knew the knock, and she forced cheer into her voice.

"Good morning Barbara, how do you fare on these early chill mornings?"

"I do not complain, Sister. A little discomfort teaches us humility."

The prioress smiled. Barbara continued to make conversation.

"Shall we see the Thames freeze this winter?"

The Prioress peered out to the grey morning.

"No. It must be much colder for that to happen. But truly, last winter, before you came, it froze all the way to Greenwich."

"To Greenwich? That you could walk across the water?"

"Yes, they sledged on the river."

"That must have been a wondrous sight."

Prioress Philippa finished her herring and put down her spoon. Barbara lifted her plate, and as she did so, her hand brushed against that of the prioress.

"Holy Mother of God, you are as ice girl."

"It matters not Sister."

"Nonsense. What are you wearing under your habit?"

Barbara gazed down, embarrassed. The prioress took her to her private quarters and opened a chest. She brought out a thick woollen shift and held it up against her.

"Put this on. I am not having you dying of cold. You were almost lost to us after your fit."

Barbara crossed her self and shivered as she went behind a screen, undressed and put on the shift. It had a solidity she was not used to, and its weight offered an almost instant shield from the cold.

"Thank you Sister."

They returned to the Prioress's desk.

"Tell me Barbara, you have not been outside St Sepulchre's since your turn at the Buttermarket."

"They come to the church to talk to me, but I just want to work in the garden and the kitchens and to pray and read."

"And what do you read?"

"My old Abbess's Book of Hours, of course, and I have read 'Non Sibi Sed Omnibus'."

"Ah, 'Not for One, but for All!' A great work. I knew the writer, Hilda of Presscott, from Chestershire. A good and holy nun. I think this volume will tell you much. Is this not so?"

"Yes Sister. It is a book of medicine, but it seems to be more than this. I saw it first at Sint Jaans Hospitaal."

"Yes Barbara. This book is about care of those in need in all its forms. Hilda of Presscott tells us that when caring for someone, it is important to touch the person, to speak of things not of their complaint, to talk of their family, their worries, and to comfort them. In the end, there is little else to do. Herbs and medicaments can help, but when it comes to it, it is the caring voice and the human touch that gives relief from suffering. This, and the belief that the person caring has an absolute empathy, and offers a mirror to their own suffering. One's own concerns were always secondary to those in need of succour."

"I think that Hilda of Presscott could be speaking to me."

"You are correct, Barbara; she is speaking to you. There is so much more in it than medicine. This book tells us not only to care for those in need of physical care, but to care also for those in torment. Whether it be the torment of the mind, where a soul cannot see the world for the distorting veil of one's own worries and twisted beliefs, where those worries may be unfounded, not bound in reality; if it be the moral torment of the person who has done wrong, but cannot find redemption; or the torment of those who have experienced loss, or rejection. Every one in need of care can achieve succour when we employ the approach of Non Sibi Sed Omnibus."

There was a pause where the two women recognised the nature of their exchange: the satisfying feeing that exists when a teacher imparts knowledge, and the pupil eagerly absorbs it. They silently savoured this moment. In the chill air outside, the sounds of a cart rumbled on the hard ruts of Dover Street; and, unseen in the sky above, a skein of geese flew south, cackling and honking as they exchanged places in their formation, the leader falling back, and another taking its place. The reverie was broken by the Prioress.

"So, to the business of the day. I see there are some pilgrims from Bruges this morning. Why don't you show them our shrine to Saint Thomas of Canterbury? You can gabble away in Flemish with them."

"Outside the monastery, Prioress? What of the pamphlet, my prophesy?"

"Barbara. It is time. We must not be like that kind of pilgrim who runs away from his problems."

~ ~ ~ ~ ~

Barbara made her way across the town, averting her eyes from passers-by. She met the pilgrims at the corner of Sun Street and Mercery Lane, next to the Cathedral Gate where Barbara had pronounced the prophesy being repeated throughout the town about 'The Towers of Fire'. She shuddered and directed the group towards the cathedral and the shrine. They would all want their little phials filled with the blood of the saint. It rained, and they complained. She cleared her throat.

"Please dear pilgrims. Should you be dissatisfied with the weather here in Ingelân, please be patient. Wait but an hour and new weather will arrive, bringing savour and new joy."

Barbara was pleased at her jest; but the pilgrims returned her gaze, stonefaced. They had seen it all before; the locals with an eye for the opportunity to take their money; they were dissatisfied, tired, weary of fraud. They turned away from Barbara speaking angrily in Flemish and Dutch. A local man intervened. Barbara recognised Edmund Vintry from the town.

"You pissing dogs. Stop. stop, stop."

The pilgrims halted in their path in the middle of the Burgate.

"You dogs of Satan, have you no awareness of the vehicles of God's succour?"

Some women crossed the road to avoid the scene; a cat ran screeching down a lane.

"You fools, cannot you see the angel before you? This is our Barbara who prophesied the Towers of Fire!"

Vintry blessed himself; Barbara walked away, embarrassed.

"Please our angel, please forgive these fools. They are mere foreigners. They cannot have any ken of your holiness."

Barbara walked faster, down Rose Lane, back towards St Sepulchre's, but the pilgrims ran after her. Behind them was Edmund Vintry, shouting "God bless our holy Barbara!" They surrounded her, touching her, asking for blessings, and she became frightened. Their number was growing; they shouted at her in Dutch and Flemish. Barbara ran to the doors of Whitefriars Church, when, from behind them, a familiar voice called out.

"Get thee away."

Prioress Philippa Jonys's voice pierced the throng, and the pilgrims retreated. She caught the eye of the man who was shouting.

"Edmund Vintry. Why have we not seen you at Mass? When is the last time your confession was heard?"

"Prioress. Of course, I meant to, I, eh..."

"Edmund, away with you. You pilgrims, begone! Ge weg!"

The gathering dispersed, mumbling.

Barbara's shoulders drooped.

"Oh Prioress Philippa, Sister, how can I thank you?"

"You can thank me by learning to deal with these situations by your self. In Heaven's Name girl. This is not the first time I have diverted attention from you. Come Barbara, for we are friends. Why cannot you speak? Just instruct them to leave you alone; for that is all that is needed. These men, for they are all men, they await your bidding. You can say anything to them, they will obey."

"Prioress, I cannot but allow them their own voice."

"Girl, these silly men have no voice. Our words are the only power we have to protect ourselves from them, from the violence they threaten. In our words lies our strength."

Barbara spoke slower, searching for clarity in this still-strange tongue.

"But Prioress, these men are not naturally violent. None of them is evil, they sometimes act in a terrible way because they have no voice. Only if we allow them a voice, can they dissolve any tendency to evil."

Prioress Philippa considered the young woman facing her, her red hair a bird's nest of a bonnet upon her.

"You are naïve Barbara, but your heart speaks honestly."

XI

Moricambe

The Feast day of Blessed Adalbero of Wurzburg

6th October 1536

Badge of The Pilgrimage of Grace.

Jaap and Harry had been walking north for days, and here in Lancaster, the rebellion was alive again. It was as if the whole country was on the move; the inns full of soldiers and King's Commissioners' men, with their bits of armour, one sword for three; this tag and rag bunch torn from their families by their duties to their lords, willing to fight: not for the King, nor for their lord, but for the right to return to the piece of land they farmed, and to their family. In the main, they did not talk of a cause, nor of glorifying their King, They grumbled about being away from home, their Lord's wealth borne on their own backs, their fear; some even expressed quiet sympathy for the rebels. These dissatisfied soldiers had travelled from all parts, bitter at the repeated musters for no reason, anxious about preparing for a fight and then being told to stand down again and again.

But the despondency of these soldiers was not shared by the King's Commissioners; men like the ambitious Doctors Legh and Leyton, who were appointed by Thomas Cromwell, Chancellor of the Exchequer, King's Secretary and Master of the Rolls, Vicar-General, Lord Privy Seal, Baron Cromwell of Oakham. The remit of the King's Commissioners was to dissolve the monasteries; but in reality, each had his own interest, seeking opportunities of riches and land.

On the other side, the rebels in these parts were different to those in Lincoln and Louth. These men were full of the virtue of their cause, with their banners of the Five Wounds of Christ and their Captains of Poverty. They had the support of the nobles and were well organised. They gained confidence with each day, crossing the counties, administering the same oath Jaap took in Louth. There were stories of monks and abbots being restored to their monasteries. In large part, this rebel army consisted of young men, taking pride in their cause, exhibiting their energy and valour for the good of God.

Jaap tried to keep this all from Harry, who was becoming more excited and spoke constantly of Thomas Cade and of going to battle. He had to get the boy to safety, away from the danger that hung in the air.

The two had slept fitfully in the dark room they shared with drunk militiamen, exhausted by walking and lack of sleep. In the morning, they rose and passed through the marketplace, with its keen stallholders, and overflowing taverns full of soldiers, still drinking from the previous night. When they left Lancaster, Jaap was pleased to have this place behind them. There was relief as they walked away from the castle and the soldiers who filled the streets, offering menace in the everyday.

As they walked west, Jaap remembered fondly the Delftman speaking of Moricambe, where they made salt with sand, the sleeching – he remembered the word, among many new words. Yet, for all the incomprehension Jaap felt when he arrived at Lynn, the names of things came easier, so many the same in English as in Dutch and Flemish. He learned to guess words by using a word from the tongues he did know. Sleeching, yes, there seemed to be safety there. He could understand sleeching. They would get to Moricambe in a few hours.

With Lancaster behind them, they walked along the cart road, out into the country. They came to a covered, hard earthen path, of the sort they had seen many times on their journey; a road formed by hundreds of years of footfall pressing the earth. Sometimes the path was so worn by the passage of feet that it dropped below the level of the ground, the roots of the trees exposed on either side. In these dark avenues they walked, sheltered from the day by the oak canopy above them. They came out into an open park, lit by the ordinary light that seemed so bright after the dim of the sunken paths. After the cold subterranean road, they felt the warmth and safety of the day.

Coming out of such a path Jaap first saw the estuary at Moricambe. He stopped to take in its scale. The sun was setting over the miles of exposed mudflats, sandbanks and salt marshes. At this distance, he could still smell the faint, familiar stench of the salt marsh. He lifted Harry onto his shoulders.

“Look Harry. Salt. We will be safe here.”

“When are we going to get there?” mumbled Harry.

~ ~ ~ ~ ~

“An' 'ere's a saltcote. This is where the brine is boiled in these 'ere lead pans. The lead makes the salt sweet. We make new pans every year. The coke makes for a hot fire to boil the sleeched brine.”

“But how do you sleech?”

“Ah, my friend, we take the water from the sea and we wash it with the white salty sand until ...”

“Until you can float an egg on it,”

“You do this too?”

"Yes, yes."

The two men nodded together. Harry was outside the steamy hut chasing ducks.

"You don't sleech where you come from?"

"No. We use heat from the sun to make the water salty and put it into ponds. We soak the sea in the salt peat until we can float an egg, then we dry it and burn it."

"What about the ash?"

"There is salt and ash mixed together. We wash to remove the ash, but the flavour of the peat remains."

"Man, you work hard for your salt!"

"You also. This sleeching is much toil."

"Indeed ' tis."

Here, at the saltcotes at Hest Bank, a short walk from their new hut in Moricambe, Jaap and Harry soon learned this new method of salt farming. The hot, enclosed saltcotes were a welcome, cleansing experience after the hard toil of the sleeching. The result was a different kind of salt, still with the familiar grey colour but sweeter, without the peat flavour Jaap knew from Sylt.

And young Harry grew in confidence and strength. He learned to light the fire, stoke it and bring coke in from the yard.

Here, a mere few hours walk from the dangers in Lancaster, stability was established, their troubles behind them. There was no talk of rebellion, or of the events of Lincoln or Louth; only the welcome humdrum of settled lives. Jaap and Harry got to know the monks from the Abbey across the estuary at Kertmel. They talked of the paths across the Kent Sands at low tide, and they heard the stories of carts and horses and men being swallowed up by the quick-sands. Jaap and Harry walked out, crossing with the monks, and learned the safest routes, to recognise signs of danger.

~ ~ ~ ~ ~

A few weeks later, Harry woke and went to Jaap's side. He shook him awake and whispered:

"Jaap, Jaap. I was dry all night."

Jaap woke without pain. He stroked Harry's head.

"Good boy Harry. Well done. This is good news. No dreams?"

"No Jaap. No dreams."

"I too slept well. This place is good for us."

Jaap made Harry's covers tight.

"You dreamed before that you had a faerie uncle."

"I didn't dream it. I was stolen."

"How long did you live like that?"

"I don't know. He was good. His hands were warm, but sometimes he was mad with the ale. He beat us."

"And you had a friend?"

"Yes. My friend Rodger died. We did things for my faerie uncle, but then Rodger died. One morning he was gone and I ran away. Then I saw you. You are not like my uncle, are you?"

"No Harry, I am not."

So it was that Harry and Jaap made a home in Moricambe. They bought bread and met people at the market, and their lives were governed once again by the slowly rotating tides; thus they would sleep and rise later each day. So their comfort went, their bodies keeping time with the rhythm of the earth and the moon.

But one morning, Jaap heard the awkward peal of troubled bells and their peace turned topsy-turvy. They went to the market square where they saw a troop of men bearing pikes and halberds. Some had helmets, and others, odd bits of armour; some on horseback, some with carts. At the top of the square two men directed others. Jaap kept Harry at the rear.

"What are they saying, Jaap?"

"Husht, Harry."

A man next to them spoke.

"Them's the Doctors, Legh and Layton, the Kings Commissioners. They are suppressing every abbey they can; the Crumme is writing the law to let them do it."

Another laughed:

"And they will be rich men at the end of all this."

Jaap touched one of them on the arm.

"Pray tell, sir. Who is the Crumme?"

"By God's Arms man, what rock have you been hiding under?"

"Shhh!", said his neighbour. He lowered his voice to a whisper.

"The Crumme. You know; Cromwell; The King's Chancellor Thomas Cromwell who writes the law."

The man's partner put his finger over his mouth.

"You have said too much. Let us go. It is not safe here."

Harry and Jaap moved in the gathering, Harry gripping Jaap's hand. They heard a familiar voice. Harry called out:

"Thomas!"

Harry let Jaap's hand go, and he ran to Cade, but before he reached him, Jaap called.

"Harry, come here. Now!"

Harry returned to Jaap, but not before Cade had seen them.

"God's Arms! My friends! Good to see you."

Jaap hesitated:

"So Thomas Cade, you came from Lincoln."

"Aye. I left your friend the good Captain Cobbler in his ridiculous coat. Yes, your friend! I saw you together."

Jaap coughed.

"He was not my friend. He helped me once."

"Methinks you took his pernicious oath too?"

Jaap looked out over those gathered around.

"I did not. I am but a salt farmer."

"I am glad to hear it; for here you are in good company. At any rate, the rebel Captain will be arrested. He is for Tyburn to be sure. Lincolnshire is for the King again, God be Praised."

Jaap pretended a lack of interest.

"So what are you to do in these parts?"

"Well, my friend, we have monasteries to suppress. These Doctors, Legh and Layton are fine men. They are the kind of forward thinking men with vision that will bring this country progress and prosperity. Everyone will benefit. We all complain about taxes, but with the monies the King can get from selling off the monasteries, he can reduce the tax burden on the common man and create prosperity for all."

Cade gestured over the throng.

"Come, sit over here and we can talk. Tell me, Have you heard of Robert Aske?"

"No."

"God's Skin, man! As the King's virtue is, the vice of Aske is as an antipode, a person who walks on the other side of the globe, an opposite."

Thomas Cade would remember that phrase when he spoke to the men. They sat on a wall and he continued:

"How have you not heard of Aske? He is a one-eyed donkey who has stirred discontent among ordinary folk. He has called these foolish rebels "Pilgrims of Grace". They follow him like sheep; sheep following a donkey, Ha, ha! But he, too, will go the way of the silly Captain Cobbler."

Jaap shuffled uncomfortably.

"So you follow Legh and Layton now?"

"No my friend. We do not follow them. We are not like those rebel sheep. We are men who have chosen; the Doctors are good men doing the King's bidding. Aske is a treasonous monster. He deserves to hang. It is he who is responsible for these dogs who force good folk to take that blasphemous oath."

Jaap looked down at his feet and back at Cade.

"Was this man Aske in Lincoln?"

"Yes, but his real hunting ground is here, north of the Humber."

Cade waved to men walking past.

"God Bless King Harry!"

The men mumbled in response.

"You know, Thomas, some of the men in the King's army don't have your enthusiasm."

"These men are tired, they need leadership."

"And you will lead them?"

"You know, some think we are just destroyers. Do you also think so, my Dutch friend?"

Cade examined Jaap's face as he answered.

"I know not. I am but a foreigner."

"And I am interested in what you think, because Doctor Legh says these suppressions are not wanton. They are necessary to bring us to a new world; away from superstition, from thieving, fornicating monks working in the lee, and protection of, the church. This destruction is a civilised destruction; a necessary destruction. What do you say? Do you see our goal?"

"I am but a Dutchman. I have no opinion here."

"I see. You have no opinion. Methinks that perhaps you took their oath?"

Jaap shuffled his feet as Cade smiled, while surveying the passing mass of jostling rebels and reformers.

"Do you know of the Abbot Adam Sedbar, of the Abbey of Jorevall?"

"I do not know this man."

"Well, he is our next problem. He is a danger to our way forward. Everyone has taken the oath in that part of the country; we have to act fast. Doctor Legh and Doctor Leyton want Jorevall suppressed. The Abbey is to be made an example of, but first we have to do more work for the King. We are to suppress Kertmel tomorrow. We have promised a pension to one of the monks to guide us across the sands. Join us my Dutch friend. You can bring your boy."

Harry beamed.

"Oh, can we Jaap, can we, can we?"

Cade rubbed Harry's head, Jaap flinched.

"No. We have salt to farm Harry. We must be up with the tide."

Harry sulked; Cade grinned.

"Don't worry son. Everyone has someone to tell them what to do."

Harry grinned back.

XII

Kertmel

The Feast Day of St Philip of Fermo

22nd October 1536

The Destruction of a Monastery

Harry was not in his cot. Jaap stretched the aches from his bones, dressed and went down to Hest Bank, next to the salt cotes. There, Thomas Cade and about thirty men were waiting to cross Kent Sands with a large black horse harnessed to a dray. They were to dissolve the monastery at Kertmel. Cade was talking to a monk, whom Jaap knew to be a guide who knew the sands. The group walked down onto the puddles on the sands; Jaap could see Harry, lifted high on Cade's shoulders. The sun was coming up on the outgoing tide, and they carried on across the sands, with the water often up to their knees. They were guided by the monk and had clear sight of the priory spire of Kertmel in the distance. After about four hours, they arrived at the other side of the sands, at Kents Bank. Jaap followed the men inland, moving from group to group, avoiding attention. They came on the massive church, surrounded by the cloisters, refectory, infirmary, dormitory, and other buildings. The men set to work immediately, splitting into groups in an exercise of organised violence. Some sought out books and ledgers, vestments and altarware, others set to chiselling and smashing the faces of the statues of the saints. Some took buckets of lye and whitewash and painted and scrubbed the frescoes and woodwork until the life was torn from them.

Jaap avoided the men silently coming and going at the priory as they threw the gold altarware, the books and other holy things on the cart. In their industry, Cade's men sidestepped bewildered monks pleading, weeping and prostrating themselves in front of the holy things.

Jaap observed this almost silent destruction in awe. As if on a blank canvas, the sounds were of hammer against stone, the tearing of wood, the breathing of men, sobbing of monks. But, pitched above it all, birds sang, and the breeze brushed the trees. Jaap stood as if outside the spectacle, watching men deliberately smashing these revered things. It didn't matter what Jaap thought about saints, or idolatry; it didn't matter what the reformers thought. Jaap was clear: these things had a profound meaning, a presence in the lives of many, even if he did not share their beliefs. It was a crime to be part of this destruction. On the other hand, the quiet violence Jaap was witnessing gave example to another human form of engagement that he could not identify. He had no words for this. In all his experience: his grief for Gertje and Anders, his memories of the Cordelière, the burning of the woman at Lynn, these silent events at Kertmel offered an insight into the powerlessness of a single man to effect change, when that change is executed by the force of so many acting in concert. They were voiceless creatures, their souls separated from their mouths. None could speak of their actions; there was only silence; silence and the inchoate human desire to enact this meaningless change.

In the commotion, Jaap saw his opportunity. He lifted Harry and took him into the trees. Harry struggled and shouted and cried, tears dripping from his nose and chin.

"I'm sorry. I ran away."

Jaap remained silent and held the boy tight until the sniffing stopped. The two held hands, watching the breaking and burning. The cart they used to cross the sands was filling with the contents of the monastery; the vestments, the altarware, and the books. The horse gave a snort and shook his head from side to side.

"Marcuccio."

The horse blew in its muzzle.

"Do you know this horse?" asked Harry.

Jaap approached and rubbed his ears.

"This is Marcuccio. I knew him in Louth. Marcuccio is a magical horse, a performing horse. They say he sang."

Marcuccio pawed at the ground.

"A horse, singing. That is wondrous magical. But here he is muzzled, tied to a cart."

"I know Harry. It is not right."

"Look. There is blood at his mouth."

"The bit is too tight. It has cut into him."

Jaap was horrified to see the bloody gouge across the animal's tongue. He loosened the bit and made the animal more comfortable.

Cade came near and Jaap and Harry moved into the trees. As Marcuccio whinnied, they watched as the cart filled with vestments and gold chalices, ciboria and other items from the altar. Some monks were running away. One sat on a low wall, weeping. Marcuccio whinnied as Cade took his bridle, and directed the cart back to Kent's Bank, down on to the sands once more.

"By the Rood, have a care men, these sands are dangerous, but we have to cross. The light is fading."

"Why don't we go back upstream? There's a crossing there."

"It would take too long, the tide is right. We have time to get back to Moricambe before nightfall if we cross the sands now."

"God's Wood! Where's that monk to guide us back?"

"He ran off."

"I paid him. God's skin! Monks; who can trust them? Never the mind, we can find our own way back. God willing, He will be found and tried."

Thomas Cade attempted to guide Marcuccio across the sands, but the horse resisted, and pulled away from Cade's direction. He and another man beat the animal until blood appeared on his hind quarter. Marcuccio whinnied and shook his head, his ears pinned back. The horse relented; he picked up speed, slipping, splashing in the puddles, the cart rumbling over the hard rippled sand, the wheels skidding and bumping over the undulations. Cade shouted to the followers on horseback and the few on foot who kept up.

"I told you, there is nothing to worry about. We will be back at Moricambe and we will drown ale together. God be praised!"

"God be praised", they shouted, nervously.

The troop of Commissioners' Men was an elongated body along the return route across the sands. At the front there was the cart laden with the contents of the priory, followed by men on foot including Jaap and Harry. They slowed as the sand turned muddy underfoot, their progress reduced to a walking pace. Marcuccio changed from a trot to a walk, each step sinking into the moving sand. The wheels of the cart buried themselves with each rotation, making it more difficult for the poor horse to pull his burden. The men beat Marcuccio again; his steps now more laboured, each one burying his hooves deeper in the mud. Inevitably, Marcuccio stopped. As he tried to raise his hooves to maintain balance, he sank further, inch by inch into the living sand. As the cart moved back and forth with the motion of the horse, it also came to be lodged axle deep in the mud. Marcuccio was snorting and whinnying pathetically; Cade moved towards the terrified beast, took the reins, and pulled. The bit tore into the horse's tongue, and blood bubbled from the poor creature's mouth. This made him struggle more, causing him to sink to his belly. Thomas Cade observed in horror his own legs sinking into the greedy sand and panicked. Shouting and flailing his arms, he tried to step out of the mud; with each movement he was sucked into the ooze. The cart tipped over on its side, the contents spilling out on to the grasping quick sand. The others looked on, silent, horrified, frightened to approach Cade, or the gold, or the sinking cart, or the doomed horse, Marcuccio shrieking horribly; he shook his head, nostrils flaring, with wide eyes, the blood foaming at his mouth. Jaap came from the rear to witness the scene. Cade was up to his chest in the liquefying sand, screaming:

"Sweet Jesus, Oh God in heaven, help me!"

Such was the sound of the awful harmony uttered by Cade and Marcuccio in the setting sun. Jaap examined the sheen on the quick-sand and kept a few feet away. He could get no closer to Cade, but was close to Marcuccio, who tossed his head at Jaap, showing the whites of its eyes, ears pinned back in terror. The horse knew he would never again dance, or trot, or canter. Jaap leaned over and rubbed the top of his mane, and he settled, his snorting breathing providing a pulse to the scene. Jaap crouched towards Cade who whimpered, his chin on the sand.

"Thomas. Listen to me."

Cade attempted to lift one hand out of the mire.

"Help me man."

"I can't come any closer. I will be sucked in, but I can help if you do as I say."

"God in heaven man, just get me out of here."

"I can't get you out. Only you can do that."

"In God's name how can I get out? I am a dead man."

"Stop moving."

"What! If I stop moving, I will sink deeper. Oh Jesus God, I am going to die. Oh Holy Sweet Jesus."

Thomas Cade prayed in short breaths:

"Ave Maria, gratia plena, Dominus tecum...."

Marcuccio snorted and shreiked again. Jaap raised his voice.

"Listen to me. Stop moving."

"Sweet Jesus, ... The Lord is with thee."

"Be still. Be still."

"Sweet Jesus, Sweet Jesus, Sweet Jesus..."

Cade stopped struggling, and he stopped sinking. He spat the sand from his mouth.

"Look; you are not sinking now. Breathe slowly."

Cade was weeping, his words running into each other, gasping for breath.

"Benedicta tu – in mulieribus, et ben – et benedictus fructus...."

Jaap spoke in a softer tone.

"Thomas. I promise I can get you out. You must trust me."

Cade sniffed.

"I will do as you say. Please hurry. Sancta Maria. Mater - Mater Dei."

As Jaap spoke to Cade, poor Marcuccio continued his struggle, but the creature was exhausted. His body was almost submerged; his heavy, terrified panting and snorting dictating the rhythm of the dreadful events. The shrieking became less regular, and more pathetic as the animal sank in the mire. Everyone kept their distance, shuffling and fidgeting, unable to help. Dusk was upon them.

"Thomas. Get on your back."

"I can't. I'll sink."

"Thomas. Listen to me. Arch your back; keep your face to the sky. Make slow gentle circular movements with your hands. Keep your fingers together, push against the sand. Lift your hands slowly and do it again. You must get onto your back."

"Ora pro nobis pecc – peccatoribus, nunc..."

Slowly, Thomas stretched his head and in a series of gradual motions, got his head and chest out on to the surface of the sand. He was drained with the effort.

"I can't. I can't go on. et in hora mortis nostrae. Oh Sweet Mother of God, at the hour of our death. Oh Jesus, Jesus, Jesus, don't let me die."

"Rest for a moment. You will not sink if you stay still."

Cade whimpered his prayers in short bursts. All the while, Marcuccio snorted with each breath, turning his head first to one side, then to the other. Then there was quiet; Cade's whimpering stopped as he caught his breath. The only sounds were from gulls crying overhead and the distant ripple of the tide. There was a cold breeze across the estuary. Marcuccio inhaled, deliberately and slowly, and now let out a sound that was discordant, disturbing; a shrieking whine that silenced all there; a cry manifest in the keening, the meaning clear in the air. All who heard Marcuccio that evening on Kent Sands knew his cry to be what it was: a curse; a curse upon them all; a curse upon all mankind, upon rebels and reformers alike, a scourge that would infect all men from that moment on.

As the vestments and altarware disappeared in the treacherous sand, the terrified men shuffled around blessing themselves, praying, frightened to move on the unreliable ground. Marcuccio was up to his jaw in the sand, his deathly song fading; his breathing fast and shallow, bubbling through the blood and foam that covered his mouth and nostrils. The group watched, dumbstruck, as the horse attempted to move his head in a last effort to escape his fate. Marcuccio gave a feeble snort and twitched, blinking one eye as the silent mire closed over him.

The cart and the altarware disappeared, leaving a single gold threaded vestment lying on the greedy sand.

"Tis not so deep as a well."

People blessed themselves. Jaap peered to the west and recognised a new danger. He had seen this before; the tide would come in as fast as a horse could gallop. He and Harry saw the depression in the quick sand left by Marcuccio. He placed both hands on the boy's shoulders and faced him directly.

"Harry, you remember I told you how to see the quick sand?"

"Yes Jaap."

"I want you to take these people back over the Kent Sands to Moricambe."

Harry's eyes widened.

"Me?"

"Yes. Look for the signs I showed you."

"The different shinyness of the sand?"

"Yes. Walk quickly. Do not stop. Do you understand Harry?"

"I understand."

"Good boy. I know that you can do this."

Jaap hushed the group who were mumbling and fidgeting.

"You must all go with Harry. He knows the way. You must get back before the tide comes in, before it gets too dark."

Harry took charge.

"Follow me. Don't step on this sand over here. Walk in my footsteps. Do not stop."

The group moved east. Jaap turned again to Cade, lying on the quick sand, covered in clay and mud, his eyes showing in the dimming light, shivering in the cold.

"Thomas, I want you to turn on to your back using your arms, like before."

Cade nodded and mumbled his prayers as he breathed. He moved with laboured effort as Jaap had instructed. The horse was gone. A priestly garment was all that was left on the sand. The air was quiet but for Thomas Cade's grunting and praying, his hips almost at the surface. As he continued in his efforts to get his body free of the sand, they heard the distant gurgling of water in the quiet night.

"Thomas. You must keep moving."

"I can't get my legs out. When I lift them, they are sucked back. Sweet Jesus, Sweet Jesus!"

"You must move slower. Make circular movements with your feet."

In the distance, the glinting moon reflected off the surface of the incoming sea. At last, Cade lay spread-eagled on the sand, on his back, covered with glaur.

"Thomas, you must move your body over the sand to me. Stay on your back."

Jaap could see the tide, closer, rippling in the light.

Cade was now close to Jaap's feet; he reached down and helped him up, his clothes fully caked in sand and clay, and breathing heavily. Jaap pointed to the approaching tide, and the two men picked up their pace over the sand. Cade stumbled, his movements restricted by the heavy mud encasing his body. The sound of the rippling water was closer, Cade slowed his pace, weeping as he tripped in a puddle.

"Thomas. You must be faster."

"I can't," he sobbed. "You go. Just leave me."

"No Thomas. We can get back, but you must keep going."

Cade and Jaap trotted together across the flats, stumbling in the pools of water. The sun was well set behind them; the moon bright above their heads, lighting the puddles and the line of tide to their right. As they ran, they came on a crow who called to them:

"There is no time. You will die here. This is the hour of your death."

The huge bird flew up into Cade's face, the black feathers brushing his mouth. He felt the dusty texture on his tongue. In that moment, he saw nothing but the black fluttering mass shutting out all else. Cade fell face first into the mud and wept.

"I can't. I can't. Ave Maria..."

Jaap helped him to stand, their feet in water that reflected the dimming light. All around them, the sand was under water.

"Look."

Jaap pointed east.

"There is Moricambe."

They saw the church spire lit in the moonlight.

"Dominus tec..., The Lord is with ..."

They carried on, splashing in the water up to their knees. Cade stopped again, his prayers a fragmented incoherent mumble, accompanied by the chatter of his teeth; his eyes fixed on some distant invisible point. He was breathing heavily, his shoulders slumped, his arms hanging at his sides. Jaap screamed:

"Thomas. Move!"

Cade was unresponsive, and Jaap slapped him on the face. Cade blinked, Jaap slapped him again and shouted:

"Move man. We are nearly there. Move!"

The two men waded through the cold water up to their waists, swinging their whole bodies from side to side, fighting against the fast moving current. The sounds were of the water and their chattering teeth.

Jaap became aware of the water level dropping; it took a few moments for him to realise that it was shallower because they were at the shore. They stumbled and staggered up Hest Bank to Jaap's hut and opened the door. Harry had tried to light a fire, but couldn't get the wood to catch. He ran to Jaap and hugged his waist.

"Jaap, Jaap, you are safe."

"Yes Harry. And so are you."

"You are cold. Look."

Harry pointed to his effort at laying a fire, the little pile of wood with a few embers. Harry looked down, and up to Jaap.

"I brought the people across the sand."

"You are a good boy Harry, a very good boy. Where are they?"

" They all went away."

Jaap fixed the fire and warmed himself while Thomas Cade shivered and whimpered at the door.

"Poor Marcuccio is dead."

"Poor Marcuccio."

Cade stooped by the fire, his teeth chattering, mouthing prayers.

"...fructus ventris ... et in hora ... Ave Maria..."

His eyes were half closed, as he shivered and mumbled. His coat steamed. They fed him some bread and beer, which he took silently. Crumbs fell from his mouth; he dribbled the beer.

Jaap and Harry undressed Cade and wrapped him in a blanket. He lay in the corner and Jaap took the other blanket for himself. Thomas Cade was almost catatonic with fear, a fear that would last a long time, a fear that could turn a man mad. He rolled over to face the wall and sobbed quietly, mumbling.

"...et in hora mortis nostrae – at the hour of our Death..."

XIII
Correspondence and Notes
Winter 1536/7

Signa

ture of Thomas Cromwell

Letter from Prioress Philippa Jonys to Lücke von Sandbeck, Abbess of Porto Coeli.

Probatissimos abbatissae

Opto tibi tui scientia novitiatus nostris sanctae Barbarae Cant nobiscum in monumentis. Et factum est a SintJaan Hopital Bruge in quo fuit domus peregrinorum apud infirmum et transiit Dovere mox septimana.....

My dear Abbess,

I wish to give you knowledge that your obedientary, Barbara, is with us in Canterbury at our little Priory of St. Sepulchre's. She came from SintJaan's Hopital in Bruge where she was sick, and crossed to Canterbury with the pilgrims just after Whit week. We are glad to have her with us. She Prays for You each day.
She took a fit in the middle of the town in a storm. She lost her senses and she spoke in tongues. The people of Canterbury have taken to her as a Holy Prophesier but this places her in peril. Our King, Henry – may God continue to Bless Him – has Forbade Prophesies concerning His Self and has made them Punishable by Death. Poor little Barbara does not know what is to become of her and is beside her self with worry.
She is recovering from her fit, but when the weather changes I shall speak with her concerning her fate. I understand you have tasked her with finding the Dutchman. She thinks he is on the road to Skotlân and wishes to follow him. She is constantly in my prayers.
Go with God's blessing in these changing times.

(Sgn'd) Prioress Philippa Jonys
St Sepulchre's Nunnery, Canterbury

Letter from Abbess Lücke von Sandbeck to Mjastro Seimen, Sylt.

Amicus Seimen,

Quod voluntas Dei, ut spero te bene litteris invenit. Ego autem in domo mea Sylt frequenter. Memini terrae pluviam et Haar aestatis calidae. Ego antiquum Sylt diebus illis quid deesset. Sed iam adest vitae meae, in Portu Romano destinátus, eo quod non sit Deus tuus in quo positus me nolebant.

My friend, Seimen,

God Willing, I hope this letter finds you well. I think on my old home of Sylt often. I remember well the earth after the rain, the hot summer and the haar. I miss those old Sylt days. But my life is here now, at Porto Coeli, and that is where God has placed me to do His Bidding.
I was saddened by your letter concerning your parishioner, Jaap van der Staen. I spoke of the matter to Our Great and Holy Prince Archbishop and He was instructed that a capable young woman is to bring the dutchman to be shrived. Van der Staen is with the pilgrims for Sanct Anders in Skotlân. They left Holstein after Easter and she will find him on the pilgrim roads. I received communication from the Prioress of a nunnery in Canterbury where she stayed. With God's Blessing, our appointed servant will continue her task.

Abbess Lücke von Sandbeck
Porto Coeli Monastery
Himmelpforten

~ ~ ~ ~ ~

Coded letter from Jan Starter (knotted beard) to Martin Reiff, Provost of Porto Coeli.
(Translated from code)

VATER,
JDII BCFE FOLP MMBO EFS+ EBTE VNNF NBED IFOH FTFI FOEF SOBS SIBU NJUF JOFN KVOH FOBV GHFO PNNF OEFO FSFS EGOL UJTU TFJO TPIO....

Sire,
I have seen the Dutchman and the stupid girl. The fool has taken up with a lad he thinks is his son. I heard he broke a monastery in Kertmel with a King's man called Thomas Cade. I think they will travel together. I will follow van der Staen him to Skotlân as you directed, and I will deal with him in that forsaken place.
The Himmelpforten girl was sick in Bruggen, and in Ingelân, she spoke a prophesy to a crowd at the Buttermarket in Canterbury. It was like the time in Himmelpforten when she spoke in tongues. I tell you she is a witch sire. But we need not think on this for the King of Ingelân has forbade prophesies so I think she will flee. The king's men will do our work for us. They will find her and burn her. It is her fate.
I say to you honestly sire, that I am good for this task. I shall follow the girl and I shall see justice done to the Dutchman for he has taken a life from mine own family in his murder of my cousin Gertje.

I have written for you sire, a new quartet of Alexandrine couplets titled The Gallant Swordsman and His Shepherdess. I will send them separately.

Yr. Obedient Servant
Jan Starter
Norwych,
Ingelân

~ ~ ~ ~ ~

Letter from Abbess Lücke von Sandbeck to
Prince Archbishop Christoph von Braunschweig-Wolfenbuttel

Ex Archiepiscopo Beatissimi Apostolorum Principis

Ego quoque fama de Priorissa de Ingelân crimen nostrum, Barbara, qui fuerit in praesentem orationes….

Most Holy Prince Archbishop

I have had a report from a Prioress in Ingelân concerning our charge, Barbara, who has been present in my prayers. I am told that she arrived at Canterbury where she has been looked after by poor sisters after her journey. I believe she still thinks her task to find the Dutchman is correct.
I pray daily for her soul and I think sorely upon what have we done.

Abbess Lücke von Sandbeck
Porto Coeli Monastery
Himmelpforten

~ ~ ~ ~ ~

Letter from Thomas Cromwell to mr. Spilman and mr. Candish (King's Commissioners in Canterbury)

Sires,
After my harty commendations, thiese shall be to aduertise you that the kinges graciousr pleasure is that ¬with convenient spede ye repairing to the Monastery of Saynct Sepulchre shall for certayn reformation and other considerations Which his grace intendith as well there as in other places, dissolue and take the same to his vse. ....

Sires,

After my hearty commendations, these shall be to advertise you that the King's gracious pleasure is that with convenient speed you repair to the Monastery of Saint Sepulchre, shall for certain reformation and other considerations, which his grace intends as well there as in other places, dissolve and take the same to his use. And by your discretions considering the age qualities conditions and towardness of the persons there shall assign unto them their annual pensions, and all other things do according to his graces commission to you in this behalf directed. Not omitting to put my Lord Chancellor or his depute in possession of one of the said monasteries, and Mr. Chancellor of the augmentations or his depute in possession of the other to our said sovereign Lord the King's use accordingly. Thus Fare ye heartily well. From London the vi th of November the XXX th year of his most noble Reign.

Your loving Friend

THOMAS CRUMWELL

Addressed to To my Loving Friends Mr. Candish and Mr Spilman

~ ~ ~ ~ ~

Thomas Cromwell's injunctions to The Clergy (Extract)

Item that ye shall make or cause to be made in the saide churche and curry other cure ye haue one sermon every quarter of a yere at the least wherein ye shall purely and syncerely declare the very gospell of christ ...

Item that you shall make or cause to be made in the said church and curry other cure you have one sermon every quarter of a year at the least, wherein you shall purely and sincerely declare the very Gospel of Christ, and in the same, exhort your hearers to the works of Charity Mercy and Faith specially prescribed and commanded in scripture, and not to repose their trust or affiance in any other worker devised by men's phantasies beside scripture, as in wandering to pilgrimage offering of money candles or tapers to Images or relics or kissing or licking the same, saying over a number of beads not understood not minded on or in suchlike superstition For the doing whereof you not only have no premise of reward in scripture but contrarywise great threat & maledictions of God, as things tending to Idolatry and superstition, which of all other offences God almighty doth most detest and abhor for that the same diminishes most his honour and glory

~ ~ ~ ~ ~

Provost Martin Reiff of Porto Coeli Monastery to Prince Archbishop Christoph von Braunschweig-Wolfenbuttel

De Barmhartige en heilige aartsbisschop
Ik dank u voor het vat wijn. Ik ben vernederd door uw vrijgevigheid die ik niet verdien...

Most Gracious and Holy Prince Archbishop

I thank you for the cask of wine. I am humbled by your generosity which I do not deserve.

I have had a report from Starter, my man in Ingelân. He tells me the girl, Barbara, is a witch and she will be burned by their King. So our problem is resolved. My man will find the Dutchman and deal with him as a private matter. This episode is ended.

Starter continues to send me his poesy. I have a dozen of his rhymes with some classical and pastoral themes. Mostly, they are drinking songs and wedding songs to be sung. I know nothing of these things and I know not what to do with them. I shall send them to you.

I continue to be your most humble servant

Martin Reiff,
Provost, Porto Coeli,
Himmelpforten.

~ ~ ~ ~ ~

Robert Aske's Manifesto (Captain of the Pilgrimage of Grace)

Louing Neighbours, The King by mouthe has declayred to me that the pardonne granted at Doncaster shalle extend to all, and that your reasonable pettitions shalle be ordered by Parliament.

Loving Neighbours, The King by mouth has declared to me that the pardon granted at Doncaster shall extend to all, and that your reasonable petitions shall be ordered by Parliament. His Grace, for the love he bears to this country, intends to keep Parliament at York and have the Queen crowned there. His grace esteems the commonwealth of the realm and the love of his subjects more than any other earthly riches and will send down the duke of Norfolk to minister justice until his coming.

NB This letter was found at Aske's lodging when he was committed to the Tower of London. (Added to the foot of the letter in another hand)

~ ~ ~ ~ ~

Nicholas Melton (Captain Cobbler), writing from Prison to Eliza Jane Foster,

My dere Eliza Jane,

I wryte in good spirits. I knowe Godde is withe me & I have yr. luve which feeds me eu'ry day...

My dear Eliza Jane,

I write in good spirits. I know God is with me & I have your love which feeds me every day. How fare our sons? Robert must take care for his safety & not follow my path. Does Arthur practice his archery? How does his Latin? You must keep me abreast of these matters, for they are what I now live for.

I am sore sorry for the hurt I have brought you in these troubled times. Forsooth, I know not how else I could have acted. I am compelled to do what is right & you above all others know this of me.

My only regret in these dealings is trusting the Nobles. What whoresons we were that we had not killed the gentlemen for I thought always that they would be traitors

Do you remember the horse, Marcuccio? Strangely, at this time, I 'member him well, Eliza Jane. I wonder how he fared. What a specimen he was. I know I shall not see his like again.

I shall write again when my guard gives me paper.
the xxviii th of March 1537

yr. loving man,
Nicholas Melton

~ ~ ~ ~ ~

Written into the end page of Barbara's Book of Hours:

The life of this world
Is ruled with wind

The life of this world
Is ruled with wind,
Weeping, Darkness
And hurting:
With wind we bloomen,
With wind we comen,
With wind we passen,
With wind we beginnen,
With wind we enden,
With wind we dwellen,
With wind we wenden.

From Hilda of Presscott 'Non Sibi Sed Omnibus' ('Not for One, but for All').

~ ~ ~ ~ ~

XIV

St Sepulchre's

The Feast Day of St John Camillus the Good

10th January 1537

St Sepulchre's, Canterbury

Barbara was digging in the frosted ground of the kitchen garden when she heard the sound of men on horses. Out on the Dover Road, two gentlemen on palfreys led some men clinking in harness; behind them, a cart. They dismounted and, without speaking, walked straight into the chapel, leaving one man with a halberd looking after the cart, glancing after her. She wiped the soil from her hands and followed them.

"Sires, what do you want in this, God's house?"

A man with a squint, wearing a helmet, placed his hand on his sword and eyed Barbara up and down.

"Be off with you, girl."

She sensed menace. The Prioress appeared at the door.

"By the Holy Virgin! You! You men."

One of the gentlemen addressed the Prioress.

"We are the King's commissioners, Mr....."

Philippa Jonys interrupted.

"You are Mr Spilman; and you, Mr Candish; you came to count our holy things for the Valors Ecclesiasticus."

Mr Spilman ignored her and unrolled a document.

"I, Mr Spilman, Serjeant-at-Law, have been empowered by Our Most Gracious King Henry the Eighth to enact the Dissolution of this monastery. This Priory has been designated as one which has been destined to be dissolved by the Grace of Our Majesty, King Henry, and by the Parliament of England. We are employed by the Lord Cromwell to carry out this task."

"What are you going to do?"

"We are going to do what is necessary to dissolve this monastery."

"But sire, this is but a little priory. We have nothing. All we do is what we do for those who are in need. How are we to perform our function? Why can you not wait?"

Mr Candish spoke.

"What; and have you squirrel away all your riches?"

"Riches! Sire we have nothing. We are a poor order."

"You are an order of whores and thieves. We are familiar with your kind. You have had children out of wedlock and are guilty of fornication."

The Prioress spoke in a measured tone.

"Sire we are all of us sinners; we are all entitled to seek forgiveness and obtain succour. Let he that is without sin cast the first stone."

Mr Candish assumed a distant air.

"God's Death, woman. Here is the law: this monastery has been valued at a sum of money less than two hundred pounds; as such it is to be dissolved. So that is the end to it. Leave us to our work!"

"Two hundred pounds? Sir, we have not two hundred pennies."

"You couvetous woman, look around you. These candlesticks, the gold altarware, the gilded statues."

"But these things are not ours, they have no value, they are for the glory of God."

"You sicken me. You drain the pockets of good, honest, hard working men and women, and you live off their gift. In the meantime, you want for nothing. You are parasites, Look, my patience is complete. Get out; let us do our work, or you might be hurt."

"What work do you refer to?"

There was menace in Mr Spilman's eyes; he stared fixedly above her head and sneered.

"I have said before, we are to dissolve this monastery. Men, to your work."

In a moment, the men moved among the women, taking down statues and candlesticks; the chalices, ciboria and ornate monstrance. Barbara was dumbstruck as the men took all the holy furnishings of the chapel. Some of the ladies fell to their knees.

"God In Heaven, forgive them."

One of the sisters tried to take a chalice from one of the men. The Prioress intervened.

"No Sister. I will not have my ladies fighting for these holy things. It is not becoming."

Some of the townsfolk gathered outside as the men filed past with vestments and altarware. A voice shouted.

"Shame on you. For shame."

The man with the halberd gestured his weapon towards the group standing around.

"Who spoke?"

In the cold air, the words came out of his mouth in a menacing cloud of breath. The assemblage remained silent, shuffling nervously, mumbling as the men filled the cart with the various paintings, statues of wood and marble from the chapel. Barbara watched, frightened to speak.

"You. Girl."

Barbara turned towards the helmeted man with a squint standing at the cart.

"You were the one at the Buttermarket. You uttered the prophesy."

"Pardon sir?"

"I see you. You are Barbara."

"No Sir."

He whispered roughly in her ear:

"I know you. You spoke of the Towers of Fire. I was there."

She glanced from side to side. Had anyone heard?

"You are mistaken sir. Please, do what you have come to do."

He glanced around and took her arm. She stared him in his good eye. He released his grip and dropped his voice.

"Follow me. We have but a minute."

The man led her across the road to Nunnery Fields, out of sight of the King's Commissioners.

"I tell you girl. I saw you; I heard you."

He moved towards her; removing a piece of paper from his sleeve, he opened it out. It was the pamphlet.

Barbara felt the flush of blood to her face. Her heart raced; she took a step back, but she became aware of his squint as he came closer, his face almost against hers, blocking out the light from her vision.

"Here are your words." He pointed to the pamphlet.

" ... not my words, not my words."

Barbara swayed, light headed. Across the road, the cart was loaded with the contents of the Church. She breathed deeply, sucking the cold air into her chest; she felt his breath on her cheek.

"I must tell you that you must be careful, for you surely know that the King, our Holy King Henry, has forbade prophesies. You spoke a prophesy that threatens the King; you are in danger. The King's ministers have you a marked woman. You must flee or hide. Otherwise you'll burn like the others."

"Like the Maid of Kent?"

"Yes, Elizabeth Barton, They executed her at Tyburn, you know. God have mercy on her soul. She prophesied against the King too."

The man blessed himself; Barbara's heart pounded in her chest.

"But I said nothing. I made no prophesy."

"Everyone who was there heard you. I was there. I heard you. See here."

He followed the pamphlet with his finger as he read:

"'Towers of fire, The King's power is but a flower in the night'. These are wicked words."

She gasped for air.

"But, but I did not say these things."

"Nonetheless, you have to see that you are in great danger. You must flee."

He glanced over his shoulder.

"I cannot be seen talking to you. I have said enough."

The man crossed the road, returning, looking from left to right; he took his place by the side of the cart, now piled with the paraphernalia from the priory. Amongst the bibles and missals Barbara saw Hilda of Presscott's book – 'Non Sibi Sed Omnibus' . The Prioress also noticed their books of accounts; she spoke to Mr Spilman, mounted high on his horse.

"Sire. Why do you take our ledgers? They can be of no value to you."

Spilman took in the sky above the Prioress and spoke in a tired drawl.

"Madam, can you not see that we intend to make you disappear?"

"Disappear? How so?"

"It is simple. In years to come, the world is never to know that you, or your antique, pernicious ideas ever existed. That is all."

~ ~ ~ ~ ~

The cart rumbled over the ruts, and disappeared down Dover Road, through the Riding Gate and into Canterbury. Barbara, Philippa and the sisters returned to the empty, now soulless Chapel. Outside the sky had clouded over; the light was dull in their tiny Chapel; no glint of hope, no presence of joy.

"So. This is the way it is to be."

Barbara wiped away tears. She considered the walls, devoid of ornament, and made the sign of the cross. She remembered the warnings of the man at Nunnery Fields.

"Our beautiful little St Sepulchre's. How will the sisters do their work? How will the needy obtain succour without the priory?"

"There are other monasteries for now, but these are going to be hard times. What did that man say to you?"

"Oh sister, he had the pamphlet. He says that my ramblings are a prophesy, that the King has forbade prophesies and that I must flee or be burned for treason."

She hung her head; her tears dropped to the rushes covering the floor.

"I am so frightened."

"Mine own girl, I am so sorry."

The prioress embraced her for a few moments. Then she held her at arms length.

"This will not serve. We need to be strong."

Barbara sniffed.

"Yes Sister, but what am I to do?"

"You must do as the man said. You must flee."

"But where? Where can I be safe? Am I to suffer the fate of the Maid of Kent?"

"Soft my dear. Let us not run towards our troubles. Let us retreat to primorum principiorum, shall we not?"

Barbara used the sleeve of her habit to wipe her eyes. Philippa Jonys patted her arm.

"Remember, my dear, your task, the task given you by your Abbess?"

"To find Jaap van der Staen. But you said..."

"If you are to be safe, you must go north."

"To Saint Andries?"

"Perhaps."

Barbara wiped her nose.

"Yes. Yes, I can go to London, then north."

"You must not go to London. You will be in peril there."

"I do not understand."

"In London, too many will know your prophesy. It is not safe for you. You must go to Norwich. There is a woman there you should speak to. She is an Anchoress; her name is Katherine Mann. She can advise you. You will find her anchored to Blackfriars Priory in Norwich."

"Anchored, like a hermit?"

"Yes. She is a wise woman."

Barbara sniffed.

"But where is Norwich? How can I find this place?"

"I know a man who can take you there. His name is Jerome. I will give you a letter for him. You must get to Margate. You will find Jerome at the Waterman's Arms. From Margate, you sail to Norwich where you must meet Katherine Mann. She will advise you; perhaps then, you might follow this man to Scotland. You can be safe there."

"But they are savages in Skotlân. They live there among the dog heads."

"Listen, my dear, they are not destroying the monasteries in Scotland. Their King James is not a reformer. You may find the Dutchman; the further you get away from this part of the world and its horrors, the safer you will be. You still have your credentials from Porto Coeli; I will write you more."

The Prioress took up her quill, speaking as she wrote.

"On your road, there are other monasteries where you can be safe. They can't close them all."

Barbara agreed. Over the winter, since her vision in the Buttermarket, she had thought of little but her own worries. Was she to suffer the same end as Elizabeth Barton at Tyburn? She had lost sight of her task in this place where she felt so at home. She thought again of the vow she had made to her Abbess at Himmelpforten and she knew what she had to do. She had to put aside her doubts about the success of her task, to trust to her fate. Philippa Jonys folded the letters and gave them to Barbara, and kissed her on the forehead.

"Go with my blessing and be safe. Tell Katherine Mann that I think about her."

Barbara ran out into Dover Street, north, to Watling Street. She did not stop.

~ ~ ~ ~ ~

The woman sharing the cart with Barbara repeated the Latin recitations, moving her beads with a flick of her fingers, each iteration solidifying her guarantee to a place in the Kingdom of Heaven. She was to be like like this all the way to Margate, praying as the cart bumped and jostled along the rutted road. Barbara wrapped her coat around her against the February chill. When the driver stopped to water his horse at a tavern, Barbara stretched her legs, but the pilgrim continued her prayers, ignoring all around her. Barbara envied her single-mindedness. This woman had her task and, for her, nothing else seemed to exist.

When they arrived at Margate, Barbara warmed her self in the Waterman's Arms, and took some cheese and beer. She tugged on the strap of her old biggin to keep it firmly on her head; keeping her eyes averted from the others in the tavern. Even in this place, she might still be recognised as the prophesier of the 'Towers of Fire'. She approached the innholder.

"God's Day sir. I am looking for a man with a boat. His name is Jerome."

The innholder jerked his head to a corner where there sat a quick, wiry man in a smock.

"Sir, are you Jerome?"

Barbara's coif was worn, and curly strands of red hair stuck out. He smiled.

"I be Jerome, but who be you my girl? Arn't you the little Joan of Arc? I'd say you ain't from round 'ere?"

She liked Jerome's open manner, with his melodic voice and its long drawn syllables

"I am Barbara, from Himmelpforten. I have come from St Sepulchre's in Canterbury. Prioress Philippa Jonys said you would help me."

Jerome looked up from his bench and beamed.

"Ah, my good friend, the Prioress. How is my dear Philippa?"

Barbara was shocked that a stranger should refer to her Prioress by her Christian name; it seemed inappropriate.

"I have to tell you sir, they dissolved St Sepulchre's."

"By the Rood! What's to become o' us. Poor little St Sepulchre's."

"Indeed sir. My Prioress is sore worried about the poor sisters and the lay helpers at the nunnery. They have no home."

"Ain't no thing sacred no more?"

She handed over her letter from her Prioress. Jerome examined the seal, broke it, and read.

"Ah, so. I be taking you to Norwich! I shall tuck you away with my wool and my felt. Tell me more of the suppression."

~ ~ ~ ~ ~

The sun warmed the cold air as Barbara and Jerome sailed from Margate, tacking north, across the wide estuary of the Thames, against the flow of traffic east and west. Out in the open water, they saw whales and porpoises. In the late winter breeze, Barbara felt that the danger was behind her. North was to be her direction. The boat hugged the coast, passing Southwold, Lowestoft, with the shipyards of Great Yarmouth to their left. They sailed inland on the long River Yare across the fens, towards Norwich, where the sailing was easier, and the little boat steadied to its rhythm in the happy calm waters, away from the constant chop and swell of the open sea. Either side of them lay flat land, church steeples and windmills piercing the broad sky. Here they relaxed, talking without the need to shout over the sound of the waves, their breath mixing between them in the cold air.

"I have seen other boats like this here. This mast is well to the fore."

"This be the Amaranth, my girl, a Norfolk wherrie."

"At home we would have a lee board on a boat like this."

"Ah."

The Amaranth gurgled and splashed as Jerome sailed between the marshes and through the narrow channels. Out over the fens, signs of the land being reclaimed could be seen; men on the flat horizon silently created polders and dykes, little windmills drained the land.

"How do you know Prioress Philippa?"

"I were a monk."

"A monk? By the Virgin! Why did you leave? I have never heard such a thing. Such a life could have kept you."

"Truly, I didn't take orders. I had no calling, see. I was weary of the playacting an' the silliness."

"No sir, it is a noble thing, to pray for the souls of others."

"Not for me. Forbye, 'twas all down to Philippa Jonys, see; for she wanted for God, not man."

Barbara's eyes widened. However, she thought to say no more. This conversation was exceeding prudence. The two passed some time in silence. The cold breeze died down; in the sky was a sound Barbara had not heard since she was small.

"Kwartelkonig."

"Well, girl, he be corncrake 'ere. Funny old sound ain't it."

"You ken birds?"

"Surely, I do."

She pointed at a group of cranes taking to the air.

"I call them Kranich; and there, in the long sea grass, a reiger."

"A heron."

He pulled on a sheet, examining the blue sky with its bundles of soft white cloud.

"We'll see snow before the end of the week, I reckon."

Barbara nodded, breathing in the cool spring air..

"Jerome, what is your favourite bird?"

"My favourite bird, well, that'd be the barnacle goose."

"I do not know this bird."

"'Tis a wondrous bird, for 'tain't a bird, it be a fruit."

"By the Virgin, sir, a bird that is a fruit?"

"Yay. Ye can eat it on fasting days. It comes from a tree that overhangs water. When the fruit of the tree drops into the water, it become a barnacle, and it grows. When it gains wings, it flies away. It'll never mate the way birds do; it is borne of the barnacle tree. When you see them barnacles, they be the beaks of the goose. Ye can tell by their markings an' the growth of the goose's neck."

"But sir, this is a fantastical story."

"It be a story I learned from my time as a monk. I read it from Gerald of Wales."

"Have you ever seen this bird?"

"No. Truly, it is a sight I long to take in."

As they watched the other waders and seabirds, Jerome named them.

"Why are you going to Norwich?"

"I am to meet a woman."

Jerome chuckled.

"Well, my girl, I know lots an' lots o' women in Norwich. What is the name of this woman ye're to meet?"

"Her name is Katherine Mann."

"God's Arms. The Anchoress?"

"So I am told. Yes."

"And what business do you have with her?"

Barbara waited. She couldn't expose her self as the 'Towers of Fire' prophesier.

"My prioress at St. Sepulchre's..."

"Philippa?"

"Yes."

Jerome grinned as he pulled on the tiller; the huge gaff sail answered with a small lurch of the wherrie in the breeze.

"Yes. Philippa Jonys counselled me to seek her advice about my path."

" Curious choice of adviser."

"Why so?"

"Where do I start? Katherine Mann; she be one of the most powerful women in England. She read Tyndall y'know. Almost put to the stake for it, she was. Poor Thomas Bilney burned for it; but they let her live on in her anchorage."

"Does she really live in a walled up cell?"

"Yes. Some cells be so small, they can't lie on the floor. Katherine Mann's situation be not so. They say she has two rooms and pays two servants. The older one is like to a Moor, but she be Norwich born 'n bred. She be her secretary; there's a younger woman who tends to what we might call her worldly needs."

Jerome tied a rope around a cleat on the side of the wherrie.

"Y'know, I met her one time, before she be anchored."

"What is she like?"

"She 'as good bearing, but she never took orders. She knowed her own mind – very critical of the old church. Some say she be an 'eretic, but I should say no more. Tell me my girl, why do you seek her guidance, if I may be so bold?"

Barbara told Jerome about her Abbess, her vow to apprehend Jaap van der Staen, of her journey, her time in Sint Jaan's Hospital, about reading Hilda of Presscott, and she spoke of her doubts. She said nothing about her prophesy, nor the danger she was in. Jerome adjusted the gaff again.

"You shall have an interestin' talk, I think."

~ ~ ~ ~ ~

Thomas Cade drew his sword and struck at the soft-falling snow.

"For the Glory of God!"

Just ahead, sheltering under a tree, Jaap held Harry close. In the silent blanket of white, the only thing to be heard was the dry, unresonant, sound of Cade's laughter as he swiped the weapon in the air. Jaap watched as Harry observed Cade's duel with the snow. Despite everything, Jaap could see that the boy still felt a loyalty to Cade that obliged him to do his best for the mad soldier.

"I think poor Thomas is sick, Jaap. The quicksand made him sick. He follows us everywhere."

Jaap watched Cade swiping at the air, thick with snow.

"We will take him to a monastery where they can care for him. I heard of a monastery called Jorevall: they have a hospital where they can make him still. Stay close to me. He is sick, but he is dangerous."

"A monastery, you say, Dutchman! What so? I hear you. I ken your mind. Take me to a monastery and I will do God's Work. Give me a monastery and I will take it. I will break it for the King. Give me a monastery. Death to idolators!"

Cade's eyes were wide as he gazed along the length of his sword. He swung it up towards a point directly above his head, towards the origin of the snow falling all around him, enveloping him in a silent white illusion. As though he was being lifted into the air, speeding through the snowflakes, propelled by his sword. He screamed spittle into the blizzard:

"For the Glory of God!"

XV

Norwich

Feast Day of St Mel

6th February 1537

Norfolk Wherrie

Barbara was looking forward to meeting Katherine Mann. Back in Porto Coeli, there had been no Anchorite. There was Cedrik, of course, the old holy man who lived under the trees who took food given to him, but Anchorites were different: attached, anchored to a church, living their solitary life in public. Townspeople passed their little cells in the street, they spoke with them, taking succour from their piety and wisdom.

In the morning, the Amaranth arrived in the middle of Norwich and moored next to a throng of boats in the narrow river channel. Barbara had seen such bustling crowds only in Bruggen. There was the tang in the air from the breweries, the tanneries and the bakeries; the pungent smell of people going about their business. Jerome helped her off the boat.

"This be Fye Bridge; Blackfriars be yonder, just up Elm Hill on your right, see."

"Thank you Jerome. I hope you find your barnacle goose."

"God willin' Barbara, God willin'. Good luck with the Anchoress."

"God's Bye, Jerome."

Barbara had no difficulty finding Katherine Mann's Anchorage, attached to the north side of the huge black and white flint-stoned structure of Blackfriars Priory. People passed up and down Elm Hill just feet away from her cell, handing food or drink in through an opening. Barbara saw her hand take the offerings and bless the almsgivers in return. As she approached, her way was barred by an older woman, about the same size as Barbara, in a wimple. She had the dark skin of someone from the East.

"God's Day my girl. How be you?"

The woman spoke in the same drawl Barbara recognised in Jerome's voice.

"God's Day to you, madam. I am well thank you. May I speak with the Anchoress?"

"On what matter?"

"On the matter of my path in my life."

"Indeed girl."

"I have a letter from my prioress, Philippa Jonys of St Sepulchre's. My name is Barbara."

"And your voice tells me you're from the Low Countries, I be thinking."

"Yes, Madam, from Himmelpforten, in Holstein."

"I think you have come a way."

"And you, madam?"

"Not me. I be Norwich born. I will see that the Anchoress reads your letter. Come back at noon."

~ ~ ~ ~ ~

Barbara walked through the sinuous lanes and streets of Norwich, churches and monasteries at every corner. Racing children weaved their way between priests and pilgrims, among the mercers and hawkers and tradesmen. She made her way past the Trinity Cathedral, along Holme Street to the Hospital of St Giles, where she heard the singing of a Benedictus. Inside, she glimpsed the coloured light from the massive stained windows, illuminating the hall lined with altars and little chapels, and in the centre, row upon rows of beds. Each bed had two patients, served by sisters and lay helpers. Barbara was reminded of Sint-Janshospitaal, of her time in Bruggen, but this morning, she would not stay to study the beauty of the place. She went to the cloister, opened Lücke von Sandbeck's Book of Hours and read the words of a Psalm:

Heal me Lord, because all my bones be troubled.

And my soul is troubled exceedingly.

Turn thee O Lord, and deliver my soul.

The bells rang Sext; Barbara looked up to the midday sun. She closed the book, returned across the city to Elm Hill, and waited to see Katherine Mann. She was met once more by her secretary.

"Ah, my child, the Anchoress shall see you."

Barbara approached the small cell opening; she saw a woman in her fifties with good teeth, wearing a light coloured linen habit. She could feel the warmth from her little cell spill out into the cooler air.

"You are Barbara, from St Sepulchre's."

"Yes, Madam."

"May you be blessed."

The older woman proceeded to make the sign of the cross as Barbara bowed to accept it.

"So you are a prophesier, a young woman who speaks in tongues, who has visions."

"Madam, I am aware of nothing when I am in such a state. I only know what others tell me. They tell me I am holy, but this means nothing to me. I am but a simple girl."

"Simple, is it? Simple enough to control violent men; simple enough to be sent on a Holy Mission by your Abbess in – where is it?" The Anchoress consulted the letter from Philippa Jonys.

"Yes; from your Abbess in Porto Coeli."

"I am gratified my Abbess has trust in me. As for the other thing, I just tell the truth. These men need love, to be shown that love can be there for them if they choose to accept it."

"Interesting; you have found this approach successful?"

"It is not for me to say, Madam."

Katherine Mann held the letter to the light.

"So; my old friend, Philippa, speaks well of you. Tell me, how is she?"

"She fares well, but I have to tell you that St Sepulchre's is suppressed. I saw it."

The Anchoress blessed her self and said a silent prayer.

"And so it begins. I had suspected as much. Tell me what happened."

Barbara told the Anchoress about the removal of the holy things from St Sepulchre's, of the shock of seeing their little world destroyed; the quiet violence of the act, the intimidation, and the uncertain future. Barbara was shaking as she told her about her prophesy and the threat of execution.

"I worry my name is known by the King's men. I worry I will suffer the fate of The Maid of Kent."

"I understand your fears, but I can see you are not like Elizabeth Barton. She was easily led; you are prudent."

The Anchoress reached out of her cell and held Barbara's trembling hands.

"Oh Madam, what is to become of me?"

"Settle, my dear; let us think on your situation. What of this task in the letter, the task given to you by your Abbess?"

"I no longer know Madam. I am told I am on a fool's errand. How am I to find one man in this land? What if I am arrested for false prophesy by the King's men? I think day and night on the Maid of Kent at Tyburn."

Barbara wept silently. Passers by saw the scene: a girl bending down at the Anchoress's cell, her chest heaving as she sobbed, her straggly red hair peeking out of her cap. One person touched her shoulder as he passed. Katherine Mann took Barbara's shaking hands in her own. Barbara wanted to be comforted, to be held by someone strong, but the situation limited their physical contact. The Anchoress spoke softly, uttering reassuring words: pieces of advice mixed with the odd words of scripture, or a prayer, the cadence of her beautiful voice embracing Barbara; the music coming from her mouth encompassing Barbara's being. Her sobs ceased, and they said nothing in their silent pose, Barbara bent into the small opening of the cell, Katherine Mann holding her hands.

"So, it seems you are as a little boat without a rudder."

Barbara laughed through her tears.

"Madam. I am but a rudderless wherrie."

"A wherrie indeed! Well my girl. We shall talk again, but I can say no more today. I need to ponder upon your predicament."

Barbara wiped a tear away with the strap from her biggin.

"Come again tomorrow."

Barbara walked away from the Anchoress, feeling light as she breathed in the autumn air. She found her self at the fish market at Mountergate, where there was an open smokery, pushing plumes of scented smoke into the sky. Her stomach grumbled, reminding Barbara that she hadn't eaten, so she bought a smoked mackerel and a heel of bread. She approached some women talking at a table.

"Ladies, may I join you?"

"Of course girl. You sit 'ere now."

They bunched up; Barbara sat, listening to their conversation.

"Like I was just saying, my boy, Tom; that's him all over. Idle as the day is long. When I kick him out of the house, all he does is stand around talking with his friends. Why can't he be like your boy, Frederic?"

"You know Anne, I be blessed with that boy, but I can't say why he be different. Your Tom is a good natured lad; there be no harm in him." The woman speaking saw Barbara's interest.

"Girl, you be too young to understand these lads."

"Not so, madam. Back in Himmelpforten, I met many such boys."

"Back where? You ain't from 'ere."

"No Madam. I am Barbara, from Himmelpforten, in Holstein."

"Well, Barbara, from Himmelpforten, I've never heard of this place."

"Holstein is north of Bremen. When I was a novice, soon to be obedientiary, at Porto Coeli Monastery, I went into the town, administering to the poor. These families often had boys just like those you speak of. To be sure, some were little saints, running errands, working, bringing home bread for the rest of their kin; but others, sometimes in the same family, rootless, playing pitch and toss all day, or just standing around; you have seen them, their backs to a wall, with one knee bent, a foot against the wall."

"To be sure, I have seen these lads here. What a nuisance they be."

Barbara carried on:

"No matter if they went to Mass, or if they were instructed, these boys just seemed to gravitate together. They were as lodestones to each other, unaware of the worry of their families. Of course, when they play acted in the street, whether they were shouting at a fool, or kicking a ball, they had no idea of the fright they caused the townspeople. You get one of these boys alone and they could be blessed, but when they troop together, they know not what they do."

"So you say girl, but how do you answer these boys?"

“Why, I only talk to them. I go into their groups and make friendly talk. I was never turned away, or set upon. It is fear of them that makes the danger.”

“You speak sense young woman, but, what of their fathers, coming home drunk, you know what that turns to.”

They mumbled in agreement.

“This I know, ladies. It is a scourge of our cruel times.”

Barbara regarded the women, speaking softly:

“Forgive me; may I ask, do your men beat you?”

The women glanced nervously at each other. One woman held out her hand.

“One time he...”

Another said:

“He used to”.

“But you ladies, you two, have your men laid such a hand on you?”

They paused.

“Girl, you speak in your strange voice, and you are near presumptuous. You ask us, whom you have never met, you ask us such things, and ' ere we are telling you.”

“I am sorry, I have no wish to pry.”

“No dear, you misunderstand. We be 'appy to tell you.”

The other women nodded approving.

“I wish to answer your question. My man has never touched me––he never would. But, you know, and God forgive me, I never told anyone this before, but, you know, once I beat him.”

“No, Jessica!”

“Yes. I was so ashamed.” She sniffed.

Barbara reached over and touched Jessica's finger on the table. She took a hankercher and wiped a tear.

"What makes us into a person who does such things?"

"It be God's will. Are we not at his mercy? We can but pray."

Barbara coughed.

"Ladies, we can have control over our lives. We can love each other and we talk to each other. We must always talk about little things, and when difficult things have to be said, we do not stay silent. We do not create this vessel for discord, this seething cauldron that creates the violence in us and in our loved ones. Ladies, we must love one another, and communicate."

She paused, and slowly lifted a piece of bread to her mouth. Jessica placed her hand over Barbara's.

"God Bless you, girl."

Barbara's hands did not shake; she was calm.

"So; it is said."

"Truly, you speak honest words."

"Forebye, we must be to our work."

"What is your work, ladies?"

"We are semsters."

"You say so?"

Jessica leaned towards Barbara.

"I hope you don't mind my dear, but I see that your little biggin is torn. Allow me to give you this one; methinks it will be a goodly fit. I made it by my own hand."

Barbara took the cap from Jessica.

"Madam. I am grateful. It is a beautiful green."

"Not at all girl. Go with God."

"Go with God, ladies."

~ ~ ~ ~ ~

The next day Barbara arrived again at Katherine Mann's cell.

"Ah, my little Barbara. You have a new coif. I have to say, the old one was well worn. You are brighter. The green shows your lovely hair."

Barbara blushed. Katherine Mann continued.

"Tell me, do you know Tyndall?"

Barbara glanced around her. No one seemed to notice the mention of his name.

"I have heard of him."

"You should read his Bible."

Barbara lowered her voice.

"But Madam, this is dangerous talk."

"My girl. Do you know who I am? You have met me but once. From this little cell, I can instruct thousands. I engage in theological argument among scholars in this kingdom, and across the waters."

"I am sorry Madam, I did not wish to assume...."

"My dear, I just wish you to see my situation. We women, anchored so, have such a tradition here in Norwich. Do you know of our Dame Julian? Such thoughts she had—have a hazelnut."

Katherine Mann held out a little bowl.

"So I ask again. Have you read Tyndall's Bible?"

Barbara chewed on the nut, was aware of passers by, walking inches from them.

"No Madam, I have not. But why should I when I can read my Bible in Latin? Why should I read in a foreign tongue?"

"You make a good point my girl, but to have it in the common tongue allows others to benefit from the word of God."

"Madam. I have no wish to read in English. My Latin is stronger than my English. Also, this book was translated by a mortal man — this man Tyndall. It is not the direct word of God. It is at once removed by the act of translation, and also by the act of interpretation."

"By the Virgin, my girl. You are good at this!"

They conversed further into the afternoon, discussing theology while the townspeople busied themselves feet away from talk that encompassed the dangerous ideas of the day.

"But Madam, we have not addressed my predicament."

"Perhaps not, my dear, but we have had a healthy exchange of ideas. You have a dilemma. Do you follow this man you have promised to find, or do you find a path of your own? Well, I would never be able to answer that; I never give advice so directly. You know that the answer is in your heart. Perhaps God might point you in the way, but the decision is yours. What I see in you is a fine young woman who is capable, who can make her own choices on God's earth. You have no need of advice from me or anyone else. Have confidence in your inner counsel. May God Bless you."

Barbara accepted the blessing of the Anchorite and left her. But now, she was even less sure of her way forward. She realised that here was another option. She was so impressed with Katherine Mann and her piety that Barbara saw that perhaps she herself might perform such a function to God and to others. Could she become an Anchoress? Or should she follow Jaap van der Staen? If God would just give her a sign. Barbara walked around the town, amazed by her predicament. The more she considered Katherine Mann, the more she felt a connection with her. But could she allow her self to be locked away? She imagined giving counsel to scholars, succour and sympathy to people in need. She could be safe from the danger of arrest; and what a way to serve God. Barbara ate and went to sleep, but dreamed of enclosure and duty, of walking along a dark road, turns at each side, visible only when they were behind her. She woke early and decided to visit Katherine Mann once more. She would become an Anchoress.

Barbara walked with new purpose towards Blackfriars where she met Jerome loading the Amaranth at the Fye Bridge.

"Well met, Barbara. I be glad to see you again. Well met!"

"And it is good to see you. Jerome. Did you sell your wool and felt?"

"I did so. Good business was done. But I have something to tell you. I have met someone who has information you will find interesting. You must meet him. He is at The Ribs of Beef."

"But I must see the Anchoress once more."

"Visit her later. She will still be at home."

Jerome laughed.

"Still at home! She ain't goin' nowhere! Do you see my joke? Ha ha!"

Barbara allowed her self a smile.

"Let us go to meet this man."

They walked the few yards to the Ribs of Beef on Wensum Street, overlooking a curve in the river, little wherries moored below. The tavern had the sweet smell of yesterday's beer and stale rushes on the floor; men still drinking from last night's cups. Jerome directed Barbara to a man sitting at an open window at the rear, looking out to the river. At his feet lay a sword in its scabbard, its belt lying loose. The man was writing with a quill on some pieces of paper, chewing on the feather end. He picked at bits of food from his tangled beard and placed them in his mouth; he chewed with his mouth open and spat on the floor. In the light from the window, Barbara could see he had strong green eyes. Jerome spoke.

"Thank you for waiting. This is the girl I told you about. Barbara, this is Starter."

The man with the beard studied Barbara.

"This little thing."

He held one of the pieces of paper to the light from the window and slowly beat time with the heel of his hand on the table as he read:

"Cupid, how have you cheated my love?

Her heart is cold as ice, all fire cleanses the eyes,

Now you are in my heart; it cannot be true again:

Because his flame has burned the wings of this house."

He spoke in a heavy accent, Barbara thought it was Flemish, but he spoke in English.

"So Girl. What do you think? A little melancholic perhaps? Will I sell it?"

Jan Starter put down his quill and took a draught from his cup.

"In the Frisian tongue, it was a happy alexandrine, but in English; it cannot serve. Alas, I cannot get the measure of the feet."

"Sire, I do not understand..."

"Husht."

The man began to untangle his beard with his fingers. He nodded to Jerome.

"So this is the one who is to apprehend a killer and bring him to account? God's skin."

He chuckled.

"Look at her. She couldn't..."

Jerome coughed; Starter spat again. He put down his comb, and separated the beard into little bundles, rolling and pleating it. Jerome placed a coin on the table.

"Tell her what you told me."

The man gazed at the little pieces of papers on the table and sighed.

"I need rhymes. Give me a rhyme. It must be sung."

He held the end of his beard in one hand, lifted his cup and drank. He placed the cup back on the table, adjusting it until it was over the ringmark. He returned to pleating his beard.

"I saw Jaap van der Staen."

Barbara opened her mouth.

"What? Where is he?"

"He was in Lynn last week, him and his boy; working on the salterns. They have gone north."

"A boy, you say. What boy? His son is dead."

He leaned across the table and met Barbara's stare.

"He was with a boy. He is a Dutchman. He is following the pilgrims. He will work on the salterns on his way. I heard say he was for Saint Andrews in that God forsaken country."

Starter fingered his now-knotted beard and spat again.

"I spit on Scotchmen."

"Did you speak to him?"

"No, but Lynn is small. Everyone knows everything that goes on. They burned a woman. That's where I saw van der Staen and the boy."

"They burned a woman? What woman? Why?"

"I don't know. God's breath, girl! She was just some damned woman."

"What does the boy look like?"

Starter stood and glared at Barbara.

"God's teeth, where are my rhymes?"

He placed a hand over his poems and closed his eyes.

"I don't know. He was a boy like any other boy. Enough questions."

Jerome rose and pushed Barbara out of The Ribs of Beef once more into Wensum Street.

"But I want to ask more of that man."

"Forbye Barbara, you have all the information you need."

"How does he ... what did he mean about his rhymes?"

"Enough. He be telling you everything you need to know. Follow the Dutchman."

Back in the tavern, Jan Starter smiled and picked up his quill.

On Fye Bridge, Barbara stopped.

"Follow the Dutchman, you say. Yes, But I don't know if I want to. I think I might like to be like Katherine Mann. I think that I would wish to be an Anchoress now."

Barbara's voice faded as she spoke. Jerome laughed.

"You. An Anchoress? When did you decide this?"

"Last night, this morning, I eh...."

Again Barbara's voice fell away, and as Jerome laughed, she realised the possibilities of what lay ahead for her. She saw that Jaap van der Staen was a real person, and that her task might still be accomplished. She weighed her Abbess's Book of Hours in her hand, feeling the thick, embossed binding under her fingertips. She remembered the triptych where she saw her self as an angel at SintJaanHospitaal in Bruggen that she took to be a sign; but here was more. It was proof; more than a sign. She could escape from her prophesy, and the dangers it brought. She knew more about van der Staen. He was travelling north, working on the salt farms, a young boy in tow. Who was this boy? Was he safe with such a man? How could she protect him from the evil that van der Staen presented? This was something new. Here was a child whose safety she had to guarantee. She realised that her wish to be like Katherine Mann was but a whim. Barbara's path was clear. All was distraction but for the pursuit of Jaap van der Staen. If he was with a young child, there was added urgency to her search. She would drive north.

Jerome bent over, slapping his sides with laughter.

"An Anchoress? You? I think not! You are too full of life my girl!"

XVI
Marrick
St Monan's Day,
1st March 1537

A Nun at prayer

Barbara had walked two hundred miles, each step taking her away from the risk of arrest, towards safety; each step towards resolution. During the journey, she had experienced wind and rain and mud, and both the threat and the generosity of strangers. She could sense danger at a distance and knew how to protect her self. Her feet had become hard and calloused, comfortable walking on rocks and gravel and ruts. She knew how to eat from the land and picked nuts and berries and roots as she walked. She also knew to rest, and the value it gave her; and she knew to accept hospitality. No longer would she become sick by failing to look after her self.

~ ~ ~ ~ ~

Barbara came to Marrick by way of Richmond where the colours changed around her. The early bloom hung on the trees and the bare wood thickened with new green. The first chestnut blossom showed white, the cold gossamer dew clung to the grass.

A smiling girl approached Barbara and prodded her in the ribs. She had bare feet and scabs on her knees; she played with Barbara's red hair.

"You have bonny hair. Art thou a sheep? Your wool is a nice colour."

Barbara smiled.

"I am not a sheep. I am like you."

"I was a sheep. But now I am a cat. Look at me be a cat."

The girl crouched down, hissed, and said, "Meeow." She pounced at Barbara, who stepped out of the way.

"My, you are indeed a goodly cat."

The girl's eyes lit up.

"Are you for the sky?"

"No, I am for Marrick."

"Bless me. I know the Prioress. She is Christabella. She was a swan once, but then she was a prioress. I am Alys."

"God be with you Alys. I am Barbara."

They walked together along the path, Alys skipping unevenly, pointing.

"There is a leaf. It makes such a tiny draft. All the leaves move together and make the whole wind; and there, look, a feather. Feathers make the birds fly."

"You are a quick girl Alys."

Alys smiled and walked tall, the two of them striding down to Marrick Priory, commenting together on Alys's observations. The Priory lay in a protected dale, lit by the afternoon sun. The church had been cared for, but the other buildings were in poor repair. Barbara saw, as she had seen in all the female monasteries, a level of poverty not present where the monks were accommodated. Nuns were denied the income available to the monks since they were not permitted to offer indulgences to reduce the time a soul could remain in Purgatory.

Barbara and Alys passed through the fields and approached the main accommodation building. It was quiet; a handful of nuns and lay helpers pottered in their various activities. Alys said 'God's Day' to all she passed.

"Here is the Prioress."

Alys picked up a stick and went off, skipping in her broken gait, in the direction of a duck pond.

Prioress Christabella Cowper was in the church, kneeling at prayer. Barbara waited at the door for her to finish, but she ignored her, making no indication that she was available for interruption. She carried on her meditation aware that someone was waiting to speak to her, but in the sure knowledge that her prayer, her little conversation with God, would continue as long as it needed to. Her spiritual health took priority over all else; and who would have argued with her? Certainly, not Barbara.

Barbara knelt at the rear of the church and set to prayer her self by a tiny altar with a single crucifix. She took a few minutes to relax, her heart still beating strong from the last fifteen miles of walking. She breathed and grew into a rhythm by reciting a Pater Noster, followed by ten Ave Marias, and a Gloria. She did this three times, fingering her rosary beads as she progressed through the cycle of prayer. Before long, she was in a mellifluous mental state, separated from any physical concern, from fatigue, from want of food or drink, or need of comfort. When she had completed her silent recitation, she looked around but the prioress had gone. Barbara rose, blessed her self, and went to look for her. She heard the sound of raised voices and Alys's cackling laugh from the refectory, where Prioress Christabella Cowper was berating a nun for some error in her tapestry, a small piece, stretched on a frame, of St Jude holding an epistle and a club.

"You stupid wretch. These stitches are loose, uneven; here look. They will not serve."

Alys laughed and pointed.

"They will not serve, they will not serve, ha, ha!"

The prioress faced Alys, raising her stick.

"Get away foolish girl."

Alys ran out of the room, cowering in anticipation of an expected blow. At her back, the Prioress castigated the unfortunate sister nervously picking at her tapestry. Once more, she raised her stick in mid air, but lowered it as she saw Barbara.

"Who are you?"

"I am Barbara. Here are my letters of credentials."

Christabella Cowper put down the stick and took the letters. She scanned them and handed them back.

"How do you think we can accommodate you? We have no money."

"I can look after my own self, Prioress. I seek only shelter."

"I suppose we are obliged to accommodate you for a single night. But do not think you can impose upon us. We have nothing here. You will leave as soon as you can. You will have no role. Your letters are of no use here. You may pray, but may not join the other sisters in any of the holy offices. You may observe. That is all."

"Of course Prioress."

That night, she attended as the sisters sang the hours at Compline. As instructed, she remained silent, but she mouthed the words, breathing the phrases of the music. The next morning, after Terce, she ate the food she had brought and helped with milking the sheep. She kneaded dough and assisted the lay helpers. They did not communicate with Barbara, and it seemed the Prioress had discouraged any association. This was not a happy monastery. Barbara sought out the sister at her tapestry.

"God's Day. I am Barbara. Forgive me, but if you so wish, I could help you."

"Thank you, girl. I can no longer see the stitches. I am old and my eyes fail me. My name is Anne."

The older sister peered at her work.

"Sister Anne..."

The woman looked at the girl in front of her: scruffy, her red hair unkempt, and holes in her skirts.

"They call us as Dame here. I am Dame Anne."

"Ah, Dame Anne, may I suggest a solution?"

"A solution? A solution to what, indeed? I suppose you may. Pray continue."

"You may wish to turn the piece to the light. But why do you work in such a room? There is no window here. You can never see where your needle will show in this light."

"Why, you are correct my girl, I have surely pricked my finger countless times."

"May I try?"

Barbara put her self to the tapestry, placed the needle down through the top side, counted the stitches and pressed it against the back of the cloth. In the better light, she could see the raised area where the needle appeared.

"You have a gift for this my dear. I don't know why the Prioress always asks me to do the tapestry work. I feel as if I have my fingers on the wrong hands."

The women worked together in silence, enjoying the rhythm of the task.

"You have come from the south?"

"I have, Dame Anne."

"They say there have been suppressions of monasteries."

"That is so. My own little St Sepulchre's is gone."

"Ah, so you say; you should be careful my girl. The King's Commissioners have also been here."

"No! I thought to escape from all that."

"Have no fear, all is as it should be my dear. Our Prioress has dismissed them for the moment."

"Dismissed them? How so?"

"Our Prioress Christabella may be strict, but she is also zealous. She has friends among the nobles; she will not allow men to suppress the monastery, despite its parlous state. She will keep this unhappy monastery functioning for as long as she is able."

Dame Anne stood at the open door of her cell, looking around at the high fields surrounding them. Barbara peered inside at her bare room; unadorned, no hint of ornament, just her cot, and the remains of a spent candle. Her bed was a bare wooden frame, filled with straw, covered by a single sheet. In the background, the river burbled and birds sang.

"Yonder is Calva Hill. To the right is the dale of Arkils Garth; to the left is Swale Dale. I have lived in these dales all my life."

"Truly, Dame Anne, this is a goodly part of the world."

"Have you been to Jorevall?"

Barbara looked again to Dame Anne, taking in the view over the fells

"Jorevall? No I have not."

"It is the greatest of our Abbeys in these parts."

Behind them, Alys had appeared from nowhere, nodding enthusiastically;

"The greatest. Yes. Jorevall."

She, turned around, and ran away again, giggling. Anne shrugged.

"The Abbot at Jorevall is called Sedbar. He is a good man, a strong man. If anyone can protect us from the reformers, it is the Abbot and our Prioress. We need these courageous men and women to reject these forces. Sedbar had an attack at Jorevall by reformers just a few weeks ago."

"I should like to visit this Jorevall."

Alys's voice came from the doorway.

"I can show you the way. I ken an owl."

"Thank you Alys. I would like that."

Dame Anne shook her head.

"Alys is a daftie, but she knows her way. You'll be safe with her."

Alys appeared beside them and held Barbara's hand.

"Jorevall is a half a day's walk. If you see my brother Gerard, please tell him I pray for him, and that I am well."

"Thank you Dame Anne. I shall. I wish you well with your tapestry and St Jude. He is the patron saint of impossible causes."

"Indeed he is, my girl, indeed he is."

Both women laughed, and Alys joined in with her soft cackle.

~ ~ ~ ~ ~

Barbara and Alys set out for Jorevall; Alys limping along, making observations about the clouds, wild dogs, horses and all she saw. Barbara didn't mind the constant chatter, and she warmed to the girl. She saw the world in a different way, but Barbara had also seen the world differently during her own little absences. Who among us would claim to know a real world? Was it the seeming firm ground underfoot? Or was it Alys's faerie world where cause and effect could be exchanged in a moment? Was it the governed world of the church, or was it pure gossamer, untouchable and infinitely elastic? 'Each of us inhabits a different world', thought Barbara, 'and that world is real to us at the time we live it'. Barbara was seeing Alys's world and was enjoying the visit.

The roads wound round the hills and dales on the way to Jorevall, sometimes placing the women in shade from the warmth of the spring sun. On taking the rise of a hill, Barbara felt the welcome heat on her face as she walked south. The great North Road, its throng of travellers and carts, was far away.

When they came to Jorevall Abbey, Barbara was astonished at the size of the site. Larger than Porto Coeli, it was a whole town built up around the Abbey buildings with industry and people, with the familiar smells of tannery, brewery, and bakery. The surrounding fields lay on a plain that stretched in all directions, sheep and cattle grazing all around. As they entered the church, the monks sang Vespers. Alys ran off and danced in the light from the coloured windows, weaving her hands in the motes lit by the coloured beams. Barbara stayed still under the centre of the hammerbeam roof, listening to the sung office. She observed a group of men waiting, their heads bowed. When the singing ended, they blessed themselves and picked up their tools. Barbara watched as they busied themselves at each end of the massive Rood Screen, working quietly, softly sawing and hammering gently at the timbers. Nail by nail, support by support, they meticulously separated the huge structure from the pillars. Barbara gasped in realisation of their task. They were removing the Rood Screen from the surrounding stonework. Alys appeared again, smiling and nodding.

"What is happening?", Barbara asked. The man next to her lowered his hammer.

"The King's Commissioners intend to suppress us tonight. They have been taking the altarware for the past week. Since the mob attacked, Abbot Sedbar has told us to protect all the holy things."

The Rood Screen shuddered as the men unfixed it from the stone.

"Jorevall is to be dissolved tonight?"

"Yes."

"Tonight", repeated Alys. The man shooed her away.

"But how can they suppress such a grand monastery? My little priory at Canterbury was suppressed, but this place? This Abbey serves a whole town; so many workers. You men, where will you all go?"

"We know not what lies ahead. The brothers will receive pensions, but we are to get nothing. These are such uncertain times. We fear for our future. We do what we can and we do the bidding of our good Abbot, Adam Sedbar. We are to take this Holy Rood Screen along the road to Aysgarth, out of the way of the Commissioners."

People congregated around the open church doors as a fog descended on the plain, hiding the top of the spire.. The murk rolled in, up the nave, chilling those inside. They shivered and rubbed their hands together to keep warm. Alys held on to Barbara's sleeve as they watched the huge coloured structure unhitch from its fastenings. The light of hundreds of candles illuminated the scene, each little globe of vapour shimmering in the draught, each with its own aura in the foggy wet air. A score of men carried the huge holy object down the nave. Townsfolk at the door stood aside as the Rood Screen was carried through the main church entrance. The Abbot sang a Benediction and held up the Monstrance, and they all joined him:

Tantum Ergo Sacramentum

Veneremur cernui:

Et antiquum ducumentum

Novo cedat ritui.

Barbara recognised the familiar Segen from Porto Coeli, sung here, so many miles away from her home, in these dreadful circumstances; and she wept, praying through the tears.

"Did you ever think to see such a thing? The world is truly topsy-turvy."

"Topsy-turvy", said Alys; she nodded and blessed her self.

Light rain fell, and the drizzle created a glassy film on the Rood Screen, so vulnerable out in the open. Barbara saw a glint of gold reflect a candle flame, and the green and the red and the blue took on a different hue out in the dull foggy daylight. The upper part of the screen had various animals picked out in gold leaf: strange creatures biting their own backs, an elephant carrying a castle, a pouncing fox, and a dragon baring its teeth. Priests swung thuribles which distributed the incense on the breath of the breeze.

"What is to become of us? Such a thing, to dismantle a church."

Candles sputtered and hissed as raindrops came into contact with the little flames. A monk went around the screen with a taper, re-lighting each candle as it was extinguished. The Rood Screen moved like a huge ship in the fog, flanked by priests and monks and lay helpers, all singing the holy words. Priests drizzled holy water on the screen, which mixed with the rain. It was as if the inside of the church was becoming the outside. All the contents no longer bound by its walls, and the colours and the smells out in the open, exposed to the rough elements. The Rood Screen and the procession progressed out through the buildings and streets surrounding the Abbey. The men carrying it were led by a tall heavy-set man, silently encouraging them; gesturing, guiding them if they seemed out of position, moving back and forth, ensuring that the structure was supported. They were followed by the Abbot Sedbar and the monks and lay workers.

The sight of the Rood Screen carried on its side, moving through the town, shook all those watching it. This surely proclaimed the end of the world. How could this event, so imbued with disruption, but done in dignity and grace, how could it not portend an end to the old ways? When the Screen passed them, some knelt, praying at the doors of their homes and workplaces. They wept as they prayed in the rain, their words lost in the mist. The whole town was frozen, immobile, drowned in the stopped moment.

Barbara saw and smelled and heard, and she blessed her self. In the cold of the rain, she felt a familiar warmth, and tasted iron in her mouth.

~ ~ ~ ~ ~

"Where are you for, girl?"

Barbara scanned in the haze around her. Where were they? How had they got to this place?, Had she had another episode in the rain? What had happened in her absence?

"I say, where are you for?"

She couldn't identify the voice; it was raining and the light was failing. A few feet away, Alys stooped under a tree in the shadows, shivering.

"Barbara, Barbara. I want to go home to Marrick. I am cold. I want my supper." Barbara was lost; wherever they were, she knew they would never get to Marrick before nightfall. She wept.

"Girl! I say! Where are you going? Is this fool with you? You cannot be about on such a night."

The woman standing in front of Barbara was plump and about her own height.

"I am lost', mumbled Barbara.

She pointed to Alys under the tree, whimpering and shivering.

"We saw the Rood Screen taken from the Church. We are lost and tired."

"I know my dear. We are all sad, but you have to keep out of this weather. You will catch your death of the cold. Come with me; you and your friend. I am Miriam."

Miriam gestured towards her little wooden home, smoke rising from a central hole in the thatched roof into the drizzling night sky. She opened the door to a lively home, warm and noisy. There was an entanglement of small children, playing and crawling over each other; all that could be seen was a jumble of little pink limbs. In the heat from the little fire, Barbara's senses returned. Alys took bread and ate, shivering by the fire. She sneezed. The woman sat her down.

" God Bless you my dear. Some broth?"

They took the hot bowls and sipped.

"Thank you. My name is Barbara. This is Alys."

"I am Alys; I was a cat." she sniffed.

Miriam grinned. Barbara tried to count the children.

"Where is your husband?"

"He was one of the men helping to move Rood Screen. He will be home late."

Barbara finished her broth.

"Where do you wish to go, my dear?"

"We are returning to Marrick Priory."

"Heavens, girl! You cannot not get there tonight. It is a half day's walk."

"Yes, but I..."

"You must stay here tonight."

"You have not the space. Your husband will be home."

"Worry not, my dear. We can find space for you and your friend."

"I thank you. God Bless you."

Miriam bustled about the tiny home, moving children, fixing the fire, stirring the broth.

"My man, Mark, will need to be warmed when he comes in. We are going in the morning to hear Mr Aske speak against the reformers. Come with us."

"Who is Mr Aske?"

"Mr Aske is the leader of our cause. He calls it our 'Pilgrimage of Grace'. He is sure to stop the reforms and the suppressions."
In the corner, Alys started her soft cackle.

"Yes. I would like to hear your Mr Aske speak."
The jumble of children were quiet and breathing softly together. For now, the tingling on Barbara's skin had gone.

XVII
Jorevall
St Timothy's Day
5th March 1537

Fragment of Rood Screen

Barbara woke to the squealing of children and the smell of cooking. Outside, Alys giggled as she chased a goat. Barbara knelt with her Abbess's Book of Hours. She thumbed to the pages of Saint's Days and found the brightly coloured image of Saint Barbara holding a little tower and read her prayer:

Beata Barbara

Tua scripta est in caelo fabula

Per cartam et aquam benedictam.

The sky above was overcast with the threat of heavy weather; little squalls blew leaves around in momentary spirals that renewed themselves in little sentences of moving air, each cadence the start of a new thing. Barbara blessed her self and closed the book.

"Bestir your self my dear. We leave for Bedale to hear Mr Aske. All our friends will be there. Here is Mark."

A man with a broad smile greeted Barbara. She recognised him as being the leader of the men carrying the Rood Screen. He shook her hand in his, which was hard and calloused, but, at the same time gentle. Behind them, there was bustling and movement, and in a seeming moment,

Miriam had all her children dressed and ready. Alys joined them and they set out; the warming sun giving their step a spring.

They joined others at the market cross in Bedale. Stallholders sold food and drink, calling to their customers; jugglers juggled, singers sang, and a man scratched at a hurdy-gurdy. Weaving through these brittle sounds could be heard the growing clamour from horses' hooves and the clatter of carts as the troop entered the market. Barbara tried to identify Mr Aske who was to stand against the King. She saw a man on the lead horse, with no semblance of authority. Alys laughed, and pointed.

"Look, look. He has only one eye. Ha ha ha!"

"Be soft, Alys."

"But I was only..."

"I know, but you must husht now."

Alys hung her head and sulked. The horsemen came to a halt at the market cross. Amidst the clap of hooves on cobbles, and the clink of harness, of swords and pikes and breastplates, there was muffled talk as they dismounted. Barbara was carrying one of Miriam's smaller children, little Margaret, on her hip; she couldn't see above the heads of those around her. After a few minutes, she caught another glimpse of the man with one eye climb the six steps of the market cross. He held on to the pillar and raised his hand. People cheered.

"That is Mr Aske", said Miriam. "Husht! He speaks."

"Pilgrims, my friends, we Pilgrims, for that is what we are; Pilgrims of Grace."

They cheered. A woman threw her arms open and called:

"For it has been prophesied:

'Forth shall come a worm, an Aske with one eye

And after that there shall be no May'."

Alys pointed again.

"It's him, it's him. I told you, I told you. He has one eye, Ha ha!"

Barbara gripped Alys's hand; a man next to them spoke:

"And it has also been prophesied:

'The power of the King is a flower that will wither.

The Towers of Fire will rage like flowers in the night'."

Barbara gasped in shock. These words; from her vision in the storm at the Buttermarket in Canterbury, spoken here, so many miles away. She realised once more the danger she was in; but here, forbye the fact that it was forbidden by law, these rebels spoke her prophesy out in the open. There were no King's men here. Alys was jumping up and down, pointing.

"Husht, my dear. We must not draw attention."

Barbara looked around to be sure no one recognised her as the prophesier. They were listening to Aske's words:

"No, my friends, for we are not rebels; we are not disloyal; we are willing subjects of our Holy King Henry. We are asking our King to listen to us. We have no quarrel with his divorces and with his right to tax us. We are his loyal subjects. We merely wish the suppressions of our monasteries to halt."

Barbara saw Aske pointed into the air;

"And, my friends, we wish him to dismiss his low born advisers."

Up came a roar of approval.

"Burn the Crumme!"

"Damn Cromwell. He is a dog!"

"He is a dog", Alys said in her soft cackle. Aske continued his address:

"We have succeeded in restoring some of the monasteries..."

The audience gave up a roar.

"... and we are turning this tide. From the Humber to the Tyne, we have men of all ranks, together, side by side, ready to take arms. But this is not what we wish for. What we want is to talk to our King: to show him our love and duty."

They applauded and cheered:

"God's Blessing on you Robert Aske!"

Aske raised his hand; there was silence.

"However, my friends, my Pilgrims, we have a sorry task tonight and we seek your help. The King's Commissioners are to suppress Jorevall."

They gasped, and cursed and shouted.

"Sweet Blood of Christ!"

"Damn the Crumme!"

"No!"

Aske raised both hands in the air and they became quiet again.

"My friends, we are not powerless. We can respond. We can be led by our Captains of Poverty. We must support the Abbot Sedbar and go to the monastery and halt any attempt to destroy it."

Once more, the they cheered.

"My friends, let me tell you. This is our greatest opportunity to reverse the tide of reform. The eyes of history will be upon us, so I must order you so: there will be no fighting."

The gathering grumbled approval.

"... And there will be no drinking."

There was the odd snigger, followed by "Shhhhh!"

"We must be ready to meet Cromwell's Commissioners on the field, and our force of numbers will cause them to turn back, for they are weak and without our resolve. For you men must buckle your harness and have your good wives to give you boiled bacon for your pockets."

The rebel supporters roared and cheered.

It was raining again and Barbara felt a tingle on her skin.

~ ~ ~ ~ ~

The smell of the lightning pervaded the thickening air. Barbara was sweating and weary after the walk back from Bedale to Jorevall. She was feverish and the white light appeared brighter. She felt the electricity on her skin, and the taste of iron in her mouth. Out of the door of Miriam's home, she saw only the grey mist. Alys sat on the floor, whimpering. There was a rumble of thunder, and shouting and calling could be heard from the Grange. At the sound of breaking glass Barbara ran to the Abbey Church, followed by Alys, limping along. Barbara turned a corner at the old infirmary where an angry mob gathered around a fire. At their head, she saw the Abbot, Sedbar, trying to speak, his words lost in the maelstrom. Monks attempted to pacify them, but the energy of the horde wielding sticks and torches was palpable. Barbara shivered; a bolt of lightning lit the incoherent scene, followed by more thunder. Alys tugged at Barbara's sleeve.

"Please Barbara, I want to go home. I am afrighted. I am not a cat now."

Someone threw a rock at the East Window, shattering the lower half, and as it lost its structure, the whole wall of glass fell in on itself, sliding to the ground in a shocking heap of colour and lead. There was silence for a moment; just the dripping of rain; the crackle of flame. A rumble of thunder broke the moment as the Abbot and the monks blessed themselves and fell to their knees. The mob cheered and ran past the clerics into the church, some drinking from flagons. A man spat on the floor of the Chantry Chapel. In the middle of the nave, they stared at the new light. Without the coloured glass, the open East window lit the whole church in an uncoloured grey void. The dull light drained the brightly painted walls of their colour. Wood-carvings and candlesticks were torn from their mounts, tapestries were pulled from the walls, and some set to smashing the rest of the windows. In the crescendo of violence, the Abbot, Clergy and their supporters tried to save relics, but were overpowered by the mob. People danced uncontrollably, jerking, shouting and throwing their hands in the air. Outside, the thunderstorm increased in intensity.

Barbara moved in the throng of confused, angry, intoxicated men and women, entreating them to stop. Before, she had been able to communicate, but here she was impotent in the face of the momentum of destruction. They ignored her or casually looked over the top of her head as if she wasn't there. Barbara felt the tingling on her skin, the haze of white light became bright to her eye, the shouts of the mob became a series of booming thumps; and she tasted iron. She watched as they sang and danced in the aisle, their movements slowing. Alys joined in, stumbling along, circling and flailing in the heavy air. As Barbara passed, they pulled at her, forcing her into their torpid frenzy. She knew not how she danced, but that she did so in this seeming dream, shared with the rest of the horde, the slow spinning roof above their heads.

A man took a torch and set light to a tapestry that had told the story of the destruction of the temple. The fire took, and the tapestry held licks of flame that sparked and spread rapidly across its entire width. Within minutes, the wooden statues of the apostles were also consumed by the fire. The sheet of flames quickly created a barrier right across the church. The fire rose with such anger and speed, tearing, cracking at the timbers, raising itself to the roof. The rabble cheered and danced and clapped and drank. Out of the fog of her perception, Barbara saw Alys's face lit up with an ignorant joy, her eyes shining in the light of the fire, her laughter lost in the slowing, pounding, maelstrom.

At the sight of the flames, Barbara knew she had to escape from the mad dancing, but two men with torches pushed her out of the way. One looked back at her. He was tall and lithe and there was something unusual about him. Her confusion fell away, and all became lucid in that instant. For no reason, she addressed him:

"Jaap van der Staen!"

At her ear, Alys screamed in laughter. The man stopped in his tracks, in the moment, startled; still in the fire, silent in their mutual shock. The chaos around them seemed to diminish; all was silent except for Alys's cackle. Their eyes locked together in a strange mix of incomprehension and recognition. Barbara's body was twitching, her eyes blinking. She lifted her hand and pointed at him.

"You have murdered your wife and son."

Alys nodded vigorously and jumped and danced between them. All around, people lolloped and skipped, their hands making random movements in the air. They sang, their eyes wide, seeing nothing.

Jaap stared at the young woman accusing him, between them a deformed fool, limping and swaying; around them, the falling masonry and burning timbers. Her mad eyes rooted him to the spot. He froze until his companion shouted above the pulsating roar of the flames:

"Come my friend, we have idolators to burn."

Jaap van der Staen turned to his accomplice.

"No, Thomas. Wait."

Van der Staen had to choose; to engage this young woman accusing him or to follow Thomas Cade; between them, this mad dancing fool. Barbara shouted over the sounds of the flames and breaking glass:

"Jaap van der Staen. You must come with me."

Thomas Cade's wide eyes reflected the inferno around them. He raised his torch into the air.

"For the Glory of God!"

Cade ran further into the building, towards the fire; Jaap ran after him, ignoring Barbara. The noise grew and she lost sight of them in the mass of bodies and chaos. The mob sang and danced, their steps dictated by the flames. Barbara tried to make sense of what had happened. Was what she had just seen been a part of another of her little silences? She could taste iron, and her skin shivered. Had Barbara just dreamed a meeting with Jaap van der Staen and another man; or had they really just run into the flames? In her confusion, she trembled as the song of the inferno blazed, governing the actions of all present, drowning sense and memory. It spoke to them:

"Be not still; be frightened; be frightened of my power. I am the one power. I alone will empower you. I will give you glory."

Barbara felt the weight of her fit, her uncertain senses. Alys tugged at her sleeve. A woman screamed into Barbara's ear: "To the Glory of God!", her eyes wide and manic. Barbara shouted back:

"Look what you have done."

"The devils deserve it."

The Abbot and monks tried to get the people out of the church, but they carried on, singing and dancing in circles, illuminated by the fire. There was a rush of wind as the blaze sucked air from the open East Window, and the ground shook as the thunderstorm grew in intensity. Parts of the roof fell to the ground in flaming fragments. The windows that remained were cracking, the glass shattering fragments into the air; rain came in through the gaps in the roof, at the same time steaming on the fire, and splashing at the feet of the dancers, slipping and sliding on the on the puddles on the tiled floor. The intermittent light of the inferno lit the mist inside the church, the lightning creating blinding flashes of illumination. Outside, were now running from the heat.

Alys shouted to Barbara, her words lost in the noise. She pointed. The woman with wide eyes was frozen in fear, her eyes fixed as if she were taken by a trance. Barbara screamed:

"Get out!"

"To the Glory of God", the woman repeated, her voice lost in the fury.

"Look, Towers of Fire."

Barbara heard the words amidst the shouts and singing and the roar of the flames. She blinked hard in the heat, looking for a way out. The West entrance was blocked with burning roof timbers, the East Window framed in flaming debris, the roof above obscured by the evaporating rain that created a cloud over their heads. The flames lit the scene with such terrifying authority that they feared for their immortal souls. The fire chose its own direction; it chose what to consume next. Lead dripped down from the roof and splashed, black, onto the tiled floor.

Barbara was sheltering at a pillar, Alys clutching her waist; the woman with wide eyes remained motionless and upright in the middle of the blazing chaos. Here, they were in a part of the church that was unfamiliar; where once only the monks had been allowed. The door had been covered by a tapestry that was now fragments of burning material. Barbara took a candlestick and used it to swipe away the remains of the burnt fabric; but the candlestick was scorching, and she could feel the skin sear on the palms of her hands. Smoke rose from the surface of the door: she shoved it open against the force of the incoming cold air; a gale of wind and rain rushed in, feeding the inferno behind her. Barbara pushed the senseless woman out in front of her, and Alys followed, crouching and stumbling, cowering and whimpering.

"I am but a little spider..."

There was a huge roar of the fire behind them, and Barbara fell out of the church, stumbling into the cloister, as a piece of the burning tapestry fell on her head. Her scalp was burning, and she beat at the flames in her hair with her hands. Alys laughed uncontrollably and pointed:

"See; so! A burning angel."

~ ~ ~ ~ ~

All that Barbara could hear was the dull guffaw from Alys. Everywhere in her vision, she saw the hazy white of her fit; the smell of sulphur from her burning hair, and the taste of iron. Alys danced around her with manic steps, pointing and screaming in her mad mirth and her short staccato cackle. Barbara ran towards the fish pond in the centre of the cloister garden and threw her self in. The carp dashed about, splashing beside this new creature, seeking solace somewhere in the confined pool. The cold of the water was shocking and she couldn't breathe. Above the sound of the fire and the screams, Barbara could hear the low pitched pulse of the flames. She lay in the water, outstretched, breathing heavily as the fish darted around. She slowly opened her eyes. The white light faded, and the orange light of the inferno surrounded her. She experienced an intense leaden throbbing in her head and on her burned hands. The light came and went in a drowsy mist. As she lay in the pool, the cool water offered relief. There was a strange sensation on her burnt hands as carp nibbled at her fingers. Two monks appeared and lifted her out of the water.

"Come with us."

Alys was quiet as she held her hand over her mouth, mumbling:

"I am a fish, I am but a tiny fish..."

Barbara perceived the ponderous rotation of the world as from above, outside of her own self. The rhythms of breathing, of walking, all decelerated to this slow viscous flow of events, pulsating with the sluggish movement of her thoughts. Each moment lasted an age. Barbara felt the white light return again as she was lifted out of the pond.

"Come girl, come with us. It is not safe. You are burnt."

Barbara arose and became erect, her eyes wide. She pointed at the church, and again, observed her surroundings as from above. There was no pain, just a distant awareness of the lethargic motion of the dislocated events around her.

The monks brought Barbara out of the cloister and down the side of the Frater and lay brothers' quarters. Inside, men levered at the supporting columns with iron bars. As they shifted the columns, the roof moved and collapsed, the timbers, lead and slate, falling so slowly, floating down to the floor, where they disintegrated in a cloud of dust and steam. As the men ran out of the building, the final pieces of the roof fell. They took Barbara into the infirmary.

"I am Brother Gerard,"

"And I am Brother Gerald. Come this way."

Alys pulled on Gerard's sleeve.

"Can I come?"

Gerard pushed her away.

"Away, daftie. Can you not see this girl is hurt?"

"But what about me, what about me? I am but a fish. I am too hurted."

Alys avoided Gerard's kick when they saw Barbara become motionless. She slowly lifted her hand and pointed at the church spire. As her eyes rolled to the back of her head, there was a huge explosion accompanied by a flash of light. She remained standing, but everyone else took shelter as more debris filled the air; lead and glass and pieces of slate from the spire dropped from the sky. Men and women took shelter and shouted, unheard in the silent chaos; their ears ringing, numb to the destruction. Gerard and Gerald guided Barbara, mumbling, to the pharmacy; they filled a bag with herbs and liniments. As they left, there was a crash as men smashed the windows of the infirmary, and broke down the door. Alys clutched at Gerald's habit, whimpering as they escaped the destruction.

"I am but a little fish. Sweet burning Jesus, help me."

Barbara felt a background throb and an intense pain in her right ear. She opened her mouth and jabbered. The monks led Barbara away from the monastery buildings, to the town. They stumbled down a lane, past the sound of crying children. A few houses along, they opened the door and went into a home with no candles, only the light from the dying embers in the hearth. Gerard whispered:

"Martha?"

"Gerard, Gerald. I worried so."

She embraced the two monks.

"I saw the fire and the explosion."

"They blew up the church."

"Sweet Jesus, what will it all come to? Who is this?"

"A girl. She is burnt. And she has a fool."

Martha looked at Barbara, standing with her shoulders drooping and her eyes blank, mumbling incoherently. She moved her burned hands in front of her, as if gesturing, swaying lazily from side to side. Martha examined her, moving her head to see into her eyes in the dim light.

"I know you girl. You were with Miriam; you and your daftie."

Barbara moaned softly. Martha assessed the girl's red and scorched head and hands. Most of her hair had been burned away, and her right ear was an unrecogniseable lump of scorched skin. They took her to a room lit with a single candle. Martha and Gerald took comfrey, ivy and larch and prepared a poultice and applied it to her head and hands.

Alys knelt, facing in to the corner, nodding her head and crossing her self. Barbara was motionless all the while and allowed the poultices to be applied.

"Poor child."

"She is blessed. She feels no pain."

Barbara muttered; Martha put her ear to the girl's mouth.

"What was that? Say again."

Barbara mumbled. Gerald and Martha exchanged glances.

"It is the prophesy. The Towers of Fire. I heard it in the village. It is what we saw tonight."

Barbara's body shuddered and shivered as she settled. She closed her eyes and felt warm – strangely in control; she gibbered.

"What did she say?"

"She speaks of Towers of Fire, and people dancing in the flames."

~ ~ ~ ~ ~

Jaap van der Staen sat slumped on a piece of broken masonry. The carnage of the night lay around him. The rain had stopped, but puddles had formed in the broken floors and between the smouldering wooden pillars and statues. In the wreckage, figures scavenged looking for souvenirs, silhouetted in the glow from the fading fires.

He remembered Harry. He had left him at the inn and he had to know he was safe. As he got to his feet, his knees and hips felt like the open ends of his bones grated against each other. He winced as he moved one foot in front of the other amongst the rubble. The pain jarred with each step, as he walked past the homes; the little homes with fearful people, awake in the night, trying to, keep safe behind their fragile doors. Behind him, odd pieces of masonry dropped to the ground, and burnt timbers creaked and crashed as they moved away from each other and fell.

When he arrived at the tavern, some men were still drinking, but there was no sign of Harry. Jaap went to all of the rooms, holding a taper to see by, and he finally came on the boy, asleep, curled up by a dying fire. As Jaap carried Harry out of the room, he placed a coat over the boy; he woke up:

"Where is Thomas?"

"Thomas won't be coming with us."

"Is he dead?"

"Yes."

"He was sick?"

"Yes."

"Will we go north tomorrow?"

"Yes. Tomorrow."

"Tell me another story about salt."

"I'm tired Harry."

"Please Jaap. I'll be good. I promise."

Jaap stroked Harry's head and told the rest of the story of the city of salt, his voice whispered, monotone:

"After many years, the city of salt was governed by men who had no time to play with their children. They met early in the mornings and talked about matters of great importance. They talked about government and their future and their worry about what would happen if things changed. They knew, you see, that they had been left an important legacy by Kinga and the other old ones who went before; it was such a legacy that they had to preserve it for the peace and security of the citizens.

But they didn't account for the deluge to come. How could they? How could anyone have known that a mountain would collapse into the sea and create a wave so huge that it would wash away the whole city? The citizens woke in the middle of the night to the sudden surge of water that engulfed every man, woman and child. They all died in the flood; all of them. The water took away almost everything, and it took away most of the salt buildings. It took away the palace and the city walls and many of the fine homes. It did leave the cathedral, but its great spires were washed away. The clear transparent walls became opaque with green and brown algae. No one who saw them would have known that they were made of salt. Now they looked like any old stone.

And, you see, that was the end of the city of salt. If you saw it now, you would never guess that it was once so special, so wondrous. There is nothing left of the gleaming spires and the fabulous pillars and temples. All you would see are some old ruins, streaked green and blue and grey, rotting in the hot desert sun. They still live in the city, but they would never be able to tell you anything of their past. They know nothing of Kinga and her virtue, and of the many achievements of the governors in the years of the city's existence. They know nothing of the beauty of the great shining salt palaces that pilgrims had come from far and wide to regard with awe. All was now gone. All was gone, and that is the end of the story of the city of salt."

XVIII
Richmond
The Feast Day of The Forty Martyrs of Sebaste
10th March 1537

Medieval City Gate

Jaap's worries consumed him. What was to become of Harry? What would happen if he ran away again; or if he was ill, how could he care for him; the bedwetting, the bad dreams, how could he make it all stop?

Harry skipped a step beside him and halted, pointing.

"Jaap. Look at those birds fighting."

Jaap grunted under his breath. Would they ever get to Sintanders?

"Look at that cloud, Jaap, it is the shape of a puppy."

Jaap gazed up to the sky. He saw nothing. They crossed a brook on a pair of logs.

"Look at the little fish, Jaap."

Jaap considered their journey. The horrors of the destruction of Jorevall behind them, they would walk to New Castell, and on to the

Northumbria Salt Roads; but how long would it take them; would they be safe? These were the questions he worried about. Through it all, he thought: 'am I right for this boy? Am I fit to be a guardian to Harry with my past? I am a sinner'. Strangers in the street see it. The man in Lincoln with the Knotted Beard, Starter – he said to his face he was a sinner, a killer, even. Through it all, Jaap could not erase the image of the girl in the fire. Who was she, and how did she know about the death of Gertje?

They stopped to rest, and Harry started playing fivestones, tossing the little stones in the air, sweeping them up, one by one.

"What was your wife like, Jaap?"

"Eh. What is it you say?"

"Your wife. You said that she died; and you had a little boy."

"Anders."

Harry now swept threw a stone in the air and picked up those on the ground, two at a time.

"Did your wife love him?"

"Eh? I suppose she did, why yes, she did."

"And Anders was like me?"

"Yes he was."

"Sometimes you call me Anders."

"Do I?"

Harry saw a squirrel and gave up his game. He ran a little way. Jaap caught up after a few steps.

"What is it like to have a mother? You said she loved him."

They crouched down to watch the creature place a nut in its mouth and scramble up a tree, a flash of rust against the bark.

"Anders was a happy boy, Gertje was a happy mother and I was a happy father. We didn't talk about love, we were happy."

"And they died."

"Yes Harry. They died."

"Do you love me Jaap?"

"We are happy, Harry."

Jaap held Harry's hand and picked up the pace.

~ ~ ~ ~ ~

Barbara made a slow recovery, cared for by Martha, Gerald, and Gerard. She was eating more and walking around. She tried to put together the images and sensations of the fire at Jorevall, and the explosion, but she couldn't separate hallucination from reality. Did she really see Jaap van der Staen? It seemed impossible that in this whole country, she had seen him there, with his mad friend. Did they die in the fire? Where was the boy? But these were things she couldn't fathom. If a resolution to all this was to come, it would be in time. Right now, thinking about them did no good..

Barbara got to know more people in the village in the aftermath of the destruction of the monastery. Alys stayed too, running errands, chasing the new lambs; but theirs was a fragmenting collective. Families were lost and broken; their society no longer had a centre, only a huge pile of rubble and fallen masonry and glass that was once the great abbey. Others began the process that would rebuild their communities, using the stones that had made up the monastery, seeking the security of new strong homes. But this would take many years. For now, some sought employment elsewhere. The saddlery, tending the animals and the land, the cheesemaking, the repairing of vestments, all the work of the abbey that gave them commonality, all had dried up overnight. Lay helpers sought alms, while monks still tried to sell indulgences, but were shunned.

The mood of the village grew despondent, but Barbara, although still recovering with her burns, tried to keep spirits up. Again, she became something of a mascot. Some came to her at Martha's home and told her their woes and their troubles. On this afternoon, she was woken by Martha. She whispered:

"Barbara, Miriam is come to see you."

Barbara lifted her head from the pillow, careful not to disturb the poultice on her head.

"Martha, I had the dream; I saw the man I seek in the fire."

Martha puffed up the pillow.

"You have had this dream before. Did you really see the man in the fire?"

"Do you know, I cannot be sure. Methinks I cannot separate dream from sensible. Forbye; Miriam, my dear, how do you fare? It is good to see you. How are the children, and how is Mark, that fine man of yours? God be with you all."

"Little Barbara. Look at you. You are cared for by our friend Martha here, and you still ask after others. I want to hear about you. We have not spoken since the destruction of the monastery."

The three women blessed themselves.

"May God forgive them for what they have done."

"Some are taking the holy stones from the ruins to build their houses."

They shook their heads.

"In such times we live."

Alys whispered from the shadow:

"Such times."

Barbara continued:

"Miriam, tell me about your children. How are they all? How is Joanna? She is like a little mother to the others; and tiny Margaret?"

"The Virgin be Blessed, yes, Joanna is a great help to Mark and me. We have been helping the cause, but things are not good. The Pilgrimage of Grace is all but over. The men were ready to fight, and they would have won, for God was on their side, but the nobles failed us. They worried about their land and their favour with the king and the court, and they disagreed. Mr Aske went to London for an audience with the king, so we await his ruling. My Mark says it does not look good for us Pilgrims of Grace."

"But if Mr Aske has spoken to the King, and he has told him of your loyalty to him, the king will see reason. He loves his subjects, does he not?"

Miriam dropped her voice.

"Barbara, the king is a cur. He is deceitful. We cannot trust anything he says. Our good Mr Aske may yet end in the Tower, or worse."

"The King is a cur," mumbled Alys.

Martha put up her hand.

"Husht, Alys. Miriam, my friend, you cannot say such things. You must hold your tongue."

"Martha, you know this to be true; but you must not say so, for you cannot place Gerard and Gerald's pension in jeopardy."

Martha looked to the floor. Barbara spoke:

"My friends, we must be strong together. Miriam, you are upset. Are you in some danger?"

"It is for my Mark I worry. He sleeps with a bodkin for fear they come for him in the night. That it should have come to this."

Miriam wept. Barbara and Martha comforted her; Alys held her hand, but Miriam pushed them away and wiped away her tears.

"No, my friends, we need to be strong. We must put weakness beyond us. I am no good to Mark and the holy cause of the Pilgrimage unless I can be strong. Martha, did I see you picking nettles?"

"You did, Miriam, you did. I shall make a tea."

~ ~ ~ ~ ~

A few days later, Barbara had been picking mushrooms with Alys, when she heard the awful sound of wailing from Miriam's house. Alys held Barbara's hand tight. They found the door open, and Miriam moaning wretchedly, the children sniffing, whimpering in the corner. Alys sat with them rocking back and forth, mumbling prayers. Barbara took Miriam's hands.

"My dear, dear friend, what vexes you?"

"Oh, oh, oh."

Barbara could not console Miriam's weeping. She scanned the home in its chaos; there was no warmth in the hearth, yesterday's potage lay on the cold ashes, straw from the beds strewn loose on the floor; no water drawn to wash the children, now fearful, cold, shivering and crying. This was not the home that Miriam had kept warm, busy, and full of joy. Barbara lit a fire and set to dealing with the children. She cleaned and dressed and fed them, helped by the oldest girl, Joanna, who copied Barbara's actions. Barbara attended to the children's needs, instructing Alys and Joanna to fetch water and clean. Gradually, they settled down. Slowly, warmth returned to the household. Miriam, however, still wept, and moaned softly.

"Tell me the matter my friend?"

"The matter is my Mark. They have, oh, sweet Jesu, they have taken him. He is lost to me."

Miriam sobbed again, Barbara put her arms around the larger woman.

"Where is he? What did he do?"

"He is taken with others for carrying the Rood Screen from Jorevall, and for other things he has done for the Abbot Sedbar."

"Tell me, Miriam."

"Oh it is so much worse than you ken, my friend."

Miriam hung her head.

"What Miriam, what?"

"Oh. Oh Sweet Jesus in Heaven; he is to be hung in chains at Richmond."

Barbara gasped and held her hand to her mouth.

"No, no, no."

Miriam wept.

"Wait Miriam. When is this to be?"

Miriam let out such a wail that the children whimpered. Barbara brought her outside, leaving Alys and Joanna to settle them.

"Miriam. Tell me, when is this to be?"

Miriam spoke and spluttered between sobs.

"This morning. Oh my Holy God, what is the time, has it happened yet? Oh Holy Mother pray for us. What is to become of us? What is to become of my love? What of his immortal soul? They will not confess him. He is to die unshriven; they will not allow his burial in consecrated ground. He will hang from a stinking gibbet until his bones fall from his body."

Barbara froze in horrified silence. She had heard of such practices. Men were hanged, their bodies covered in pitch and molasses, encased in a skeleton of steel. The crows and vermin would feast, the body would rot for all to see, their immortal souls never to see the Gates of Heaven.

Barbara calmed her friend as best she could. They completed chores and tended to the children. This was as much as they could do today. The small tasks of the moment, significant and sufficient, those tasks that created stability, that would maintain the home and feed the children until new decisions had to be taken. So went the sombre day. At its end, Barbara and Miriam sat down together.

"I must save him."

"But Miriam,"

Barbara held Miriam's shaking hands.

"It is too late to save him."

"No, Barbara, I must save his soul."

"But how?"

"I can cut down his body and bury him. I know a priest who will say a mass."

"But how will you do this thing? How will you do this?"

"My friend, I will need help."

Barbara couldn't hide her horror at the realisation of what was being asked of her.

"You mean, go with you to take down Mark's body from the chains?"

"Yes. It is the only way to save his soul. He cannot enter the kingdom of heaven with a body that is rent asunder. We can get Martha to help."

Alys, who had been listening, spoke up.

"I can help. I am strong."

Barbara embraced Miriam; at the other side of the room, the children slept.

~ ~ ~ ~ ~

For four hours, Miriam, Martha, Barbara and Alys pushed a cart to Richmond in the rain along rutted tracks, the puddles reflecting the troubled moonlight; they trudged on, their skirts heavy with mud, their hair plastered to their faces.

"I be a little fish. A minnow it is that I am."

Alys peered up into the rain, and nodded her head up and down, repeating:

"Yes a minnow it is that I am."

"Shhh, Alys."

"Sorry Martha," Alys whispered. "Verily, a tiny quiet minnow I am, that not a soul can hear me." Alys nodded, silently agreeing with her self, satisfied. The rain soaked through her clothes and she sneezed. From inside the old city walls, they heard the sound of a horn.

"It be the Richmond watchman. What if he should see us?"

"We only have to get to Galowbrawghe. That's where we will find him."

No one was about when they arrived at the Gallows gate at the northern entrance to the city in the middle dark of the night. They had tools, a knife, ropes and a winding sheet. Through the rain, there was the stink of putrefying flesh which increased as they approached the city walls. Hanging from the tops were the odd shapes of arms and legs; those of poor unfortunates whose body parts had been cut from one another, who had been quartered. Each of the women blessed themselves and tried to look away from the shocking sight. Among the horrifying shapes were four bodies, silhouetted against the moon; hanging, encased in their iron bounds, the rain pouring through and around them. The wind came up and swung the bodies together, their chains creaking in a harmony of death.

"I do not like it here."

Barbara squeezed Alys's hand.

"Say an Ave Maria."

As Alys recited her little prayer, Barbara peeled away the sodden bandage on her head; the poultice now washed away. She felt the cool rain, each drop drumming on her scalp. She touched the remaining hair stuck to her face. She peered up at the bodies, blinking at the full moon shining through the rain.

"Which one is Mark, how can you tell which is he?"

Without hesitation Miriam pointed at the body on the right.

"How can you tell?"

"That is Mark."

"That is Mark", repeated Alys, seriously.

The four women entered the gate and climbed the city wall from the path on the inside. The sound of their breathing mixed with the rain and the intermittent crows clicked and called to them with their kraa:

"You should not be here."

Alys whispered:

"I am but a tiny mouse. I am a mouse."

There were no sentries by the city wall, and the women made their way around to the top where the bodies hung. Some of the bodies had been there for some time, and now, closer, the fetid stench was stronger. In the white light from the moon, they saw crows pecking away, busy, slipping on the wet surfaces, losing their grip on the wall, wheeling around in the rain, and returning for another peck. Miriam reached over the wall as Martha and Alys pulled at the rope from which Mark's body hung. Alys took the whole weight of the chained body and heaved.

"I am a horse, and I haul."

The rope was wet, slippy in their hands; they swung it and it creaked, and the carrion birds flew away in irritation. They understood the call of the crows:

"We will return. You will not deny us. We are but messengers."

Miriam and Martha and Alys were strong women, but they could not lift the weight of Mark's body and its iron shroud. Barbara helped, her own hands still scarred from the fire; but the body would not be raised, they could not lift it.

After fifteen minutes of tugging and pulling, they rested, exhausted. Barbara felt the pain of her burns.

"How far is it to the ground?"

Alys whispered:

"Yes."

Miriam was aghast.

"What? No."

"Yes, cut him free and let him fall."

"But it will hurt him so."

Barbara touched Miriam's hand.

"Miriam, Mark is beyond physical pain."

Miriam sniffed in the rain and took the knife from Martha. Again Alys took the weight and Miriam began cutting the rope holding Mark's chained body. The cage moved backwards and forwards with each cut of the knife. As it swung, the sweet rancid smell of death wafted up to them. As each core of the twined rope was severed, it sprang away from its neighbours with little sprays of water; the remaining strands strained, throwing off more water as each chord vibrated silently in the night. Barbara, Martha and Alys tried to hold the rope to make the cutting easier; Miriam was sweating at the effort of each stroke. As she cut through the last piece of rope Barbara felt it fly through her scarred hands, and the encased body crashed to the ground, thirty feet below. The iron skeleton that protected Mark's fragile body had kept it in one piece. The women went back down to where the iron frame lay outside of the city wall, and rolled it, splashing in the rain, to the cart. With terrible effort, and Alys's strength, they heaved the cage containing Mark's body onto the dray. It took all night for them to push the cart back along the puddled, rutted road to Bedale and home.

~ ~ ~ ~ ~

The next day, Miriam was first out into the dewy morning. There was no sign of the torrential rain from the previous night, the warm sun betrayed no hint of the horror of their night's work. She went to where Mark was lying, covered under a lean-to, and worked to remove the iron strips that held her husband's body. She ignored the rope burns on her hands and her fatigue; she had not slept. Tenderly, she washed him; when her work was complete, he smelled of lilies and rosemary, and she wrapped him in a pristine shroud. Miriam went into the house and roused the others. They all rose, Gerard and Gerald, Barbara, and the children, and brought Mark to the church. Alys followed, limping behind. She sneezed, and they all said "God Bless You."

Inside the little church, others who had heard came in and blessed themselves with holy water at the little piscina by the door. The priest waited as some men placed Mark's body on a bench. Assisted by

Gerald and Gerard, he said a requiem mass, and they sang 'Requiescant in Pace' together.

During the service, Barbara's senses were overwhelmed by the smell of the candlewax and incense. Her thoughts returned to the night of the fire at Jorevall, meeting Jaap van der Staen; her promise to her prioress in Porto Coeli.

Outside, after Mark's burial, while the children ran around, a little one fell over, and was tended by Joanna, who rubbed her knee and said an Ave Maria. Alys ran after some hens. Miriam, Martha and Barbara gathered together.

"What is to become of us?"

"There is nothing for us here."

They watched as another family left the town, following their belongings piled on to a cart, pulled by a horse.

"This place is dying. We cannot stay. God does not live here any more."

"But where will we go?"

Martha looked at the ground.

"Gerald may find work in York. He can read and write; he knows something of the law."

"And I must take the children away from here. I too will go to York, and we can be together. Barbara, come with us."

"I cannot. I know what I must do, but it pains me."

Alys left her hens and stood by, sensing the anxious women speaking, examining their faces one by one. Martha spoke to Barbara.

"What must you do?"

"I must follow van der Staen to Sintanders. I am to follow the salt roads to Skotlân."

"But it is dangerous there. Scots are savages."

"But we have seen savagery here, have we not?"

Martha and Miriam acknowledged agreement.

"And you know about my promise to my Prioress. I am sorry not to be with you, but you will be strong together."

"Our little Barbara, you are the strong one. You must follow this man; go with our love."

"I am for Scheles. There are salt roads there. The Dutchman will take the salt road to Skotlân."

"But what about our Alys? She has helped us so."

Alys beamed, and she sniffed, and sneezed once more.

"I want to follow Barbara, for she will look after me. I will follow you to Skotlân."

Barbara embraced the muscular frame of the small girl.

"You must go with Martha and Miriam to York. You will be safe there. As for my own self, I know not what is before me."

Barbara, Martha and Miriam embraced and kissed Alys. Alys held Barbara's hand tight, as they were lost in the enfolded arms of the larger women.

XIX

New Castell

The Feast Day of St Aldelmus of Sherbourne, 5th May 1537

Coat of Arms, Goat's Head

Barbara followed the salt roads, accompanied by memories of the sore troubles of her absent friends – her little tribe. She was alone now, without the towering strength of Miriam, and Martha, and without the small joy that Alys brought to each moment.

She had come on the North Road, stopping at Durham, and had arrived at Goat's Head, from where she could see the light from the lantern in the spire of the Church of St Nicholas, across the Tyne river, high above New Castell. Crossing the old bridge, mixing with pilgrims and townspeople, traders and stockmen, and the constant stream of rebels fleeing the king's wrath, Barbara went up the hill, passing Blackfriars and Greyfriars monasteries, and came to St Bartholomew's in Nunn Street. She showed her letters of credentials to the sister who opened the door, entered, and was confessed. Barbara soon re-acquainted her self with the regularity of the singing of the Canonical Hours. From Lauds to Compline, she immersed her self in the familiar rhythm of praying and working that made her forget her problems. She moved around the nunnery, and conversed with the ladies, discussing matters of everyday, the everyday that was, for now, cocooned, and detached from the horrors of burning and death and suffering.

Barbara still felt the pull of the friends she had left behind. Martha and Miriam had cared for her after the fire at Jorevall, and they had shown her love in the most awful circumstances. In particular, she felt a duty to Alys. So simple and wise, she would now be protected by Miriam and Martha, but Barbara knew the girl had wanted to be with her. She should have allowed her friend to accompany her. If she was honest, she would say that she had not wanted Alys with her. She told her self that her high minded quest was to seek the Dutchman as instructed by her Prioress in Porto Coeli; but she was aware that in her own desires, she was placing her self before others. This was the pride she abhorred in her self. How difficult would it have been? Such was her betrayal of Alys; and such was the matter of her first confession at St Bartholomew's. As he was to do in subsequent confessions, the Priest consoled her, and told her the life of the nunnery was to be her saving. What was to come was to come. Having hope in God's design for her was all there was in these times.

Hope, hope, hope. Barbara pondered on this advice. If she were to give up all to hope in God's will, she could not govern her own destiny. She had become strong in her journey, and had learned from the wise counsel of others: her Abbess, Philippa Jonys, Jerome and his Amaranth, Katherine Mann, Miriam and Martha, her reading of Hilda of Presscott, even Alys who had taught her so much through her strength and her simple love. Their wisdom showed her that it was in her choices that she found the will to do good. Waiting for God to show the way was dutiful, but after a few days of the rhythm of life at St Batholomew's, she was becoming distracted with thoughts of her destiny. She had to choose: to stay, or to follow the instruction of her abbess at Porto Coeli and find the Dutchman. This was the only reliable course of action; all else was but habit, hoping for God to offer a way. But Barbara was starting to see that her destiny might down to her own choices; mere hope a misguided philosophy that froze her and sucked the life from her.

But how did a life governed by her choices balance with her responsibility towards others? Should she have gone to York with Miriam and the others? There was fortitude in that group of women. They would have protected each other and cared for Alys who had been as a shadow to Barbara, a reflection of her own needs. These women had shown Barbara a life of support and strength outside of the confined life she had known in the monasteries. They showed her how to have belief in her self; but how would she temper this course of action with a duty to others, to the principles of care she had learned from Hilda of Presscott? How could she offer succour to others? Barbara knew now she had betrayed Alys by pursuing the Dutchman on her own.

These problems consumed her, and with her new confessor at St Bartholomew's, she found a sounding board for her troubles, an exploration of her self, how to grow, to flourish and be virtuous? During these confessions, the Priest was mostly silent. He interjected with short pieces of scripture, a prayer here and there, or just by nodding his head. He never offered advice, which allowed Barbara to crystallise her thoughts. She became even more convinced that her destiny lay not in a futile hope, but in the embracing of her own choices; each little decision governed by a comparison with the example of others; and in the practice of making these choices, she might attain that same virtue. It was a matter of each time, simply doing the correct thing.

~ ~ ~ ~ ~

The rain pattered on Jaap's cape as he paced over the wet ground, west, towards the sea, to Scheles. Harry struggled to match his step. With each stride of his longer legs, the man covered more distance, and the boy had to trot to keep up.

"Jaap, I walk with your steps, but you are always quicker."

"I am sorry. I go slower."

"No. I can keep up."

Harry skipped a few steps until he a was at Jaap's side once more. Jaap shortened his gait.

They came to a large waterlogged plain, covered by reeds and long grass. Without speaking, as they had done a hundred times before, Harry fell back and Jaap went in front. He pushed the reeds with his feet, making them flat on the watery surface, creating a carpet to walk on, like the rushes on a clean floor. Harry followed in his footprints, observing the gurgling water filling the spaces left by Jaap's feet, the gentle rain making little ripples on the surface of each new puddle. Over this flat landscape they kept a good pace, and once again, fell into the slower, comfortable monotony of their steps. The rain was not unpleasant, its rhythm inducing an almost hypnotic state in the two of them. They didn't speak; the sounds were of the rain, of their breathing, and of the sloosh and gurgle of their steps across the sodden heath. From behind, Harry would see only Jaap's large back, glossed and steaming with the heat generated from his exertion. Harry wondered if he also had his own little cloud of steam. He could imagine them as from a distance, over the flat expanse, one a miniature version of the other, perfect, and perfectly in step, each with their own little cloud above their heads.

Harry felt safe in this open place. They were never lost and Jaap would always show him the way. These thoughts in Harry could never have been articulated; they existed by way of his relaxed state, how he became happily distracted by little things, a bird taking flight, a tiny creature in the grass, by a snail crossing their path. He could concentrate on such things because he was not in need of food, he was comfortable, he was safe. These three things made up his whole world of need. Jaap gave him these things.

The rain ceased, and the new sun warmed the wet grass; a low fog lay on the ground to knee height. They walked through this low lying veil that billowed gently, creating fresh eddys with each step. Harry trotted to walk at Jaap's side and the song of the rising linnets was heard against the clearing air that smelled of wet soil. The ground was muddy underfoot despite the new warmth, and they descended into an old part of the road, just wide enough for a cart and horse. Here, the weight of the footfall of teams of pack horses and people over the years had lowered the surface of the path a good ten feet below ground level; earth and roots either side, the leafy canopy above.

After a while they heard the sound of a little bell, tink, tink, tink; then the snorting of horses coming their way, the dull thud of their hooves on the compacted dirt, and the rumble of cartwheels. In the dim, the intermittent sun glinting in the leaves above, they could see but a short distance ahead. Out of the leafy chamber, approaching them in the enclosed tunnel of trees and roots, they found themselves face to face with a massive pack horse pulling a dray, loaded with barrels, that filled the full width of the road. It was led by a man with a stick; behind, more horses and carts; the sound of snorting and breathing, the clatter of more hooves on dry earth, and the clinking of harness, all adding to the subtle menace in the confined space. There was no room either side of the animals and their burden to allow Jaap and Harry to pass; faced with the unstoppable mass of horse bearing down on them, they had no choice but to turn back.

Jaap swiftly hoisted Harry onto his shoulders and turned around to face the way they had come, walking briskly in front of the lead horse, driven by a man flicking a switch. They felt the animal's breath on their necks. Harry spoke into Jaap's ear.

"He is like Marcuccio."

Jaap glanced back. Indeed, this was a draught horse, and dark, but he had none of the bearing of Marcuccio. This beast was born for burden, not for joy. This poor creature would never dance or sing.

"Yes Harry, but this horse will never fly."

"Poor Marcuccio."

"Yes. Poor Marcuccio."

Behind them, the driver grunted, and gestured them out of the way with his stick, but there was no room at the sides of the narrow tunnel. Jaap was breathing heavily as he kept his pace ahead of the column of horses and drays, keeping a distance ahead. He turned his head and raised his voice over the sound of the clatter and the rattle of hooves and carts.

"How many animals do you have today?"

The man appeared to glare at Jaap in the poor light.

"You not be from 'ere."

"No. I am Dutchman."

The driver gave a hawk and a hem and spat to the side of his cart; Jaap tried again:

"You are carrying salt? I am salt farmer."

The man peered ahead into the dim burrow, surrounded by the trees above, and the dark roots on either side.

"Jaap. Why doesn't he want to speak to us?"

"Shh."

Above the rumble of hooves, and the rattle of wheels on the compacted earth in this buried road, behind them they heard the constant tink, tink, tink, of the bell on the lead horse, propelling them in the wrong direction, away from Scheles. Jaap was tiring of the fast pace, but they came to a junction and ducked into the side, out of the path of the pack horses. Harry came down from Jaap's shoulders and they stepped back into the gap as the train of horse and cart passed them. The driver raised his hand.

"God's Day tae ye sir."

Jaap and Harry looked on as he led the twelve pack animals, their hooves thundering past them, out of the low road and west to the markets, where they would sell their salt; salt from the pans at Scheles, where Jaap and Harry were now headed.

"Jaap; that man wouldn't speak to us."

"No Harry."

"But why did he say God's Day?"

"I don't know Harry. These Ingelânders confound me."

Jaap and Harry rested and ate some berries before returning into the low road, back towards the sea, and Scheles. This time, as they were entering the dim tunnel, they encountered another train of pack horses going in their direction, at a slower pace, towards Scheles. Jaap hailed the new driver, grinning, walking at the side of his lead animal.

"My friend, are you for the salt pans?"

"Aye, sir; by the Rood, I am. Come with me to Scheles?"

"Thank you sir, we would like that. We have walked the road twice today."

"Were you stuck with the train coming in the other direction?"

"Yes sir, and led they were, by the most ungracious of men."

"Ah. That be blind John."

"Blind John?"

"Aye. He be most ill mannered, but he plies these Galloway pack horses three times a week, often at night. It makes no difference to him; day or night."

Jaap pointed east.

"You carry coal for the pans?"

"Aye. Coal one way, salt t'other. The animals are full loaded with coal, an' light wi' salt. The salt makes us the money and gives the 'orses a rest."

Jaap and Harry and their new guide walked side by side, along the low road, listening out for oncoming pack horse trains. Harry saw a fine old hazel tree with low boughs and strong exposed roots.

"Jaap. Jaap; can I climb that tree?"

"No Harry, we must keep going."

"But Jaap, please."

Jaap took Harry's hand and pulled him on.

"We can find another tree."

"Promise, Jaap?"

"Promise."

"Look Jaap."

At the side of the path lay an empty barrel.

"Aye. From one of the salt carts", said their guide. They carried on, with the fading daylight showing dull through the trees above them. After a short time of walking in the leafy tunnel, they came out into an evening sun. There was a fork in the road.

"Scheles, you say? You go right, mannie."

"Thank you, sir."

Jaap and Harry arrived in South Scheles in the dusk that showed the fires of the salterns illuminating the coast as far as the eye could see.

XX

Scheles

The Feast Day of Saint Serenidus and Saint Serenus, 7th May 1537

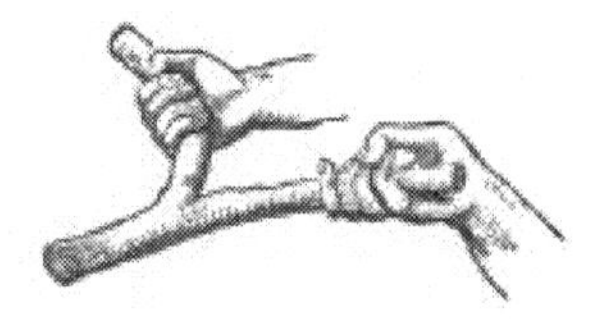

The Divining Rod

As Jaap moved in his cot, his thoughts and his pain stole sleep. He held his breath, trying not to grunt, as he turned on his side so to ease the ache in his back and hips. He opened his eyes in the dark, he saw nothing; he closed them and still saw nothing. He shut his eyes tight and made out dull shapes that lingered on his retina, but faded before he could make them out. In the intense dark, it didn't make any difference whether his eyes were open or closed. He looked to where he heard Harry's shallow breathing, but saw nothing. Outside a fox yelped and an owl hooted, and the void was silent once more. Jaap peered all around him to see just a glimpse of light. Even the dead embers in the hearth offered no respite from the dark. He stared towards the shuttered window looking for some hint of starlight in the moonless night. All was black.

But here, with this boy, in this room, warm and dry, there was no feeling for the cold outside. Harry stirred, gave out a small cry and sobbed for a few breaths. Jaap got up and squeezed his hand.

"Be at peace Harry. I am here. You are safe now."

"Safe now", Harry mumbled.

Jaap felt his way back to his pallet and lay with his eyes open. His thoughts turned, as they often did, to Gertje. Without her, on his own with each decision, he had no touchstone; he had no one telling him that such-and-such was a silly thing, or that this way was better. Jaap felt alone; but with Harry, he found some decisions clearer – not easier, but clearer. Above all, he had to keep Harry safe. Also, here in this dark, he allowed himself to think about his Anders. Harry was very like Anders, if a bit older, more assured from years of living on the street; each boy answering Jaap's need to provide.

Some heard their departed loved ones speak to them, but not Jaap. He never heard her voice, she never appeared to offer advice, but Jaap so would have liked to listen to her all the same. His eyes drooped; the shapes he had seen behind his eyelids re-formed and this time they lingered. He made out a figure in the distance, walking through the dark towards him; a figure whose walk he would have known anywhere. He thought he heard her words as he drifted off.

~ ~ ~ ~ ~

Once more, Harry found himself in the suffocating crowd and the smell of smoke, and the taste of ash, unable to see. He sank into the dark, gasping for breath, and woke. He opened his eyes and watched Jaap rise and go outside, and return to lie on his pallet. Waiting until Jaap's breathing became regular, Harry rose and left their hut; walking away from Jaap into a world to which he was drawn; a world of danger and excitement where no one would tell him what to do; not even Jaap. Unable to stop his self, or to know why he was doing it, he stepped out into a lighter night, where the moon had come out to show his way. He traced his steps back along the salt road and found the barrel and the hazel tree. He climbed the tree, placing his bare feet and knees against the rough bark. He heard the sound of a horse's bell, tink, tink, tink, and the rumble of the hooves of a train of pack horses. In a moment there was the lead horse, driven by the old Blind John from the day before. As the train passed, he looked up to the hazel tree Harry had climbed. Blind John stared, his white eyes cutting right through him. He grunted, spat, and flicked his switch at the lead horse and passed, leading his twelve horses along the dark road.

Harry sat in the tree, frozen in fear. He waited until the sound of the last horse disappeared, and there was silence in the moonlight. In moving to get down the tree, he disturbed a pair of nesting pigeons who fluttered and hoo'ed before settling. Harry stayed where he was. At the sound of the birds, he saw a female figure stumbling towards his tree. She sneezed. Harry hid in the branches – he did not want Jaap to know that he was out alone in the night. The girl limped to the spot underneath Harry's perch and raised her head to see the source of the noise. Harry could only make out her unkempt hair. He kept still, breathing through his mouth in order to remain silent. Then he saw another swaying figure approach, a man, about the same size as Jaap, but with a beard. The man spat on the ground and whispered to the woman. Above them, at first, Harry could not understand the words the man spoke; they sounded like the foreign words Jaap spoke, but then he thought he heard words he knew, and then he couldn't hear them. All of a sudden, the woman shouted – "No!" and she stumbled away. Harry watched as the man followed her. Their pace quickened, and he saw her start to run in her unusual gait. The man ran after her and she tripped on a root, lying where she fell. Harry saw the man bend down and speak in those strange words, and shake her, but she remained motionless, like a doll. In the dim light, Harry saw him look up and down the low salt road, drag her to the barrel, and place her in it. He rolled it away from the path, into the dark of the undergrowth.

Harry felt a small waft of air on his cheek. It was a bat, and then it was many bats, flapping and clicking in a confusing cloud of movement. Harry flailed his arms, trying to keep the creatures away, but all he saw were tiny black things in the night. He knew they were bats; those strange birds that flew on a breath, without feathers. Then there were more that made a tiny storm around his head. The bats didn't fly, but directed themselves from point to point within the blinking of an eye. He kept still, his eyes shut tight, holding his breath, hoping not to be discovered by whatever danger these tiny creatures offered. Suddenly, the bats settled, and Harry opened his eyes and saw the silent shapes of the night. He exhaled and panted for breath. He peered across to where he had seen the man put the woman's body. Had he really seen it? Did he dream it? Anyway, Harry didn't think about it; the man had gone. He blessed himself, waited for a minute in the silence and came down from the tree. He ran, ignoring the dread contents of the barrel, looking neither left nor right, back to their hut and the warmth of his cot, next to Jaap. There, he closed his eyes, and made himself sleep.

~ ~ ~ ~ ~

The next morning, Jaap and Harry shared some bread and small beer.

"Will we go back and climb that tree you liked?"

Harry said nothing.

"There is time. It is but a little way. Come on Harry. Let us go."

"No. I don't want to."

"Don't be foolish, Harry."

Jaap took Harry's hand and then let go. Harry dawdled behind as they made their way along the low tunnel of foliage, back the way they had come the previous night. They came to the tree.

"There Harry, you can climb the tree."

"No. I don't want to."

"But Harry, you wanted to yesterday. Come on. I'll climb it with you."

Harry burst into tears.

"What is it Harry? Why do you cry?"

Harry told Jaap what he had seen in the night; of Blind John, the limping girl, the man and the barrel. Jaap held the boy in his arms.

"I'm sorry I ran away from you again."

"You are a good boy for telling me Harry. We must find a Bailiff."

~ ~ ~ ~ ~

"I am called John Whyte, the Bailiff; this man is the Dowser."
Jaap led them to the hazel tree, and Harry told them his story.

"And you didn't dream this, boy?"

Harry kicked his feet.

"No sir."

"Because if you did ... if you are wasting my time ... I will beat you full sore."

Jaap spoke up.

"He doesn't tell lies, sir."

"Hmm!"

Harry glanced up at Jaap, following the Bailiff. It might have been a dream. How could he be sure? Would he be beaten? He had not been beaten since he took up with Jaap, except that one time...

The Bailiff and the Dowser studied the dim tunnel as another train of horses hauling salt rumbled past.

"Where did this man put the barrel?"

"Over there."

Harry pointed across the path, to the undergrowth. The Bailiff and his assistant examined the tangled tree roots and found the barrel in the hedging. They rolled it out and tipped it up. Harry closed his eyes tight shut. A pile of clothes fell from the barrel onto the road, but then appeared mis-shapen limbs and a mass of hair. The men blessed themselves.

"Do you know who this is?"

Jaap scanned the body. It was that of a young woman, stout and short, lame. There was nothing familiar about her.

"No."

"And you, boy, is this the woman you saw last night?"

"I think so, sir. It was dark."

It had not been a dream. The Bailiff examined the body and found a deep gash at the side of her head, her hair plastered to her face with black brown blood like a cap.

"Boy. You said that they spoke in a foreign tongue."

"Yes sir, no sir, I am not sure."

Harry held Jaap's hand.

"He spoke a tongue like this man here?"

"Yes sir. Like Jaap's, He sounded like him, but then ..."

"And he was the same size as this man?"

"Yes. In the dark, he was the same, like Jaap."

Harry looked up at Jaap and smiled nervously.

"It is good Harry. Just tell the man the truth."

"And you; foreigner. You are a Dutchman I think."

"Yes. I am Jaap van der Staen."

"You say you do not know this girl."

"I do not."

The Bailiff and the Dowser spoke together in a low voice, and in a sudden movement took Jaap by the arm. Confused, he allowed them to direct him to the cart.

"Where are you taking me?"

"To the Goat's Head Bridge gaol. You will be tried for the murder of this girl at the next assizes."

Harry tried to hold on to Jaap with both hands and started to cry.

"Oh no! Oh no! Please don't take him away. Jaap, don't go, don't go."

~ ~ ~ ~ ~

They tied Jaap's hands and took him west, away from the sea and the familiar stench of the salt marshes.

At every turn, they passed thatched triangular huts, each with the mixed smell of woodsmoke and cooking food wafting from their open doors. Jaap had not eaten for many hours.

The Bailiff and the Dowser drove to Goat's Head, to the old bridge from New Castell. The Goat's Head Bridge was built on fourteen pillars, stone and wooden buildings and huts had been built on either side, so the bridge appeared as another jumble of structures protruding out from the city, as if the wide river were no obstacle. The central street was mobbed; on either side a varied collection of little churches, writer's stalls, bakers and bankers, tailors and tanners, fishmongers and metalworkers; women bought from traders stalls supplied from either side, and all along the bridge, crossing back and forth was a solid mass of bodies crushing past each other. Today, the main flow was of people travelling north–pilgrims, and rebels fleeing persecution following the Pilgrimage of Grace.

The Bailiff and the Dowser took Jaap from the cart and entered the bridge below a stone carving of a man's face. The carving had a beard pleated in two tails, with long curly hair carved at the side of the face. On the right of the bridge was a stone structure with iron bars on the windows. They entered; by the door was a fat man pouring ale from a large jug.

"God's day, gaoler. This Dutchman is to be held for the murder of a young woman in Scheles.'

The gaoler belched and pointed to a cell with several inhabitants. He passed a key across the table to the Bailiff who opened the door and pushed Jaap inside. The Bailiff took the quill from the gaoler and wrote in his book.

Some hours later, Jaap was given some thin ale and gruel. He had tried to rest on the stone ledge at the side of the cell, but could not get comfortable. He had no interest in communication with the other inmates, and they had no interest in him, each engaged in their own miseries. Jaap sniffed out of the barred window. There was no smell of salt farms, just the stink of the waste that had been tipped into the river, mixing with the stench of old urine.

As the light faded, Jaap attempted to sleep. He picked up a moth eaten blanket, and, wrapping it around him, sat in a corner on the stone shelf, but he couldn't sleep; his pains were constant, piercing the night; he merely slipped in and out of consciousness for moments at a time. Out of the fog of his exhausted mind, he worried about Harry. Where was he? Was he in danger? Jaap sat in pain, weary, his eyes burning. After the long, numbing night, he watched the sun come up through the tiny opening in the cell. He could smell the smoke from a nearby fire when the Bailiff and the Dowser came for him.

"Where are we going?"

Jaap had difficulty mouthing the words; his dry tongue stuck to his palate.

"By God's legs, we will test you by the rods today. We are to meet a priest at St Edmund's Hospital."

They tied Jaap's hands, and he was bundled back through the crowds on the bridge, back in to Goat's Head, up the hill to the old hospital.

"What about Harry?"

"Don't you worry about the boy. He will be cared for. You should pray for your own damned soul."

They walked up the hill to St Edmund's where they met a priest who directed them into one of the outbuildings. At the far end of the room, was a body covered in a sheet.

"This is the mortal remains of the girl in the barrel. Your boy showed it us."

They blessed themselves.

"We have his testimony that the man who killed her looked like you, and spoke like you. Do you have anything to say?"

Jaap shook his head. He had no spit to talk.

"Do you understand the charge against you?"

Jaap nodded slowly and breathed deeply. With this he experienced a lift from his exhaustion and in his spirits. As if a fog of desperation lifted, he became lucid, strangely alive to his predicament. Now he knew in the cloud of his own tired mind that, at last, he was to be accountable for his sins; for the Cordelière; for Anders, for Gertje. He was calm; someone else would decide his fate, and finally he would be answerable for his past.

"I say again, do you understand the charges against you?"

Jaap relaxed.

"I understand."

"Why do you smile, Dutchman?"

Jaap didn't answer.

"You are sure to hang, Dutchman. Let us see if you smile when you have a noose around your neck."

The Bailiff gestured to his companion who bent down and chose two 'L' shaped twigs, still green, and about the length of his forearm.

"This man will test your guilt."

Jaap looked on bewildered as they said a prayer and crossed themselves. The Dowser held the two sticks in front of him, balanced on his forefingers. They remained still as he walked around the room. He approached in turn the Bailiff and the priest, and then he approached the body. As he did so, the twigs jumped in his hands until, when he was directly over the body, the rods crossed from left to right and over each other. The priest blessed himself.

"Sweet Jesus. I have never seen such a thing."

The Bailiff agreed.

"Indeed, I have observed this manifestation many times, and I am still dumbfounded."

The Dowser moved away from the body and the rods became quiet once more.

"Now we shall see the guilt in this Dutchman."

Jaap's eyes were fixed on the Dowser's sticks as he approached; they remained motionless. He walked around Jaap, and yet they did not move. Jaap's shoulders dropped and he breathed out. The Bailiff shook his head.

"Fie, this will not serve. What is the matter with your rods, Sir?"

The Dowser spoke softly.

"Sire, the rods never lie. They are quiet in the presence of this man. He is not the man you are looking for."

"But the boy's testimony does not concur. There is something amiss. We can test again where the girl was killed?"

"Indeed we can, sir, but it is a way back to the low salt road."

"That is of no matter. Murther has been committed. Go; bring the boy."

~ ~ ~ ~ ~

They made their way back east to the hazel tree in the dark road with its tangled tree roots where they met Harry. He raced to Jaap's side.

"Jaap, Jaap, I am with the monks. They will not let me see you."

"Quiet boy. You said that the man who killed the girl resembled this Dutchman, and that he spoke like him?"

"Yes, but it wasn't Jaap."

"Enough, boy." He addressed Jaap.

"You are the only Dutchman in these parts."

"I think not sir, since I did not kill this girl. Another Dutchman is guilty."

"God's Eyes man. I see what I see. A Dutchman killed the girl, and you are that Dutchman."

The Bailiff gestured to the Dowser who set to work. This time, he cut new rods from the hazel tree and moved around the site. At the foot of the tree, the rods vibrated in his hands. They continued to do so as he traced the path towards the salt barrel that had contained her body. He then approached the priest and the rods stilled. They remained still for the Bailiff; as he approached Harry, the rods trembled.

"It is usual for a witness to bring movement to the rods."

The Dowser approached Jaap. All eyes followed the rods that remained immobile in the Dowser's fingers.

"Well Dutchman. The Holy Rods appear to proclaim you innocent of this crime, but I am confounded. The boy's testimony made your guilt clear. Perhaps you are correct. Perhaps there is another Dutchman here. I shall discover this truth."

In his exhausted state, Jaap felt cheated. He was not innocent. This was an opportunity to pay for his sins, to be answerable for his actions, for his part in the deaths on the Cordelière during the Sea Battle of St Matthieu; for the deaths of Anders and Gertje. This was the punishment he sought; but then he regarded Harry. His own concerns and his own guilt were subsumed by the profound sense of duty he owed to this boy; how could he protect him under these circumstances?

The Bailiff indicated for Jaap to be untied; Harry went to his side and held his hand tight.

"Dutchman, I cannot release you until I investigate whether there exists another Dutchman here who is guilty. In the meantime, you will return to the prison to await trial when the Assizes sit at Michaelmas."

"But that is four months away. I cannot be in prison until then. What is to come of my ... what is to come of Harry?"

"The boy will be sent back to the Dominicans at Stowell Street. The Blackfriars will look after him."

XXI

Goat's Head

The Feast Day of Saint Helladius of Auxerre,

8th May 15

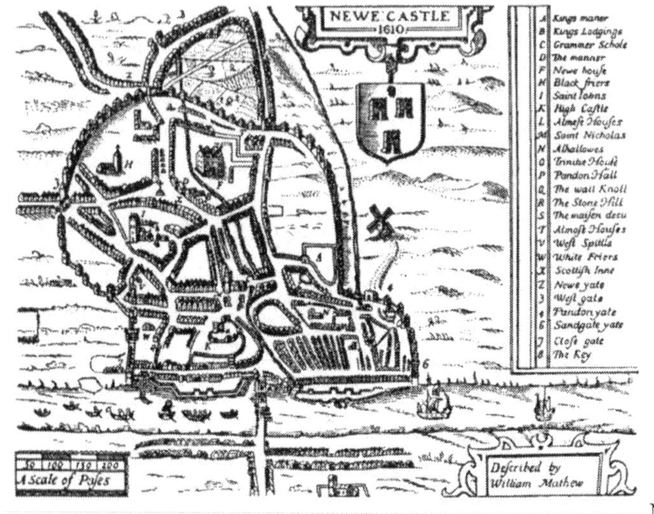

New Castell, with Goat's Head Bridge in Foreground

Sext had ended, and Barbara stood at the door of the church at St Bartholomew's at Nunn Street, chatting to one of the older lay sisters.

"Will they suppress your monastery?"

"We were suppressed last year, but In March the King re-founded it and so we continue for now. If you ask me, I would say poor St Barthlomew's has little life left. We have no money, and no one will leave us tithes anymore. The monks do the praying and earn all they get from benefactors buying their way out of purgatory."

A boy came along Nunn Street, shouting:

"Innocent Virgin Killit on Salt Road."

Barbara stopped him.

"A girl killed?"

"Buy my pamphlet."

The sister looked over her shoulder, squinting at the shapes on the paper.

"What does it say, what does it say?"

"A girl was murdered. Buy my pamphlet."

Barbara blessed her self.

"Sweet Jesus. Where? Who?"

"Yonder, in Scheles. She was following the horses on the salt road, and she was killed. Buy my pamphlet."

Barbara gave him a penny and read:

Ane gorey and wickit death of a Littel One upon the Salt Rode

Tae yonder Scheles,
Frae ower West,
Ane innocent travellt so.
Where she was to go?
We will never knowe.
She was knocked on the head
Bye a eville Frogge
And left in a filthey barrell

Kinde Bailiff John Whyte
founde the Frogge gude right
and heir had him testit
With Holy Rods
And the testimmonie
Of ane honeste boye,

This Gude Boye Saith

'Twas a Flemish who Killt her oh sir,
She so lovelie

And the Kinde Bailiffe
Did so test the holy body of the innocent
And founde nae name and nane merks
Sae nane could sayit whom She was.

Small and light, and lame was all he say'd
Forbye, butte he cought the Frogge
And hid him testit wi The Dowser's Holy Rods
Which answered naught.
Butte he was seen by the boy
And the Gude Bailiffe did sae
Take the Eville Frogge
To the Bridge Prisonne
Where he layes.

And from thence to Assize
For trial at Michaelmastide
And so justis will be seen fit.
As he, the Eville Frogge, will not admit.

She blessed her self once more. A murdered girl; from the West. A lame girl. She felt her stomach shrink. The sister made the sign of the cross.

"Who was the girl? What was her name?"

"I don't know. It does not say. A stranger, a pilgrim, perhaps?" The lay sister held her hand to her mouth.

"Who would carry out such an evil act?"

"It says that the Bailiff, John Whyte, arrested a Frogge, but the Dowser found him innocent. What is a Frogge?"

The sister sniggered.

"Don't you know nothing? You foreigners are all the same. You are called a Frogge my dear! A Frogge is a Dutchman."

"By my oath! A Dutchman. It says his guilt was not found by the Rods. So where is this Dutchman now?"

"Down in the Bridge Prison to await the Michaelmas Assizes."

"Michaelmas? That is four months away."

~ ~ ~ ~ ~

Barbara walked down the Flesh Market, past St Nicholas with its lantern, around the castle, down Side and along Sandhill, past St Katherine's Maison Dieu. and the bridge, south towards Goat's Head. At the little chapel on the bridge were traders, their wares spread on the ground; monks and priests moved back and forward, pushing and shoving and shouting amongst the smells of cabbage, faeces, smoke and urine. In the crowds, children darted around and dogs sniffed at middens. Fleeing rebels travelling north, some still carrying their flags showing 'The Five Wounds of Christ'. At the side of the bridge, people ate and drank ale, and talked and bartered. Barbara pushed her way through, and suddenly, right in front of her was the man with a knotted beard, carrying a sword. She recognised Jan Starter, the man that Jerome had introduced to her in Norwich.

"You were at the Ribs of Beef, near the Fye Bridge."

The man ignored her, addressing her in Flemish.

"You have found Jaap van der Staen?"

Barbara hesitated; surprised at the sound of her language she had not heard for months. She responded in Flemish.

"He is in the prison at the end of the bridge."

She held out the pamphlet.

"Here. They say he killed a girl."

Jan Starter spat.

"You have seen him?"

"No. Someone saw the girl killed by a man who spoke Flemish, but the Dowser's Holy Rods did not find him guilty and they are looking for another man who speaks Flemish."

She held out the piece of paper.

"It is written here."

Starter scanned the pamphlet and flinched.

"It is not well writ. Cannot this man count his feet?"

Starter examined the leaflet.

"But it says that van der Staen is in prison?"

"Yes. I told you. Come and see. The prison is just there."

Without warning, Starter moved forward and pushed past Barbara, and in the blink of an eye, disappeared in the throng, towards New Castell.

Bewildered, Barbara carried on until she got to the prison. At a table by the door, the gaoler was asleep. Behind him, figures moved in the murk and someone moaned. Barbara held her sleeve to her nose against the smell. Water dripped down the walls, and as she approached the bars, a rat scurried at her feet. She whispered:

"Jaap van der Staen?"

A figure appeared out of the dark.

"I am Jaap van der Staen."

Barbara stepped towards the cell, into a muddy puddle in the stone flags. She spoke in Flemish.

"I have been sent by The Abbess Lücke von Sandbeck of Porto Coeli to bring you to confession, to seek penance for your sins."

Jaap looked at the diminutive girl in this dark place, one half of her face scarred, with bestraggled hair; here, in this strange country, speaking Flemish to him in his dank prison. He started laughing, first chuckling; he laughed out loud.

"Stop. You will wake the gaoler."

Jaap held his mouth, but continued his muffled laughter with his eyes starting to stream.

"What? You? Here? You want to take me to confession?"

"What is funny?"

Jaap's mirth subsided, but still had the odd uncontrollable chuckle, holding on to the bars for support; at his desk the gaoler snored.

"I am expecting to be tried and executed for a murder I did not commit; and you tell me that you are here because of my sins, and you have to take me for my confession?"

"By the Virgin, I am."

"So, then; you are not here to talk about the girl who was killed?"

"I think I know her."

"By the Holy Wood, you say you do?"

Barbara handed the pamphlet to Jaap. Here in this gloom, she recognised him; there was no doubt, this was the man in her dream, in the fire at Jorevall. Surely this was God's Will directing her? Jaap van der Staen scanned the piece of paper, turning it this way and that, and gave it back. Barbara put it in her sleeve.

"Does this not trouble you?"

"No."

Barbara made the sign of the cross.

"But this states that you are guilty of murder."

Jaap looked surprised.

"And what else does it say?"

"You cannot read?"

"No."

Barbara read, holding the paper to the light; Jaap looked out beyond the girl to the daylight, and the figures passing by outside the prison. He was no longer laughing.

"I did not kill this girl."

"If not, who did?"

"Another Dutchman."

"How do you know this?"

"Harry heard him speak Dutch, or Flemish. Harry is a good boy. The Bailiff took him to the Blackfriars in Stowell Street."

"Wait. I am confounded. Harry is the boy in this pamphlet? He witnessed the killing?"

"Yes, I must see that he is safe."

"And this boy is not your son."

Outside, men and women went about their business, buying food or wares; pushing past each other in the narrow space between the shops and other buildings that clung to the bridge.

"My son is in the ground in Sylt with my wife. She is Gertje."

The gaoler sighed and twitched in his ale-fuelled dream. Barbara whispered:

"We must speak of this anon."

Then she remembered the man who had spoken to her a few moments before.

"This other man who speaks Flemish, the man who killed the girl, did he have a knotted beard?"

"I don't know; but Harry would. He saw the girl killed."

"Harry? The boy who witnessed this murder? You say he is with the Blackfriars?"

"Yes, yes, yes, but I have to tell you that the Bailiff is convinced that I killed her. He doesn't believe that there is another Dutchman."

Standing in the dark, Barbara was surprised at her self, becoming complicit in this man's troubles. She blessed her self nervously.

"A few moments ago, a man spoke to me on this bridge in Flemish. His name is Starter. He knew of my business. How so? I am a stranger here. No one knows me. He spoke Flemish, and he had a knotted beard."

"Which direction was he heading?"

"North, I think."

"Did he have the bearing of a soldier?"

"I would say so, yes."

"I, too, have seen this man. Yes, Starter, I saw him in Lynn."

"He told me he saw you there, with the boy."

"Yes, I was with Harry."

Barbara took a moment to take in this new information. Jaap was beginning to see a way of escaping from his despair.

"This man Starter, with the knotted beard, he has an interest in us. Why so?"

Barbara coughed.

"He must know I was sent to have you confessed."

Jaap shook his head. Barbara caught his eye in the dim light.

"I was sent a dream. You were in the fire; methinks I saw you in Jorevall."

"What?"

"You were burning the church."

Jaap took a deep breath and paused. On the other side of the door to the cramped, filthy prison, past the sleeping gaoler, women bought bread, talked about day-to-day things, children played, and people loved and bickered. Just a few yards away, life went on, but inside these damp, moss laden walls, surrounded by suffering souls, fearful for their fate, Jaap saw his past in a blur.

"You saw me at Jorevall?"

"Yes."

The gaoler groaned; Jaap's head was spinning. Just off the street, in this strange town, so many miles from Sylt and that other life; in this situation, in this cold, dank, prison, this girl comes and speaks to him, telling him that she saw him at Jorevall. What was he to make of it?

"We must talk of these things later. John Whyte, the Bailiff must be told of this man, Starter. Can you find him? Can you tell the Bailiff?" Barbara glanced at the gaoler and the other prisoners. For the first time, Jaap noticed her burned face, and patchy red hair.

"What is your name?"

"I am Barbara."

Jaap took her hand through the bars. She flinched and tried to take it away, but let it stay – he was cold. She saw beyond, to the shadows moving in the fetid cell, and to Jaap's white eyes, blinking in the dark.

"They say I am to be tried at the assizes at Michaelmas." Behind him, another prisoner mumbled something incomprehensible. Jaap whispered:

"I cannot stay here until Michaelmas."

Barbara fidgeted as she considered her situation. Before her was a man of whom she had dreamed and now knew to be the man that burned the church at Jorevall. Her Abbess told her that he had killed his wife and child, and had buried them in unconsecrated ground. But what could she do; what should she do? She was in a prison, and behind her a gaoler, appointed by an officer of the law. There, in that moment, she realised the peril she was in. She had tried to distance her self from the Towers of Fire prophesy she had uttered in Canterbury; and here, in this place, she realised that she was still at risk from her words. Inside this prison was a very dangerous place to be. As for helping this man; what was she thinking? She was in no position to do anything for him. She removed her hand, and was turning to leave, when the gaoler grunted and jerked awake.

"God's Eyes! Who the Devil are you?"

"I am sorry, sir. I..."

In an instant, the gaoler took a leather strap and struck Barbara on the body. She raised her arms to protect her self, but he continued to beat her.

"Stop. Stop", shouted Jaap. The gaoler's belt rose and fell, and rose and fell. The belt struck the bars, and Jaap grabbed it. The gaoler struggled with Jaap, who shouted to Barbara.

"Get out, get out."

Barbara ducked under the gaoler's arm and ran out into the milling crowd, the gaoler cursing as she fled.

~ ~ ~ ~ ~

Jaap lost all sense of the passing of time. As well as the pain in his joints, there was now the permanent ache of hunger. Since he had struggled with the gaoler and the girl had run away, he had been given no food. His sense of smell was changing and he could tell what a person had last eaten by their odour. He sucked the moss on the walls to slake his thirst. He didn't speak to his fellow inmates; in the dark, they were as ghosts. He could not be sure how many there were. One day, a man had died, and the gaoler took the body away. Though they did not speak, the prisoners shared the same fears; of sickness, hunger, pain, loneliness, and death.

In the cold night, Jaap tried to pray, but could not bring himself to believe that he was at the mercy of a bountiful God, who could intercede by the facility of prayer. In his snatches of sleep, he dreamed of the dying souls on the Cordelière, the screams and torment of the women and men and children, the searing heat, and the freezing cold water. And he saw poor Marcuccio, drowning in the quick sand, neighing and shrieking, lit by the flames of the Cordelière, cursing as he died, mute bystanders unable to respond, with no answers to the accusations of the dying creature. And, in the light of the fire, he saw the faces of Gertje and Anders, looking out to him, their arms open, pleading from their grave, lit by the grey light over the Wadden Zee. In odd moments of lucidity, Jaap understood why he was in this dirty wet, smelly cell. He was here because of his sins; his sins and those of none other. Perversely, this offered him comfort; a logic that made more sense to him than the actual circumstance – that he had been falsely arrested for a crime he had not committed. He thought of Starter, the man with the knotted beard. Perhaps he had killed the girl, but Jaap could not focus on any of these questions for any length of time. All these ideas appeared to him, melded together in waking dreams, interrupted by spasms of pain, and he tried to make sense of them as the images faded into each other, merging in the persisting nightmare.

The constant pain in his joints and in his stomach, the cold and damp and hunger, starved him of the nourishment of sleep. His exhaustion made him forget about his sins and his punishment. His only concern was for the moment, the survival in each breath, whether wakeful or in his half sleep. His dream world fused with the real world around him. He thought he saw Harry, and then woke to the quiet torment around him, and the unfathomable sense that outside the door of the prison, on the bridge, people were leading ordinary lives, while in this stone room, men descended into madness and death.

Jaap found a spider and ate it. He sat in his corner, watching the shadows creep across the floor, and fell to a sleeping consciousness. Harry was walking beside him, laughing and chasing sheep. Out of the dark, he heard his voice.

"Jaap. I have food for you."

While Jaap was pleased to have him in his dream, he knew it to be a cruel trick of his mind, but in the dream, the boy stayed. They were holding hands, crossing a green park, the horizon a long way away. Harry's voice came again.

"Jaap, Jaap where are you? I have food."

"No Harry. You are in my dream."

"Jaap. It is me. It is Harry."

Jaap sat bolt upright and groaned from the throbbing pain in his back. Silhouetted against the light from the open door was Harry, carrying a pie and an apple. Behind him, the gaoler stood, his arms folded, a full jug of ale on the table, beside the large key.

"Harry, Harry. God in heaven, you are safe, thank the Saints."

Jaap blessed himself and took the food, eating with his fingers, gulping greedily.

"Barbara said you must eat slowly."

Jaap paused, holding a piece of pie.

"Barbara, but..."

Jaap forgot his question, took another bite from the pie and drank the ale. After a few mouthfuls, he could eat no more.

~ ~ ~ ~ ~

Harry came every day with food, and Jaap felt his strength return. Harry was safe, and Jaap felt nourished.

"So, Barbara found you?"

"Yes Jaap. She came to the Blackfriars monastery with letters and she spoke with the Abbot. She is nice. I told her all about us."

"I did not expect to see her again."

"She can't come to see you because of the, you know..."

Harry tilted his head at the gaoler, mouthing the words:

"The prophesy."

"What prophesy?"

"She says she is in danger because of it and I must whisper when I speak of it."

Harry pointed theatrically with his thumb to the gaoler.

"If they find her, she will be burned."

"Burned?"

"Yes."

"Harry. I can't stay in this place until they move me to the New Castell prison."

"Barbara has a plan."

~ ~ ~ ~ ~

Every day, Harry brought food for the gaoler: a pie, some potage, a piece of salt cod, and always ale; and they appeared to become friends. Harry played fivestones on the floor of the gaol. On this day, the boy came into the prison with beer, looking on nervously as the gaoler belched and drank. Jaap talked of Barbara, and asked about Harry's life with the Blackfriars, but Harry kept glancing at the dozing figure at the table. The man shuddered in his beery dreams, and hesitantly, Harry approached him, not breathing, and gently lifted the key from his belt. Together, Harry and Jaap gently fiddled the key into the lock. It creaked as they turned it, and the gaoler grunted. The other prisoners whispered behind, pushing forward.

"Silence!", whispered Jaap.

They waited until the gaoler settled once more, and Jaap and Harry opened the cell, gripping the hinge to stop it creaking. The other prisoners rushed past them, out into the open, and disappeared into the crowd. Harry's and Jaap's hearts pounded together as Jaap stooped in pain, the bones in each joint grating with each step as they crept out of the prison into the bustle of people. They turned right, and North.

XXII

Salt Priestown

The Feast Day of St Fortunatus of Trier

7th June 1537

A—Trench. B—Vat into which the salt water flows. C—Ladle. D—Small bucket with pole fastened into it.

That summer saw mild days. The flowers lit the green fields, and the birds flew in song. The lambs grew sturdy, and the sky was a daily sheen of blue with whispers of cloud. These days knew long periods of soft calm when the sun would shine strong, or there might be just one or two clouds, or perhaps just a few drops of light rain. This pacific weather soothed people's outlook, and, the further north you went that year, the more temperate was the climate.

After the English rebellion, humiliated communities responded with resignation. Following the brutal punishment of the rebel leaders, people wanted only peace; they had had enough of men stalking the country, having to make account for one's self by the swearing of oaths, worrying about claiming allegiance to reform or King; They were weary of the menace in the air. They put rebellion behind them and returned to their crops, to their tanning and baking, to their children, and the feeling of warmth at night.

Many rebel supporters went north, to Scotland, where the flames of reform had not yet taken. There, King James V and his new young French wife, Madeline of Valois, had no appetite for the implementation of a dangerous experiment with such potential for unrest.

After New Castell, Jaap and Harry had lost sight of Barbara, and they took their own journey north. They travelled on the salt roads of Northumbria into Scotland, finding work in the numerous salt farms along the east coast, all the time creating distance from New Castell. Their journey took them from disruption, towards peace; their destination set once more for St Andrews. The good weather and the lack of threat eased their steps until they settled once more at Salt Priestoun.

~ ~ ~ ~ ~

It was dusk when Barbara arrived. The smells were of breweries and baking bread, but it was the stench of the salt marshes that told her this was where she might find van der Staen and Harry. She quickened her pace as the setting sun dipped, throwing huge rays into the red sky. The dimming light showed up the many fires along the shore, upwards of a dozen in this area alone, and dots of light from saltpans visible all along the coast.

In the town, she was shown to the Grange, and given a room and a cot where she took some beer and cheese. After a night's rest, she attended a Mass in the chapel. She enjoyed the familiar peace of it all, the ritual and the habit that she had not known since St Sepulchre's. The drift of incense and music and Latin encompassed her like a blanket in the small church. After all the danger and destruction she had witnessed, there was no talk of reform here. She came away from the mass refreshed and chatted to one of the Monks.

“There is salt farming here?”

“Ye mean the 'pans?”

The monk gestured towards the landscape east, west, and north, full of ponds set into the marshland, with channels cut between them; figures moved about, carrying, raking, and working in the little huts, stoking and heaving coal. Each hut poured smoke and steam.

"Jist look aroon ye, hen."

Barbara tried to understand this new voice, different to the sounds just twenty miles away. She blinked and listened hard.

"Pardon Sir, could you say again?"

He rolled his eyes.

"Aye. The 'pans. Ower there, wan fur each fire ye c'n see. Ye canny miss them. C'n ye no smell the reek?"

Barbara sniffed the unmistakable sulphurous tinge. She nodded. Now she could see more pinpricks of light, the red fires of the salt works along both shores of the estuary.

"What is the name of this place?"

"They cry it the Firth, ken."

"The Firth?"

"Aye, the Firth o' Forth."

Barbara repeated, struggling with the consonants. The monk grinned.

"Dinny fash yersel' hen."

Barbara flushed.

"No sir, I shall not. Can you tell me, do you know a tall Dutchman and a small boy?"

"Aye. Jaap an' wee Harry. A'body kens them. Fine wee boy. Guid workers."

Barbara smiled, but felt the same worry she had when she met the Dutchman in the Goat's Head prison. How was she to face this evil man once more, this sinner who had killed his wife and son, but whose escape she had arranged from prison? Her doubts remained. Here in

Skotlân her prophesy had not been heard; she was confident she could speak to Van der Staen and cope with any danger he might pose. If he had been travelling with the boy for the past few months, it was not likely he would be a threat. On the other hand, she still could not understand why he associated with the rebels who destroyed the Abbey at Jorevall.

"What 'pans' does he work at?"

"Ower there. Just this side of the girnel hoose."

"The girnel hoose?"

"Aye, where they store the salt; for market, ye ken."

The monk pointed to a stone construction next to a group of open pans with scummy boiling water. She approached the pan-house, and saw Jaap van der Staen – tall, lithe, covered in muck, towering over the small boy as they stoked the fires together. The Dutchman took a cask full of a dark liquid and poured it into the pan. They stirred the boiling mass, then let it settle. He took a large paddle and skimmed the surface of the boiling water until it was clear, putting aside the thick glutinous scum. Barbara shouted over the noise of the fire:

"Gottes Dag, van der Staen!"

Jaap started at the sound of Barbara's voice, his body and shirt streaked in black and red. He put down the paddle and wiped the sweat from his head. There was a powerful stench of blood that combined with the stink of the salt beds. Barbara spoke in Flemish.

"You have poured blood into the water?"

He paused and replied in the same tongue:

"It takes away the bitterness; sweetens the salt."

Jaap paused and savoured the sounds of the Flemish in his mouth.

"Well met girl. Well met. I did not know if we were to meet again. I owe you a great debt."

At the entrance to the pan house, Barbara was lit both by setting sun behind, and, and in front, by the fires of the pans. She wore a pale coloured smock and cape, and a biggin that almost covered the burn mark on the right side her face. Some of her red hair on the right side had grown back in and stuck out like straw. Jaap now noticed a slight nervous tick.

"You are burned?"

She twitched.

"Yes."

Harry saw Barbara and ran to her. He hugged her around the waist.

"Barbara, Barbara! You found us!"

"Yes, Harry, I found you."

She bent and kissed him on the head.

"By the Virgin, it is good to see you. Are you eating well?"

"Yes, Jaap and I cook together every night. I can cook a potage."

"You are a clever boy Harry."

"Barbara, You talk funny, like Jaap."

Jaap rubbed the boy's hair, catching Barbara's eye. He remembered her voice at the prison; the soft sound of the familiar plosives and her pleasant cadence. After such a long time, he enjoyed the release from English:

"You arranged my escape."

"It could not have happened without Harry."

"He is a brave boy. I owe my life to the two of you."

Harry tugged at Jaap's sleeve.

"Jaap, Barbara, what are you saying? I can't understand."

"I am telling Barbara how brave you were."

Harry beamed and held Barbara's hand. Jaap addressed her in Flemish:

"But what now, Barbara from Porto Coeli Monastery? Will you do what your Abbess has asked you to do?"

Jaap smiled once more at the thought of this diminutive person, so young, being sent to find him. Aware that Harry was listening, Barbara spoke in their shared tongue.

"You know the answer, Jaap van der Staen. My instructions are to bring you to a monastery to be confessed."

"Ah, confession. And why do you think this is necessary?"

"Because you are a sinner."

Jaap took a poker and stoked the fire, which answered with a roar of flame. They felt the raw heat on their faces.

"There is no doubt about it. I am a sinner."

"They say you killed your wife. There are other sins, I think."

Jaap's body was streaked in filth, the heat of the fire caking the blood on his skin and clothes. He pointed Harry towards a pan encrusted in lumps of dried salt. He gave him a wooden shovel and spoke in English.

"Harry. Please break new salt."

Jaap smiled without showing his teeth. Henry knew that this strange conversation was not to do with him. Jaap would tell him if he had to know anything. He took the shovel.

Jaap directed Barbara out of the building into the fresh cool summer air. He went to the edge of the water, stepped into the sea, and cleaned the muck and old blood from his body. He removed his shirt and rinsed it, the scum dissolving, making a small cloud in the cold blackening water that swirled and coalesced as he moved. He stepped onto the sand, squeezed water from the shirt and shivered as he put it back on.

Barbara continued in Flemish.

"I have seen a letter from Majstro Siemen..."

Jaap recoiled at the mention of the name.

"I see you know of whom I speak. His letter says that you are guilty of the murder of your wife, that all the people of Keitum knew of it, that you buried her and your son in unconsecrated ground; that you burned down your own home."

Jaap was quiet as the girl twitched; she was bright and scarred, her cap lopsided, wisps of thin red hair poking out at the side.

"And, and I have heard ...I have heard more."

Jaap gazed west, towards the reddening sky.

"And you; what do you think?"

Once more, Barbara considered van der Staen. Now he was looking right at her, his gaze unthreatening, an opening, a channel offering truth, or so it seemed.

"My Abbess ... she was a good woman and she would not have sent me on this journey without cause. I believed her."

"And now?"

Barbara was uneasy at the uncertainty that Jaap's response had created in her. She had prepared her words for this conversation, and now, when faced with this man, her words failed her.

"Eh, I ... I do not know. Prioress Philippa at St Sepulchre's said I was on a fool's errand."

"Barbara?"

She blushed at the sound of her name.

"Barbara, all of this is in the past. This is now. What do you believe?"

She found her confidence failing; what did she believe? Behind her, she felt the heat of the pans, but here, she felt the air cooler as the sun sank into the horizon.

"I know what I want to believe."

"If you want to believe, believe."

"But there will always be doubt."

"Yes. We will never know anything truly."

"I was talking about the charges against you. What are you talking about?"

Barbara hesitated; these words she had spoken seemed so unreal, here in front of Jaap van der Staen. This situation was not an abstract collection of arguments on paper, or of tales told. It was a charge against a real person; and more: this person did not fit the description given to Barbara by her Abbess. Barbara had met violent men before, in Himmelpforten; she had a sense for threat and danger. But now all she felt was confusion in the contradiction between what she thought she knew, and the reality before her; the same as she had faced in the prison on the bridge at Goat's Head. Here, facing van der Staen, she asked her self: could she trust her instincts, or should she act on information given by others?

"Do you think I did this? Do you think I am capable of such deeds?"

"I am instructed by my superior to take you to be confessed..."

"I know, I know, you said this. But do I look like someone who..."

"I heard things. I saw you at Jorevall."

Jaap paused.

"Ah! Jorevall."

"You despoiled a monastery. You burned it down. People died."

"And you think I was part of this?"

"I was there. I saw you."

"Yes. You did."

"It was in a dream, but I did see you. It was real. You were with another man. He said he was going to kill idolators."

"His name was Thomas Cade."

Jaap looked north across the wide estuary, past the islands. If he took the crossing over the Firth, he could get to Crail and St Andrews in a few days – in less than a week.

"You knew him?"

Jaap remained silent. The sounds in the air were of the crackling fire in the hut, the bubbling brine; the muted thud of Harry's wooden spade chipping salt off the pans, the lapping of the water on the sand.

"They make good salt here."

"I am asking you...",

"They say they can make eight or nine hundred bushels in one week with these ten pans."

"But..."

"They use iron pans. They last longer than our lead pans, the stones from the ground burn hot so that the brine boils quickly."

He faced Barbara.

"You do not know me. You have seen me once before, and you have heard things about me. The story behind all these things is not straightforward. We sometimes do not know how we have come to where we seem to be. I don't know how you got here, but I am sure you could not tell your story simply. Whose life have you destroyed?"

Barbara gasped. She thought of Alys. Was it she who was done to death on the salt road to Scheles? Did van der Staen know? How could she be sure of Harry's story of the murder? Did he know that she abandoned her friend at Richmond, leaving her to her bloody fate? Barbara looked up to the tall figure, and out to the sea where he was gazing.

"What will we do? I have made a promise to my Abbess. I have a duty."

"Ah, yes, your Abbess."

In the silence between them, there was only the sound of the crackling fire, of Harry's dull chipping, the plash of the soft tide, seals singing out on the water; and the moving air on their faces. Jaap spoke.

"Let us start by speaking this new, odd tongue. Come, let us talk with Harry."

They walked back up to the pan house. They spoke in English, like wearing new clothes, and they felt cleansed. These words, once foreign to them, appeared now to offer a clarity of sorts; a clarity of purpose that seemed to resolve, for a time, their doubts. They watched

Harry for a few moments, struggling with the oversized spade, hitting the salt encrusted pan. Barbara spoke to him.

"Harry, what you are doing?"

"I am breaking the salt rocks. I have to be careful not to break the pans, so I have a wood spade."

"By the Virgin, You are a clever boy."

Harry beamed.

"Jaap taught me."

~ ~ ~ ~ ~

Barbara went back to her cell at the Grange that night, but was unable to sleep. She lay in the dark and reflected on her journey, and on the wise counsels of the women she met: of her Abbess, the sisters at the Sint Jaan's Hospitaal, Philippa Jonys, Katherine Mann, and from the writing of Hilda of Presscott. She thought on her friends: Jerome with his wherrie; Miriam and Martha and Mark, and gentle Alys; yes, gentle Alys. At the thought of her friend, She started to recite an Ave Maria, but again her thoughts turned to the events of the last year.

She wondered on the tingling on her skin, her silent moments, which she had now not felt for some time, and on her unwitting prophesy, 'The Towers of Fire', and of the dangers that came after. In the dark, she fingered the creased skin of her burns, and tucked a straggle of hair back under her biggin. All these things had happened to an ordinary girl, all in a single year. Yes, she was that same silly girl who spoke to the people in the marketplace in the storm at Himmelpforten, but now, after such a journey, how could she not be changed? She had learned much; she had become a woman.

Such a journey? But her amazement was tempered by the fate of Alys. The more she thought about it, the more she was convinced that it was her friend who had been killed on the salt road. She remembered conversations at their farewell in Richmond, and then the words from the pamphlet from the boy in New Castell:

The innocent one travellt so,

Where was she to go?

Now Barbara was sure that Alys had been following her. She had not travelled to York with Martha and Miriam. She was dead, and Barbara was responsible. She had abandoned this sweet soul to her cruel fate. But for now, she was to choose what to do about Jaap van der Staen. Against all odds, she had found him, but she could not have anticipated her current difficulty. Was he guilty of these crimes? Having met him, she was not so sure; she was not so sure. The maze of memory and circumstance became a blur. Slowly, the comfortable fog of sleep enveloped her.

~ ~ ~ ~ ~

A few days later, they were sitting on rocks, eating oysters; warmed by a midday summer sun, looking out from Salt Priestown, north to Fife. In the daylight, the Firth of Forth offered a very different landscape. Here there was a continuous view of the estuary. Inland from the salt farms, as far as the eye could see, there was the wild stretch of untended land: gorse, impenetrable heather punctuated by stumps – the remains of old woodland. There was not a tree to be seen. In the scrub, there were random runrigs on the sides of the hills – little 'S' shaped patches of well-drained cultivation coloured green or brown. Next to these were low stone-built hovels, smoke lifting straight out of their turf roofs. Such were the signs of habitation along the firth.

Jaap watched Barbara work a shell open and slurp an oyster into her mouth. She saw him looking at her and wiped away the drips of salt water.

"When we met, you said that we all have a story that cannot be told in a moment."

She took a knife to another shell.

"I wish to hear about how you came to Jorevall."

"Ah."

Barbara tapped another shell with the heel of the knife, waiting for his response. Jaap placed an empty shell on a pile and spread his hands on the sun-warmed rock. He started to tell her about their involvement with the rebels, with Captain Cobbler; with Thomas Cade at Lincoln and Louth; the confusion and fear having to befriend rebels and King's men when Harry ran away. He told her how they came to Moricambe to escape the rebellion, and once more came on Thomas Cade, who lost his reason on the sands; and about the death of poor Marcuccio. He took the knife back and gently prised open another oyster shell.

"We tried to look after Cade, but he would not be spoken to. He talked of nothing but rebellion, about how he had work to do for his king. But, truth to be told, he was mad. He wouldn't eat; he fought imaginary enemies. He unsheathed his sword in the house; he was dangerous. He needed someone to try to calm him. Harry did that, but I had to look after Harry."

Barbara held out her hand, Jaap handed over the knife.

"One day, Cade ran off with a group of rebels to go to the suppression at Jorevall. When we arrived, Cade was lighting fires and breaking windows. I tried to stop him. That is when you saw me. I was trying to stop Cade, to stop him harming himself and others, but it was to no avail. He was overtaken with the devils in his broken mind, and he ran to the flames."

Barbara blessed her self.

"By the Virgin. Where did you go?"

"We took the salt roads to Scheles."

Barbara hesitated:

"Where the girl was killed, and you were taken to the prison on Goat's Head bridge?"

Jaap reached for another oyster and paused, tapping the shell with his forefinger.

"That was a bad time. Goat's Head was my Hell; but do you know, at the time, I felt I deserved it."

"But you didn't kill Alys ... I mean, the girl. Harry saw someone else do it, another Dutchman."

"Prison was punishment for my past sins."

"For your wife, and Anders?"

"I have committed many sins. I thought about them a lot in prison."

Out in the Firth of Forth, the sun came out from a cloud, lighting a large ship, its sails blazing in the sunshine.

"After Goat's Head, we joined the pilgrims and headed for St Andrews. When we arrived here at Salt Priestown, we learned their ways of making the salt. They are good people here. It is safe."

"Will you stay here?"

Jaap pointed across the Firth.

"We are for St Andrews."

"To pray for your son?"

"Anders? Yes."

Barbara ate an oyster and spat out a piece of grit. Harry was climbing the rocks towards them.

"Was your son as Harry is?"

"Perhaps a little."

Harry got a footing on the rock, placing his hand on Jaap's knee for balance.

"Can I have one?"

Barbara opened a shell. He tipped his hread back and she slid the salty flesh into his mouth. He grinned and wiped the water from his chin.

"Let us walk together, Harry."

They jumped down from the rocks, running ahead of Jaap, Harry sang:

"Cock a doodle do!

What is my dame to do?"

They played and pointed, and made pictures in the sand.

"My master's lost his fiddling stick."

They ran, laughing and breathless, to some rock pools.

"You speak funny, just like Jaap."

"Do I? "

Harry picked up a stick and poked in a pool, disturbing tiny shrimps and crabs. Barbara watched him as he turned and stared at her. He stared for a long time, without speaking.

"Are you his friend?"

Barbara blushed.

"Your ear looks funny. What happened to your face?"

"I was in a fire."

"Oh."

Harry climbed on some rocks and examined another little pool of seawater.

"Are you burned under your coif?"

"Yes."

"Can I see?"

Barbara removed her hat and showed Harry the burns on the side of her head, and the missing hair where her skin was white and whorled.

"Can I touch it?"

Without pausing, she said said, "Yes". Harry stroked the burned, creased skin.

"It feels lumpy and soft at the same time. Is it sore?"

"Not any more."

Barbara replaced her cap and Harry returned to the rockpool. He found a small crab and lifted it out.

"Careful".

"It's all right, Jaap showed me how to hold it without getting nipped."

He examined the crab.

"I can climb trees."

"I am sure you are a good climber."

"I climbed that tree I told you about in New Castell, remember? It was at night, in Scheles; A woman fell in the dark; there was a man just like Jaap, but it wasn't. The Bailiff thought Jaap pushed her, but he didn't."

"Who pushed her?"

"No one pushed her, she fell."

"What did she look like?"

"It was dark. She limped."

Barbara flinched and blessed her self.

"Alys!"

Harry nodded:

"Yes, he called her that; that was her name. I had forgot."

Barbara put her head in her hands and rocked gently. Harry carried on:

"I saw a fire once."

Barbara sniffed.

"Did you?"

"Yes. A lady was burned and lots of people watched and some people were angry and some other people were laughing and they shouted a lot."

Barbara sat down on the rocks beside Harry and dried her eyes with the corner of her biggin.

"You saw a lady burned?"

"No, I couldn't see, but I heard her shouting. It was raining and they had to make more fire to make her burn faster."

Barbara put one hand to her mouth and the other on Harry's arm.

“That a child should witness such things.”

“A man told me that I would see a woman burn again. He said I was to remember it. The smoke smelled funny, but all the people squeezed me and I felt sleepy and I fell down, but Jaap came and saved me. “

“Do you like Jaap?”

“He keeps me safe.”

“How long have you been together?”

As Harry opened his mouth to speak, Jaap caught them up.

“What are you two talking about?”

“I'm showing Barbara my crab.”

Together, Barbara and Jaap raised their eyebrows.

“I'm going to take it home and keep it by me. I will teach it tricks.”

XXIII

Edenburg

The Feast Day of St Ralph of Bourges,

21st June 1537

Barnacle Goose Tree

Jaap found a tree by the side of a river. He crouched down and moved some rocks, rubbing the roots; he looked into the sky. Barbara stopped beside him.

"What are you looking for?"

"I think this is the Goose Barnacle tree."

"Ah. I have heard of the Goose Barnacle. Is this such a tree?"

"It might be."

He stroked the bark and examined the branches.

"I have heard say that the Goose Barnacle tree lives here in Skotlân. It grows by the water. The branches grow fruit that look like the beaks of little geese. If the fruit falls on the ground, it will rot; but if it falls in the water, it attaches to roots or stones and be's a barnacle. It grows, gaining strength from the wood and the sea. When it becomes strong enough, it turns into a barnacle goose and flies away."

Barbara examined the tree, remembering Jerome on the Amaranth telling her the same story. Jaap bent down and fingered some shells in the water.

"They say that the barnacle goose is good to eat on fast days because it is not born like other animals. It is but a fruit."

"By the Rood, a fruit that flies."

"So they say."

" Is nature not such a great book of the world to be read, a bright glass of creation?"

"I see your meaning. It is indeed a book open to me, wherein lies the content of this great ball."

Barbara rubbed the bark of the tree with her thumb.

"When was the last time you were confessed?"

Jaap stepped back from the tree.

"Not since Anders died."

Barbara gasped.

"By the Blood of Sweet Jesus, you are unshriven. All this time your soul has been in jeopardy. If you had died, all your sins would be unconfessed."

"It matters not. I will receive what I receive and I will accept."

"Come with me. You can be confessed now."

"No."

"But your..."

"No. I will not."

Barbara could not understand. Jaap was risking eternal damnation and suffering for reasons she could not comprehend.

"Is it pride that stops you from attending confession? Is it shame?"

"No. I will deal with the consequences of my sins on their own terms. I do not accept the cruel explanation that my Anders and Gertje suffered for my sins."

"You are making a wager with your eternal soul."

"Yes. My wager is that if God punishes me, he will punish me alone."

Barbara wiped away a tear.

"But your soul."

"Do not fret."

Jaap put his hand on Barbara's shoulder and she became quiet. In this simple act, with the touch of his hand, she was calm. It was the first time anyone gave her relief from her troubles. Before this, she would give succour to others, but here she was receiving it in this small touch.

"Thank you. But why are you going on a pilgrimage if not to seek an indulgence?"

"I'm looking for my Anders. I think I will find peace for him there."

Harry came running to Jaap. In front of him, he rolled an iron hoop from a barrel, tapping it with a stick, propelling it forward. He left it to travel a few feet where it wobbled and fell over.

"Jaap, Jaap; I found a game. My new friend Dugald calls it a gird and cleek. "

When he saw Barbara, he ran to her and held her hand.

"God's Day to you Harry. You are very good at your new game."

Harry flushed, then let her hand go. He took up the hoop and rolled it, guiding it with his stick. He ran after it, following the rotating iron wheel.

"Dugald. Wait for me, wait for me."

Jaap, had the smallest smile on his face.

"Tomorrow, we should go to Edenburg."

~ ~ ~ ~ ~

Barbara and Jaap travelled west to Edenburg, through Musselburgh, past the lump of Arthur's Chair, and ahead of them, the old castle on the hill. It started to rain as they entered the city through the Netherbow and walked up the crowded high street, tall tenements on either side, a grey damp sky above. In the busy Lawnmarket passers-by spat and threw old vegetables at a miserable young man, sitting in the mud, chained in the 'juggs'.

Jaap and Barbara separated at the St Giles' Collegiate Church, where she walked back down the hill, and he towards the castle. As he approached the Mercat Cross where the road forked, a group of men came out of the Isle of Man Tavern at Cant's Close.

"Jaap van der Staen!"

Jaap recognised Jan Starter and sensed menace. The man with the knotted beard staggered as he approached, and threw his half full cup aside. Gripping the hilt of his sword, he spoke loudly in Flemish.

"Where is the girl?"

He came close, and Jaap smelled the sweet reek of ale.

"She is not here. Why are you here? Why do you follow us?"

Starter peered at Jaap through half-shut eyes and spoke through gritted teeth.

"Where are my rhymes? Do you know where lie my rhymes."

"Speak sense, man. What is your business with me? I think you have followed me since Hamburg."

Starter stood straight and swayed a little.

"Hamburg?" Starter laughed. "You see nothing. I know you. I know your sins and you know nothing."

Starter spat into a puddle at their feet.

"I am sent by the Provost of Porto Coeli to ensure you seek absolution for your sins."

The rain was heavy now. Jaap wiped away the water from his head and smirked.

"I already have someone who is to see to this."

"The girl. Yes, yes, yes; but I am to make sure it happens."

"Who is this Provost?"

"He is appointed in Bremen by the Prince Archbishop Christoph von Braunschweig-Wolfenbüttel in temporal matters of the Monastery of Porto Coeli."

"From Bremen? You have come a long way to see his instructions are followed. Your loyalty is exemplary."

"There is more. I am from Sylt. Gertje was my cousin."

Jaap stood still at the mention of Gertje's name. In the moment he took in his surroundings, the rain pattering on his bare head, the dull light from the sunless sky, Starter standing unsteady before him, holding his beard with one hand, and the hilt of his sword with the other. Across the busy street, some boys were poking a stick at a beggar in the mud, surrounded by a small pack of barking dogs. He examined the face of the man glaring at him.

"I too lived on Sylt, but I do not know you."

"I grew up with Gertje. Her parents took me in; we played together. I left to go to war, and I worked for the Provost and now you have killed her, I will never see her again."

"Now it is you who know nothing. I know you. You were in Lynn. You beat me outside the cathedral; you stole my things – and in New Castell, I think that you were the other Dutchman. By the Virgin, it was you who killed the girl in Scheles."

Jaap moved out of the way for a woman in a scold's bridle, led by a man with a rope. People shouted at her as she stumbled, whimpering, down the hill from the castle. Starter hawked and spat again onto the mud between them. Jaap looked Starter in the eye.

"So, Provost's man from Bremen, what are you going to do now? I tell you, I know you killed the girl on the Salt Road to Scheles."

Jan Starter rubbed the hilt of his sword with his thumb and shook his head.

"She said she knew where Barbara, the Himmelpforten girl was. She was just a fool, an idiot girl. She told me her name was Alys."

"An idiot girl? In the name of Jesus Christ! I was to be tried for your crime. I was in prison because of what you did."

"God's Blood, man. Don't shout at me. You escaped, didn't you?"

Starter stuck his finger in Jaap's chest.

"And I tell you that I am here, I am here because you killed my beloved Gertje."

"You know nothing", said Jaap.

The two men were getting the attention of a small group who gathered close, offering opinion and encouragement in the rain:

"Speak English, you damned Frogges."

"Fight and have done with it."

Jaap and Starter screamed at each other in Flemish:

"You know nothing."

"I know what you are; bastard murderer. May your soul rot in Hell."

"You know more about murder than I. You killed the girl on the salt road."

Jan Starter and Jaap van der Staen were forced together by the onlookers, face-to-face, unable to grab each other with their wet clothes, fending off each other's fists. Each could feel the other's spittle on their cheeks. The crowd of spectators gathered even closer, restricting their movements. A little cloud of mist appeared above them in the rain.

"It's two Frogges."

"What are they arguing about?"

"The Devil knows; my money's on the one with the beard."

"Go on. Give him one for Saint Nicholas!"

The growing crowd crushed together, passers-by joined the pack, peering from the rear. Starter reached for his sword, but the density of pushing, shoving bodies restricted his movement, and he couldn't free the weapon from its scabbard. Jaap saw the danger and, in an instant, brought the heel of his hand hard up against the other man's nose. There was a splash of blood, and Starter fell to the mud. The onlookers roared and laughed and pressed closer. Jaap pushed out through the soaking, cheering, muddy mass. Knotted Beard shoved through, staggering into the open, blood pouring from his broken nose. He drew his sword, raising it into the rain, screaming nasally:

"I shall find you van der Staen. Gertje shall be avenged!"

~ ~ ~ ~ ~

When Barbara left Jaap, she walked back down the high street in the wind and the rain to St Andrew's Port. She turned down Leith Wynd, past the Trinity Hospital, to the Trinity Collegiate Church that sat in the dip between the hills to the north, south and east. Barbara came to the Great West Door, and looked out past the Physic Garden, west over the Nor' Loch. Did it always blow such a wet wind here? Was it never calm?

She entered the warm church. A Segen, a Benediction, was ending; everyone knelt to receive the final Blessing. The priest raised his right hand, and sang: "In nomine Patris", then lowering it slowly, and moving it from left to right: "et Filii et Spiritus Sancti", finally joining his hands: "Amen".

Barbara knelt in private prayer as people bustled about the church, but her thoughts drifted. Had she done the right thing in helping van der Staen get out of the Goat's Head prison? It felt wrong going against the instructions of her Abbess, but what was she to do? She could not leave a man in that terrible place when she believed he had not killed the girl; especially when she heard Harry's story.

Barbara tried to return to her prayer, but once more became distracted. She took in the colour of the fabulous surroundings of the Trinity Church. The Monks sang, their quiet consonance filling the space like a cloud, the soft echoes rolling from nave to chancel, along the aisles, across the transepts; in the apses of the chantry chapels, and in the wooden space above, among the rafters with their little medallions and carved figures peering down on all below. The music made time slow down, it encouraged all present to step into the reverberations; to feel the vibrations on their skin; to experience the wonder around them. She approached the beautiful main altar, behind which was a glorious triptych, the execution clearly the same as the paintings in Sint Jaans Hospitaal in Bruges; so similar, but perhaps without the clear light of the Bruges piece. She made the sign of the cross and gazed at the images. How did it come to be here, like her, all this way from the Low Countries? They opened the doors of the triptych; Barbara put her hand to her mouth at the beauty of the central panel as it lit up with the light that permeated the whole church. The panel showed the Madonna and Christ Child, surrounded by angels, but Barbara was struck by the depiction of St Catherine, holding her tiny tower, and an angel playing a little organ behind her. Barbara gasped. It was the same angel from St John's Hospital in Brugge. Surely, it was that same angel, but here it was in Edenburg. How? She was wearing a different dress, a green dress decorated in golden ears of corn; it was Barbara's own image. When she had seen the painting in Brugge, she was convinced that she saw what she did through the sin of pride, but here, this was as direct and as accurate a portrayal of her self as could be. She examined the painting. Yes, the hair was perfect – of course, she would never again have the possibility of having such hair since the fire in Jorevall – but it was the same red colour as the few tufts she saw at night when she removed her coif. Her smiling features were as she imagined her own. There was no doubt in her mind. In the painting of this angel was her own likeness. But what did God mean by this? She often thought she was in some way gifted, and those she helped told her as much. Did she have a holy mission that transcended the things of the every-day? Why would God have shown her something like this, if not to indicate to her that her path was true, that her choices had been true? Her worries about Jaap van der Staen faded into the background.

Barbara genuflected and walked out of the Trinity Church. It no longer rained and a rainbow framed the old castle on the hill.

~ ~ ~ ~ ~

Barbara was entranced by the joy around her. She approached the eastern shore of the Nor' Loch, breathing in the smell of the wet earth, warmed by a new sun, when she heard her name. It was Jaap, panting and running after her.

"Barbara, I..."

She put her hand on his arm.

"Soft, Jaap, soft. I must tell you that I saw my own self in a painting in the church, over the altar. I was as an angel, an angel with red hair. It was my own likeness. Is this not a message from God? It can't be coincidence."

Jaap looked down at Barbara; she had tears in her eyes, tears of happiness. She stared at him in such a way that his agitation diminished. She took his hand, and they walked along the side of the loch, stepping past the ducks and swans, dogs and geese. She spoke lucid words of joy, love, and prayer. Anyone observing them would see a man listening to the soft chatter of a young woman; then taking two or three steps, stopping to gaze at the loch and the city on the hill; above them, the pacific clouds in the sky. They walked together like this to the park on the western side of the castle. Barbara pointed, showing Jaap the tiny things of beauty around them: birds singing, a deer over the way, or the colour of leaves, a tree, a flower. The afternoon sun shone in their faces. Jaap placed his hand on hers.

"Barbara, we cannot stay here."

~ ~ ~ ~ ~

"I saw Jan Starter. We fought in the rain. We were seen."
Barbara let go of Jaap's hand, and looked him up and down.

"Are you hurt?"

"No, but do you not see? Starter is dangerous."

"Yes, yes. We must get a Bailiff."

"No, we cannot. This is Skotlân. They will not try a man for a crime in a different country."

"But he must pay for the murder of the girl, Alys, the girl in Scheles."
Barbara froze; her mood transformed from joy to fear.

"It is true then, that you say so. Her name was Alys. Harry also told this to me in Salt Priestown."

"That is what he called her, the girl murdered on the salt road, for he told me that it was he who killed her. He said her name was Alys."

Barbara staggered. She reached for support. Jaap held her arm.

"Sweet Jesus in Heaven. Oh no. Please God Forgive me."

"What is it?"

She sat on a rock and held her head in her hands.

"I have killed her."

"Not so. It was Starter. He told me so. Harry saw him with his knotted beard."

"But it was me; I put her there by neglecting her."

Barbara told Jaap about Miriam and Martha, and Alys, the things that happened at Richmond, and of their parting.

"Little Alys wanted to come with me, and I wouldn't let her. If I had, she would be alive today. "

Barbara sobbed. Jaap hesitated, and then placed one hand on her shoulder, and then the other. She allowed him to hold her, and her tears slowly subsided. Jaap held her even after she settled.

"Starter, the man with the knotted beard, was Gertje's cousin. He thinks I killed her. That is why he is following me."

~ ~ ~ ~ ~

Harry poked at a fire as the sun set.

"Barbara, Jaap told me about you. You are from a place called Holstein, and when you talk funny, you call it Flemish."

"Truly, that is so."

"He says you are a novice in a monastery with a long name."

"Yes, it was a beautiful place called Porto Coeli, in Himmelpforten. In your tongue it is Heaven's Gate. I was tithed there by my mother when I was a girl, just about your age. I was to take orders."

"You would be a nun?"

"I know not what I will do. So many things have happened."

"What kind of things?"

"Oh, some good things, and some bad things. I learned about healing at Bruggen when I was sick, and I met a wise woman in Norwich, and I read the book of Hilda of Presscott, but I have also seen bad things. Sometimes, I have visions and I say things I don't understand."

"What kind of visions?"

"I see a bright light and it pulls me. It feels warm. It might happen when there is a storm, or a fire."

"Does God speak to you?"

"I could not say."

"Are you a saint?"

Barbara laughed.

"I am not. I am a simple girl."

"Jaap likes you."

"Oh?"

"We're going to St Andrews. We're going to pray for Jaap's other little boy."

Across the room, Jaap busied himself putting things in his bag. Harry saw Barbara watching him.

"Jaap. We must talk?"

"Of course. Harry, please go outside."

Harry ran out of the door with his gird and cleek followed by a barking dog that jumped up at him. Barbara sat on a small stool near the fire; she picked up the poker and moved some burning coals, the rising smoke turning to flame.

"How did your wife die?"

"It is not your concern. God took her away."

"And you had no part in it?"

"My sins are my business."

Barbara touched Jaap's sleeve.

"You know that my Abbess received a letter from Majstro Siemen in Keitum."

"Him! That man is a dog."

"But he wrote that you buried them in unconsecrated ground. How could you do that to those you loved; commit them to an eternity of suffering; deny them access to the kingdom of Heaven?"

"Gertje and I agreed to it."

"What? How could you? And little Anders, did he agree?"

Jaap lowered his voice.

"He was never baptised."

"What?"

Barbara could not hide her shock.

"So your son, Anders, is in the state of Limbo? He will never get to the Kingdom of Heaven."

"This is not how we saw things."

"How did you see things?"

"I'm not so sure. I used to be sure. I was so certain in the old days. First, I believed it all. My doubts had no place, but there is more, so much more. I did a terrible thing. Oh sweet Jesus, I did a terrible thing."

Jaap wiped his eyes and Barbara touched his hand.

"Jaap van der Staen, it will be a good thing if you tell me."

Jaap swallowed. The fire spat and crackled, and then settled.

"Fifteen hundred people died because of me."

"What? No, that is impossible."

Jaap held up his hand.

"I was a youngster on a fighting carrack, the Cordelière. Today they would call me a powder monkey. I carried the gunpowder and shells for the men to load the cannons; all those people died."

"I do not understand. What is the Cordelière? What happened?"

"The Cordelière was in a sea battle, near Brest, on St Lawrence's Day. I was a boy. Fifty ships engaged; they talk about it even now. The captain of the Cordelière was a man called Portzmoguer; he put to sea not expecting combat. They entertained visitors on board; landsmen and ladies who should never have seen battle. The English surprised us when they fired on us with their new, powerful cannons."

Jaap's shoulders dropped as he exhaled.

"Portzmoguer, ordered our men to use grappling hooks and board the English ship, The Regent. Our decks were awash with blood. Everyone was in the melee, even the visitors, men and women in their fine clothes, fighting with swords and staffs. All the time, we fired on the Regent, our guns so hot that we had to pour water on them to keep them cool. I ran, carrying gunpowder and shot for the gun crews; I was afraid."

Jaap's hands trembled as he spoke. He breathed in:

"A cannon recoiled across the deck in front of me. I tripped and the gunpowder fell to the floor. A spark from a fuse ignited, and there was an explosion and I was thrown into the sea. The Cordelière sank and dragged the still-shackled Regent to the bottom. An old sailor took me from the water. Even yet, I dream on it. They said the explosion could be heard for miles around. I tell you, fifteen hundred people died."

"When did this happen?"

"I was a boy; maybe eight or nine years old."

"They had children carrying gunpowder?"

"Yes."

"And you think that you are responsible?"

Jaap nodded.

"But you were a child. You could not have been responsible. You fell. That is all."

"That is what Gertje said."

"Alas; it is true."

"But I was responsible. If I had not tripped, the fire would not have started and the magazine would not have exploded and all those people would not have died. It was because of me and no one else."

Barbara made the Sign of the Cross. God in Heaven.

"What an ordeal. What an awful and terrible thing to live with."

Jaap sat, slouched; Barbara touched his knee.

"I understand this terrible thing that happened to you, but what does it have to do with the death of Gertje and Anders and their being buried in unconsecrated ground?"

"Because this was my sin and no one else's. I alone am responsible for what I did. They should not suffer for what I have done."

"But Jaap, it was an accident. By the Holy Virgin! You were a child working in the danger of battle. You should never have been there."

"But I was there. I have to pay for this sin. Who else is to pay for it?"

"Why, no one. It was an accident."

"It was my fault."

"Jaap, Jaap, this is too much. This is dreadful. You have lived with this all your life? What a burden for you to carry alone."

"It is indeed my own burden."

"But Jaap, I ask you again, how has this to do with the souls of Gertje and Anders?"

"They are not responsible for my sin."

"Why do you think they are?"

"The priests say they are."

"How so?"

"They say that if a soul is suffering in Purgatory for their sins, if they are suffering in that half world between Hell and Heaven, they say that I can ameliorate that suffering by praying for them, so there is a connection between their sins and my prayers. There is a connection between my prayer and the immortal soul of another."

"Yes."

"But one person alone is responsible for their own sin. They must suffer the consequences alone. I, that is, Gertje and I did not want others to pay for our sins."

"I'm not sure this follows..."

Barbara saw fault with Jaap's argument. She thought briefly of a debate with Katherine Mann on the subject, but this was not the time to dispute. Jaap continued.

"If Gertje and Anders never get to Purgatory, they will not suffer. Gertje agreed to this. I saw her suffer for months before our bountiful God took her away. Barbara, she was in so much pain; and she wanted me to help her into death; I was not to allow someone to pray for her soul who did not love her."

"Sweet Jesus in Heaven, Holy Mother of God. What is that that you say? She wanted you to help her die. Is that what you just said?"
Jaap paused. He rubbed eyes, raised his head and looked away.

"Yes."

XXIV

The Binks at Queenis Ferrie

The Feast Day of St Procopius of Scythopolis

8th July 1537

Queenis Ferry, with the island of Emonia

The sun had not yet penetrated the summer haar and the cold damp seeped into Jaap's bones. They waited at the Binks at Queenis Ferrie, just by the stone pier. Around them, fisherfolk and workers and shirkers went about their business. Jaap blew on his hands to keep them warm. He and Barbara and Harry had risen early in the dark, walking west from Edenburg, to travel on the morning ferry-boat. All the way there had been an uncomfortable silence between them.

"Jaap, you must tell me more."

Jaap ignored Barbara's questions and walked away, out to the rocks. He kicked at some loose shells. Out in the mist could be heard a number of ships, large and small, with the dipping of oars, the lapping of water on their sides, and the flapping of sail in the light breeze; the clunk of yard and rope, and the shouts of sailors. But further out was the unmistakeable sound of a larger ship, a carrack, perhaps. Jaap cupped his ears to listen to the familiar noises of metal and timber and sail, to the shouts of a crew. Unseen in the murk, its approach could be felt in the still air.

"Can you hear it? A big ship, I think." Jaap smarted at the sound of Jan Starter's Flemish behind him.

"Stay away. What are you going to do? Draw your sword again?"

"I wish to speak with you. I have taken no drink. Here."
Jaap took a leaflet, glanced at it and handed it back.

"You do not read?"

"I do not need to read."

"It is poesie. It is spoken as a song. I have found a rhyme for it."
Jaap regarded Starter, clean and washed. He was not wearing his sword.

"You wanted to speak to me? About what matter?"

The two men listened as the ferry boat approached, a spectre in the haar, half full of people, two monks hauling at the sails. Starter put away his paper.

"That girl on the Salt Road. I didn't kill her."

"Alys. But she is dead."

"But I did not kill her. The stupid girl fell. She hit her head on a rock. I didn't kill her."

"How can I believe you?"

"I swear it, on my immortal soul."
Along the beach, a crow found a mussel shell and waddled to a rock to open it.

"They found her in a salt barrel. Did you put her there?"

"That was foolish."

"Why didn't you tell the Bailiff in New Castell?"

"He would not have believed me."

"No, he would not."

"I am haunted by her spirit."
The crow took the mussel shell in its beak and hit it against the rock, repeatedly, clumsily; left and right, left and right.

"You have killed before, I think."

Another crow joined the first, and they fought for the shell, slipping on the wet rocks and seaweed.

"I am a soldier; this was different. She was an innocent. She was frightened when I spoke to her, and she ran away."

"You spoke Flemish to her?"

"Yes. I thought, I don't know, in the dark..."

Back at the growing crowd on The Binks, Barbara and Harry talked together as the ferry-boat approached. Starter lowered his voice.

"You know, I shared a home with Gertje when we were children. She was as a sister to me when my parents died of the sweating sickness. Her mother became my mother; her father became my father."

"Yes. You told me."

"Did you kill her?"

"Gertje was very sick."

One of the crows won the mussel shell and flew up over the rocks. In mid air, it released the shell from its beak, dropping it to the ground, the way it had seen the clever gulls do. The shell fell not on the rocks, but on the sand. It remained closed, the mussel safe inside.

"You are good with that child. I have seen you."

"Harry is a fine boy."

Starter kicked at a limpet stuck to a rock.

"How did you become virtuous?"

"Ha!" said Jaap, "Virtuous; me? I think you have the wrong man."

He stopped smiling.

"I am not virtuous. I have sinned grievously, but I try to act virtuously. I try; I fail. I have much to atone for; we are all sinners."

As the two men watched, two gulls wheeled in the clearing air, calling to each other, laughing at the efforts of the crows. Jaap turned to Starter.

"Barbara knew the girl on the Salt Road. She thinks her actions to be the cause of her death."

"Holy Mother of God. It was not her fault."

"She thinks it was."

The ferry-boat landed, crunching and splashing on the stony beach. The two monks jumped to the gravel and went through the little crowd to a stall and took some small ale. When Jaap looked back, Jan Starter had gone.

~ ~ ~ ~ ~

Jaap went back to Harry and Barbara, chatting amongst the others waiting to clamber on to the grounded shallop rocking in the surf. A trio of pilgrims sang psalms; Barbara hummed along while Jaap and Harry played, pushing each other around. Others were heading for the Lammas Fair market across the river in Inverkeithing and tended to their sheep.

There was a hawker's stall loaded full of pilgrims' trinkets; tiny devotional altars that would be carried in a leather pouch, staffs with inlaid scallop shells in the handles; little tin badges with images of St Andrew, St Cuthbert, and St Margaret; there were Breviaries, tiny Books of Hours, phials containing relics and holy water. The pilgrims flocked around the stall, fingering the goods. The stallholder, dressed in a habit, called out:

"Get your relics here! Get your holy relics here! St Margaret's fingernails, guaranteed!"

The locals shook their heads. Barbara approached the stall:

"You should be ashamed; taking money from poor folk."

"Go and piss, girl. I sell the most Holy relics in Scotland. People want, I sell."

He gestured to a man examining some items on his stall.

"Yes sir. That is truly a fine cap. Note the scallop shell design. It will keep the rain from your head on your Holy Journey. Thank you sir; may St Cuthbert light your way."

Harry pointed to one of the badges that showed St Andrew on his X-shaped cross.

"Jaap, can I have that one? Please Jaap."

"Go on sir, let your boy have the badge. I will bless it here and now."

"Please Jaap. Can I, can I?"

Barbara dragged Harry away.

"Come away, come away. This man is nothing but a swindler."

Harry started to cry.

"Barbara, please?"

Jaap gave the hawker a coin and took the badge. The hawker winked.

"God Bless you sir. May St Andrew's blessing go with you. You've got a hard woman there."

Jaap gave Harry the badge. He whispered "Thank you Jaap". Jaap put his finger to his mouth and gestured towards Barbara.

The monks finished their breakfast beer. They yawned as the sheep were pushed among the passengers on to the open topped boat, a shallop with fore-and-aft sails, unfurled, ready for the breeze. Jaap and Barbara and Harry clambered aboard with everyone else, splashing and shoving in the surf, and the ferrymen heaved the boat off the shingle. The exposed boat was cramped, forcing everyone into happy companionship. Harry found another boy, and they took fun in sticking sticks into the sheep. The shepherds shouted at them; Jaap and Barbara pretended not to notice.

The sun was clearing the fog, warming their backs, and people squinted into the depth below and out to the prospect ahead, whether it be a good price for their produce at the Lammas Fair, eternal succour through their pilgrimage, or the ordinary pleasure in a daily crossing to say hello to friends or relatives. For any or all of these reasons, the travellers settled into a contented silence as the canvas sail stretched in the breeze and the water turned white at the shallop's bow. With the wind brushing their heads, the air to their cheeks and the sun on their faces, they felt good on this fine day, the softly creaking boards between them and the water below.

In the busy quiet, and the splashes of water against the hull, porpoises played alongside, and seals sang on the islands to the east. The regular travellers noticed it as they might notice a cabbage on a stall, or a piece of tripe from a butcher; but the others, the newcomers to this crossing, they ooh'ed and ah'ed and said "What is that? Is it singing?" and the locals answered that it was the seals. The visitors peered at the shapes on the rocks.

"They sound like angels."

The locals rolled their eyes. Harry tugged at Jaap's arm.

"Are they angels, Jaap, are they, are they?"

Barbara looked out across the water. Jaap smiled at Harry and rubbed his head.

"But, are they Jaap? Are they like the angels you heard grinding salt at the big quern under the water?"

"They were witches, Harry, not angels."

"Oh yes, I remember."

Among these noises of seals and little boats on the water, Jaap heard again the distant familiar sounds of a larger ship, with the calls and orders to the crew. Around the headland, a large Carrick was disappearing into a harbour.

" What is the big ship there?"

" That is the Salamander, out of Leith; the King's ship."

As seagulls passed overhead, they accompanied the seals' song until the shallop came to rest on the beach at St Margaret's, at the North Queenis Ferry. The traders and the sheep and the pilgrims and the locals jumped off the boat and paid the ferryman their penny. They split up and then became lost to each other after their enforced intimacy. None said God's bye, but all comprehended their shared moment and its demise.

~ ~ ~ ~ ~

Jaap and Barbara held Harry's hand between them as they joined the company of traders in the walk to Lammas Fair at Inverkeithing. They remained silent, but spoke in turn to Harry. When they got to the market, Harry held his hand tight.

"Don't worry, Harry. Nothing bad will happen here. There is no danger here."

Harry relaxed his grip on Jaap's hand. He saw a small dog.

"Jaap, can I pet the dog?"

"Yes you can Harry. I stay here."

Harry ran to the dog and the group of children playing around it. Barbara stood closer to Jaap.

"Jaap, I..."

"Not now."

"When?"

"Maybe later."

"I am sorry Jaap. You are a good man; I want to understand you."

Barbara touched Jaap's forearm for a second. At the touch, Jaap felt the hairs on his arm rise. He was aware of a brief glance, her eyes somehow opening up her whole self; their look, a channel between them that said everything in a momentary silence. In that instant, there was no guile or artifice. That look changed everything, and if asked, they would both say that they knew it. By the time he realised that this thing had happened, she had removed her hand and was looking away from him. They heard a voice calling.

"Hail, friends!"

A man with an aristocratic bearing gestured to them. He wore an elaborate red scarf.

"Where are ye for? Methinks ye be pilgrims?"

"We are for St Andrews."

"A fine city. Ye'll be tended well there. Whence d'ye come? I can tell that ye are not my countrymen."

"I am a Dutchman, Barbara hails from Holstein, and Harry over there is English."

Harry had found more sheep, and practised his new skills, poking them with a stick.

"Ah Harry; a fine name. That is what my uncle is called. Ha ha!"

"And what is your name, sir?"

"Ah, the direct question of people from your parts. How refreshing. Why my friends, I am a mere merchant. I am Gudeman of Ballengeich. I travel the land and I learn from my people."

"That is a noble activity sir."

"Noble? Perhaps. ... Well, aye."

The Gudeman breathed deeply, his countenance sinking, his shoulders sagging. For a moment, he fingered his staff, but then stood straight; he put on a smile. Barbara saw that he was distracted.

"Sire, methinks you are troubled."

He stared across the wide water to Edenburg.

"Ach, my dear, by the Holy Rood, I am sairley troublit."

"Sire, pray tell."

Barbara touched his ruffed sleeve. He took a silk kerchief from his cuff and dabbed his eyes. His bearing softened.

"Forgive me my friends. I have a new wife, such a delicate gentle flower, so fragile. She is ill, you see, and this day, she lies abed. Sometimes I fear..."

He blessed himself. Barbara took his hands in hers and their heads bent together. They said an Ave Maria together, as people in the market place milled around, while children played, and dogs barked, and merchants called their wares. Their little prayer ended, and Barbara held on to his hand.

"Sire. Go to your wife."

The Gudeman cleared his throat and composed himself.

"Aye, my dear. Ye are richt. By the Virgin, ye are richt."

He smiled and lifted his head. He took in the sights of the market. He saw a beggar and bent to give him alms. As he stood, he stared at the marks on Barbara's face.

"Ye have been burned, young woman. Is this not so?"

"Sire, I have to tell you that we have travelled England and seen terrible things; such burnings and destruction. Terrible, terrible."

"Ah yes. I have heard these things told, and they frighten us all. There is a threat in the air in the country of our neighbours. They are now executing the unfortunates who rebelled, even the abbots and priors and monks. Only last month, an Abbot was hanged, drawn and quartered at Tyburn. An abbot; imagine, such a thing? His name was Sedbar."

Jaap and Barbara glanced at each other.

"From Jorevall?"

"You know this man?"

"We know who he was. We saw Jorevall suppressed."

Barbara turned her gaze to the ground.

"It is where I was burned."

Jaap tried to catch Barbara's eye. The Gudeman blessed himself.

"You were burned at Jorevall?"

"Yes."

The Gudeman took their hands.

"Terrible times; these are terrible times. But you know here in Scotland, our King James is a man of the old faith. He is happy to adapt, but there is a way to it. We shall reach trust and compromise."

"Have no monasteries been destroyed in Scotland?"

He coughed into his kerchief.

"Not in Scotland my friend. They say that the Lord Cromwell, The English king's Chancellor, approached our King to ask him to pursue a similar path, but our Godly King James has no interest in the pursuit of material wealth at the cost of the happiness of his people. They say he is a Monarch Blessed, who loves his countrymen."

"You seem to know a lot about your King."

"Aye, tae be sure. I have met him on many occasions. In truth, he is another Gudeman, Ha Ha Ha!"

"So can we live in peace in here?"

"As long as this King rules, I can guarantee peace in this country."

"Thank you sir, you cannot know how happy this makes us, hearing from a man who has known the King."

"Indeed I have, little madam, indeed I have."

He peered out to the Firth, towards Edenburg.

"But I think I must to my poor wife."

Barbara and the Gudeman bowed to each other.

"God's Blessing on you, my dear."

"And on you and your wife, Sire."

The Gudeman made his way through Lammas Fair crowds, down the hill to the harbour where the brightly coloured Salamander lay at anchor.

Barbara and Jaap walked around the busy town square while Harry chased a dog. They took in the smells of smoked fish and enjoyed the sights and colours of the marketplace, the vegetables and fruit, the sounds of talk and laughter. They stopped to look at a juggler, and a luter played, the sound almost lost in the noise of the crowd. Harry found them and took their hands.

"I've found a unicorn! I've found a unicorn!"

He took them to the centre of the town square; there was a tall post topped with a unicorn, painted blue and red and yellow. Harry pointed.

"Look, there it is, a unicorn, a unicorn."

A woman passing by stopped and rolled her eyes.

"Aye son, it's a unicorn."

The woman took in the threesome in front of her: Jaap sturdy and bald, in need of new clothes; Barbara, bright eyed, with spindly tufts of red hair poking out of her cap, the burn marks, her left ear all but gone; the scallop shell and badges pinned to Harry's coat, his face grubby but happy.

" I told you it was a unicorn, I told you."

She grinned as Harry jumped up and down .

"Where are you for, pilgrims?"

"Saint Andrews."

"And where have you come from?"

"Sylt, and other places."

"I do not know this place. It is unusual to see a family on a pilgrimage."

"A family, I suppose we are. Yes, a family on a pilgrimage."

"Will you stay with the Greyfriars here at Inverkeithing? There is a fine hospital," the woman pointed, "just there."

"No. we are for a place called Abyrdower."

"Ah. Sisterlands?"

"What is Sisterlands?"

"Sisterlands is St Martha's; the wee Hospital in Abyrdower. Just by the Earl of Morton's keep. Ask anyone."

Barbara interrupted.

"Is it a nunnery?"

"Yes. They are Franciscans. They are good folk."

~ ~ ~ ~ ~

Jaap, Barbara and Harry headed east out of Inverkeithing, across the open green parks, towards Abyrdower, and Sisterlands. They walked along the shore with the breeze at their back, and then higher along the avenew with its views across the Firth, showing the road they had come that day. They observed the Salamander, the huge four masted carrick, sailing east, towards Leith, back on the other shore. The three crossed the mudflats and the open stretches of sand and passed by the Abbey of Emonia, on an island in the firth, its squat spire clear between its two little paps, smoke rising from the monastery buildings. At the closest point to the island, they came to a cave in the hill, away from the stony beach. Inside were three monks.

"Come in friends, have some beer?"

The monks shared their beer and bread; Harry played on the rocks below.

"We were at the Lammas Fair. Inverkeithing is a fine town."

"Aye, truly."

"We met a gentle; he was called the Gudeman of Ballen-something."

"Aye. He wid be The Gudeman of Ballengeich."

"That was his name."

"Well, I should tell ye that ye've met our king."

"No, this man was a merchant."

"I tell ye, our King James comes amang us. He often visits the markets."

"What, alone, with no retinue?"

"Aye. He travels aroon', meeting commoners. Indeed, there he sails, on his Salamander. A wedding present frae the French, ye ken."

They stopped to observe the brightly coloured ship veer south towards Leith.

"That is the King. But this is wondrous. He must be a truly virtuous monarch."

"He is indeed virtuous. He's a gey popular man."

Another monk spoke from the back of the cave.

"Aye, except he raises taxes on us poor churchmen."

"Dinny listen tae him."

"Take it from me, oor time will come."

There was silence while they ate their bread. Jaap spoke to the first monk.

"This man, the Gudeman, said his young wife was sick."

The monks blessed themselves; Barbara and Jaap followed suit.

"Aye, that is so; the beautiful Madeline is sickly. Some say she is not long for this world. Oor summer queen."

"The poor man must be distraught. She was so delicate, ye ken. She shouldn'y hae left France. She arrived in Edenburg just last Whitsun."

The monk nodded to his companion, sipping his beer.

"Brother Robert, ye remember a' they French and Scots ships a' thegether at Leith?"

"Aye, aye! It wis the first time we saw the Salamander."

"They say the wedding in Paris was a wondrous affair."

The monk at the back of the cave grunted.

"Aye. Wi' so many poor in the world, they spend all their gold on such affairs. It's no richt, Ah tell ye, it's no richt!"

"If God sees fit tae tak oor gentle Queen Madeleine, oors will be a sair loss. The joy she brought, 'twas like a piece of French sunshine, so it was."

There was another grunt from the rear of the cave. The Monk at the front pointed.

"Brother, our boat for the Abbey is here. My friends, it has been good to speak."

The monks blessed them, touching their heads.

"In Nomine Patri..."

Jaap offered them some coins.

"That's no needed, my friend."

They watched the monks rowing over to Emonia, and waved, before carrying on east.

~ ~ ~ ~ ~

"When are we going to get there?"

"Soon Harry, soon."

From behind, Barbara watched Harry and Jaap walking in step. Jaap slowed his pace to allow Harry to catch up. Harry, on the other hand, had to skip or run, or lunge to keep the pace. She watched this odd pair tripping together as they had done for months. Over the wide heaths and parks, and muddy paths; in the sun and the rain and the dark and in the dull days, they kept together in their lumpy, ever-correcting synchronisation.

On this long day, Harry was tired and lagged behind. Jaap had long since ceased to become frustrated and simply waited for him to catch up. With no exchange of words, he swung Harry high into the air, where he sat astride Jaap's neck. He ate an apple, threw away the core and rubbed his hands on Jaap's head. Jaap picked up speed, striding across the ground at this new, more satisfying pace. Barbara quickened her step to keep up.

On Jaap's shoulders, Harry was a happy boy. He loved this new rhythm, the loping step that made him feel as if he was flying on this huge man. Harry could see for miles as he travelled. He had to duck for the branches of trees, with no worry about puddles and soft ground. He felt close to the birds flying just over his head; he could see the white backs of sheep grazing in the parks to the north of the road. Up here, he was free from fatigue, happy in his timeless state, his legs around Jaap's neck, playing with his ears and resting his cheek on his warm head. In short, Harry was the happiest boy; safe and fed and comforted. He dozed, his head resting on Jaap's.

"He is asleep?"

"Yes."

"I am sorry I asked you those questions."

"I want to tell you."

"You don't have to."

They paced along together, Harry sleeping on Jaap's shoulders. They stopped, and Jaap placed Harry's sleeping form on the grass.

"Your wife suffered?"

"Gertje. Her name was Gertje."

"Gertje."

The late-afternoon sun lit up the Firth. They could see all the way they had come; from Edenburg in the south, and west along the road to the South Queenis Ferrie. The long day's travelling was almost over. They had covered a lot of ground, both completing the day happier than when they started. Harry twitched, dreaming on the soft ground. Once again, seals sang in the firth.

"She suffered greatly. It was dreadful to watch; I could do nothing. She asked me to help her die. When she first said it, I thought that she meant me to ease her pain at death, but she asked me again. I could not but ease her pain. It was such a little thing for me to do, but she was so grateful. She was so grateful."

Jaap wept. First, softly, and the weeping consumed him. He remained quiet so as not to wake Harry, but the silent sobs took control of his whole body as he shook with the force of his grief. Barbara put her arms around him. She remained silent, and just held him while this uncontrollable fit of loss coursed through him. He cried for a long time. Very slowly, the force of his tears diminished. Jaap was left intermittently sobbing as he regained his composure. Barbara held him as his breathing became regular. She whispered to Jaap.

"She asked you to do this because she loved you?"

"Yes."

XXV

Abyrdower

The feast Day of St Macrina the Younger

19th July 1537

L'homme Armé

Ahead of them was a high walled fortalice, and just beyond, masons worked on scaffolding that surrounded a newly constructed tower. Smoke came from the chimney rising to the sky in a single tall column, lit by the late sun behind them. A heron flew across their path, and to their right, was the sound of calling seals. On Jaap's shoulders, Harry grunted in his sleep, and Jaap shifted his position to ease his creaking back.

"Have you seen the dog heads here?"

Barbara took a skip to be in step with Jaap.

"No."

"I thought to see people with dog heads who walk and talk and appear as men and women. I heard they lived in Skotlân. I dreamed them."

"I have also dreamed of them. Perhaps they live further, in the north?"

They passed an oak tree, singular and huge, and walked on east to a bridge over a burn. On their right was a path, and out in the firth, little boats came and went. On their left, was a long hedge of hawthorn and gorse with the odd remaining yellow flower. A drystane dyker was working on a wall.

"God's Day to you!"

"Hail, pilgrims. Are ye for Saint Andra's?"

"Yes."

"Are we there yet?" said Harry, drowsily.

"Ah, this wee man is keen to arrive at his destination."

"We are looking for Sisterlands, St Martha's."

"Aye, the Pilgrim Hospital. It is here on the Mains."

"The Mains?"

"Aye. The Mains o' Abyrdower; jist here. This wall and this hedge enclose Sisterlands. The hospital is just there on your left o' the Mains."

To their left, was a long slope covered with riggs full of kale, and carrot, and leeks. Ahead they saw, above the hedge, a hospital building with high roof and smoking chimneys. There was a neat church, monastery buildings and beyond, an orchard with a timber doocot, lifted on stilts. Above the door at the street was a wooden carving of the Virgin. Barbara knocked. The woman who answered had rosy cheeks and rough hands, and she wore a grey habit. Barbara adjusted her coif to cover her burn.

"God's Day, my lady. Can you give us shelter tonight?"

The sister looked at the three, weary from their walk.

"I'm sure we can squeeze in your wee family."

Barbara smiled; Jaap blushed.

"I am Sister Agnes Wright. The Prioress here is Isabella Henryson, and we have three other sisters. Please come this way."

They were shown their pallets, in separate areas for male and female; Harry was to stay with Barbara.

"Can't I stay with Jaap? You snore."

Barbara and Sister Agnes grinned at each other.

"The refectory is over there, the chapel that way. Compline is about to start."

Jaap, Barbara and Harry went to the chapel where a sense of the familiar encompassed them. Incense and Latin and the singing from the four Sisters, led by their Prioress, washed over them; but Jaap heard something else in the music. A lower voice was singing a harmony, but the harmony part was a tune.

The armed man should be feared.

It was 'L'homme armé', the song from that night, in a different world, when he was drunk, singing with Geoff and Bent in Hamburg. But now he was in Skotlân; that he had come so far, to be returned to the memory of that night by this music. Embedded in the harmony of this sung mass was his old drinking song.

After Compline, in the late evening dim, Prioress Isabella showed them the physic garden. Jaap rubbed the leaves of a large sage bush between his thumb and forefinger.

"Prioress, the singing."

"Yes my son, our Sanctus; our lovely Gloria Tua."

Jaap sniffed at the sage.

"It reminded me of a song."

"Yes. L'homme armé."

"You know it?"

"Our friend Robert Carver from Scone gave us this music. He wrote it for the King. He told us they sing that song in France..."

"...And Holstein and the Low Countries. It is a common song."

"And now we use the tune in our devotion. Is it not strange that we use it so."

They approached a tree in the middle of the garden. Jaap gazed at it in amazement. Someone had placed rocks between its three intertwined trunks, which had grown around them, forming a single entity of tree and stone. Jaap touched the trunk with the palm of his hand. It was identical to the quikbeme near St Severin's in Sylt with its embedded offerings and trinkets; where Jaap had once spread salt for Gertje on the morning of her death.

"What is it, Jaap?"

"This is Gertje's tree. It came from Sylt; across the sea. But this is Skotlân. I am confounded."

Barbara held Jaap's hand, and they remained silent, standing, taking in the quikbeme, ordinary and universal, a tree that must have been there forever.

"How did it get here?"

~ ~ ~ ~ ~

The evening was warm and Harry trotted behind Jaap and Barbara, away from the hut they had taken next to Sisterlands, turning right on the Mains towards Abyrdower. They passed the Earl's keep on the left, and the lands of Neuton of Abyrdower on the right. They arrived at the wester side of Abyrdower, where, in the open area in front of the tower of the Earl's keep, people gathered, chatting around a few stalls with hot food and beer. The local folk nodded and smiled at Jaap and Barbara, the new family that they all now knew, who stayed near Sisterlands.

Some musicians had set up at one side of the area, in front of the keep; two luters, a piper and a drummer. They spent a minute tuning, glanced at each other and started to play. One or two couples got to their feet, followed by others; soon the area was full of dancers. Jaap and Barbara watched the steps, bewildered. It seemed as if the whole of Abyrdower was dancing in time.

"Come away you two. Hae a reel wi' us."

Harry ran away to play, but Jaap and Barbara walked out onto the open area and allowed themselves to be positioned for the next dance. The music had a strange, rocking rhythm and they imitated the moves of the other dancers, tripping and bumping into each other, laughing at each little collision. They looked an odd pair alongside everyone else, with Jaap towering above Barbara, floating above the little sea of people. The pair bounced and lurched, laughing and dancing. They were becoming more confident in their steps when the music ended. They then dispersed and went to eat some food. Jaap and Barbara had a cup of beer and congratulated each other on their new skills. Harry came up to them.

"I saw you dancing. You were the best."

"Thank you Harry", said Jaap. "Now, you do it with Barbara."

"I can't do that."

"Neither can I", said Barbara, " but we should try."

"I don't want to."

The music played again and Barbara took Harry's arm, laughing.

"Come on, my little man."

"No, don't make me."

Jaap smiled as the two disappeared in the throng, lurching among the dancers, laughing and skipping to the music.

"So Jaap. You are happy in Abyrdower."

It was Hamish, one of the merchants, grinning, pouring fat on to a sheep roasting on a spit.

"Yes my friend. Abyrdower is a haven. You are blessed to be living in such a place."

"Indeed. Outside of this place, the world is disturbed and all is change, mere fashion and fangle, but here we can be at peace."

They watched as the dancers whirled and spun their web of contentment, propelled by the musicians.

After the dance, they all stood around one of the luters waiting for him to play. He sat on a stool, taking time to tune. He bent his ear to the instrument, adjusting the pitch of each string, repeating the process until he was satisfied with the consonance. Then he played, moving with the music, his body reflecting the phrasing with subtle twitches of his head and shoulders. The strange melody rose and fell, the chords driving the music on. The luter and his instrument were as one, the sound controlling Jaap's breathing, his exhalations permitted only when each phrase was complete. The musician lifted himself off his seat, nearly rising to his feet as the tension grew to be almost too much to bear, the air thick with this music that made the audience gasp in excitement. The luter played into his cadence, allowing them to relax, and he made the music quiet, so that Jaap and the other listeners strained to hear more. He allowed the last note to die away and everyone was hushed. Some had already walked away, immune to the power of the music, but those who stayed, one or two with a tear in their eye, were fixed, immobile in this new silence, a silence that could never be like any silence that preceded it. They were aware that they had breathed together in this prolonged moment, in this little tryst between the luter and the listener, that was such a thing that words could never capture. They looked to the musician who bowed his head and put his instrument to the side, then stood up to walk away, and they followed him.

"Can ye no play more music?"

"Later. I hae tae eat."

The listeners followed him.

"How did ye do that to a'body?"

"It was the music."

"But how?"

"I did nothing. They were just notes."

"Can you no tell us?"

"I dinna hae the words."

"But ye must know what you felt."

"I'm sorry. I hae tae eat."

~ ~ ~ ~ ~

The sun was setting, and the dancing continued. A fire threw flickering shadows in the dimming light. Over their heads, at the top of a little rise, Jaap was watching the happy gathering, when he became aware that a figure had been staring at him for some time. As he approached, he recognised Jan Starter. He spoke in Flemish.

"You again?"

"You know me?"

"By God's Holy Bones, I do. You have troubled me sore. I thought to be rid of you at Queenis Ferrie."

"I told you. I am The Provost's man, from Himmelpforten. I am to make sure you answer for your sins."

"This is what you wish, to see me confessed; shrived and absolved?"

Starter did not answer. The two stood on the raised piece of ground, where they could see the dancers, rising and falling together.

"I have watched you, and I have followed you. We are alike. You must know this. If you know me, you know your self. You know I write poesy?"

"No, but.."

"I like the alexandrine form. It is formed of couplets, each line has two halves, each of six feet. Each half is separated by a caesura. Sometimes, they allow for rhyme, and sometimes, they do not. You see; symmetry, but not always agreement. You and I are like these two halves."

"This is nonsense. Why do you speak as you do?"

"I say these things because they are true. We have both done things. I know that you have sinned most grievously – like me. We have lived each other's deeds."

Jaap heard Harry's voice.

"Jaap, Jaap?"

Jaap placed his finger on Starter's chest,

"I do not know what you have done. Stay away from me. Leave me alone."

"I tell you we share a past, and we share a destiny. My friend, you will always seek me. We are tied together."

"I will not seek you."

Starter handed some papers to Jaap:

"Here is a song for you. I wrote it for you and me. I like the allusions in it. It could be a drinking song."

Jaap looked at the papers and turned them around, top to bottom, and back to front. He offered them back.

"I do not read. I cannot understand your words."

"Keep them in any case. Look here, at the refrain:

'We sing our song at the fire, and we dance at the fire

Our words in the sweet smoke, our love warm in the hearth'."

Jaap turned away and back to the group where Harry was calling.

"Did you see me dance, Jaap?"

"I saw you. You are a good dancer, Harry."

Jaap turned back to where Starter had stood. There was only the bare ground. Barbara was laughing.

"Yes, my little man was the best."

Once again, the people formed themselves into groups of six in circles around the fire. The music played, and they went round first in one direction and then the other. Jaap, Barbara and Harry moving as a trio, joining and splitting, joining with another group, repeating the steps governed by the music. And so they continued splitting and combining and rotating again and again into the night, lit by the fire and the moon.

They returned to their hut next to Sisterlands. Jaap carried Harry, still sleeping, and placed him in his cot. Barbara and Jaap lit their fire and sat in its warmth, chatting about nothing to each other in Flemish, happy in their night.

~ ~ ~ ~ ~

Barbara was picking vegetables in the Sisterlands' kitchen garden when Prioress Isabella approached.

"It has been good to have the help at St Martha's since Jaap and you and wee Harry arrived. More pilgrims will come, who need to be fed and sheltered, and your treatment for sore eyes is successful."

"You know that it is simple, Prioress. It is not a miracle. I take some fresh water from your well and dissolve some of Jaap's salt, and apply to the eye with a cleaned mussel shell. It is an little thing."

"Don't tell anyone how simple it is. We are getting more and more pilgrims arriving, complaining about their eyes. The word is getting around that this is what we do, so the more we can help the better."

"Prioress, we all know that this is not a cure. We can do nothing for blindness. It is but a mere treatment to salve eyes that are swollen and with a crust under the eyelids. That is all."

"Just so, but with belief, God can work miracles. If there is faith, miracles can happen."

"Perhaps, Prioress."

Barbara felt a tingle in her back and the taste of iron was in her mouth

~ ~ ~ ~ ~

The next day Barbara met some pilgrims gathered in the chapel for the eye treatment. The first woman was rubbing the broken skin around her swollen eyes, which ran with tears and blood. They entered the pharmacy together, where they knelt and said an Ave Maria. Barbara poured fresh water over her eyes, wiping away the dirt and dried blood. She took some of the water from the well, added some grains of pure salt prepared by Jaap, and a drop of witch hazel. She mixed the liquid and put a few drops into a large clean mussel shell. Barbara directed the pilgrim to sit with her head forward. She applied the shell with the mixture to one eye and moved her head back.

"Amen. Now, open your eye and let the fluid wash your eye."

"No, no, I cannot."

Barbara kept a firm but comforting grip on the pilgrim's shoulder.

"My friend. Your eyes are sick. We can help; but you must do as we direct."

The pilgrim opened her eyes and the cold water came into contact with her eye. She struggled and gasped, but Barbara held her firmly.

"You must stay like this and you must blink to wash the inside of your pained eyes."

The woman relaxed and allowed the mixture to soak into her swollen eye. Barbara repeated the process for her other eye.

"Thank you my sister. My eyes are cured."

"No my friend. Your eyes are not cured yet. You must repeat this act at morn and even, until the swelling subsides."

Barbara gave the woman a phial of the fluid and a pair of mussel shells. She called the next person and repeated the process.

Such was the relief given to the pilgrims by Barbara and the other sisters at St Martha's.

~ ~ ~ ~ ~

The late summer weather on the East of Scotland can be humid and warm: 'close', as they say. The sun would be obscured by haze, and the dull heat of the day made people perspire. Anyone familiar with the climate would know a storm was coming. It was 'close' on this night; Barbara threw off her cover to cool down, but she still shivered. Jaap snored next to her, long and soft; across the room Harry was quiet in his pallet. The heavy rain thudded on the roof and the wind howled down the Mains in a low drawl. She turned over and closed her eyes against the growing white light in the dark, but within a few minutes she sat up. She knew what was coming, with the feeling of electricity on her skin and that old taste of iron; and after such a long time. Not since Jorevall had she felt one of her episodes.

"Jaap, Jaap."

She heard her voice as if in another room, each long syllable hanging in the air between them. She felt her eyelids close over, and then open in the dark, all the while filling her vision with the white light. Her head rolled from side to side, like a pendulum, slower and slower. She watched as her arm moved to shake him awake.

"Jaap, help me."

"Go back to sleep."

Barbara got out of bed, mumbling incomprehensibly. Jaap woke to see her shaking in the dark at the end of their cot.

"Barbara, what is it?"

She jabbered and pointed out to the sea. Through her gabbling, Jaap heard the word "wrack".

"A wreck? Where?"

With the slight hint of dawn in the sky, Jaap watched as Barbara tilted her head back and opened her mouth. She started to wail, as a siren, starting low, and rising in pitch.

Harry woke and put his hands over his ears. He shouted:

"What is wrong with Barbara?"

"It is one of her visions."

People were woken in the other huts, stirred by the noise. They called for sleep, but Jaap shouted:

"Listen to her. There is a wreck."

Barbara stopped screaming and raised her right hand and pointed south, towards the Firth. The storm stilled, and they heard in the distance shouts and screams and the sound of breaking timber.

"It's coming from White Sands – the rocks."

The people stirred; they ran down from Sisterlands towards the beach and the sounds of the wreck. With the rain beating down, the haar was thicker the closer they got to the shore. As they approached the rocks, the air resounded with the sound of the howling gale, the splintering wood, and people shouting and splashing. Barbara followed, stumbling in incoherent steps, dragging herself, her wailing reduced to a persistent moan like a banshee in the night, mumbling sounds of Latin and Flemish. Harry ran alongside Jaap.

"Harry, the rope in the workshop, can you bring it?"

"Yes Jaap. What about Barbara?"

"She will be alright. If a boat is stricken in the storm, we will need help. Wake everyone up."

Jan Starter appeared and ran beside Jaap. They exchanged glances, but said nothing. At White Sands, the wind died. They saw bodies lying on the beach; people from the ship wandered in the mist like ghosts on the sand. Jaap heard the deadened shouts and calls of men and women, shrouded in the grey mist; the unmistakable sound of Dutch and Flemish voices, the whimpering of a child; but even this close, with the sound of terror and chaos around him, there was little to be seen in the murk of the early grey dawn. The ship was invisible, despite the proximate sound of breaking timbers. The wind rose again, and the rain blasted their faces; behind him Barbara wailed. Then, out of the haar, right in front of him, as if it had been placed there that instant, close enough to touch, there appeared the hull of a huge ship, tipped on its side. Jaap saw that she had foundered and de-masted at the stern. The massive ship so close was a terrifying sight; keeled over, rocking and creaking with each thundering wave. In the cacophony of the storm, in the roar of the wind and the crashing of the breaking wood, a man leapt from the moving deck into the water and disappeared. Jaap couldn't see any sign of him, or even if he lived. Some from the ship tried to wade on to the beach, hand in hand, with the rain pummelling their faces, but the huge waves knocked them down, their bodies smashing onto the side of the ship, or onto the rocks. On its side, so close up, Jaap recognised that the wreck was a caravelle. Men and women and children could be heard in the clamour, their cries fading and rising as the howling wind drowned their calls.

"Help us, for the Love of Jesu, help us."

In the murk and torrent, Starter shouted into Jaap's ear, and others screamed, pointing at the survivors and the wreck, directing each other, their actions coalescing into a surge of manoeuvres executed in the chaos.

Jaap tied a rope around his waist and walked out into the surf. The merchant, Hamish, directed men from the shore, and they fed the rope out to Jaap as he approached the ship. He held on to an exhausted woman and guided her back to the beach, the two of them falling and tripping in the waves. Jan Starter followed Jaap's lead and the two men waded out and repeated the operation, again and again, finding one survivor after another, returning them away from the wreck.

Jaap came upon a man standing in a space in the rocks, up to his waist in the water, praying, buffeted by the spray and wind. His heavy cloak, covered with pilgrim's badges and pins, was saturated, weighing him down. He fell to his knees, overpowered by the waves. Jaap reached him, removed his cloak and carried him to land, trembling, mumbling his prayers.

The two men worked together, faster and faster, guiding and carrying survivors up the beach. Jaap saw Starter carrying three children, their terrified father splashing in the heavy surf behind them.

They worked close to the wreck, helping a man stranded on the rocks. Jaap placed his hands on the hull to steady himself when it lurched in the heavy surf. The name of the ship was above his head. He leaned back to read the blur of characters, the letters meaningless to him; but he recognised the shape of the words. He knew this ship. A wave knocked him down, and as he found his footing once more, it came to him. This was the Sanctus Andreas out of Purmurend – from the town of his birth – the ship he had seen in Hamburg. At the realisation, Jaap pointed to show Starter, but as he did so, he slipped on some seaweed, and they both fell into the water. The hull rolled, unstoppable, and the desperate current sucked them below, tossing them in the eddys between the rocks and the stricken ship. Jaap found the rope and heaved, dragging the two men together. Exhausted, desperate for air, they held each other but were again separated by the force of the moving water. Above them, the ship bobbed and rolled; they held their breath and waited to gain the surface, thrown by the current again and again, against the hull and the rocks; grasping for a purchase on anything that seemed secure. They were swept back and forth in the current, their attempts at stability, futile. At one surge, they came together and saw each other's faces, wide-eyed in fear and struggle. With each failure to gain the surface, they felt the uncontrollable urge to breathe in the water, the desperate need just to breathe; to open one's lungs, just once. After one more pull of the waves, Jaap's chest felt it would burst, and he succumbed and sucked the water into his body. There was relief, and he no longer needed to breathe, and there was peace as his body was swept back and away. He could hear singing. He released his grip on the tether and became subject to the swirling water. Above he saw light, varying in intensity with each surge. The colours changed from green to blue; below him he saw little fish, sheltering between rocks, protecting themselves and their young from the torrent. Jaap looked in the direction of the singing and there, standing strong in the storm, smiling and holding hands, were Gertje and Anders, gesturing for him to come close.

"But my sins; what of my sins?"

He inhaled the cold water once more. Starter, also fighting the desire to breathe, held on to him, as he went limp. Starter gained the surface and hauled Jaap's immobile form across the lathering surf. As the ship lurched again, he smiled:

"It rhymes, it rhymes…"

Then he spat, and in that moment, a loose piece of timber struck him on the head. He gasped, and the air left him as he dropped under the surface. Hamish was now with them and he grabbed Jaap, pulling him to the shore, before going back to find Starter.

Barbara stood nearby, mumbling, by a large rock, attended by Prioress Isobella and Sister Agnes. As the wind dropped, she opened her eyes wide.

'Jaap', she called; and she called again to the open air. The dawn was offering light, and the haar was clearing. Harry appeared out of the drizzle.

"Barbara. You must come."

Barbara looked around her, bemused, unaware of how she had come to be here. Harry pulled at her sleeve, and she shook her self alive.

"Come with me, It's Jaap, you must come."

Barbara ignored the tingling still on her skin and ran, stumbling, splashing with the boy down to the water's edge. She saw Jaap, lying on the sand surrounded by onlookers, some praying, all soaked and tired. Barbara and Harry pushed through. The pilgrim whom Jaap had saved was bent over saying a prayer in Flemish, rocking backwards and forwards in the pouring rain; Barbara pushed him out of the way.

She bent down and touched Jaap's cold white cheek. He was motionless.

"It be the will of God," said the pilgrim.

Barbara tipped Jaap's head back and opened his mouth. The onlookers gasped.

"Sweet Jesus, leave the man. He is in a better place."

Barbara cleared the dirt from his mouth and instinctively pushed down on his chest. Water and silt came from his mouth as he exhaled, but he remained lifeless. She covered his mouth with hers and breathed air into him.

"God in Heaven, she is kissing him. Come away girl. Have pity."

The survivors looked on, shivering. A man bent over to pull Barbara away from Jaap's body.

"No," shouted Harry, "Leave her."

Sister Agnes stopped the man's hand.

"Leave her."

"God's Eyes, this is madness" said the man, making the sign of the cross. The little congregation gathered around Jaap's body, speaking in different languages, making the sign of the cross, shivering in the rain and wind. Some turned away from Jaap's prostrate form, and towards shelter in the Mains.

Barbara pushed hard on Jaap's chest again and again; there was a small puff of air and gurgling from his throat, but no sign of life. Once more, she sealed her mouth over his cold lips, blowing life into him. Some shook their heads, others blessed themselves.

"Shame. For Pity's sake, leave him be."

"Bring him back," Harry whispered in Barbara's ear.

Barbara pushed on Jaap's chest once more and forced her own breath into his lifeless form. She slapped him hard and screamed spittle on to his face.

"Jaap! Come back!"

XXVI
Sisterlands
The Feast Day of the Fourteen Holy Helpers,
8th August 1537

A Shipwreck

Barbara pushed hard on Jaap's chest. He coughed and his body convulsed. The crowd gasped as one.

"God's Resurrection!"

"He quickens!"

"Holy Mother of God. He lives."

Jaap's back arched, his eyes wide in terror; he coughed but couldn't breathe in. Barbara and the other sisters sat him upright. He spewed water as his face turned from white to blue. As his eyes rolled back into his head, Barbara clapped his back, there was a rasping sound as he sucked in the air through his constricted throat. He clawed at the empty space in front of him staring wildly at Barbara and Harry. He took several huge breaths, and as he recovered, he looked around him.

"I thought..." he croaked.

"I know," said Barbara.

"A miracle!" said a woman.

A few yards away, the body of Jan Starter lay on the sand, his limbs lying askew; grains of sand on his open, sightless eyes, seaweed entangled in his knotted beard.

~ ~ ~ ~ ~

Out in the Firth of Forth, past the rocks, the daylight grew and the colours became clear. The crewless Sanct Anders from Purmurend drifted out into the Firth, its hull part submerged, its remaining mast vertical, its tattered sails blowing like leaves in the breeze. The storm was abating and crows landed on the cross-trees. The clouds parted and a golden shaft of sunlight lit the upright mast of the ship as it drifted sideways, silently, away from the shore.

"It be the will of God."

Some blessed themselves. Barbara and Harry supported Jaap and walked back towards Sisterlands.

Harry brought a blanket.

"Jaap, I thought you were for the deep."

~ ~ ~ ~ ~

After the shipwreck, there was much to be done. Local folk helped the survivors bury the dead; but the stories repeated up and down the coast that year told of the courage of the tall Dutchman, and his young wife's vision, that had alerted everyone. She was the saviour of the day, but when they talked of how she revived Jaap, they would make the Sign of the Cross, saying:

"Ye ken they are Sidhes; faerie folk. That yin's been tae the ither side."

Jaap was quiet after his experience. When he walked, people would not hear him coming. His breath was silent, and anyone watching would say he moved differently, as if he glided over the earth. He was slower, and he watched things. In particular, every day, he would observe young Harry, playing and learning, and flourishing. Harry thrived in this place.

From their small hut adjacent to Sisterlands on the Mains, they continued helping the sisters. Barbara worked with the pilgrims and in the running of the hospital, treating those that came with eye problems. Jaap farmed salt again, and helped in the physic garden, and with the keeping the buildings; and Harry attended the new school run by the sisters. Such was the slow rhythm of their new life together. In the aftermath of the shipwreck was a crystallisation, a stillness and a welcome stability following the traumas they had experienced since arriving on these islands.

They sat by the Dower Burn. Jaap made circles in the water with a stick. He spoke in a near whisper.

"I met a man in last year in Louth, one of the rebel leaders. His name was Captain Cobbler. When he heard that Harry was lost to me, he gave me Marcuccio. I will never forget Marcuccio; a magnificent horse. That was a hard time and Captain Cobbler helped me greatly."

He faced Barbara and spoke softly.

"I heard that this man was hung, drawn and quartered in London. He was a good man, Barbara."

Barbara touched his arm.

"I too have heard of such executions, nobles and commons: the abbot, Sedbar, Miriam's man Mark; and the man with one eye, Robert Aske, the Great Captain of the Pilgrimage. My friends Martha and Miriam loved him. They executed him in York last month."

"So many fine people killed at the whim of a wicked king."

"These are great events we have seen. We can do nothing to stop these things. We protect those whom it is in our gift to protect. We can only do the best we can, one day at a time."

No one noticed them as they walked up the side of the burn, swinging their arms, their hands brushing as they stepped together, leaving no prints on the uneven grass. They headed in the direction of the fortalice, on to Sisterlands.

"Barbara, you know more about me than any living soul. I still do not know anything about you."

"I am a simple girl. All I want is to do something to ease the pain in others. I want for nothing. When I was a novice, I wanted to take orders, but that seems a long way away now. I have seen things, the burnings, the suppressions, the deaths. I don't want what I wanted before."

"What are your talents?"

"Talents? Why, it is not for me to say. I talk to people."

"Yes truly, you have me speak about things I thought I would never say."

Barbara held Jaap's hand tight and released it. They paused, watching the water of the Dower Burn play on the rocks and then looked back upstream, up the hill to Neuton. In front of them, some deer stopped and turned their heads, fixing them with their silent gaze. Jaap approached them, and they stayed still. He stroked each one and blew softly into their ear, whispering, before turning back towards Barbara. They walked on to a bend in the river where ducks played among the reeds, exploring, and returning to their little family group, dipping their heads in the weed. A flash of blue darted through the air.

"Did you see that? Like a little piece of lightning in the air. An ijsvogel."

Barbara pointed. The streak of iridescent blue darted over their heads and out to the Firth, in a large circle, and back to the clump of vegetation where the river bent.

"Here, it is a halcyon. They say the female will carry a wounded male on its back for its whole life."

"I too have heard this story. I have heard say it charms the wind and waves so they can raise their young in peace."

"There is no way of knowing when it will return. Its nest will be out at sea; a nest of fishbones so it will float on the water."

Barbara and Jaap watched blackbirds and linnets and crows, but they waited in vain for the return of the halcyon.

Barbara considered this sky, full of birds with different names. She listened to the sounds of wings and wafts, and song and silence; and felt a small flutter on her skin, a murmur. It had been some months since her fit at Jorevall, and she was feeling better after the vision of the shipwreck, but she was watchful for any such signs that might forewarn of another little silence: that electricity on her skin, or the white light that warned her that she was about to be lost in that other world, and waken to be told of unknown actions and words. But then, she thought of the consequences: her prophesy and her close brush with such danger, and she shivered. Others said she had a gift, but for her it was a curse. Maybe she would be cured; she hoped the complaint might just vanish, or perhaps God in his wisdom would decide that she no longer had to endure these moments.

~ ~ ~ ~ ~

Jaap went out to the doocot past the kitchen garden. It was a round timber hut on low stilts with a cone shaped roof and an opening at the top that allowed the birds to come and go. He bent down, opened the low door, and entered to the din of hundreds of agitated birds, fluttering, filling the small space, raising the dirt from mounds of pigeon droppings. Jaap coughed in the dry cloud of dusty dung and they settled quickly. Slowly, he reached in, took two birds and dispatched them in a soft explosion of feathers. He returned with their dinner and met Barbara in the kitchen garden of Sisterlands, standing before the quikbeme tree. As she cleared the space around the tree, Prioress Isobella Henryson approached.

"God's day to you, my friends. You see our quicken tree."

"The quikbeme?"

"Yes, a tree of life."

On a branch of the quicken tree, somebody had hung a coat turned inside out; next to it, there was a pair of open scissors. Someone had scattered broken eggshells on the grass around its base, and pieces of linen hung like leaves. A child's shawl was draped over a low bough. The Prioress touched Jaap's arm.

"Jaap, how are you my friend?"

Jaap looked down at the two warm birds he had chosen for their meal. He placed them on a small stone table set near the tree.

"Ah, sister, I fare well."

"Indeed, you appear to flourish, but I wonder: you have not been to Mass."

"No Prioress."

Barbara coughed and looked away. She placed her hand on the tree, tracing the bark of the three intertwined trunks.

"You know they talk about you, since your drowning."

"We cannot help this."

"I know Jaap, but they say things about you. That you are returned from the afterlife, that Barbara brought you back, that you are Sidhes."

"Sidhes?"

"Aye, creatures of the other world, trolls, faeries."

Jaap gestured towards the items on the quikbeme.

"And these things, the scissors, the eggshells?"

"They are charms."

Barbara took Jaap's arm.

"Come, I must show you something."

The Prioress went with them to their hut. Barbara pointed to a cavity in the wall, high up. There, in the shadow, above their bed, was something Jaap couldn't identify. She reached up and took down a pair of pig's trotters, grey and desiccated; she handed them to Jaap.

"To ward off evil spirits."

The Prioress blessed her self. Jaap examined the trotters, old and dry, covered in dust.

"They must have been there for years. Just put them back."

"Jaap, if they think you are a Sidhe, a creature that has come from the other side, and you Barbara, your healing powers are known..."

"Prioress, this is not important. We can do nothing about what people think. The tide is almost out, I must go to the salt, and we will have these doos for our dinner."

~ ~ ~ ~ ~

Jaap and Barbara climbed to the top of Hawkry Hill, looking south over the Firth, across to Edinburgh. The outline of Arthur's Chair and Samson's Ribs were visible, and they could see the incline of the High Street, rising to the keep. Wisps of smoke rose from the houses, straight into the still air. To the east, there was the smoky mess of the salt workings.

"I will work the salt here."

"What did you do when you buried Gertje?"

"I said a mass."

"A mass. Holy God, Jaap, How?"

"I said the words, like the priests do. I used holy water."

"How?"

Jaap's shoulders sagged. He put a hand on Barbara's arm.

"Barbara, my love, I am tired of these questions. I have said enough. I just want peace."

Barbara stood with her back to the Firth, facing north, to the clear air and the bright green parks. She did not know what to say. This man's way of seeing the world was borne out of old suffering and love.

The true understanding of Jaap van der Staen was beyond her. Despite his new calm, she could neither settle him, nor could she explain it to her self. His was a world far from her own understanding of things. They walked to the harbour where the burn came down from the hills and entered the open estuary. A man was attending his nets.

"Look, a set of swans."

They watched the huge birds gliding on the calm surface despite the swift undercurrent. So it was that the swans played: dipping their heads in the reeds, or preening each other's feathers. Thus they lived, looking out for themselves as the clouds passed above them, as first the sun, then the moon, rose and set, and the water moved below their webbed feet. The swans caroused around their nest, a great mound in the middle of the river, and their white feathers shone in the murk as they circled each other around their construction; the fiddle of twig and moss that was raised above the water, dry and warm for new incumbents in the spring. One took a leaf from the surface and placed it on the nest, slowly and deliberately. The other dipped its head deep down into the water, its neck disappearing until only the torso remained. The tail upended as it sought the deep, and then the creature reappeared, lifting its head proud. In its beak was a mush of moss which it shook dry and placed on the nest. The mate came close and the two intertwined their necks, spiralling themselves around each other in a geometric embrace. They floated together like this for several minutes, drifting with the current; then separated and carried on with their nesting.

"They say the king owns all the swans in this country."

"But Jaap, that is silly."

"It's what they say."

~ ~ ~ ~ ~

Barbara and Jaap sat at their hearth. Barbara fingered the pages of her book of hours, contemplating the text, the notes in the margin, examining the little coloured pictures of people working in fields, or praying, or tending to animals, or engaging in conversation; and the images of animals and plants and trees and birds. The sound of her turning the page lived in the silence of their companionship. At her feet, Harry played fivestones, sweeping up the little pebbles from the floor. Outside, a dog barked. Jaap rose, and walked to the door, gently moving the rushes spread at their feet, releasing the mingled scent of rosemary and herbs. The still air stopped all sound. Jaap opened the door, the metal clasp rattled as he pulled. Out in the warm air, the clouds hung motionless, and a flock of geese flew overhead. The whoosh, whoosh of their wings could just be heard, while over at the doocot, the doos took turns at their wooden calls; do doo, do, do doo do. There was a soft rustle of leaves, as a single movement of air, an eddy, brushed them. That same movement made the light from the candles flutter. Jaap closed the door and blew them out, leaving one candle lit between them. He poked the fire and resurrected some flame from the embers.

"Well, Barbara."

Barbara smiled. They picked at the last crumbs of bread on the table and swirled the last of the beer in their cups.

"What has become of us? We have changed, haven't we?"

"Maybe," said Jaap.

"Is this what God had in mind for us?"

"I'm not sure he had any idea. We were to end in St Andrews."

"Yes. You wanted to go for Anders."

Jaap considered the dregs of beer at the bottom of his cup.

"I no longer wish to go to St Andrews. The spirit of Anders is here."

"In Abyrdower?"

"Here, by this fire."

In the silence, Barbara relaxed. Jaap watched as her head drooped, and her eyelids closed. He finished his beer and stood, watching her movements as she dozed: her twitching, the small, slow pulse at her neck below the creased skin of her burned ear. What was to become of them? They disagreed about many things, but this girl comforted him. She pacified him and made him feel complete. Jaap van der Staen would never be as he was.

Harry was watching as Jaap poked at the fire and brought it to life. He built the sticks and peats into a pile.

"Look, Jaap. Just like a little tower of fire."

Barbara stirred and caught Jaap's eye and smiled.

"Yes, a tower of fire."

The warm hearth eased the ache in Jaap's bones. Barbara rose and put a pot over the heat. Harry continued to stare into the fire.

"Look you can see little people dancing in the flames."

Jaap and Barbara smiled.

Here was the true redeeming warmth, not the corrosive redemption of the fires of purgatory; but a recognition of this moment of comfort and companionship, under a roof celebrating this eternal point in time, freed from the past, and whatever was to come. Change would continue as the world turned. It was but a series of moments; moments just like this one, inseparable from the last, and from the one to come.

Jaap stirred the pot and the smell of cooking filled the home.

The Quicken Tree

Epilogue

Sisterlands

Some years later

I am standing at the quicken tree in Sisterlands. Its three intertwined trunks are gnarled with time, and some of its branches are dead. It will stand for a long time yet, but as it dies, it will give life to the small creatures that live from it. I can easily put my arms around one of its trunks, but not the three trunks together. There are scars on its bark, and many of its branches no longer produce the bright red berries. They say that it is a magical tree, and it keeps evil spirits away. I don't know about that, but I know I have grown with it, and I have touched it every day.

My mother and father spoke little of their lives before they adopted me, and I remember little of the events you have been reading about in this story. They still live in Abyrdower. Mother never again had any of her absences, and she is a healer now. They help at Sisterlands, and still they lapse into Flemish, which, even now, I cannot understand. After the shipwreck on White Sands, my father changed. He was quiet and avoided people. Locals called him a 'Sidhe', one of the elvin folk, one who has returned from the dead. He still farms salt, and, do you know, he takes a horse called Marcuccio to help him with the work. Poor Marcuccio; I will never forget his cry on the sands at Moricambe; it was as if he knew what was to come.

I also remember my father's stories about the city of salt and the princess Kinga. I know this was just a story, but to my young mind, it was real. In my head I can still see the beautiful city of Taghaza, with its gleaming palaces of salt. For me they will remain; for me they never faded. For me the city of salt was real. I could touch it and taste it, and I saw its realm of wonder and beauty, devoid of harsh reason. This world now lies, for me, forever in the past.

The reforms? Well, you know, my mother says that they come and go. She says there are no monasteries left in England, and she says that the wind of change is here in Scotland too. Despite the King James's intentions, men seem bent on destroying holy things, regardless of the law. They have burned Reformers here in Scotland, but this is no way to respond to these great changes from Europe. I wonder, can the King resist such a tide in the sea of history?

I am in my twelfth year, and my father's friend, William Boyd, the captain of The Earl's keep, has sponsored me to be schooled in Glasgow. If I can go to Paris, I would like to be a law man; my mother has already taught me my Latin and my numbers.

So it is that I am to leave Abyrdower and may not return for many years. I am sorry to be leaving my mother and father, but some day I will return to touch the quicken tree again, and they will still love me.

My mother says that the answer lies within us all, the simple need to share. All we need to do is love one another. All there is, is love.

Harry Staine

Summer 1540

Abyrdower

Historical Note

Abbess Lücke von Sandbeck, Prince Archbishop Christoph von Braunschweig-Wolfenbuttel, and Provost Martin Reiff lived in Holstein and were associated with the Porto Coeli Monastery in 1536/7. Philippa Jonys was the prioress at St Sepulchre's in Canterbury. Captain Cobbler (Nicholas Melton) and his adjutant Great James were principal characters involved in the Lincolnshire Rising which preceded the Pilgrimage of Grace counter-reformation rebellion. Robert Aske was the Captain of this rising. Melton was executed at Tyburn, and Aske at York, in the spring of 1537.

Elizabeth Barton was the 'Maid of Kent', a nun at St Sepulchre's, who was executed at Tyburn in 1534 for prophesying against King Henry VIII. Mr Spilman and Mr Candish were King's Commissioners responsible for the destruction of St Sepulchre's. Doctor Legh and Doctor Layton were the Commissioners who managed the destruction of Kertmel (Cartmel) Priory. Katherine Mann was an Anchoress at Blackfriars in Norwich. She narrowly escaped burning at the stake in 1531 for promoting Tyndall's (English) Bible.
Christobella Cowper was the Prioress of Marrick Priory. Adam Sedberg was the Abbot of Jorevall (Jervaulx). John Whyte was a Bailiff at Newcastle. The Prioress of St Martha's – Sisterlands, in Aberdour – was Isabella Henryson.

The dates of the reformation in England, and the counter-reformation – the Pilgrimage of Grace – are as the dates in the chapter headings. I have assumed a degree of licence with respect to the actual dates of the destruction of St Sepulchre's and Cartmel. Similarly, the destruction of Jervaulx took place over several weeks, but I have compressed the event into a single night. Adam Sedbar carved his initials on the Rood Screen at Jervaulx, which was removed prior to the destruction of Jervaulx and can still be seen at the church of St Andrews, Aysgarth, some five miles from the site of the abbey.

The Battle of St Mathieu took place in 1512 near Brest, as part of the War of The League of Cambrai, and involved forty-seven ships including the Mary Rose. The Marie la Cordelière (or simply 'Cordelière') and the Regent sank together following an explosion, killing more than fifteen hundred people, including women and children, who were visiting the Marie la Cordelière to celebrate the feast of St Laurence. Portzmoguer was the captain of the Cordelière. Legend has it that he cried 'To the Glory of St Laurence' as his ship sank. The cause of this explosion is not known. The wreck of the Cordelière still lies submerged, somewhere off Pointe Saint Mathieu, near Brest.

Jan Starter was a Friesian soldier and poet who lived from 1593 to 1626. The extract in Ch 15 is an adaptation of his poem "Cupido, hoe heeft u mijn liefs gesicht bedrogen?" from Friesche Lusthof (Friesian Pleasure Garden), 1621.

I invented Hilda of Presscott, in recognition of HFM Prescott, author of 'Man on a Donkey' (London 1952). Christobella Cowper of Marrick Priory and Robert Aske play major parts in Prescott's book.

All other characters are fictitious.

The Author

Francis J Glynn Lives in Aberdour, Fife, on the site of the old Sisterlands Nunnery. In his garden, there is a quikbeme tree with three intertwined trunks.

I am indebted to Barclay McBain, Hamish Whyte and John Mortimer for their advice. Thanks also to Kerry Houston and Andy Redman for their guidance on graphics. Mostly, thanks are due to Shirley for her patience.

Glossary

Canonic Hours of Divine Office. - The order of daily worship in a monastery. They comprised Lauds, Prime, Terce, Sext, None, Vespers, and Compline.

Doo - pigeon

Emonia - The name that was given to the Monastery on the island in the Firth of Forth now called Inchcolme.

Fortalice - A small fortress or fortified house.

Halcyon - A kingfisher.

Hospital - a place of rest, where people received hospitality. Sometimes, these hospitals catered for the ill or dying, in which case, the care of their souls was the priority as they passed from this life.

Scrip - Bag carried by pilgrims

Segen - German name for the religious service known as a Benediction; a blessing.

Shallop - Scottish coastal fishing vessel.

Sidhe - One of the elvin folk or faeries. Pronounced 'shee', as in banshee.

Image Credits:

Cover: Photograph from iStock.com/Quangpraha ©, By kind permission of Quang Nguyen Vinh. Processing by Kerry Houston, 2018.
Page Opposite Page 1, and page 349 Quickbeme/Quicken Tree. Courtesy of J T Irvine, © 2018.
Page 2: Naval Battle, 'Dated at Sea off Dover the 4th. of May 1647.' From The Project Gutenberg EBook of The Pictorial Press, by Mason Jackson.
Page 4 Map After Blaeu - Atlas of Scotland 1654, *INSULAE ALBION ET HIBERNIA* (after Ptolemy) [Public Domain]
Page 5: 'An amberfish and an amber tree' from Ortus Sanitatis, published in Mainz in 1491 by Jacob Meydenbach. From Project Gutenberg's Herbals, Their Origin and Evolution, by Agnes Arber.
Page 17 'A Benedictine abbess and nun'. From The Project Gutenberg eBook, Scenes and Characters of the Middle Ages, by Edward Lewes Cutts.
Page 32 After 'The Great Drinkers of the North', 'Histoires des Pays Septentrionaux", by Olaus Magnus, Antwerp, 1560. [Public domain], via Wikimedia Commons.
Page 42 After 'A hospital ward in the Hotel Dieu.' Sixteenth Century. Credit: Wellcome Collection. CC BY
Page 52 Measuring Salt. Facsimile of a woodcut of the "Ordonnances de la Prevoste des Marchands de Paris", in folio: 1500. From The Project Gutenberg EBook of Manners, Custom and Dress During the Middle Ages and During the Renaissance Period, by Paul Lacroix.
Page 63 After 'The Domesday Book' from Andrews, William: *"Historic Byways and Highways of Old England"* (1900) [Public domain], via Wikimedia Commons.
Page 74 From Georgius Agricola, De Re Metalica, Basel 1556. [Public Domain] EBook via Project Gutenberg.
Page 88 The first European picture of Timbuktu.From a drawing in Caillé's *Tomboctou*, 1829. In A Book of Discovery, by Margaret Bertha (M. B.) Synge, [Public Domain] via Project Gutenberg.
Page 101 After Antonio Tempesta, 'Rearing Horse', from 'Different Animals (1590?), Harvard Art Museums/Fogg Museum, Gift of Belinda L. Randall from the collection of John Witt Randall, by exchange.
Page 114 'Mapp of Canterbury', 1640 by John Speed, published in 'The Antiquities of Canterbury', by William Somner. Reproduced courtesy of The Chapter of Canterbury reference WS11/14
Page 123 Badge of The Pilgrimage of Grace. From The Project Gutenberg EBook of The Story of the East Riding of Yorkshire, by Horace Baker Browne. [Public Domain] via Project Gutenberg.
Page 132 Nuremberg (1525-1527), Von Scheurl-Bibliohtek Katalog Nr 147Ausst. Kat. Strasbourg, Karlsruhe, 2001
Page 143 Signature of Thomas Cromwell.

Page 154 After an Etching of 'The Nunnery of St Sepulchre.' From 1879 "Canterbury in the Olden Time" by John Brent F.S.A (1879), by kind permission of Tina Machado.
Page 168 From The Norfolk Wherry Trust. Courtesy of 'The Wherry', Autumn 1973
Page 182 After St Bridget of Sweden, From The Project Gutenberg eBook, The Invention of Printing, by Theodore Low De Vinne. [Public Domain] via Project Gutenberg
Page 195 Pennant Melangell Church screen. From Archaeologia Cambrensis, The Journal of the Cambrian Archaeological Association, Vol. III, Sixth Series, London, 1903. [Public domain], via Wikimedia Commons
Page 210 St John's Gate, Clerkenwell. From the cover of The Gentleman's Magazine, January 1731. [Public domain], via Wikimedia Commons.
Page 223 Sixteenth Century Coat of Arms, Gateshead (Goat's Head) [Public Domain].
Page 231 The Divining Rod. From Curious Myths of the Middle Ages (1866) by Sabine Baring-Gould, [Public domain], via Wikimedia Commons
Page 242 John Speed, Map of Newcastle (described by William Matthew), 1610) Reproduced courtesy of Newcastle City Library
Page 255 'Producing salt by evaporating natural brine by pouring it into a pit of burning charcoal.' After woodcut illustration from *De re metallica* by Georgius Agricola, Basel, 1556. Copied by unknown artist, 1550s [Public domain], via Wikimedia Commons
Page 271 'Barnacle Geese' Cosmographie Universelle" of Munster, folio, Basle 1552 [Public domain], via Wikimedia Commons
Page 287 After Alciati, *Emblematum Liber* (Augsburg, 1531), Emblem 75 (Sp Coll SM18, folio D7v) by permission of University of Glasgow Library, Special Collections.
Page 303 Agnus Dei II, from Josquin's *Missa L'homme armé super voces musicales*, (Venice, 1502) as reprinted in the *Dodecachordon* of Heinrich Glarean, Basel (1547). [Public domain], via Wikimedia Commons
Page 319 Stones, 'Shipwreck'. Ortus sanitatis (1497), Strasbourg. Wellcome Collection CC BY

Text Attributions:

The Poem "The life of this world …" on page 147 is taken from 'The Man on a Donkey', by HFM Prescott, page 139 Grafton Press, London, 1992. See also the Digital index of Middle English Verse, London, British Library Harley 7322, f. 136v

The stanza on page 168 is the author's translation of an extract from 'Cupido, hoe heeft u mijn liefs gesicht bedrogen?' by Jan Starter from Friesche Lusthof (Friesian Pleasure Garden) of 1621.

All other texts and translations quoted in this book are by the author.

Printed in Great Britain
by Amazon